DUMBARTON OAKS
MEDIEVAL LIBRARY

Jan M. Ziolkowski, General Editor

THE WELL-LADEN SHIP

EGBERT OF LIÈGE

DOML 25

DUMBARTON OAKS MEDIEVAL LIBRARY

The Well-Laden Ship

Egbert of Liège

Translated by

ROBERT GARY BABCOCK

DUMBARTON OAKS
MEDIEVAL LIBRARY

HARVARD UNIVERSITY PRESS
CAMBRIDGE, MASSACHUSETTS
LONDON, ENGLAND
2013

Printed in the United States of America

Library of Congress Cataloging-in-Publication Data
Egbert, of Liège, active 1010–1026.
The well-laden ship / Egbert of Liège ; translated by Robert Gary Babcock.
page. cm.—(Dumbarton Oaks medieval library ; 25)
Includes bibliographical references and index.
ISBN 978-0-674-05127-0 (alk. paper)
1. Proverbs, Latin. 2. Proverbs, Latin—Translations into English. I. Babcock, Robert Gary, 1958– II. Title. III. Series: Dumbarton Oaks medieval library ; 25.
PN6418.E34 2013
398.2′0471—dc23 2013007293

Contents

Introduction

The Well-Laden Ship is a collection of medieval proverbs, fables, and folktales written in Liège (modern Belgium) at the beginning of the eleventh century as a schoolbook for young boys. A poem of over 2,370 dactylic hexameters, it is divided into two books and survives in a single manuscript in the Cologne Cathedral Library.[1] It has been called a "document of the greatest importance for the comparative study of popular sayings," and "the most ancient and pure source of our knowledge of a notable part of the folklore of the tenth century."[2] The poem includes medieval versions of many still popular proverbs, for example, "Don't look a gift horse in the mouth," "When the cat's away, the mice will play," and "The apple doesn't fall far from the tree." It also has early variants of many fairy tales, nursery rhymes, and animal fables, including "Little Red Riding Hood," "Jack Sprat," and various tales connected with Reynard the Fox. *The Well-Laden Ship* provides illuminating insights into the educational practices of the period and also sheds light on broader aspects of the instruction and transmission of knowledge to children outside schools; for it is based, in part, on stories that children learned from their mothers and nursemaids before entering a formal classroom. The work has never before been translated and will fascinate and amuse anyone interested in proverbial wisdom or folklore.[3]

The Well-Laden Ship was compiled by Egbert, a cleric living and teaching in Liège in the first quarter of the eleventh century. Egbert drew his material not only from oral proverbs and tales but also from a wide range of literary sources: the Vulgate Bible; the Church Fathers, especially Augustine and Gregory the Great; and many works of pagan literature, in particular the poems of Horace, Juvenal, and Virgil. He intended the work to replace two of the standard introductory schoolbooks of the day, the *Disticha Catonis,* a collection of short proverbs attributed in the Middle Ages to the Roman statesman Cato, and the animal fables known in Latin translation under the names Avianus and Romulus, and derived ultimately from Aesop.

In compiling *The Well-Laden Ship,* Egbert realized that he could help students in their study of Latin by producing for them a Latin version of the vernacular nursery tales and proverbs that they would have heard from the cradle. For they would already know the contents of the tales and could use that knowledge to help them unravel the abstruse vocabulary and complicated syntax of Egbert's poem. Their knowledge of his poem would, in turn, put them in good stead to read the classical poets and, more importantly, the Bible and the Church Fathers.

Beyond its storehouse of proverbial sayings and fables, *The Well-Laden Ship* also contains much other material: satirical sketches of cuckolded husbands, nagging wives, gluttons, dandies, starving monks, and greedy clerics; observations on the human condition; rules concerning proper manners and behavior; anecdotes about class distinctions, law, and politics; and catechetical material intended to teach basic Christian principles, often through the examples of Old Testament figures. Egbert frequently rails against vices and especially assails the rich and powerful for their un-Christian greed. Another of his favorite themes is the decline of learning. A true believer in the good old days, Egbert bemoans that the students are getting lazier, the teachers stupider, and the world in general less interested in learning.

One of the most tantalizing, and at the same time most frustrating, aspects of Egbert's work is that he preserves the kernel of many medieval folktales that do not otherwise survive. Egbert provides only the names of the characters in these narratives and the salient lesson to be derived from their experiences, but their stories are completely unknown to us. We encounter Magfrid, who acquired a fortune by sitting; Hyringus, who became so feeble in his old age that a fly knocked him off his stool; Poles, who when he finally acquired power, used it to slit his own father's throat; Radbod the Frisian, who issued a decree without the king's support; Billardus, who was killed by an ax and a pickax; and Butzo, who consoled his master but foolishly put his trust in words alone.[4] With these tales Egbert pulls back the curtain, allowing us to glimpse a lost world of medieval narratives and the characters who inhabited them. But we can only guess at the details of their adventures.

Perhaps the most bewildering thing about *The Well-Laden Ship* to a modern audience is that Egbert also incorporates into his work grammatical rules, vocabulary building exercises, and anecdotes from the daily life of his pupils. His goal was, first and foremost, to make a book to use in his own classroom. Like any good teacher, he varied the material regularly (and, in his case, widely) to keep the students' attention and interest. He instructs them on many aspects of Latin language and thought, and he provides as well lighter material to entertain them (for example, vv. 1575–80 on the Latin terminology for the various secretions and excretions of the body). Many modern readers will be baffled by a work intended for preteens that combines pious religious teaching with coarse, even crude, anecdotes employing barnyard language. But people in the Middle Ages were often more down-to-earth than their counterparts in the modern world are, and schoolchildren still delight in scatological language and jokes. In puzzling over the diversity of Egbert's material, we should not ask, "Why is such stuff here?" but rather, "Since it is here, what does it tell us about the daily routine in Egbert's classroom?" A less surprising feature of Egbert's poem, alas, is the extreme misogyny and anti-Semitism sprinkled throughout the work. We may dismiss these passages as typical of Egbert's time, place, and station in life, which they certainly are. But that such poison was being fed to children is still disturbing.

Besides an extensive and esoteric vocabulary, Egbert frequently uses common words in very uncommon ways. His odd lexicon is designed to further his students' ability to analyze words and phrases in multiple ways, and to appreciate words in senses that go beyond the literal. One of the primary reasons for teaching proverbs is that they are metaphorical. They require the students to analyze metaphors, similes, and allegory. "Don't look a gift horse in the mouth" is not about horses but about accepting and appreciating what we happen to have for what it is.[5] Similarly, the study of fables instructs students in searching for deeper meanings in texts, especially moral lessons. The grammatical and lexical exercises included in Egbert's treatise make more sense in this context: they aid the students in learning complicated Latin words and phrases, in understanding fine distinctions between similar words, and in comprehending that words have different meanings in different contexts. The first stage in learning to interpret extended narratives and their meanings is to decode individual words and their usages.

Through ancient proverbs and fables as well as through biblical and Christian stories, Egbert taught his students to extract allegorical and moral meanings from texts. That he considered folktales and folk wisdom equally capable of providing edifying lessons to his students is one of the most fascinating aspects of his poem, and of his teaching philosophy.

The unusual and varied nature of his source material, his desire to get his students to read beneath the surface, and the contorted syntax that resulted from his effort to render his material into short (often single) verse segments, probably account for the enormous difficulty of Egbert's Latin. It is rarely straightforward, frequently tortured, at times impenetrable. His students, indeed, must have found the ancient authors comparatively easy reading after they had struggled through Egbert's Latin—not, it must be admitted, necessarily an undesirable outcome. That the author himself could use the work effectively in his teaching, we may well believe; but other teachers must have found it tough going indeed. It seems likely that the difficulty of Egbert's Latin is responsible for his poem not having been widely transmitted during the Middle Ages,[6] and not having been translated until now. In offering the present translation, I cannot claim to have solved all of the problems of the text, or to have produced intelligible renderings of every passage. But I hope that this translation will win many new readers for Egbert's poem and that the deficiencies of my translation will inspire a new generation of readers to study and analyze it—it needs their attention and deserves their efforts.

The Author

The author of our poem is nowhere mentioned in the lone surviving manuscript. His name was preserved by Sigebert of Gembloux (ca. 1030–1112), who describes Egbert's poem in his *Catalogus de viris illustribus* (Catalogue of Illustrious Men). Other than the brief account of Egbert's poem by Sigebert, the only information we have on Egbert's life is what we can glean from the work itself, in particular, from the *Letter to Adalbold.* And that is very little. The *Letter* does tell us that the author was a priest and the dedicatee, Adalbold, a bishop at the time of the writing of the letter. Adalbold was bishop of Utrecht from 1010 to 1026. The letter also tells us that the work is intended for the schoolroom, and from that we might infer that Egbert was a schoolteacher. Another thing we learn from the *Letter* is that Egbert and Adalbold had been fellow students at an early age.

From the first of these data, we may conclude that a draft of *The Well-Laden Ship* was completed during the sixteen-year time span from 1010 to 1026. Egbert's description of the poem in the *Letter* makes clear that he is referring there to the second edition of the poem, not the first. How much earlier the first edition was written we do not know.

Voigt argued that *The Well-Laden Ship* was completed toward the very end of the period of Adalbold's bishopric, that Egbert was born around 972 of noble German parents, and that he taught in the cathedral school at Liège. While none of these claims is necessarily wrong, there is little to support them, and they have been rejected by some scholars.[7] What we can say with confidence is that the second edition of the poem was completed between 1010 and 1026, that Egbert and Adalbold had studied together as children, and that Egbert was later a priest and schoolteacher somewhere in Liège.

Adalbold is known as the author of various works: he corresponded with Gerbert of Aurillac on mathematical questions; wrote a *Life* of the emperor Henry II, in whose chancery he had served before he was elevated to the bishopric; and composed a commentary on a section of Boethius's *Consolation of Philosophy.* Unfortunately, we know very little about Adalbold's schooling and education. In the period before he served in the imperial chancery, he was associated with the cathedral of Liège, where he is recorded as archdeacon in 1007.[8] He is said by Anselm of Liège (writing shortly after 1050) to have been a student of Bishop Notger of Liège,[9] one of the most powerful figures at courts of the Holy Roman Emperors Otto II and Otto III. Notger was a zealous supporter of education and was responsible for making Liège a leading center of learning in the West at the end of the tenth century.[10]

At an earlier period in his life, Adalbold was also connected in some fashion with the Benedictine abbey of Lobbes (in Hainaut, roughly fifty kilometers south of Brussels) or with its abbot Heriger (990–1007). Lobbes was the leading center of monastic learning in the Liège diocese in the tenth and eleventh centuries and had an impressive library.[11] Heriger wrote a dialogue in which he made Adalbold his interlocutor.[12] From this circumstance, it has been argued that Adalbold was a student of Heriger's, or that he was a teacher at the collegiate church of St. Ursmarus in the town of Lobbes. Heriger had a close relationship with Bishop Notger of Liège, so we can safely state that Adalbold belonged to the circle of Notger and Heriger. And we can deduce from the *Letter to Adalbold* that Egbert was educated in this same circle. Where he later taught is less clear. At the beginning of the eleventh century, Liège had not only a cathedral school but also schools in seven of its collegiate churches.[13] Egbert may have taught in any of these institutions, but we have no information on the subject.

Sigebert's *Catalogue* is a medieval continuation of *De viris illustribus* (On Illustrious Men) by Jerome, a bio-bibliographical work on Christian writers. Fortunately for present purposes, Sigebert especially focuses on writers from the period immediately preceding his own, and on writers from his own region. Gembloux lies within the diocese of Liège, and writers affiliated with Liège appear prominently in Sigebert's work.[14] As it is the only independent source for information about Egbert, it is worth quoting in full: "Egbert, a cleric of Liège, wrote a book in meter about the sayings (riddles) of country-folk. Originally it was a brief book, but with the scope of his subject expanded, he wrote a second larger book on the same subject, also in meter."[15]

Sigebert does not give the title of Egbert's work; instead he describes it. The term he employs to describe the contents of Egbert's poem, *aenigmata* (riddles), is used in the Middle Ages as a synonym for "proverb" or "parable."[16] It is frequently used of allegorical stories, which need to be unraveled.[17]

Beyond confirming that Egbert was a cleric in Liège, and identifying him as the author of our poem, Sigebert also provides important information about the two editions of Egbert's work. The surviving manuscript confirms Sigebert's account, for the first, shorter edition is still apparent from the prayer that appears at verses 1005–8 of Book 1. This was originally the epilogue of the entire work, and it consisted, therefore, only of the one- and two-line proverbs. The later expansion of the poem to include proverbs and fables of three or more lines (vv. 1009–1768), and the further addition of the second book, which is mostly devoted to Christian teaching, constituted the second edition. The structure of the final version is discussed further below.

The Title

Developing an elaborate nautical trope, Egbert refers to his poem as a ship or vessel *(ratis)*. It has two parts (two books), just as a ship has a prow and a stern. Egbert's poem begins with elementary instruction at its head, in the prow (Book 1, *The Embellished Prow*). Just as the front of a ship may be festooned with decorations, outfitted with rigging, and ornamented with sculpture, so Egbert's *Prow* provides his students with the means of decorating their speech and ornamenting their writing with proverbs and wise sayings.

Egbert's ship ends with a loftier section, Book 2, *The Bronze-Clad Stern,* focusing on religious instruction. The stern is where the pilot, on a raised bridge, controls the rudder that guides the ship. The bronze armor of the stern protects the ship from the assaults of the sea.

The word *ratis* originally referred to a "raft," "bark," "barge," or some other small or utilitarian vessel.[18] Classical poets used it metaphorically to refer to larger boats: warships, transport vessels, merchant ships. We should understand the term in Egbert's title in both senses. He humbly refers to his poem as a little raft, a small, everyday vessel. And it is, certainly, small in comparison to the major Latin hexameter poems. It is, however, quite large when compared to the schoolbooks he sought to supplant, the *Distichs of Cato* and the *Fables* of Avianus. But Egbert's ship, unlike a raft, has an ornamented prow, an armored stern, and diverse rigging. So we should imagine a rather grand vessel. Perhaps a merchant ship, filled to the brink with goods (wisdom) from the four corners of the earth, perhaps the sailing ship of an adventurer like Aeneas or Jason, exploring the world. Perhaps Noah's Ark, preserving what is valuable in the world and delivering it to a safe harbor.

The term *fecunda* (well-laden) carries many meanings as well; these include "teeming," "well-furnished," "fertile," and "fruitful" (in the sense of beneficial). Egbert emphasizes that his ship is abundantly loaded with rich and varied—even exotic—content, such as would be brought to port from many different places by trading ships. Liège is not a coastal town, but its situation on the Meuse River made it a center of marine commerce.[19] So Egbert's students would have been familiar with the sights and sounds of a wharf, where exotic merchandise was unloaded from seagoing vessels and displayed for sale.

The title, then, may be seen as an oxymoron, simultaneously emphasizing the richness of the offering and the humility of the author. Egbert is also playing on the biblical metaphor of a ship as a means for the safe conveyance of souls through the seas of this world, as, for example, in the book of Wisdom:[20] "Thy providence, O Father, governeth it: for thou hast made a way even in the sea, and a most sure path among the waves" (14:3–4); "But that the works of thy wisdom might not be idle: therefore men also trust their lives even to a little wood, and passing over the sea by ship, are saved" (14:5).[21] Egbert's ship will transport his students, through its combination of ancient, folk, and biblical wisdom, to the safe port of wisdom and salvation.

The Structure of the *Fecunda ratis*

Egbert's poem follows, to some extent, the format of its principal models. Like the *Distichs* of Cato, Book 1 has a section of one-line proverbs, followed by a section of two-line proverbs. This Catonian section, in turn, is followed by segments with proverbs of three lines, and of four lines and longer. Beginning with the three-liners, each proverb or story has its own descriptive title. In contrast to the mostly secular nature of the first two sections, the three-line and longer sections tend more toward Christian content and spiritual sources. Here, too, the influence of Egbert's second model, Avianus, shows, for many of the animal fables and tales appear in the latter parts of the first book. Book 2 follows the format of the end of Book 1, namely longer poems, each supplied with its own title; these are overwhelmingly of biblical and Christian content. So, in general, the work starts with shorter pieces and ends with longer and more serious ones, following a pedagogical path from simpler to more complex readings. Egbert is not, however, entirely consistent about the layout, and the section of one-liners also has a few proverbs of two or more lines. The section with distichs also has four-line proverbs.

A more detailed description of the format of Egbert's work is necessary in order to appreciate the precise organization of its various parts and to understand the formatting of the present edition and translation, which differs to some extent from the layout of the only previous edition, that of Ernst Voigt (Halle, 1889). In the Cologne manuscript (Dombibliothek, MS 196), the *Fecunda ratis* begins on folio 1r with the title "Here begins the little book of the Embellished Prow. The second book is called the Bronze-Clad Stern. For Bishop Adalbold." This title serves as the introduction both to the prefatory *Letter to Adalbold* and to the two books of the poem. The title is followed immediately by the *Letter,* which is in prose and runs until the antepenultimate line of folio 1v. The penultimate line of 1v was left blank, and verse 1, with its first letter enlarged and partially filled with color, is written on the last line of that page. Verse 2 begins on the top of folio 2r, and the poem continues without any original interruptions until folio 16v, line 6, after which there is a subheading to introduce the section of distichs. Then the distichs themselves follow.

An early corrector made a necessary alteration on folio 2r: namely, he erased the first letter in verse 5 and rewrote it in a much larger module, extending well into the margin, and he also added color (a light yellow wash) to further call attention to the letter. His objective was to indicate that the poem proper begins at this point, for the first four verses are not part of the poem, but of the prefatory matter. Verses 1–2 continue the theme introduced in the *Letter* of requesting Adalbold's assistance in editing the poem. They are a coda to the letter proper and are addressed to Adalbold, not to the reader. Such metrical flourishes are found at the ends of other letters of the period from the Liège school.[22] These two verses belong to the *Letter,* not to the poem.[23]

Although the corrector made the opening of the poem proper more transparent by separating what comes before and what comes after verse 5, he did nothing to mark off or indicate the function of verses 1–2, on the one hand, or verses 3–4 on the other. As stated above, verses 1–2 form a coda to the *Letter,* and they are now printed as such. Verses 3–4 serve as an introductory distich to Book 1; they precisely parallel the distich that opens Book 2. The introductory distich at the start of each book mentions the title of that book; but neither of them mentions the other book, nor the title of the work as a whole. Although there is no separate title for the *Prow* in the manuscript to match that for the *Stern,* the introductory distich implies that there should have been one; so does the gloss in the upper margin of folio 2r. It provides an explanation for the overall title of the work, *The Well-Laden Ship.* Only this gloss preserves the title of the work. The distich and the gloss make evident that the title of the work should have appeared somewhere after verse 1 and before verse 5. It makes most sense between verses 2 and 3, and I have inserted a title at that point, based on the wording of the gloss.

From verse 5 to verse 596, the poem comprises, for the most part, single-line proverbs (although there is an admixture of two-line proverbs as well). After verse 596 there is a subheading, occupying an entire line and indicating that the following proverbs are of two verses each (though occasionally there are four-line proverbs here.)[24] There were originally no indications in the manuscript (by formatting, spacing, indentation, titles, or any other type of marking) to separate the distichs into two-line units: the formatting of the distichs in the manuscript is identical to that of the one-liners.[25] In the present edition, each distich is set off from the preceding and following distichs by blank lines.

The two-line proverbs continue through verse 1004, at which point a four-line prayer follows (1005–8). In the first edition, the poem ended with this prayer, which served as an epilogue. Discounting verses 1–4 and the four lines of the concluding prayer, the original *Prow* numbered exactly one thousand lines, a popular length for medieval Latin poems.[26]

After verse 1008, a new subheading announces the following section of individual three-line poems.[27] Each of these poems has its own descriptive title. These titles are original to the MS, but it is not clear whether they were supplied by Egbert or by a later copyist. New subheadings appear before verses 1075 and 1097, in both cases indicating that four-line sections are to follow. In the second instance, the subheading refers to sections of four lines or longer.[28] The poems of four lines and longer have individual titles, on the model of the three-liners. This section continues to the end of Book 1 (v. 1768).[29] No epilogue comes at the end of Book 1, but three lines were left blank in the manuscript, creating a division between the end of Book 1 and the title that introduces Book 2.

Book 2 begins with a new title, "Here begins the second little book of the Bronze-Clad Stern." This is followed by an introductory distich. The rest of Book 2 has the same format as the later part of Book 1: poems of four or more lines (the longest is twenty-seven lines), each with its own title. The last poem, "Concerning the End of Life," serves also as an epilogue to *The Well-Laden Ship.* It contains a prayer in which Egbert asks God to receive him when he dies. The manuscript has no indication to mark the end.[30] The ship metaphor is alluded to in the concluding poem, albeit indirectly, through the terms "hand" *(manus)* and "spirit/wind/breath" *(spiritus, flatus).* Egbert refers to the hand of God, which has replaced the hand of the pilot in guiding the ship. The wind that had provided the power to Egbert's ship is here replaced by the Holy Spirit and the breath of life within Egbert.

For the first four hundred verses, the margins of the manuscript are filled with explanatory glosses, and these are frequently crucial in understanding and translating the text. Often these glosses simply rewrite the proverb in prose, and in simpler language. In addition, some of them preserve additional proverbs or outside information of interest in understanding the text. They were written either by Egbert, or, more probably, by one of his students. These glosses are transcribed and translated in their entirety in the Notes to the Translation (introduced for each verse by the word "Gloss.") For the remainder of the work, the manuscript occasionally has a small number of short, interlinear glosses explaining a word in the Latin, usually by giving a synonym. I have not always transcribed or translated these lexical glosses, though I include them whenever they influenced my translation or interpretation, or where they seemed particularly helpful to the reader.

Notes to the Present Edition

Voigt's edition includes an extensive and valuable apparatus of parallel proverbs in a multitude of medieval languages and from a wide range of sources. These are very helpful to the polyglot reader in understanding Egbert's meaning and should be consulted by every scholar engaging with Egbert's work.

In the Notes to the Translation, I focus on the essential. These notes frequently give references to biblical, classical, or patristic passages that are certainly or almost certainly one of Egbert's direct sources, especially when the source is extensive and verbatim, or when it is especially important in understanding Egbert's lines. I rarely repeat information about sources that is provided in the *Thesaurus Proverbiorum Medii Aevi* (hereafter, TPMA). When I have introduced such references with "compare," I am signaling less confidence that the source or parallel is necessarily related to Egbert. I have added a few new identifications of sources to those made by Voigt, but these are not marked in any particular way. I have made no attempt to identify verse tags, or to reproduce Voigt's extensive collection of these, and I cite verse tags only where the context of the source text seems essential in making sense of the proverb.

Even though Voigt's apparatus is enormous and solid,

more work has been done in the 130 years since he published, and much of this is incorporated in TPMA. I give for every proverb in Egbert a reference to the section of TPMA in which that proverb is recorded. The availability of this rich collection, which provides much more by way of parallel passages than Voigt was able to do, was one of the principal reasons for not reproducing Voigt's apparatus here.

My references are normally in the form "TPMA + the keyword under which the proverb is alphabetized + the section number (not the proverb number) in TPMA." For example, "TPMA *Wolf* 2.1" means the section labeled "2.1" under the keyword "*Wolf*." I cite the section number, not the proverb number, because Egbert gives a version of a proverb, which appears in many other versions in different languages and sources. The goal is to lead the reader to this section, with the parallel proverbs, not to lead the reader to the citation in TPMA of Egbert's own line.

Sometimes, where very few proverbs are listed under a keyword, TPMA has no section numbers. In these cases, only a proverb number differentiates one proverb from another. The proverb numbers appear in TPMA in italics under each keyword, so I have rendered them in italics as well (so, for example, "TPMA *Stiefsohn 1*" means the first proverb under the keyword "*Stiefsohn*"). When I could not find Egbert's line listed in TPMA, but where there is a keyword with a section within which Egbert's line would, at least to some extent, appropriately fit, I have given the reference in the form "compare TPMA. . . ."

I am grateful to a great many people for their help and encouragement as I studied Egbert. Wolfgang Maaz first introduced me to Egbert when I was a student at the Institut für Mittellatein in Berlin in 1981; I am indebted to him and to Fritz Wagner for welcoming me there and furthering my studies. Some of my work on this volume was undertaken at the Flemish Academic Center while I was a visiting fellow of the Royal Flemish Academy for Science and the Arts in 2011 and 2012. It is a pleasure to acknowledge the support of the academy and of my old friend and collaborator Albert Derolez. Ronald Pepin has been a constant companion in producing this translation; he worked through every line multiple times with me, and I can honestly say that it would not have been completed without him. I was especially fortunate in having such able readers from the DOML editorial board, Gregory Hays and Danuta Shanzer, who corrected many mistakes, solved numerous riddles, and provided constant encouragement and support. Further advice was provided by Michael Winterbottom and by Kurt Smolak. To all of these editors and advisors I am very grateful.

It is a special pleasure to acknowledge the endless and undeserved support I received from Jan Ziolkowski: from his encouraging my undertaking of the project in the beginning to his patient tolerance of my continual delays in completing it to his valuable personal interventions with difficult passages whenever needed, he has been a faithful friend. My greatest scholarly debt is to Francis Newton, in this project as in so many others; he read endless drafts, repeatedly challenged my assumptions, corrected my mistakes, and unstintingly promoted the importance of the undertaking. All of these scholars contributed substantially to making the present volume better than it otherwise would have been; they bear no responsibility for whatever imperfections remain. On a personal level, I am especially indebted to my wife, Elizabeth, who for many years listened tirelessly to my struggles over Egbert and offered the continual love and support that allowed me to complete this volume.

Notes

1 Cologne was the archbishopric to which Liège belonged.

2 Paris, "Review," 563.

3 Maaz, "Egbert von Lüttich," 1016–17, gives a list of many of the folktale types and motifs.

4 Magfrid, 1.120; Hyringus, 1.122; Poles, 1.124; Radbod, 1.493–94; Billardus, 1.643–44; Butzo, 1.663–64.

5 It is also about proper manners in receiving a gift; and about being realistic ("you get what you pay for").

6 There is only one surviving manuscript, and the work is listed only in a single medieval library catalog, that of the abbey of Lobbes (in the Liège diocese, see below, n. 11). Beyond Sigebert, few medieval readers of the work can be named, though the author of the *Ysengrimus* is probably one such.

7 Voigt's conclusions were repeated uncritically by Manitius (*Geschichte*) and Brunhölzl (*Geschichte*) and from there have found their way into most scholarship on Egbert. But they are dubious at best and were rejected by Voigt's first reviewers, Kurth, "Review," 78–80; Paris, "Review," 559–62; and Balau, *Les sources,* 153.

8 Voigt, *Egberts,* ix.

9 Anselm of Liège, *Gesta episcoporum Leodiensium, MGH, Scriptores* 7:205.

10 On Notger's career and his promotion of teaching in Liège, compare Kurth, *Notger.*

11 On the library, compare François Dolbeau, "Un nouveau catalogue des manuscrits de Lobbes aux xie et xiie siècles," *Recherches augustiniennes* 13 (1978): 3–36 and 14 (1979): 191–248.

12 The dialogue itself does not survive.

13 Compare Kurth, *Notger,* 257–59; Voigt, *Egberts,* xxv–xxxix. There was also a school at the Benedictine abbey of St. James, but Egbert was not a monk so would not have taught there.

14 On Sigebert's writings and career, compare Manitius, *Geschichte,* 3.332–50, esp. 346–48. Sigebert's work is edited by R. Witte: *Catalogus Sigeberti Gemblacensis monachi de viris illustribus.* Lateinische Sprache und Literatur des Mittelalters 1 (Bern, 1974).

15 *Egebertus, clericus Leodiensis, scripsit metrico stylo de aenigmatibus rusticanis librum, primo brevem, sed ampliato rationis tenore scripsit de eadem re metrice alterum librum maiusculum.*

16 Compare Voigt, *Egberts,* xxi–xxii.

17 Sigebert's description is similar to that given by the MS in the gloss on the title (compare Notes to the Translation, gloss on the title of Book 1): *plena iocis et rusticis instrumentis* (filled with riddles and rustic embellishments), and we may infer that the gloss was Sigebert's source.

18 Compare also the reference to the poem as *navicula* (little ship) in the gloss preceding 1.3–4.

19 There are records of Liège merchants trading in London in Egbert's day; compare, for instance, Neil Middleton, "Early Medieval Port Customs, Tolls and Controls on Foreign Trade," *Early Medieval Europe* 13 (2005): 313–58, at 333–34 and 343–44.

20 The term *ratis* occurs three times in the first six verses of chapter 14 of the book of Wisdom.

21 Here and throughout I generally use the Douai-Rheims version of the Bible, sometimes slightly modified.

22 For instance, the letter from Notger to Werinfrid that precedes the *Vita Remacli* (ed. B. Krusch, *MGH, Scriptores rerum Merovingicarum* 5, 109–11).

23 Voigt should not have numbered these verses as part of the poem, nor separated them from the *Letter;* but it seems unproductive to renumber the entire work, as that would create discrepancies between the numbering of the present edition and the references in all previous scholarship on the poem. But I have printed verses 1 and 2 where they belong, at the end of the *Letter.*

24 The two-liners begin on folio 16v.

25 At a later date (using a different color of ink), however, punctuation was added that marked a more significant stop, and this often provides an indication of the end of a distich. The added punctuation looks like an Arabic 7, and it follows the point at midline that the original scribe had

used. It must be stated that the scribe who added this punctuation was very inconsistent in his work. A different and considerably later reader also added paragraph marks to mark the distichs between 719 and 803 (but not those before or after that range of verses).

26 Compare Voigt, *Egberts,* xxii, with a list of examples. There is further discussion of the first and second editions of the poem above in the discussion of the author.

27 This section begins on the top of folio 26r.

28 These two subheadings appear on folios 28r and 28v, respectively. Voigt combined them into a single subheading and placed it before verse 1075 (and I have followed him in this, though with reservations). Additions by later correctors result in some confusion about the placement of specific poems within these sections; compare the notes to the translation at verses 1072–74.

29 On folio 47r.

30 The poem ends on the top line of folio 63r. The remainder of the page was used for the copying of a Christmas hymn *(Dulce melos cum organo),* and folio 63v for a prayer *(O lux mentium);* compare Voigt, *Egberts,* v.

LETTER TO BISHOP ADALBOLD

INCIPIT LIBELLUS PRORAE DISTINCTAE.

SECUNDUS VOCATUR PUPPIS AERATA.

AD ALBOLDUM EPISCOPUM.

A., gratia dei episcopo, litterarum studiis admodum instituto, E., servorum dei humillimus presbiter, ut eam cui praeest ecclesiam digne in dei oculis regere, et in extremis verbo et opere cum grege suo summo pastori possit placere.

Ambo olim a pueris apud scolares alas in uno auditorio militavimus, quo magis novimus nos inter nos, et ideo confidentius privatumque malui alloqui te, quia fretus de te, hoc rustici sermonis opusculum emendandum audeo commendare. In communi enim sermone, multi sepe multa loquuntur, et plurimis ad usum necessariis exemplis, illa vulgi sententia profertur; quod quidem hausi, mecum id reputans, quod in his plurima versarentur utilia, et, si aliquatenus retineri possent, perspicua, quae quoniam nusquam scripta fuissent, quo magis memori pectore servarentur, indiligentes propterea facerent auditores. Unde ego quae comminisci per horas interdiu noctuque potui, singulis ea versiculis

HERE BEGINS THE LITTLE BOOK OF THE EMBELLISHED PROW. THE SECOND BOOK IS CALLED THE BRONZE-CLAD STERN. FOR BISHOP ADALBOLD.

To Adalbold, bishop by the grace of God, and most learned in literary pursuits, Egbert, the most humble priest among the servants of God, [sends greetings]; may he succeed in steering worthily in the eyes of God that congregation over which he has command and in the final hour may he, along with his flock, be pleasing in word and deed to the shepherd on high.

Both of us once, from the time we were boys, campaigned among the scholarly ranks in the same lecture hall, whereby we came to know one another better; and so I have chosen to address you more confidently and privately, since relying upon you, I dare to commend, for you to emend, this little work of rustic speech. Many people often say many things in ordinary language, and that wisdom of the commoners is proffered in a great many examples that are indispensable to employ. I drank from this font, thinking to myself that among these things were many that are practical and (if somehow they could be preserved) clear—things which could make listeners of those who were for this reason inattentive: that these things had been written down nowhere to be preserved better in a mindful heart. So, I have gathered up in just two little books whatever things I could think of through the hours of day and night, in single verselets,

sepe duobus, interdum tribus, uti in ordine scriptos videbis, praeterea novis atque vulgaribus fabellis aliquot divinisque paucis interserens, in duobus tantum coacervavi libellis. Nam non his qui sunt assidua lectione ad virile robur exculti, sed formidolosis adhuc sub disciplina pueris, operam dedi, ut dum absentibus interdum preceptoribus illa manus inpuberum, quasdam inter se (nullas tamen in re) nenias aggarriret, uti in his exercendis et crebro cantandis versiculis ingeniolum quodammodo acueret, tum istis potius uteretur. Quocirca si ad hanc rem utcumque opus sit codicello, eo iure in tuam sinceram commendo fidem, ut errata corrigas, superflua reseces, ut in te primo post deum permanendae securitatis quaerat asilum. Non enim quisquam ita ut sciam, et tu perliquido nosti, in ventum aliquid scriptitans, posteris monimentum de se ullum reliquit.

Nilus ut Egyptum perfundit flumine dextro,
sic tua percurrat peto lingua diserta libellum.

many times in two, sometimes in three (as you will see them written one after the other), furthermore interspersing them with some new and popular tales and with a few divine ones. For I worked not for those who are already perfected to manly strength by careful attentive reading, but for those timid little boys still subject to discipline in school; so that, when their teachers are at times absent, while that band of youths is babbling to one another certain ditties (though none of them to any purpose) in order to sharpen somewhat their meager talent by practicing and frequently chanting those little verses, at such times they might rather use these. And so, if to this purpose my little book needs anything at all, I commend it to your sincere trustworthiness, on these conditions: that you correct the errors; that you cut out what is superfluous; that it might seek in you first, after God, an asylum of enduring safety. Indeed nobody (so far as I know, and as you know very clearly) scribbling anything in the wind has left any monument of himself to posterity.

Just as the Nile pours over Egypt with its beneficial
flood,
so, I pray, may your fluent tongue run over this little
book.

BOOK ONE

The Embellished Prow

[INCIPIT LIBELLUS CUI NOMEN FECUNDA RATIS. PARS PRIOR: PRORA DISTINCTA]

Lintris foeta iocis diversa aplustria portat,
cuius Prora nitet vario distincta colore.

Sic me iuvisti velut ardens flamina tectum.
Absque suo nihil eventu consistere dicunt.
Ad cuius veniat scit cattus lingere barbam.
Omne bonum pulcre veniens in fine beatum.
Iure canes rumpunt maculantem furfure vultum.
It lupus inter oves cum sermo ceditur inde.
Rana super sedem velotius exit honorem.
Sicubi torret amor, mirantur lumina formam.
Crebra manus palpat, quo menbra dolore coquuntur.
Tecum migret honor, solus quocumque recedas.
Qui rem dissuadet caram, sibi suscitat iram.
Nam quod fastidit, perfecte nullus amabit.
Defuncti vituli senior bos tergora traxit.
Ante novam moriens procumbit cornipes herbam.
In curte est pecus adveniens nutritus apud rus.
Compescatur aqua, quod quisque minatur in igne.

[HERE BEGINS THE LITTLE BOOK WHOSE NAME IS *THE WELL-LADEN SHIP.* FIRST PART: THE EMBELLISHED PROW]

My ship teeming with riddles carries diverse rigging;
its "Embellished Prow" shines with manifold color.

You helped me like the winds help a burning roof.
Nothing, they say, exists without its destined outcome.
A cat knows whose beard it may come to lick.
Every good thing that comes out well in the end is blessed.
Dogs rightly destroy the man who dirties his face with bran.
The wolf appears among the sheep when there is talk of
him.
A frog on a throne quickly gives up the honor.
Where Love burns, there our eyes admire beauty.
The hand keeps stroking the spot where the limbs are
tormented by pain.
Let honor go with you, wherever you withdraw in solitude.
One who argues against what is dear, arouses anger against
himself.
Nobody will truly love something that disgusts him.
An older ox has been known to haul away the hide of a dead
calf.
The horse drops dead before the new grass arrives.
One reared in the country is a brute when he arrives at
court.
What a man threatens with fire should be quenched with
water.

It sero canis ad coplas senioribus annis.
Non semper pueri, nec edendi tempora mora.
Non quaecumque vides intentant nubila nymbos.
Ossa canes rodant, ubi noctis tempore latrant.
Unde oneras plaustrum, pavor in temone resultat.
Non sic veste nova, saturo quam ventre iocatur.
Quid comedat, sapit omnis avis per cornea rostra.
Qui fuerit lenis, tamen haud bene creditur amni.
Digresso pastore pecus dilabitur omne.
Quam cuperet meretrix incestas vivere cunctas!
Castigat natam "quod sum, ne desere" scortum.
Ignis ano, cibus ore licet—privignus at idem.
Non nurui placet ulla suae nisi mortua socrus.
Permissa est magnae plerisque licentia culpae.
Dum deerit cattus, discurrens conspicitur mus.
Fortis ab invalido metuat persona periclum.
Sepe leo fortis muscarum sumitur escis.
Consumptum redit in nihilum rubigine ferrum.
Venatur tristis, cui desunt crustula panis.
Qui male consulitur, melius quid suadet agendum.
Cum bove non ludant vituli per cornua victi.

A dog in advanced years goes too late to the leashes.
We are not children forever, nor is it always the season for
eating berries.
Not every cloud you see threatens rain.
Let dogs gnaw their bones where they do their barking at
night.
When you overload the cart, there is trembling in the pole
beam.
It is not so much by new clothing as by a full belly that one
is tickled.
Every bird tastes with its hard beak whatever it eats.
One does well to distrust a stream, even one that is calm.
When the shepherd has strayed, the whole flock scatters.
How the prostitute wishes that all women would live
wantonly!
A whore reproves her daughter "Stick to being what I am."
Whether there is fire in his arse or food in his mouth, a
stepson is always the same.
No mother-in-law is pleasing to her daughter-in-law unless
she is dead.
License granted to most people leads to great mischief.
While the cat's away, the mouse is seen scurrying about.
A powerful person should fear danger from a weak one.
Often the powerful lion is consumed as food for flies.
Iron, consumed by rust, returns to nothing.
He is a sad hunter who has no crusts of bread.
One who is reluctant to take advice is better at persuading
others what they should do.
Calves should not play with an ox since they are
outmatched in horns.

Bos, nisi vult, bibet invitus, dum ducis aquatum.
Vitibus ut mater, tantum nocet ipsa capella.
Promptius instabit res quisque suas alienis.
De pulcra subolent contracta piacula pelle.

Iste supervacuus tamquam poletrinus in hoste;
quem fastidimus, quinta est nobis rota plaustri.

Propter equum magis incedes secure, viator.
Cornice inmuni tollet stipendia milvus?
Gallina, ut semper, trahit anteriora retrorsum.
Tu circa puteum noli discurrere, psaltes.
Iniustis alienus amor ne crede novercis.
Dum durat follis, semper dominatur asellis.
Invidia puer et vetulus consumitur ira.
Regem habeat comitem, qui regi comparat hostem.
Debita longa trahens pro frumine solvat avenam.
Qui frustra sua consumunt, aliena catillant.
Inplet et extendit locupletem curta supellex.
In scamno fatuus tibias per inania vibrat.
Vocis in articulo stolidus dinoscitur erro.
Quo careat quis nummatus, solum superest pus.

An ox, unless he wants to drink, will do so unwillingly when you lead him to water.
As much as the mother goat harms the grapevines, so also does her kid.
Everyone will apply himself to his own affairs more readily than to other peoples'.
Sins committed in a pretty pelt still stink.

He is as useless as a pony in battle; someone we dislike is a fifth wheel to our cart.

You will travel more safely, traveler, if you go alongside your horse.
Will the kite take the tribute while the crow is unrewarded?
A hen always draws back to the surface the foremost things.
You, musician, don't run around near a well.
You who are dear to another, do not trust unjust stepmothers.
While a sack remains [to be carried], it is always the lord of the asses.
A boy is consumed by envy, an old man by anger.
One who prepares an army against a king, should have a king as his ally.
One who drags out his debts for a long time can pay with straw instead of grain.
Those who rashly devour their own stores, end up licking another's plate.
A meager property enriches and enlarges a wealthy one.
A fool on a bench swings his legs in the breezes.
As soon as he utters a sound, a stupid man is recognized as a vagabond.
There remains only pus for the rich man to lack.

Morbus ovem, quae sola gregem mox inquinat omnem.
Albior estne quidem cornix studiosa lavandi?
Famina nostra docet picam esuries imitari.
Nam livor, quibus est plenus, vetat ossa caninus.
Subsidet in tecto passer, dum migrat hirundo.
Qui picas fovere, habeant, quod dicere nolo.
Nondum venit in utre suo, iam bacchus acessit.
Qui telam orditur, telam disterminet idem.
Pluris enim constat dilatio nocte sub una.
In quo sunt similes aper et rubicundula vulpes?
Corticis et ligni medium ne fixeris unguem.
Ordea manduces, panis dum cogit egestas.
Corvus non crocitando cadaver solus haberet.
Absque suis paleis nequit ulla annona venire.
Dum flagrat vicina domus, ibi proximat ad te.
Non sincera levat, sua qui pulmenta supinat.
Ignavum mordere canem haud vereare latrantem.
Plaustra molendino ut veniunt, discedite, folles.
Pane quis attentus nimirum attentior auro.
Qualis ad aediculas, non talis in hoste voluptas.
Heu male sorbet eas, quisquis non digerit offas.

Disease infects one sheep, which alone soon infects the whole flock.
Is the crow any whiter because he is fond of washing?
Hunger teaches the magpie to imitate our speech.
A dog's envy denies bones [to others], though he has plenty.
The sparrow stays under the roof, while the swallow migrates.
Let those who have raised magpies have what I'd rather not name.
It has not yet been bottled, and already the wine is growing sour.
Whoever begins the weaving ought to finish it.
A delay of one night is worth a great deal.
How is the wild boar like the little red fox?
Don't stick your fingernail between the bark and the wood.
You should eat barley when the lack of [any other] bread compels you.
The crow, by not crowing, could have the cadaver for himself.
No grain comes without its chaff.
When your neighbor's house is burning, the fire is getting close to you.
One who drops his food, does not pick it up unblemished.
You should not fear that a cowardly dog who barks will bite.
Get out of the way, mere sacks of grain, when wagonloads come to the mill!
He who is frugal with bread is surely more frugal with gold.
There is no such pleasure on campaign as there is in our own little houses.
Whoever cannot digest the mouthfuls—oh, how ill-advisedly he swallows them!

Castrum munitum testudo facit rigidorum.
Verbera debentur pueris, reverentia canis.
Dignum conubium, proculo dum competit uxor.
Sero opici muris perit intractabile rostrum.
Sermo est vulgaris: cuneus cum pane iuvabit.
Armillam portare iuvat, quicumque meretur.
Segnius auditis malim quam credere visis.
Tergora nemo canum componit idonea melli.
Quid canis ad sacram colaphos nisi queritat aedem?
Lingere quod nequeat, tundit gallina patellam.
Rure valent oculi, densis in saltibus aures.
[Silva suas aures et habent sua lumina campi.]
Vel loto cane vel pexo non mundius itur.
Non pedes a toto rudenti vectus asello.
Non paleas vitae tutor defendit inanes.
Cuius enim est asinus, comes hunc post terga scquatur.
Solvitur in pluviam, dum canduit alba pruina.
Dat modicum comiti, sicam qui lingit inunctam.
Non rabidi canis est multus grex visus oberrans.
Sic sepes non senta, velut mulier sine vitta.
Qui pendet, nimium dilatio longa videtur.

A shield of strong men fortifies a camp.
Children deserve beatings, those with gray hair respect.
It is a worthy marriage when the wife is suited to her suitor.
The gnawing mouse's indomitable tooth takes a long time to wear down.
The saying is common: it's nice to have some white bread with your [plain] bread.
It's pleasant to wear an arm ring when one has earned it.
I would rather be slower to believe things I have heard than things I have seen.
Nobody makes dogs' hides suitable for [storing] honey.
What is a dog going to find at church except a beating?
Because it cannot lick the platter, a hen pecks at it.
In a field, the eyes are strong; in dense forests, the ears.
[The woods have their ears, and the fields have their eyes.]
Whether the dog is washed or combed, it ends up no cleaner.
One carried on a braying little ass is not entirely a pedestrian.
He who protects his own life does not defend worthless chaff.
The one who owns the ass, should follow behind it as its companion.
When the white frost has begun to glitter, it is turning to rain.
The man who licks a greasy knife gives little to his companion.
One rarely sees many stray offspring from a rabid dog.
A hedge without thorn bushes is like a woman without a hair ribbon.
To a man hanging, any delay seems too long.

Non hosti parcas, artes nec discere cesses.
Formidat passer crebris in fustibus actus.
Territus igne semel post haec puer odit eundem.
Aequa et communis non frangit sarcina dorsum.
Mel mandens patiatur acum sub melle latentem.
Nemo gravem poterit procul a se pellere fascem.
Dultior exquisita manu vindicta videtur.
Grande pedum sibi, quem cordis timor arguit, aptet.
Vertit eo caudam, qua decidit arbore, malum.
Stercus olet foedum, quo plus vertendo movetur.
Non sic latus ager quam dulcis frater ametur.
Pressus humi serpens obvolvit terga vianti.
Raro actore lupo quisquam venabitur alter.
Pix contacta sui manibus palponis adheret.
Inmundus canis inmundam sorbebit orexim.
Interdum stultus, qui stulto cedere nescit.
Magfridus meruit sua donativa sedendo.
Aes, quodcumque rubet, non credas protinus aurum.
De quo fama, dies aequat longevus Hyringi.
Prestat apes una inmensis per moenia muscis.
Accepta ditione Poles iugulat genitorem.
Non cadit in pontem sapiens equitator hiantem.

You should not spare an enemy, nor cease to learn [his] arts.
A sparrow is timid when driven away by frequent beatings.
A child once terrified by fire will avoid it thereafter.
A burden that is equal and shared does not break the back.
Let the one who eats the honey endure the sting that hides in it.
No man can drive a heavy burden very far from himself.
Vengeance acquired by your own hand seems sweeter.
The man convicted of faintheartedness had better cut himself a big stick.
An apple turns its stem toward the tree from which it fell.
Shit smells foully, the more it is stirred up by turning.
A broad field should not be loved as much as a sweet brother.
Trampled on the ground, a snake wraps its coils around the traveler.
When a wolf is in charge rarely will any other wolf hunt.
Pitch, when touched, sticks to the hands of the one touching it.
A filthy dog will swallow its filthy vomit.
Sometimes the fool is the one who does not have the sense to yield to a fool.
Magfrid earned his rewards by sitting idly.
You should not immediately assume that any reddish metal is gold.
A long-lived man equals the age of Hyringus, of whom legend speaks.
One bee in the city is preferable to countless flies.
Once he gets the authority, Poles slits his own father's throat.
A wise rider does not fall on a gaping bridge.

Quisquis opus, nam se multo prius oderit, odit.
Ipse suum tetulit, cuius porrigo, galerum.
Gratis equo oblato non debes pandere buccas.
Successus felix putat ire simillima cunctis.
Excoriare pecus qui nescit, tergora ledit.
Nec mihi munda manus, canis et non teste solutus.
Invitus canis et luctans ad balnea migrat.
Regem aliquem magna est penuria degere solum.
Nix ruat aut ymber densus, tamen hospes iturus.
Suspirat sonipes vacuis presepibus egre.
Antiqua enituere novo commissa rubore.
Extollens animus, dum nititur alta, labascit.
Sepe tholis suberunt angusta cibaria celsis.
Agris fertilibus pretiosum ceditur aurum.
Aurum odiumque dei cuncto graviora metallo.
Lux manifesta hodie, sed crastina ceca diei.
Musca sitit morbum, potor super omnia vinum.
Deinde fit informis, qui primo pulcher, asellus.
Pro sapone dato capite haec carissima merx est.
Consulit in brevibus deus his, quos somnia terrent.
Dat deus ipse boves nulli per cornua ductos.
Finditur in bivio bracis aut podice tendens.
Nidos commaculans inmundus habebitur ales.
Pelex nec factis claret nec nomine digna.

Whoever hates his work, surely hated himself first.
The man who had scabs on his head wore his cap.
When a horse is offered for free, you should not open its mouth.
One happy in his own successes thinks things go similarly for all.
He who does not know how to skin an animal, damages the hide.
My hand is not clean, and the dog still has one testicle.
A dog goes to a bath unwillingly and struggling.
It is a sign of great poverty for a king to spend time alone.
Let snow or heavy rain fall, still the guest is going to leave.
A horse snorts ill-temperedly when the mangers are empty.
Old sins have often bloomed with fresh blushes.
A boasting spirit begins to waver when it strives for the heights.
Often under lofty domes there will be meager meals.
Precious gold is inferior to fertile fields.
Gold and God's enmity are heavier than any metal.
The light of day is manifest today, but tomorrow's is blind.
The fly thirsts for disease, the drunkard above all for wine.
The little ass who at first is beautiful afterward becomes ugly.
To trade one's head for soap is a very bad bargain.
God soon ministers to those whom dreams terrify.
God himself gives to no one oxen led by the horns.
One heading in two directions is split either in his trousers or his arse.
A bird that fouls its own nest will be considered unclean.
A concubine is neither distinguished in deeds nor dignified in name.

Stultus enim tempus non vitat dampna per omne.
Fermentum populat cum pullis funditus ornix.
Omne bonum in tectis coniunx vagabunda ligurrit.
Post homines gravis et magnus conflictus equorum.
Praecarum penuria dat pro panibus aurum.
Dum tibi lac detur, cuius sit vacca, quid urit?
Pontis erit sollers aliquis cur ante capellas?
Loripes exibit liber mendace reperto.
Cum piscem pro pisce locas, olet alter eorum.
Quanto plus iuris, tanto quis plenior, haurit.
Sepius exclusum foris obliviscimur intus.
Ille opifex fertur, qui rem disponit agendam.
Hoc facit ingenium, nequeunt quod vectis et asser.
Non queritur veris mulier satis ebria verbis.
Consumenda habitis sunt nobis pascua porcis.
Nidos destituens sine pennis corruit ales.
Porci postponunt gemmas, quas calcibus instant.
Consumendo vorans alios formosior ales.
Summa minor domino multis commissa ministris.
Carus erit minime, qui, quod scit, ventilat omne.

A fool does not avoid losses altogether.
A hen with her chicks plays havoc with the milled corn.
A wayward wife slurps up every good thing in the house.
After [that of] men, the greatest and deadliest battle is that of horses.
Penury trades the most precious gold for bread.
So long as the milk is given to you, why do you burn to know whose cow it is?
Why will anyone be worried about a bridge before [he has] goats?
The lame man will depart freely, when the liar has been caught.
When you trade one fish for another, one of them stinks.
The more sauce a man slurps, the fatter he gets.
When we are inside we often forget the one excluded outside.
He is [rightly] called the creator of the work, who arranges what must be done.
Ingenuity accomplishes what the pole and the beam cannot.
A woman in her cups does not complain with truthful words.
Our pastures must be grazed by the pigs we have.
A bird that leaves the nest unfledged falls to the ground.
Pigs place little value in gems, which they trample with their hooves.
A bird grows handsomer by devouring others for food.
A sum entrusted to many servants diminishes for the master.
The one who broadcasts all he knows will not be much loved.

Qui minus inspiciunt, incauto verbere cedunt.
Rarus enim grex foecundatur in exule tecto.
Non tollit donata gelu tibi pascua nec nix.
Intendens aliud diversa et dissona profert.
Pro! molli pastore lupus turbaverat agnos.
Labitur enitens sellis haerere duabus.
Exhaustis canibus bene non venaberis umquam.
Ad pugnos vacuos crebro non advolat auceps.
Stantes sepe casas anceps fidutia vertit.
Sepe minus, quod non oculi videre, doletur.
Piscis, avis licet ossa habeant: bona rapula nullum.
Gutta cavat lapidem, consumitur anulus usu.
Assidue non saxa legunt volventia muscum.
Iuncea longinquis melior vicinia pratis.
Mollia ceduntur ferro, sed dura retundunt.

Ad nos nemo venit nisi cum rumore sinistro;
ex multo iam tempore dextera fama recessit.

Quem non alma fides, neque sacramenta tenebunt.
Frigida cum calidis duo sunt contraria calvis.
Mus massam trahit et nequit ipse subire foramen.
Non callem veterem, non oblivescere amicum.

Those who see poorly, strike with an overhasty rod.
It is a rare flock indeed that is fruitful under a foreign roof.
Neither cold nor snow takes away the pastures granted you [by God].
One who means something other [than what he says], says things that are contradictory and discordant.
Oh, the wolf wreaked havoc among the lambs when the shepherd was lax!
One striving to cling to two stools, falls.
You will never hunt well with tired dogs.
A falcon does not keep returning to empty fists.
Wavering confidence often overturns standing houses.
Often what the eyes have not seen causes less pain.
Though fish and fowl may have bones, fine little turnips have none.
A drop of water hollows out a stone; a ring is consumed by wear.
Continually rolling stones do not collect moss.
Nearby reed is better than far off meadows.
Soft things are pounded by iron, but hard things strike back.

No one comes to us except with bad tidings; it is a long time now since good news vanished.

One whom genial faith does not bind, oaths will not bind either.
Cold and heat are two opposing evils for bald men.
The mouse is hauling a mallet, and he cannot enter his hole.
Do not forget an old path or an old friend.

Quod lupus invadit, mihi crede, invitus omittit;
quem lupus asportat, feralia carmina cantat.

Aure lupi visa non longe est credere caudam.
Arcendus prius est tibi, quam lupus intret ovile.
Quam timui innatum, tam te formido minantem.
Fel terrae pallet, furit hoc absintium et ardet.
Qui retinet censum, videat ne perdat agellum.
Quo magis abruptus gradus, hinc gravior quoque casus.
Palmam militiae prefert animi moderator.
Quadrupes occumbit—quid si tu labere verbis?
Suscipitur male porticibus te limine pellens.
Quanto nobilius, tanto mage flexile collum.
Pauperis exsuperat stultum sapientia regem.
Is, qui pre manibus deus adiuvat, ille benignus.
Non fluor aut sanies manat de corpore sano.
Sanum vinxisti digitum, dissolvito sanum.
Hic probulus frater corda modulatur amena.
De cocleare cadit, quod hianti porrigis ori.
De quibus ipse locis veniat, mihi dicat amicus.
Ecce manus quae non rapiunt, tegetes tibi reddunt.
Mendicans bene non poterit cantare Camena.
Mendicans dispergit epos tenuatque Thalia.

Believe me, what a wolf lays hold of, he is loath to let go; the
one whom the wolf carries off sings funeral dirges.

When you glimpse the wolf's ear, you can be sure the tail is
not far off.
You must fend off the wolf before he can enter the
sheepfold.
I fear you threatening me now as much as I feared you in
the womb.
Gall of the earth grows pale; wormwood rages and burns.
He who withholds his tax payment should take care that he
does not lose his field.
The steeper the step, the heavier the fall from it.
He who governs his own spirit carries off the trophy of war.
Even a quadruped falls down; does it matter if you stumble
over words?
It is unwise to receive in your front hall one who drives you
from the threshold.
The nobler the neck, the more it is capable of bending.
The wisdom of a pauper excels a stupid king.
The god who is at hand to aid us is a kind god.
Pus or blood does not flow from a healthy body.
You bandaged a healthy finger; unbandage it healthy.
Here our good little brother strikes a pleasant chord.
What you extend to your mouth, even though it is wide
open, falls from the spoon.
A [true] friend should tell me whence he comes.
Whatever hands do not steal, houses return to you.
A Muse reduced to begging will not be able to sing well.
A Thalia reduced to begging destroys an epic and
diminishes it.

Esuriens Clio defrudat laudabile carmen.
Mandant Waltero fratres non reddere brachas.
Quam male nutritum melius non vivere natum.
Ingenio salso preceps violentia cedit.
Digna verecunda referamus seria mensa.

Res pueriliter insolitae carbone notantur;
olim prosperitas calclo numeratur in albo.

Labitur Asturco pedibus nitendo quaternis.
Fortes de ferro non pluris habentur inaures.

Vera videre loquens folium recitare Sybyllae;
responsis cautus, quid refert alter Apollo?

Ipse canit, quae scit, quamquam domus alta, sacerdos.
Dulce sed inmundum mel est in folle canino.
Mel posui famulis, non virus; et ulcera fovi.
Frigidus inplebit frumentis horrea Maius.
Vitalis comes est ratis in fluvialibus undis.
Scandit equum rabies cum stulto plurima servo.
Nam pennis descendit avis de nube remissis.

A hungry Clio damages a song of praise.
The brothers enjoin Walter not to surrender his pants.
It is better for a child not to live than to be brought up badly.
Rash force is inferior to quick wits.
Let us speak worthy and serious things at a respectable table.

Unfamiliar things are marked, in the childish fashion, with charcoal; long ago, prosperity was reckoned with a white stone.

Even an Asturian horse, which stands on four legs, falls.
Iron earrings, though strong, are not considered of much value.

Speaking the truth, you seem to be reciting from the Sibyl's leaf; what does our second Apollo, prudent in his responses, report?

Even if the church is lofty, the priest sings only what he knows.
Honey in a dog-skin flask is sweet but unclean.
I gave honey to my servants, not poison—and fostered ulcers.
A cold May will fill the granaries with corn.
A raft is a vital companion in a river's waves.
A great deal of madness mounts a horse along with a stupid servant.
Surely the bird [at some point] descends from the clouds on slackened wings.

Munda quidem mundus colliria querit ocellus.
Quod careat lingua, stolidus non inde tacet bos.
Ex testa qualis fuerit dinoscitur olla.
Crapula suffocat mentem, Venus ebria mersat.
Cur, qui non callet, stultus puer ambit honorem?
Nam digitus sanus lippum prevertit ocellum.
Sedulus est curagulus offitio residendi.
Quitne diu canis inmunes calcare placentas?
Confidens animi canis est in stercore noto.
In qua pelle lupus modo nascitur, hac morietur.
Hoc quoque cum multis abiit, quod Bertheca nevit.
Dum manus arte vacat, carnem scalpendo cruentat.
Rex, ubi vult, solet invitas discindere leges.

Dum cupio vitare lupum, ferus ingruit ursus;
ursum declinans offendi forte leonem.

Quod nostrum non est, immo alterius perhibebis.
Non mihi carus erit, qui profert omnia, quae scit.
Non erit inmunis culpae, qui iurat in arte.
Non suspendetur se iudice quisque latronum.
Delusor promisit apes—ego credulus!—albas.
"Ludimus antiquum" rapiens aquila inquit ad aucam.
Emendet monitoris egens iter axe citato.
Vestis carne calet, caro qua calefacta calescit.

A pure eye surely looks for pure eye salves.
It is not because he lacks a tongue that the dumb ox is
silent.
From a shard one can discern what the pot was like.
Gluttony stifles the mind; drunken Venus drowns it.
Why does a stupid boy who has no skill seek honor?
A healthy finger is more valuable than a bleary eye.
A sedulous person is intent on the business of sitting.
Can a dog tread for long on cakes without harming them?
A dog is bold on the shit-heap he knows.
A wolf will die in the skin it was born with.
What Bertheca wove has perished, along with many other
things.
When the hand lacks a useful task, it bloodies the flesh by
scratching.
A king, when he wishes, shreds uncongenial laws.

While I am trying to avoid the wolf, a wild bear attacks;
backing away from the bear, I chanced upon a lion.

Whatever is not ours, is to be regarded as another's.
The man who tells everything he knows, will not endear
himself to me.
He who swears an oath with intent to deceive, will not be
free of blame.
No thief will be hanged, if he himself is the judge.
The trickster promised white bees—I'm gullible!
The eagle snatching up the goose told it, "We're playing an
old game."
He who lacks a guide ought to alter his journey posthaste.
Clothing is warmed by the flesh; the flesh it warmed grows
warm [from it in turn].

Terra malos homines nunc educat atque pusillos,
olim maioris fidei cum robore grandi.

Qui volet esse puer centum maledictus in annis.
Nugatur promissa petens quasi debita solvi.
Idem animus non est asino pueroque minanti.
Semper habet tussis miscere calentibus egris.
Cursim currendo concurrunt famina multa.
Quippe infrunito non sufficit omne paratum.
Probrose interdum vivit, qui non numerose.
Non multum metuas matutinum hospitem et ymbrem.
De folle accipias obturans follis hyatum.
Res commissa cani: canis it committere caudae.
Unguibus arta tenet locuples de paupere factus.
Lodix plurima erit, quae clauserit ora loquentum.
Utimur inde foris, quod sepe domi recitamus.
Qui patrem occidit, non patrem reddet eundem.
Cum liquor exsuperat, pleno de margine manat.
Corrigias excide alieno in tergore largas.
Pars hominum didicit quid frangere, non solidare.

The earth now produces bad men, and small ones; once
[they were] of greater faith and of full-grown strength.

Whoever seeks to be a child at a hundred years, will be cursed.
He is talking nonsense, demanding that promises be paid as though they were debts.
The ass and the boy threatening it are not of like mind.
A cough will always attack those ill with a fever.
Many rumors, running swiftly, race with one another.
To the insatiable person everything at hand is insufficient.
One who does not live in a measured way, must sometimes live in a disreputable one.
Do not fear overmuch the guest or the rain that arrives in the morning.
Take from the sack to patch the hole in the sack.
A task is entrusted to a dog; the dog will entrust it to his tail.
A poor man who has become rich holds things tightly in his clutches.
It will be a large cloth indeed that will shut the mouths of talkers.
What we recite often at home, we then repeat outdoors.
He who kills a father, will not restore him whole.
When there is too much liquid, it overflows the brim.
Cut the belts long when the leather is someone else's.
A portion of mankind has learned how to break something, not how to fix it.

Dura valetudo certissima mortis imago;
longus item languor fatalem tendit ad urnam.

Calliditas ita grata foret, si calleat unus.
"Pauper," ait, "non vendo, immo suffragia venor."
Vertitur heus rerum mutabilis ordo vicissim.
De cane edente canem rabies acerrima surgit.
Alba videntur in albis ova inserta farinis.

Signatur de fune freneticus, unde ligatus;
et canis inde nolam subvectat, ut hinc caveatur.

In baculo pastor popularis cernitur unco.
Delictum premitur, si pena sequens timeatur.
Hic solus sapiens, quem condierit humilis mens.
Sumitur adiutor, qui consilii est onerator.
Stultus dampnatus maiori cedit honori.
In plaustro, quodcumque novum, quod inutile, stridit.
Securus, cui cuncta arrident prospera, dormit.
Quippe diu male cesus lamentabitur infans.
Nec curas sanctos neque enim curaris ab illis.
Currere festinans in asello perdit opellam.
Sola putat fatuus, quae cogitat, insita veris.
Cui satis est piperis, pultes condire licebit.

Adverse health is the most certain sign of death; likewise, a long weakness leads toward the fatal urn.

Cleverness would be pleasing on this condition: if only one person were clever.
"As a pauper," he says, "I do not sell favors; rather I seek them."
Oh how the mutable order of things turns and turns again!
The bitterest rage arises from dog eating dog.
They are like white eggs placed in white flour.

A madman is identified by the rope with which he is bound; and a dog wears a bell so that it might thereby be avoided.

The common shepherd is recognized by his hooked staff.
Crime is suppressed if it is feared that punishment will follow.
That man alone is wise whom a humble mind has seasoned.
[Sometimes] an advisor is taken who is a hindrance to deliberation.
A fool, after he has suffered harm, yields to a greater authority.
On a wagon, whatever is new, whatever is broken, creaks.
A man on whom all prosperity smiles sleeps carefree.
An infant who is hardly beaten will wail for a long time.
You care nothing for the saints, and in turn they care nothing for you.
He who tries to go fast on a little ass, wastes his effort.
A fool reckons that only the things he thinks himself are full of truth.
One who has enough pepper can season even his gruel.

Vir fugitans lites extinguit seditiones,
nam semper furiosus amat committere rixas.

Litus ama, proreta, celer surgente procella.

Ei mihi servitii perierunt tempora longi:
O salva mercede, deus, nos respice tantum!

Lapsa suam non post solidabit virgo ruinam.
Vos, ubi defitiunt iurati, herete, propinqui.
Vana superstitio est, quod non sum, velle videri.
Lumina qui dolet eruta, non gemit irrita dampna.
Allinis in vanum fundendo picem super udum.
Parci sunt cinici mollesque in carne cinedi.
Ariditas gaudet paucis, opulentia multis.
Pauperiem dilatat inops, cum vina frequentat.
Subiacet, ut semper, solitis ignavia dampnis.
Penitet ante tubas galeatum sero duelli.
Annuum ab exitibus non omne revertitur agmen.
Maxima quaeque domus servis est plena superbis.
Commendo calvum, non tota fronte glabellum.

Libertas decet hos humeros, ubi nobilis ortus;
obscura et stulta est ignavia fasce premenda.

A man who avoids conflicts extinguishes strife, for the hotheaded man always loves to engage in brawls.

Hug the coast, pilot, and be swift about it when a storm is rising.

Alas! The seasons of my long service have been wasted.
Oh God, only look upon us with the reward of salvation!

A fallen virgin will not afterward restore her ruin.
Stand by us, relatives, when those bound by oaths abandon us!
It is an empty vanity to wish to seem what I am not.
He who is pained because his eyes have been gouged out, bemoans no mean loss.
When you pour pitch over a wet object, you coat it in vain.
"Cinici" are parsimonious; "cinedi" are soft in the flesh.
Parsimony is content with a few things, opulence with many.
A poor man extends his poverty when he has frequent recourse to wine.
As always, laziness is at the root of the usual losses.
Right before the trumpets [blast], it is too late for a helmeted man to rue the battle.
The year's recruits do not all return from their excursions.
Every great house is full of haughty servants.
I approve of a bald man, not one who is hairless on his entire face.

Liberty suits those shoulders where the birth is a noble one; it is worthlessness, stupid and of obscure origin, that should be crushed under a burden.

Mantica mulorum lumbos, eques ulcerat armos.
Iustitiam opprimit invitam violentus et exlex.
Expuncta sanie solidatur sautia pellis.
Ante boves versum non vidi currere plaustrum.
Filia non recte generis datur una duobus.
Non potes uxorem quam dicunt ducere glorem.
Currit iter liquidum multo sinuamine hyrundo.
Terra tenet sulcum, levis aer et unda recurrunt.
Vermiculus lens, lendis; lens a lente legumen.
Participes sint plagarum, qui forte epularum.
Turpiter in mensa, si non sis mente fidelis.
Turpes rana sonos, nullum solet edere melos.
Ranae continuant hac tempestate coaxem.
Cur portant vituli clitellas propter asellos?
Nos iniecta gulae fecerunt ossa tacere.
Propter melle litas non latrat Cerberus offas.
Anulus in digito, digitus cenosus in ungue.
Extinguat vitium, non carnem, qui abstinet escis.
Dum pluitur vobis, nobis stillare necesse est.

The pack chafes the mule's loins, the rider his shoulders.
A violent and lawless man subverts justice he finds uncongenial.
Wounded skin heals when the infection has been expunged.
I've never seen a wagon go when placed in front of the oxen.
It is not right for one daughter to be given to two sons-in-law.
You cannot take as a wife the one they call your sister-in-law.
The swallow flies his smooth course with many a turn.
The earth retains its furrow; light air and water revert to their original state.
Lens, lendis is a little worm; *lens, lentis* is a lentil.
Those who are there to share the meals should share the blows.
It is dishonorable to be loyal to a man's table if you are not loyal to him in your heart.
A frog usually produces unseemly sounds, not a pleasant song.
Frogs continue their croaking throughout their life.
Why do the little bulls carry saddles on account of the asses?
Bones tossed in our gullets have made us silent.
For the sake of gobbets dipped in honey Cerberus stops barking.
There is a ring on the finger; [but] the finger is filthy under the nail.
He who abstains from food ought to eliminate his vice, not his flesh.
When it rains for you, it has to sprinkle for us.

Multis propter iter consurgunt tecta magistris.
Hic te rex ideo, ut loquereris vera, reliquit.
Aequos a puncto formabit circinus orbes.

Cattus amat pisces, sed non vult crura madere;
isque adeo tumidus, si non vult carpere mures.

Nulla farina tamen quamvis aliud sit in urna.
Infans ova petit non curans, unde habeantur.
Ex turpi symia ingenuus leo non generatur.
Dicitur electus de pluribus optio miles.
Quae pars in nostris dic, sodes, uclupa tectis.
Te penes, auditor, quid sit perquire vopiscus.
Velitibus iunctis equites ad bella parantur.
Milvus edit pullos, quamvis non foverit illos.
Non emitur tuto tibi clausa pecunia sacco.
Mus inpune satis mendici in folle superbit.
O puer, ede, quid est et cur sit aranea vatrax.
Cymex, exiguus mus, quid sit, disce, capronus!
Lomentum, furfur sunt purgamenta farinae.
Ve, qui luxuriam moriendo nec ante relinquunt!
Mutua cum nata matrem munuscula amicant.
Dosinus est asinus genitali pelle potitus.

Houses being built by a roadway have many foremen.
The king has left you here so you can speak the truth.
A compass will form equal circles from a point.

A cat loves fish, but does not care to get its paws wet; and it
is too haughty, if it does not want to catch mice.

There is no flour in the jar, though there may be something
else in it.
An infant asks for eggs, without caring where they come
from.
A noble lion is not begotten on an ugly ape.
A soldier chosen from among many is called an adjutant.
Tell me, please, which part in our houses is the ridge?
Ask yourself, listener, what does surviving twin mean?
Knights are prepared for wars when the foot soldiers are
alongside them.
The kite eats chicks, though it did not raise them.
It is risky to purchase money tied up in a sack.
A mouse can be haughty with impunity in a beggar's wallet.
Tell me, child, what a crooked-legged spider is, and why.
Learn what a bug is, you little mouse, with your head bent
over!
Husks and bran are the waste products of grain.
Woe to those who leave luxury behind at death and not
before.
Exchanging gifts makes friends of a mother and her
daughter.
The ass who has the skin he was born in is gray.

Naribus obstrusis odi crutiale catarrum.
Incultae quam plura fovent aviaria silvae.
Curritur ad facinus tamquam ad vivaria pisces.
Uritur hinc vivus defuncti in laude mariti.
Sus inhonestat equi faleras lutulenta decoras.
Fusteus aut raro canis aut numquam bene ridet.
Sponte inarata filix in nostris pullulat agris.
Haec circum pagos et compita currit amica.
Ut te suscipiam, laetus tibi brachia tendo.
Tabida quam facili quassatur aranea tactu!
Da pueris, quod cire vocare, ciere movere.
Candidum erit, quod cura facit; natura quod, album.
Ex multis alius, de binis dicitur alter.
Non sunt accipitres pennati quique volucres.
Panificum coclear non crescit edentis in ore.
Molliter iste legit, quasi qui prunas pede calcat.
Palpat ut estivas ventus percurrit aristas.
Sunt quaedam nescire magis quam prospera scire.
Omnis obest fatienti noxia quam patienti.
Vertitur ad modicum descendens nostra potestas.
Linguam taurus habet, quamvis non multa loquatur.
Accitus si non veniat, veniat bonus annus.
It, rediit Vulteius ad haec, quae nuper omisit.
Accipiente manu potiorem iudico dantis.
Tanto plus calidum, quanto vicinius igni.

I hate a painful nose infection with stopped-up nostrils.
Uncultivated forests foster a great many aviaries.
They rush into crime like fish into feed-ponds.
The living husband is incensed by praise of the dead one.
A filthy pig disgraces the beautiful armor of a horse.
A wooden dog rarely or never laughs well.
Uncultivated, the fern grows spontaneously in our fields.
This harlot runs around the neighborhoods and crossroads.
I joyfully extend my arms to you, in order to welcome you.
The spider's feeble web is shaken by such a light touch!
Tell the boys that *cire* means "to call," *ciere* "to move."
A thing will be *candidus* if effort whitens it; if nature, *albus*.
Alius means "one of many"; *alter* means "one of two."
Not all birds with feathers are hawks.
A spoon made of bread does not get larger in the diner's mouth.
He reads haltingly like one treading on embers with his foot.
His touch is like the wind running through summer grain.
Some things are more profitable not to know than to know.
Every injurious action hurts the one doing it more than the one suffering it.
Our power, declining, is rendered insignificant.
A bull has a tongue, although he does not say much.
If the invited guest does not come, a good year should come.
Vulteius leaves, then returns to the things he just abandoned.
I judge the hand of the giver preferable to that of the receiver.
The nearer a thing is to the fire, the hotter it is.

Ligna, per occasum quod nanciscuntur, habebunt.
Flos foeni typus, extollentia nostra minaeque.
Qui fallit, coclear vacuo deprendit in ore.
Spes venientis aquae, quo iam fluere ante solebat.
Qui te audire fugit, culturae inpendia perdis.
Lancibus appositis in villam transilit ignis.
Dum calidum fuerit, debetur cudere ferrum.
Matutina viros incultos frigora mordent.
Raro audistis ovem de capra poscere lanam.
Plus sapere est quid scire malum; quid prosit, oportet.
Corbulo nomen habet tractum de corbe ferenda.
Stultus erit gnatus dolor altus utrique parenti.
Nemo potest animum invitum curare scolaris.

Luter amat fortis pelles ambire tenellas;
bever habet longe pluris munimen honoris.

Vulturibus semper sunt nota cadavera villae.
Cui bene non volumus, nec dicimus "euge, fidelis."

Filius accrescens vivi genitoris amatur;
mater habet puerum de patre superstite carum.

Inmerito auditur, qui previus ire veretur.

Trees will have whatever place they get when they fall.
Our boasts and threats are like the flower of grass.
He who deceives, takes a spoon in an empty mouth.
There is hope of water coming where it used to flow in the past.
You waste the effort of your teaching on one who refuses to listen to you.
When the platters have been served, the hearth fire skips over to the neighbor's house.
One ought to strike iron while it's hot.
The morning cold nips at men who are inadequately clothed.
Rarely have you heard a sheep asking for wool from a goat.
To know more is to know something bad; it is right to know what is profitable.
Corbulo has a name that came from carrying a basket *(corbis)*.
A stupid son will be a deep pain for both his parents.
Nobody can nourish the mind of a student who is unwilling.

The brave otter prefers to [be the] trim [on] thin hides; the beaver has a covering that is far more esteemed.

The village corpses are always known to the vultures.
We do not say, "Bravo, faithful friend," to one whom we do not wish well.

The growing son of a living father is loved. A mother holds dear the child of a father who is still alive.

One who is afraid to go first, is not worth listening to.

Pavonum caudis visuntur verrere terram:
longa trahunt fratres indignis syrmata nugis.

Pocula terna modum fatiunt, superaddita rixas.

Dicitur in medio vatum saltare Saul rex;
vidimus in clero quendam versare Saulem.

Odit adhuc deus, a quo prima superbia victa est.
Incendetur inops, tumidum dum gloria tollit.
Iustius est modicum quid divitiis sceleratis.
Unde hic promeruit laudes, hoc vapulat alter.

Consilia est celare bonum fidissima regum;
verba dei vulgare salus, sapientia, virtus.

Sarcina dura, virum qui vult tolerare procacem.
"Falsus testis," ait dominus, "non ibit inultus."

Munera, quae donat moriens, ea munera non sunt:
nulli ferme daret, si posset longius uti.

Solaris nimium calor afflat inertia corda.
Fumida comparent interdiu et ignea noctu.
Piscis aqua non sponte caret nec doctus amico.
Dum fueris felix, duri reminiscere casus.

They seem to sweep the ground with the tails of peacocks:
the brothers drag long robes in their unworthy frivolities.

Three cups make a proper measure, any more produce brawls.

King Saul is said to dance among the prophets; we have seen a certain Saul whirl among the clergy.

God, by whom Pride was first overcome, still hates [it].
A poor man will be set on fire, while glory is exalting a proud one.
A reasonable sufficiency is more righteous than dishonorable riches.
What earned this one praise gets that one a beating.

It is good to keep secret the most confidential plans of kings; to spread the words of God is salvation, wisdom, and virtue.

Whoever wants to tolerate an impudent man has a hard burden.
"A false witness," says the Lord, "will not go unpunished."

Gifts which a dying man gives—those are not gifts: he would scarce give them to anyone, if he could use them longer.

Excessive warmth of the sun favors indolent hearts.
Smoky things appear by day, and fiery things by night.
A fish does not willingly do without water, nor a learned man without a friend.
While you are fortunate, be mindful of a hard fall.

Stultus correctus monitorem protinus odit.
Res bene gesta dabit mensurae premia plenae.
Effera mors hominis, serpentis vita venenum.
In diversa vagi fiunt per singula tardi.
Indiscretus amor sotiorum crimina celat.
Diligit omnipotens hilarem deus ipse datorem.
Mucida semper apud parcum cum carne farina.
Ante oculos avium iactabis retia frustra.
Primitiis frugum regem placato supernum.
In te fidentem numquam asperneris amicum.
Omne, quod est in precipiti, stat limite casus.
Quem deus apponit, laetus servabis honorem.
Nam summi pretii melior sapientia gemmis.

Vir sapiens, ubi semper iusta monentur, obaudit;
deputat in stultis derisor dogmata sannis.

Peccati inmunes non sunt, qui multa locuntur.
Inpietatis honor spoliis plorantis honustus.

Augebit formido dei tibi tempora vitae;
inpietas mutilans vivendi proterit annos.

Corruet in fovea fidens in divite gaza.
Qui parcit virgae, sua pignora protinus odit.

A stupid person who is corrected, immediately hates his admonisher.
A thing well done will bestow rewards in full measure.
Poison is savage death to a man, but life to a serpent.
Men who range over vast numbers of things are slow about individual ones.
Indiscriminate love conceals the crimes of companions.
Almighty God himself loves a cheerful giver.
The flour, like the meat, is always moldy at a miser's house.
It is pointless to cast your nets in plain view of the birds.
Placate the King above with the first fruits of the harvest.
You ought never to spurn a friend who trusts you.
Everything which is on a steep precipice, stands on the verge of a fall.

You will happily preserve the honor that God bestows.
Surely wisdom is better than the highest priced gems.

A wise man always pays attention when just things are being taught; a mocker despises teaching with his stupid grins.

Those who talk a lot are not free from sin.
The honor of impiety is weighted down with the spoils of a weeping man.

The fear of God will increase for you the seasons of your life; destructive impiety wears away the years of your existence.

One trusting in rich treasure will sink in a pit.
The one who spares the rod, hates his charges from the start.

Mentem quisque parat, linguam deus ipse gubernat.
In linguae plectro tibi mors et vita parata.
Prudentem deus uxorem legavit in edes.
Verba beant iustum, non centum verbera stultum.
Ad bellum itur equis, dominus dat dona salutis.
Divitiis posuisse modum non infima virtus.
Cuius enim panem manduco, carmina canto.
Hanc pluviam non equiperat, quod rex habet, aurum.
Iugiter os stultum mentitur et inproba lingua.
Pleno sarcofago non conditur alter humandus.
Talliolas invisibilis vitate draconis.
Migale, cuniculus, sophorus nigredine pulchra.
Non prodest adeo tibi mel multum comedenti.
Scuta die portat, sed nocte in stercore iactat.
Pulli sunt surdi, dum trudis in horrea messes.
Calones et plena facit tritura superbos.
Pauperem apud dominum servi spes nulla opulenti.
Haec vita est oculorum, carnis, et ambitus orbis.
Qui non compatitur miseris, quid habet pietatis?
Inter aves reliquas biteriscus queritat escas.
Hoc carmen pueris "but, but" de cornibus exit.
In psalmis et laude dei torpescere noli.

Each man makes up his own mind; God himself controls his tongue.
In the strumming of your tongue lie death and life.
It is God who bequeathed [you] a prudent wife in the house.
Words benefit a just man; a hundred lashings don't benefit a stupid one.
We go to war on horses; but it is the Lord who grants us safety.
It is not the lowliest of virtues to have placed a limit on your wealth.
Whose bread I eat, his songs I sing.
All the gold that a king has does not equal this rain.
A stupid mouth and a wicked tongue lie continually.
When a sarcophagus is full, we don't put another corpse in.
Avoid the invisible snares of the serpent.
Ermine, rabbit, and sable have a beautiful blackness.
It does not benefit you much to eat a lot of honey.
He carries shields by day, but at night he throws them in the dung.
The chicks are deaf while you are shoveling the harvests into the granaries.
An ample harvest makes even the porters haughty.
There is no hope of finding a wealthy servant in the home of a poor master.
This life is lust of the eyes, of the flesh, and of the world.
One who is not compassionate to the wretched—what has he of piety?
The kinglet seeks his food along with the other birds.
This song for children "būt, būt" comes out of the horns.
Don't be lazy regarding the Psalms and the praise of God.

Difficiles sunt res, numerando quis explicat omnes?
Corvorum pullis dominus non denegat escas.
Caseus est durus, canibus quem non dat avarus.
Arguo te cedis, qui spem non ponis in armis.
Promptus ero, ut celeres sunt ad fenilia furcae.
In multis asinis nullus discursus equinus.

Qualiter adversus fortes pugnabit inermis?
Scuta dei, qui materialia non potes, obde.

Quod fuit, illud eo melius, quod non erit ultra.
Plaustra cadunt: hinc passim verba superflua crescunt.

Hunc hominem non sensus, non sapientia condit:
hunc creat ex aliquo, qui de nihilo omnia fecit.

Non hodie est minor ulla boni iactura clientis.

Aevo fractus equus saumaria ferre recusat;
bos vetulus sulcos, epiredia, vitat aratra.

Non aliter te, quam cultrum capra diligit, odi.
Vires pre gazis vegetis placuere Latinis.
Qui celare nequit, fur quo minus ut sit, oportet.
Quid videt is, qui pauper erit, mirum, unde superbit?

Things are difficult: who can explain them in his reckoning?
The Lord does not deny food to the chicks of crows.
It is a hard cheese that the greedy man does not give to his dogs.
I accuse you of murder, you who place no hope in arms.
I will be prompt, as swift as pitchforks to haystacks.
Amid many asses there is nary a horse's gait.

How will an unarmed man fight against strong men? Gird yourself with the shields of God, you who cannot do so with real ones.

What once was, that was better for this reason: that it will not be any longer.
Wagons tip over; then a flurry of words arises on all sides.

Neither sense nor wisdom produces this [thing called] man; he who made everything from nothing, creates *him* from something.

Today, no loss is of less importance than that of a good client.

A horse broken by old age refuses to carry loads; an old ox avoids furrows, harnesses, and plows.

I hate you no differently than a goat likes the butcher's knife.
Strength pleased the energetic Latins more than treasures.
He who cannot conceal, ought not to become a thief.
What does a man who will always be poor see so remarkable that it makes him haughty?

Qui laudant dominum, ne claudas ora loquentum.
Qui misere hic vivunt, his mollius ossa quiescent.

Non poterit domus aut carabus rectore carere,
quo sine nulla viget domus ac sine remige lembus.

Ardea nomen avis, nomen de ventre cacatrix.
Arcet hiemps solem, perdit plaga nostra calorem.
Ad morem cancri nunc cogimur ire retrorsum.
Saltum movisti, sed aves collegerat alter.
Bile sub obliqua geris in penetralibus anguem.

Christe, iuva miseros, sicut vis et potes et scis:
munia qui possunt fieri breviora precantum?

Felix, Leviathan poterit qui rumpere fauces
et tam formidolosos evadere dentes!

Radbodo Freso facit decretum nemine secum
et sine rege, caput procerum laudabile nulli.

Quicquid erit nimium, datur experiendo nocivum.
Vivere vult laute gallinae filius albae.
Ceditur, ut feritas paveat, canis ante leonem.

Do not close the mouths of those speakers who are praising
the Lord.
The bones of those who live miserably on earth will rest in
peace all the more softly.

Neither a house nor a boat can do without a leader; without
him no home thrives, and a ship has no rower.

"Heron" is the name of a bird; its name on account of its
bowels is "crapper."
The winter keeps the sun at bay; our region loses its
warmth.
Like a crab, we are now compelled to move backward.
You stirred up the meadows, but another collected the
birds.
Out of spiteful wrath, you are carrying a viper deep inside
you.

"Christ, help the wretched, as you wish and are able and
know how to do": how can the duty of praying be made
any shorter [than that]?

Happy is the man who can crush the throat of Leviathan
and escape those teeth that are so terrifying!

Radbod the Frisian made a decree, with no one at his side
and without the King—he's a leader of the nobles who
can be praised by no one.

Whatever is excessive—one learns by experience—is
harmful.
The son of a white hen wants to live in luxury.
A dog is beaten in front of a lion to scare the wildness out of
the latter.

Mater pro natis dolet et de pane pusillo,
tristis de multis, cum desit copia panis;
ve matri multis natis et fomite pauco!

Hic visus carnem desiderat et caro mundum.

Precessor cupidus, cupidissimus ecce secutor:
ista feros carpit sententia nostra ministros.

Inprudentis erit per singula verba minari.
Dispergendo quidem tenuabitur ampla facultas.

Mendaci, dum vera canat, vix creditur ulli;
nam quae sanctius affirmat, magis irrita credas.

Qui semper tepuit neque scit, qui queso docebit?
Turris caepta fuit, quae iam derisa refrixit.
Subditus hinc populus gemit, inpietas ubi regnat.
Vera solet canis interdum gannire senilis.

Hinc meror, quod, frater, ades tam rarus ut hospes:
quandocumque redis, iubar ex oriente videris,
iocundos agimus te presto et sospite soles.

Nemo hodie sua dat, nisi carius omnia vendat.

A mother grieves for her children and because of too little bread. She is sad that there are many, when the supply of bread is exhausted. Woe to the mother with many children and little food!

Here, sight desires flesh, and flesh the world.

The leader is greedy, and, see, the subordinate is very greedy: this saying of ours censures cruel ministers.

It is the act of an imprudent man to make threats with every word.
Even an ample supply is bound to be lessened by squandering.

A liar is scarcely believed when he is telling the truth. Indeed, the things he affirms more sincerely, you should consider more worthless.

One who has always been lukewarm and knows nothing—how, I ask, will he teach?
A tower has been begun, which now has stalled, a source of ridicule.
Where impiety rules, the subjugated populace groans.
Sometimes an old dog growls the truth.

I grieve over this, brother, that you are so rarely here as a guest. Whenever you return, you seem a shining light from the east. We spend pleasant days when you are here, safe and sound.

Today nobody provides his goods unless he sells everything at a higher price.

Tollitur insolabiliter pullis pia mater,
destituens inplumes et sine fomite nidos.

Ut phalere decuere suem, sic inprobum honores.
Proficimus, ceu lac distenditur ubere capri.

Et cocus et friget focus atque refectio fratrum:
nullus ut introeat, torpent in limine valvae.

Rite onus alternum subeunt ad pascua cervi.
Ante moras fatiet tibi, quam bene cocta sit, auca.

Dic, aquilae quis scire vias in nube volantis,
quis poterit piscis spiras tot agentis aquosas?

Nomina stellarum, numerum quis dicet harenae?
Traditur herbarum quoque inextricabilis error;
nam volucrum tegitur pictorum calculus ingens.

Qui ficte querunt dominum, non scire merentur.
Dimissus puer arbitrio confunditur actu.
Ve soli! prolapsus humi nec habet subeuntem.
Solvere qui nolit, melius non vota vovere.
Defuncto canis est melior vivendo leone.

A dutiful mother is inconsolably removed from her brood,
leaving her chicks behind unfledged and without food.

Honors suit a wicked man as ornaments do a pig.
Things are going as successfully as milk is drawn from a
billy goat's udder.

The cook and the hearth and the brothers' food are cold;
the doors at the entrance are stiff so that no one may
enter.

Deer [swimming] to pasture support each other's weight in
turn.
Before it's well cooked, a goose will cause you many delays.

Tell me who could know the paths of an eagle flying
through the clouds, who the paths of a fish making so
many watery circuits?

Who will tell the names of the stars, who the number of the
[grains of] sand? Of grasses too there is said to be an
inextricable labyrinth. The enormous tally of the
colorful birds is hidden [from us].

Those who seek the Lord deceitfully don't deserve to know
[him].
A boy left to his own judgment is confused in his conduct.
Woe to him who is alone! Having fallen on the ground, he
has no one to aid him.
He who does not want to fulfill vows, would do better not
to make them.
A living dog is better than a dead lion.

Verba viri docti stimulis et comparo clavis:
non sapiens palpare nefas sed pungere novit.

Unus sit per cuncta deus mandata timendus.
Contra consilium domini prudentia nulla.
Cuius despicitur vita, est doctrina repulsa.
Ad summum transire bonum perventio felix.
Quae tribuit deus, ante oculos non semper habemus.
Non pacem colit unius divisor amoris.
Prelata pietate metes, homo, gaudia pacis.
Redditor est patiens altissimus, aequus ubique.
Delatore Doech fit mox homicida Saul rex.
Permittit deus, et fiunt quae sepius odit.

Laudatur Moyses mitissimus esse virorum:
O quantum distant hodierni a laude priorum!

Valde logi sunt a veris ad falsa minuti.
Profitiente David gliscunt tormenta Sauli.
Serpentem spiras, cum quo tibi vita venenum.
Venalem prebes animam, si appareat emptor.

I compare the words of a learned man to goads and nails:
the wise man knows to puncture wickedness, not to stroke it.

The one God ought to be feared in all his commandments.
There is no prudence that is contrary to the plan of the Lord.
A man whose life is despised—his teaching is also rejected.
It is a happy outcome to pass over to the Highest Good.
We do not always have before our eyes the things God has bestowed.
One who rends asunder the one [true] love does not cherish peace.
When you have put piety first, O man, you will reap the joys of peace.
The Highest One is patient in retribution, just in all matters.
Because Doeg was an informer, King Saul soon became a murderer.
God permits things which he hates, and they often come to pass.

Moses is praised as the kindest of men: O how far the men
of today differ from the worth of our predecessors!

Greatly have words been diminished from true things to falsehoods!
While David advances, the torments of Saul increase.
Your breath is a snake's breath; to you, as to him, poison is life.
You offer your soul for sale, if any buyer should appear.

Speranda est spes, non habitas depromere causas.
Consequitur robusta boum iuga plurima messis.
Virtutum flores, dum vivis, apiscere, sodes.
In te, virtutum mater, discretio nulla est.
Semper in extremis bene erit dominum metuenti.
Friget amor domini regnante cupidine mundi.
Inmundi cordis molimina spiritus odit.
Lucra beatius est dare quam suscepta fovere.
Fortior est, animum, quam sit, qui vicerit urbem.
Mors metit omne caput, medium, maturum, et acerbum.
O malefactum, Gordiana secuta bubulcum!
Hesitat ergo Laban, quosnam magis eligat agnos.
Nabal, cum parcis, est durus arator habendus.
Inter cursores Asahel vexilla ferebat.
Nemo athleta bonus nisi summo in principe salvus.
Protheus, in diversa fugax, victus redit in se.
Qui trahit infirmos, infirmis compatiatur.
Pultes lactatae sapiunt, melius piperatae.
Is geminat stimulum, qui contra calcitrat unum.
Dum iocus est, bellum cessare et omittere debes.
Donatus legitur, donis evertitur aequum.

Hope must be hoped in order to produce things you do not have.
An abundant harvest follows strong yokes of oxen.
Pursue the flowers of virtues while you live, please.
Discernment, the mother of the virtues, is not to be found in you.
In the end, it will always go well for one who fears the Lord.
When desire for the world reigns, love of the Lord grows cold.
The Spirit hates the endeavors of an unclean heart.
It is more blessed to give away profits than to cherish those you have gotten.
The man who has conquered his soul is stronger than the one who has conquered a city.
Death harvests every head: the unripe, the ripe and the one in between.
O wicked deed! Gordiana got herself a plowman.
Laban hesitates about which lambs he ought to choose.
Nabal, even when you do him no harm, will prove a curmudgeonly farmer.
Among the runners, Asahel carried the banners.
No one is a good athlete unless he is saved by the Highest Prince.
Proteus, taking refuge in diverse forms, returns to himself once conquered.
One who attracts the weak, must suffer with them.
Creamed porridge is tasty; it's tastier peppered.
The one who kicks against a single goad, redoubles it.
While it is still a jest, you ought to give up war and put it aside.
The gifted one is read; justice is subverted by gifts.

Muribus est aliis mus deterior rubicundus.
Res, quae tollitur invitis, mihi preda videtur.
Noctibus occulti parent in mane susurri.
Te claudente diem vacuum subit alter honorem.
Vita quid est nisi nostra dei pietate regatur?
Non spetiosa dei laus peccatoris in ore.
Frigore et esurie caro non laetabitur ulla.
Numquam crescet in enormem formica camelum.
Munditiam servat sinceram rara venustas.
Quicquid id est, fratres, semper timeatur Ulixes.
Non est vena lupis, quae non infecta venenis.
Polipes esuriens mordere magis perhibetur.
Motio crebra viri sed non promotio salva.
Glutto parem sotium non optat in arbore secum.
Sic an sic, fratres, nos hinc transibimus omnes.
Huius enim tegnae excutiam mihi de pede spinam.
Compatribus multis sed paucis fungor amicis.
Numquid is est solitus de caulis pellere capras?
Pullulat iste puer matura ut ordea messe.
Promissis vacuis spes luditur irrita follis.

Rixantur fortes, ibi fit discordia perpes;
nam neuter neutri, non Hector cedit Achilli.

Insanum natum mater delira necabit.
Est: non; dedicat: abnegat; et facit ambiguas res.

A red mouse is worse than other mice.
A thing that is taken from unwilling people seems like plunder to mc.
Whisperings that were hidden at night become clear in the morning.
[To the Sun:] When you end the day, another [the moon] takes on the station you've abandoned.
What is our life if it is not ruled by piety toward God?
Praise of God is not seemly in a sinner's mouth.
No flesh will be made happy by cold and hunger.
An ant will never grow into an enormous camel.
Rarely does beauty maintain true cleanliness.
Whatever it is, brothers, Ulysses ought always to be feared!
There is no vein in wolves that is not infected with poison.
A hungry louse is said to bite more.
A man often changes, but he does not necessarily get better.
A gluttonous bird does not want a companion like himself in his tree.
One way or another, brothers, we will all pass from here.
I will cut the thorn of this deceit from my foot.
I associate with many comrades, but few friends.
Is he not accustomed to driving the she-goats from the sheepfolds?
That boy is growing like ripened barley at harvest time.
The vain hope of a fool is mocked by empty promises.

Strong men quarrel; perpetual discord springs from this; for neither yields to the other. Hector does not yield to Achilles.

A delirious mother will kill an unhealthy son.
Yes, no; he agrees, he refuses; and he makes things ambiguous.

Hic sensus in duobus invenitur versiculis.

Sepe molam petiere canes: in tempore fausti
ante alios, magis infelix ad dampna repertus.

Hoc canit indiculus: vector dum desit equinus,
ire pedes, si sic placeat, dignare, viator.

In suris minuebat itis: poscendo "pusillus
fundatur sanguis tenui de vulnere" dixit.

Hoc dicunt, versuta opifex quod subdola vulpes
astu rem tractat, dum roboris anxia nutat.

Cattulus inprimis stipulas imitatus oberrat,
ad quam vix veterem sollers produxeris artem.

Nam vicina quidem vulgatur ependima vestis,
interulae sed sunt propiora iuvamina carni.

Perfida quod vulpes in cauda continet ima,
inde supercilium credis tibi, stulte, politum.

Quae fuerant, canit Ada profundae carmina curae,
scilicet ut redeat, quem poscit ab hoste, maritus.

Byrrum, si sapias, adhibebis sole sereno;
fac utrum libeat pluvia inpendente, viator.

Non mirum, si forte diabolus est ocreatus,
qui fama vulgi solus dominatur in hedis.

Here the sense is found in two verselets.

Dogs have often gone to the mill: the lucky ones [arrived] in a timely fashion, before the others; the less fortunate one was left wanting.

The writ tells us: when there is no equine conveyance, O traveler, deign to go on foot, if you please.

The little bird was letting blood from his legs: beseechingly he said, "Very little blood should flow from a tiny wound."

They say that the crafty vixen, a clever artificer, does her work by cunning since she hesitates, doubtful of her strength.

A kitten roves about, following a straw; even if you are clever, you will scarcely induce an old cat to this trick.

A shawl is a garment popularly said to be close fitting, but shirts are closer aids to the body.

What the perfidious fox has on the tip of his tail, you, fool, think is an adornment for your eyebrow.

Ada sings songs of profound pain about the past. That is, she asks the enemy that her husband may return.

You will wear your cloak when the sun is bright, if you are wise. Do whatever you please when rain is threatening, O traveler.

No wonder if the devil happens to have greaves. According to the common folk, he alone is lord among the goats.

Putrida quemque magis domino sua poma tueri
quam comesta, mihi potior sententia visa.

Conveniunt quaecumque manubria sepe securi
non peiore loco quam condita fuste saligno.

Ad caveas laris ostiolo ue muribus uno!
Quo fugient, illud quando obturaveris unum?

Nam calibem faber ardentem cum forcipe versat,
ne scintilla manum vulcania comminus urat.

Moribus effulgens non pulcrius obsitus ibit;
nudus ad opprobrium, cui pessima vita, pudendum.

Credula virgo proco quae se commiserit ultro,
irrita post pretium iactabit iurgia dandum.

Spargit in autumno mulier quae prodiga fructum,
viribus effetum dabit inproba vere maritum.

Ante fames occidit herum quam forte ministrum;
quam cocus egrotet, dominus longe tumulatur.

Occupat indignata solum sine frugibus arbor,
hinc maledicta aret ficulnea stans sine ficis.

Ipse canis venaticus indignando gemiscit
longi servitii suspendia dura rependi.

Confuso labio tepuit Babylonia turris:
sic modo dissipat internum discordia templum.

It seems to me a better plan that a man guard for his master the rotten fruit, rather than the fruit that has already been eaten.

Any sort of handle is often suitable for an ax, if it is made from no worse source than a willow stick.

Woe to the mice with [only] one little door to the caves of their home! Where will they flee when you have closed off that one?

A blacksmith turns glowing steel with a pair of tongs, so that a fiery spark not burn a hand that is too near it.

One who shines in morals could not go more beautifully covered. The one whose life is very bad will go naked to a shameful disgrace.

A trusting maiden who willingly gives herself up to a suitor, will quarrel in vain afterward about the price to be paid.

A prodigal woman who wastes fruit in autumn, will wickedly leave her husband sapped of strength in the spring.

Hunger will perchance kill the lord before the servant. The master will be buried long before the cook gets ill.

A tree without fruit is unworthy to occupy the soil; hence the cursed fig tree, standing without figs, withers.

The hunting dog himself indignantly complains that cruel hangings are the recompense of long service.

The [enthusiasm for building the] Babylonian tower cooled off when language became confused; so now discord upsets a temple from within.

In virgae sonipes terretur nobilis umbra;
pellere vix potes ignavum, dum calcibus urges.

Quis poterit patulam prius evertisse patellam,
quam qui suscepit iuris ratione tenendam?

Billardum dolabra occidit comes atque securis,
quem facile exanimem ventris fultura abolebit.

Otius institui possunt comes atque magirus
quam farris duo grana: deus haec, non homo, format.

Emeritus de curte senex subeunte bacillo
mendicus perreptabit castella casasque.

Stercus et obprobrium poterit, sed nullus obambit
interitum, simul omne caput mors et metet Orcus.

Qui dominum capit, hunc firmis constringere loris
est opus: expendet, nodum si ruperit illum.

Haud facile emergit, quod primo in fune domandus
discit equus tener in freno mollisque capistro.

Quid poterit iactare suo de stamine Lide?
Subtiles posuit casses simul et male fortes.

Sibilus attollens animos instigat equinos,
atque canes simul horridulos commitigat idem.

A noble horse is terrified by the shadow of a whip. You can scarcely move a cowardly one when you urge him with your heels.

Who will be able to overturn the wide platter better than the one who rightly took hold of it?

A pickax and its companion the ax are killing Billardus, one whom the upkeep of his belly will kill dead.

A companion and a cook can more quickly be produced than two grains of corn: God, not man, gives form to the latter.

An old man retired from court, with a staff supporting him, will crawl through castles and cottages as a beggar.

Shit and shame you may avoid, but no one gets around dying. Death and Orcus together will mow down every life.

Whoever captures his lord needs to bind him with strong straps. He will pay the price if the lord breaks that knot.

A horse does not easily rise above what he learns at first when he must be tamed with a rope, when new to the bridle, and pliant to the muzzle.

How could the Lydian spider boast about her weaving? She made webs that were subtle, but at the same time far from strong.

A hissing sound stimulates horses' spirits, raising them up; and the same thing simultaneously calms frightened dogs.

Zelotipam curruca suam devinctius ardet,
suspectam excusat, prior offensacula donat.

Si poterit vulpes imitari facta leonis,
tum tu, quem falso simulas, potes esse, quod ille.

Butzo dedit domino puris solatia verbis,
spes mera cui fuit in sola confidere lingua.

Somnia quem terrent, vigilans terrore carebit,
vanescunt experrectis adversa quietis.

Iste ut pluma volatilis et stipulae levitatis,
actibus instabilis tamquam circumvagus amnis.

Dissipat hic sacros malesuada Pecunia mores;
rerum corruptrix, regina Pecunia vincit.

Hic puer induviis et pelle leonis amictus,
pro pudor! ante viros inmunda cynomia crevit.

Pollinis et fumi sunt plena tuguria stulti,
qualis erat Coridon et plurimus usque fatoclus.

Letamur nummo plaudentes munere magno,
tristamurque obulo pretio leviore gementes.

Ad caelum minus assurgunt animalia ventris,
libera nobilitant animas ieiunia carnis.

Desipiunt hi, quos inhonestant savia mechi,
ultro qui tolerant maculati scandala stratus.

A cuckold burns devotedly for an adulterous wife. He excuses her when she's under suspicion and forgives her stumblings in advance.

If a fox can imitate the deeds of a lion, then you can be what that one, whom you fraudulently mimic, is.

Butzo gave consolation to his master with pure words; but it was pure hope for him to trust in the tongue alone.

He whom his dreams terrify will be free of fear when he wakes. The things that disturb their rest vanish for those who have awakened.

He is like a wafting feather and is of the lightness of straw, unstable in his actions like a meandering river.

Here Money, which encourages evil, corrupts sacred morals. Queen Money, corrupter of all things, triumphs.

This boy is wrapped in the clothes and hide of a lion. Oh, for shame! A wicked dog-fly has risen up before men.

The huts of an idiot are full of ash and smoke. Corydon was like that, and so is many a fool.

We rejoice, applauding money as a great gift. And we are sad, groaning because of [the loss of] a penny of very little value.

Creatures of the stomach are less able to rise toward heaven. Fasts free of meat ennoble souls.

Those adulterers whom kisses dishonor are fools; even more so those who tolerate the scandals of a polluted bed.

Egregium dominum lauti decorant laterales,
atque alium quendam latus indecorat sceleratum.

Nulla quidem plerique solent nisi credere visa,
illud habet carnalis homo atque hebitudo profunda.

En quid habent, qui trituras odere scolares,
de quibus aufugiunt multi sudare sophistae?

Inprobus ad sua vana trahit documenta magister
electum iuvenem placidis in rebus adultum.

Perspicuum satis est fatuas accrescere barbas,
non omnes in pube genas prudentia condit.

Pultes exsorbet, non pulmentaria, pauper:
utitur his habitis, non illis, forte quod absint.

Er sonat in lingua, quae littera valde canina:
rumperis invidia rodentum, ianitor imus.

Urbem venalem corrupit in aere Iugurta;
ut nunc sunt multi, cecantur munere tali.

Venter ut inpletur, non verbis lingua domatur,
diffluit inde loquax luxu dominante cyborum.

Qui solis, periture, minis ignavus obibis,
condignum meritis in stercore stercus olebis.

Linque, marite, nuces, quoniam nunc competit uxor:
est ultra vires, quamvis agitaveris, hic flos.

Elegant companions adorn an outstanding lord; and a wicked sidekick dishonors a certain other one.

Most people are accustomed to believe nothing unless they have seen it. A fleshly man holds to that, and so does profound stupidity.

Do you see what they have, those who hate corporal punishment in school? It is because of them that many students avoid working hard.

A wicked teacher draws to his vain teaching a choice young man, who grew up in a soft environment.

It is clear enough that beards grow on fools; prudence does not cover all cheeks with hair.

A poor man slurps up porridge, not relishes; he uses the things at hand, not those that might be lacking.

R resounds on the tongue; it is a very growly letter. You burst with the envy of backbiters, infernal doorkeeper!

Jugurtha corrupted venal Rome with money. There are many like that now; they are blinded by such largesse.

When the belly is filled, the tongue does not control its words. When an excess of food masters it, it wags loquaciously.

You, mortal, ready to die like a coward because of threats alone, will deservedly stink of shit, for you are shit yourself.

Leave behind, O husband, your playthings since now a wife is right [for you]. This flower is beyond your strength, however hot and bothered you are.

Hic fugit ecclesiam, trahitur nidore culinae
plus quam sophiae, veneratur furta coquinae.

Concurrunt in carne modis fastidia miris,
sola salus placet et columen de corpore sano.

Callidus et sapiens motum bene temperat irae,
naviter iste modum vitae decorabit honestae.

Rem ludo (si quando fuit, mirabile dictu!):
mures haud fatiunt nidos in vertice catti.

Quicquid habet fidei lupus, in silvis latet omne;
cognatae parcit, caveat sed caetera pellis!

Dixit anus delira suo patuisse palato,
quid sapiant caules, ebulum dum coxit in olla.

Ut non respitiat, qui sic discurrere temptat,
forte cadet, quo non surgendi copia detur.

Hic fidei, quot rana pilis est edita, tantae,
aut mediae palmae vola quot consuevit habere.

Vitricus ut plorat privigni funera tristis
et pater econtra cantat, cukerella vocatur.

"Has epulas lupus inreverens sine fronte petivit,"
cum faties invisa venit, quam nemo vocavit.

Sese commendat, quem non vicinia palpat,
vicinosque sui inmemores inglorius odit.

This man avoids the church; he is attracted more by the scent of food than of wisdom. It is things filched from the kitchen that *he* worships.

Nuisances compete with one another in our flesh in wondrous ways. Only health is pleasing, and the well-being of a sound body.

A clever and wise man controls well the stirring of his ire; he will zealously honor the golden mean of an honest life.

I mock this (a remarkable thing, if ever it took place): mice don't make their nests on the head of a cat.

Whatever loyalty a wolf has, it is all hidden in the woods. He spares the hide of his kin; but let every other hide beware!

A crazy old woman said that to her palate the taste of cabbage was undeniable, as she cooked hellebore in her pot.

Whoever tries to run without looking around will probably fall where there will be no opportunity for getting back up.

This man has as much integrity as a newborn frog has hair, or as the hollow of the middle of the palm has.

When the stepfather wails sadly at his stepson's funeral and the father, in contrast, sings, we call it . . . cuckoldry.

"An impudent wolf has attended this feast shamelessly" [we say] when an unwelcome person arrives, whom nobody invited.

The man whom his neighbors do not flatter sings his own praises. And this unappreciated man hates the neighbors who ignore him.

Herba nec antidotum poterit depellere loetum;
quod te liberet a fato, non nascitur horto.

Herpica ut horridulam trivisset forte rubetam,
"Tot colaphos, quot," ait, "dominos, contingit habere!"

Vas commune vel inmundum, quod operculum omisit,
est os stulta loquens, cuius custodia nulla.

Sepe minus salsus plus iusto rem colit unam:
arguitur fatuus sua tintinnabula amare.

Nullo decipitur visu raptoque columba;
ut predam rapiat, consuete milvus hanelat.

Martius insuda fatie, madefactus Aprilis
frigidus et Maius contundent horrea messe.

Oblitum causas ne te mirere querendo:
sepe ea, quae posuit, fiscedula perdidit ova.

Diva in natura memoratur strutio menceps,
isti, doctor, avi stultum compone clientem.

Cingitur ob signum virtutis ferrea virga
regibus, ut culpas simul amputet atque recidat.

Dispice, rex portat gladium, sed non sine causa:
ut delicta premat vel poena sequens timeatur.

Semper erit murmur stulti, sicut rota carri,
foenum dum portat, numquam de murmure cessat.

Neither an herb nor an antidote can drive away death. What could free you from your fate does not grow in a garden.

When a harrow chanced to run over a scaly toad, it said, "One has as many blows as masters."

A mouth that has no restraint saying stupid things is a common or filthy vessel that has lost its lid.

One who has little wit often cherishes a single thing excessively: it is alleged that a fool loves his own bells.

The dove is corrupted by nothing it has seen and by no plunder; the hawk usually strives to seize its prey.

March with a dry face, a wet April, and a cold May will burst the granaries with harvest.

Do not be amazed that you have forgotten things while seeking them; often a figpecker loses the eggs that it has laid.

In Mother Nature there is said to exist the mindless ostrich. O teacher, compare your stupid protégé to that bird!

Kings are girded with an iron rod as a sign of their power, so that it may simultaneously suppress faults and cut them short.

Look, the king carries a sword, but not without cause: so that he may check crimes, or so that subsequent punishment may be feared.

The murmuring of an idiot will always be just like a wheel on a cart: while it is carrying hay, it never ceases to murmur.

Nulla fovere potest mortalia lucidus ether;
quae spirant mortaliter, omnia continet aer.

Spiritibus pax summa viget sine lite supernis;
si iurgant homines, properando reconcilientur.

Demonibus lis seva, reconciliatio nulla,
quorum conditio perpes discordia princeps.

Hinnulus et lepus est timidus, leo fortis et ursus:
sic puer et pauper, rigidi sunt quique potentes.

Olim rebus adhuc rudibus noviterque creatis
ad silvas feritas, pietas ad tecta cucurrit.

Eximie princeps qui cenat, lautus habetur;
qui parce, lutulentus, ineptus, funere dignus.

Otius involvunt nos dampna priora secundis;
largior adversis, iocundis est minor usus.

Tendit ad occasum, quicquid precessit ad ortum,
dico creaturam substratam legibus istis.

Nuntius iste volat tot flatibus otior Euri;
quam celer in pedibus, non tantum flumina possunt.

Fabrica concusso fundamine tota vacillat,
et capite infirmo tabescunt caetera menbra.

The clear ether is not able to sustain mortal things; the air contains every mortal thing that breathes.

The highest peace thrives, without strife, among the spirits above; if men quarrel, they should be reconciled quickly.

For demons, there is savage strife, no reconciliation; their primordial condition is perpetual discord.

A fawn is timid; so is a hare. A lion is strong; a bear is too. Likewise, a child and a pauper [are timid]; those who are powerful are harsh.

Once upon a time, when things were new and recently created, wildness took refuge in the forests, piety in houses.

The prince who dines in the finest manner is considered elegant; the one who dines frugally [is considered] filthy, inept, worthy of death.

Losses overwhelm us more quickly and sooner than good fortune. Our experience of adversities is more abundant, that of pleasant things less so.

Whatever advances toward its rising, inclines toward its setting. I say all creation is subject to these laws.

That messenger flies swifter than so many blasts of the east wind. How swift on his feet! Not even rivers can do so much.

The whole building totters when the foundation has been shaken; and the other members grow weak when the head is infirm.

Cuculus altorem iniusta mercede cruentat,
nam curruca suam fovet ova vorantia carnem.

Non mulier prudens emat a meretrice maritum,
in pretio quod non vincet, cum distrahit illum.

Divitis ingenii naturam extinguere vita;
vera prophetarum preconia spernere noli.

Laudant artifices baculum, quem flectere possunt,
et puerum parere minis senilibus ultro.

Vir fugitans lites extinguit seditiones;
et semper furiosus amat committere rixas.

Non liquide cantabit aquis infusus et herbis,
pocula nec fatient voces mellita sonoras.

Multa decent communia, sed non congruit uxor:
si communis erit, letalis fabula, mechis.

Perfidus instructor, qui lumbum tollit ab ovo;
commodior, qui grana legit tria lentis in orbe.

Acres potores a convivis metuuntur;
tanta in sumendis epulis non dampna queruntur.

Nemo tam ferus est, qui non mitescere possit,
tam sanae mentis, qui se nequeat furiare.

The cuckoo bloodies its nourisher with an unjust repayment; for the warbler cares for the eggs that will devour its own flesh.

A prudent woman should not buy her husband from a prostitute because she will not come out ahead, when she takes him away.

Don't destroy a precious character; don't spurn the proclamations of the true prophets.

Craftsmen praise a stick which they can bend and a boy willingly obedient to old men's threats.

A man who avoids conflicts extinguishes strife, and the hotheaded man always loves to engage in brawls.

One filled with liquids and herbs will not sing clearly, and honeyed cups will not make voices melodious.

Many things that are shared are respectable, but this does not apply to a wife. It is a deadly tale if she will be shared with adulterers.

It is a perfidious steward who takes the yolk from the egg. More proper is the one who collects three grains of lentil from the dish.

Hard drinkers are feared by their table companions. They do not complain of such great losses from the consumption of food.

No one is so wild that he cannot grow gentle; no one of so sane a mind that he cannot make himself mad.

Non idem sensus potoris aquae atque Falerni:
vinum sepe facit, quod non valet haustus aquarum.

Urgeat in multa te clade Canopica pestis,
qui premis Israel luteo laterumque labore!

Omnibus ira modis ad lapsum frena remittit,
omne suo fas iustitiae de cardine vellit.

Perfida corda pavent ad iudicis ire tribunal;
iustus securo poterit pertendere gressu.

Invidiae rubigo faces succendit in ipsum
vel merito auctorem, qui gestat livida corda.

Invide, tabescis, torqueris et igne cremaris,
in te nempe prior decurrit rivulus irae.

Alta serena videt mundana volutabra calcans;
et nimis infelix, qui figitur in lutulentis.

Debilitas magna est quoque somnolentia mentis,
offitio dignas quae multas transilit horas.

Non habet alma fides meritum sperare supernum,
quae visu carnis desiderat experimentum.

Unus ad assiduos adhibetur spiritus ater,
plures desidibus sotiantur, ad otia pronis.

Assurgens sermone humili compescitur ira;
concitat hausterus nimio clamore furorem.

The drinker of water and the drinker of Falernian wine do not have the same capacity for feeling. Wine often does what a draft of water is not strong enough to do.

May a Canopic plague press upon you with great destruction, you who crush Israel with the labor of mud and bricks!

Anger gives free rein to error in every way; it tears every obligation of justice from its hinges.

Perfidious hearts fear to approach the judge's tribunal. The just man will be able to step forward with a carefree gait.

The rust of envy kindles torches, and deservedly so, against its own instigator, who bears a malicious heart.

Envious one, you melt away; you are tortured and incinerated by fire. Surely it is on yourself that the first flood of your anger descends.

One who looks to the serene heights tramples underfoot the pig sties of this world; and unhappy indeed is he who is stuck fast in the mud.

Sluggishness is also a great debility of the mind; it skips over many hours that are appropriate for one's duties.

Genial faith that desires proof by seeing in the flesh does not have a hope for heavenly reward.

One dark spirit is allotted to people who are busy; many accompany slothful people who are prone to idleness.

Surging anger is restrained by a humble word; a harsh word stirs up rage with excessive clamoring.

Corvus querebat polluta cadavera in undis;
eheu, clade nova nunc carpit olentia in agris!

Non vidi faleras asini gestare leonem,
hic potius legitur redimitus pelle leonis.

Mendicans, qui dat, quod habet, sequitur peregrinum;
in vanum tribuit, quem penitet ante dedisse.

Gliscit stultorum laxo violentia freno;
quo placas magis, instigas adolere meracam.

Vivit apes bene congestis et fruge benigna,
crabrones avidis predonum more rapinis.

Fratrum census ab ungue fero penaliter exit,
ut tabes prodire solet de tergore sano.

Post epulas tarde in mensis mensalia sternis;
haec series prepostera, dum fit prima secunda.

Ni mechus foret, uxor adhuc tua virgo maneret:
cuculus hinc multis currucis nascitur heres.

Vermiculi cutis incultae nos acrius urunt,
quos alienus alit luvionis sudor olacis.

Vix ab anu pressum lac extorquetur avara,
duriter et durum canibus dispensat edendum.

The crow sought out filthy cadavers amid the waves; alas, now it plucks in the fields things reeking of recent slaughter!

I have not seen a lion wearing the trappings of an ass; rather one reads that the ass was wrapped in the hide of the lion.

The beggar who gives what he has follows the pilgrim. That man to whom it is painful to have given, distributes in vain.

The violence of fools escalates when they are given free rein. You spur them to increase their bitterness in your effort to placate them.

The benign honeybee lives well from what it has gathered and from fruit. Wasps [live] like robbers from greedy plunderings.

The wealth of monks leaves their savage claws painfully, just as disease comes out of a healthy hide.

After the feast, it is too late to spread tablecloths on the table. The sequence is backward when the second thing happens first.

Without an adulterous lover, your wife would still be a virgin. That's why the cuckoo is born as heir to many a cuckold.

The little worms of filthy skin chafe us sharply. The sweat of another, with its stinking rot, nourishes them.

It is scarcely possible to tear fresh cheese away from a greedy old lady, and she hardly relinquishes the hard cheese to the dogs to eat.

Ramus apud Stigias sis aureus—esto—paludes,
ultro me numquam post te sperabis iturum.

Nebris quae nunc est lenis, fuit hispida pellis:
exemplo hoc teritur factus de divite pauper.

"Oscula iam figes media inter cornua caprae";
ista solent proverbia proponi macilentis.

In silvis onager venatio parta leoni:
pascua maiorum sunt semper et esca minores.

Uncinus in silvis oritur silvae spoliator,
pomorum arguitur frugumque et predo parentum.

Raro omnes remeant, quot eunt ad pascua porci,
et neque de castris aties ad prelia missa.

Tempestivius ad sulcum solet ire bubulcus,
quam fratres matutinos cogantur ad ymnos.

Hoc mihi crede—vale bene!—me te velle valere:
dum spiras, ego me iam spero posse valere.

Gratis equo oblato ne contempleris in ore,
ut numeres dentes, matris quibus ubera suxit.

Hinc puer exivit, qui tectum commaculavit;
circus adhuc olet, is sua quo vestigia flexit.
Unde putas? habet a porcis documenta subulcus,
addidicit siliquas, non exercere palestras.

You could be the golden bough in the Stygian swamps—granted!—[but] you can never hope that I will follow willingly after you.

A fawn-skin that is now smooth was once a rough hide. A man once rich who has become poor is worn down in the same way.

"Now you will plant kisses between the horns of a goat." These proverbial words are usually offered to skinny people.

A wild ass born in the woods is prey for the lion. The lesser are always the nourishment and food of the greater.

A wooden pruning hook rises in the forest, [destined to be] the forest's despoiler. It is charged as a robber of fruit trees and of fruits, and of its parents.

Rarely do as many pigs return as go out to pasture, and neither do as many troops as were sent from camp into battle.

The plowman usually goes to the field in a more timely fashion than the monks are compelled to their morning hymns.

"Fare well!" Believe me about this, that I want you to fare well. So long as you are breathing, I believe that I can be well.

When a horse is offered for free, do not look into its mouth to count the teeth with which it sucked its mother's udder.

The boy who dishonored the house has departed from here. The arena, toward which he turned his steps, still reeks. A swineherd gets his training from pigs: where else do you think he would get it? He has learned to labor at husks, not at school exercises.

Corvus et accipiter rapuere cadavera, frater,
et pica, cum milvo cornix—nec mica remansit.

Porcorum siliquas contempsimus utpote inanes,
ventis inflatos, sine fructu et semine folles.

Dives verba tonat rigidissima, plena minarum;
obsecrat econtra supplex per humillima pauper.

Erue ab his, deus, et veniat vindicta ministris,
qui bona nostra secant partemque legunt meliorem!

Huc omnes veniunt vacuis ad festa sacellis,
qui nostris inhiant, cum nemo diaria portet.

Malo mori ignotus, quam sit mihi gloria dampnis;
quam presim dampnose, malo inglorius esse.

Debet episcopus, ut prosit, non querere, presit:
omnis in offitio hoc curet prelatus et auctor.

Annus abit, nostrae breviantur tempora vitae:
et quae debuerant minui, peccamina crescunt.

Quisquis divinos non vult consistere ad ymnos,
sepe foras trahit hunc tinctus carbone catellus.

Albus equus pellem celare nequit lutulentam:
albatis nusquam sordes indignius herent.

The raven and the hawk have snatched the carrion, brother, and the magpie, and the crow along with the kite. Not a speck remained.

We have despised the husks of pigs as worthless. They are dry pods inflated with wind, without fruit or seed.

A rich man speaks harsh words, filled with threats. The humble pauper, on the other hand, asks in the most submissive terms.

God, save [us] from these ministers, and let your vengeance come. They divide up our property and take the better share for themselves!

Everyone comes here to the festivals with empty sacks; since none of them brings his daily rations, they gape at ours.

I prefer to die unknown than to have glory from doing harm. Rather than rule in a harmful way, I prefer to be inglorious.

A bishop should seek to be useful, not to be in charge. Every prelate and leader should take heed of this in [performing] his duty.

The year passes away, the seasons of our life are shortened, and the sins which ought to have diminished increase.

A puppy marked with charcoal draws outdoors whoever does not want to take his place at divine hymns.

A white horse cannot conceal a muddy hide. Nowhere does filth cling more shamefully than to those dressed in white.

Magnus Alexander de se fidenter aiebat:
"Malo mori quam me regnandi iura precari!"

O terrae vermis, memorare novissima carnis;
si semper memor incedis, peccare timebis.

Non surrexit Aquis anno domus alma sub uno;
propter aquas calidas ibi structa est regia sedes.

Suadelas surdo cantabis in aure salubres:
dum castigat amor, corruptior inde fit osor.

Nos, genus humanum, dampnat caligo futuri;
quae pateat meritis nescitur ianua nostris.

Hoc pastore lupus, quicquid sibi vellet, haberet,
qui neque se plane neque scit commissa tueri.

Dulces sunt lacrimae scelerum commissa gementum,
quae celebres ludos teathrorum et gaudia vincunt.

Drances in sola lepidus confidere lingua,
militiae arguitur timidus, sermone profusus.

Vulpinat Herodes Christi a presepibus agnos,
dum mactat pueros insonti morte trucidans.

Ultima quam multis mala cladibus anticipantur!
Crebra notant preconia, quod graviora sequantur.

Alexander the Great confidently said about himself, "I prefer to die rather than beg for the right to rule."

O earthworm, remember the final end of the flesh. If you always proceed mindful of this, you will be afraid to sin.

The venerable cathedral at Aachen did not rise in a single year. A royal residence was constructed there on account of the hot springs.

You will be chanting salutary suggestions into a deaf ear: when love chastises, then the miscreant becomes a hater as a result.

The obscurity of the future dooms us, the human race. We do not know which door lies open to us deservedly.

While this man is shepherd, the wolf can have whatever it wants. He plainly knows how to guard neither himself nor what has been entrusted to him.

Sweet are the tears of those groaning over the sins they have committed. They are better than popular games and the pleasures of the theater.

Charming Drances is shown to trust in his tongue alone; [he is] timid in military affairs, lavish in speech.

Herod plays the fox to the lambs from Christ's fold, while he savagely slaughters the children by an undeserved death.

By how many disasters are ultimate evils anticipated! Frequent forewarnings indicate that more serious things are to follow.

Gens Iudea liquat culicem sorbetque camelum,
dum Christum dampnat nequam mittendo Baraban.

Angelus artifici bonus et malus ipse ministrat:
ut sit in auxilio bonus, et probet alter, habetur.

Plantari nemus in templo domini prohibetur,
ne doctrina gravis fuerit rudibusque profunda.

Haec tria nostrarum solatia sint animarum:
sancta elemosina, sintque preces, ieiunia digna.

Quicquid agas, semper vigila pro morte secunda:
prima pavenda satis, magis est tamen illa secunda.

Spuria in aede dei crescunt vitulamina et error,
discordes ubi currunt quidam ad limina fratres.

Omnis avaritiae studet et rex atque sacerdos,
a maiore usque ad minimum desistere nolunt.

Non possunt mea te, deus, inperfecta latere,
sunt oculis peraperta tuis simul omnia nuda.

Intentant animae interitum solatia carnis,
veque animae misera querenti a carne salutem!

Perspicuum decus est regis secreta tueri;
archanum proferre dei sanctissima virtus.

The Jewish people "strain out a gnat and swallow a camel," releasing the worthless Barabbas while they condemn Christ.

The good and the bad angel too serve the creator. It is said that the good one is His helper, and the other one tests Him.

"It is prohibited for a grove to be planted in the temple of the Lord," lest the teaching be burdensome and unfathomable to uneducated people.

Let these three things be the solaces of our souls: let there be holy alms, prayers, and worthy fasting.

Whatever you do, be vigilant against the second death. The first one should be frightening enough, yet the second one is even more so.

Illegitimate sprouts and error grow in the house of God when certain discordant brothers run to its thresholds.

Every king and priest alike is a slave to avarice, from the mighty to the lowest they do not want to cease.

My imperfections cannot hide from you, God; they are all simultaneously exposed, completely open, to your eyes.

Comforts of the flesh lead to the ruin of the soul. Woe to the soul seeking salvation from miserable flesh!

It is a [cause for] special honor to safeguard the secrets of the king. It is the most sacred virtue to proclaim the mystery of God.

Dum tonat, interea domini sum servus ad oram;
sublato terrore iterum me adscisco priorem.

Quindenis gradibus caelestes itur ad arces,
et totidem fuerant Solimiti ad limina templi.

Tota mente deum flagres, mediteris amesque,
esurias hunc et sitias, quia iugis aquae fons.

Christe, salutarem fratrum fatias itionem,
legati ut nobis sua nuntia fausta reportent!

Femina pauca bona est; si forte inveneris ullam,
de caelo cecidit, tessella caractere miro.

Plangit Adonidis interitum Venus algida, dudum
quem percussit aper; quatit hinc nos frigidus aer.

Qui sine commento rimaris scripta Maronis,
inmunis nuclei solo de cortice rodis.

Grammatici "similis" dicunt "illius et illi:
moribus illius distare et vultibus illi."

Si qua tuam mentem delectat spes meritorum,
at non te deterreat anxia cura laborum.

Laudatur Moyses mitissimus esse virorum,
qui vixere suis domino testante diebus.

While it is thundering, at that time, for an hour, I am the slave of the Lord. Once the fear is removed, then I again assume my former state.

By fifteen steps one gets to the celestial citadel, and there were the same number of steps to the threshold of the Temple of Jerusalem.

With your whole mind you should burn for, meditate upon, and love God. You should hunger and thirst for him, because he is a fountain of unending water.

Christ, make the journey of the brothers salutary, so that, having been sent, they may bring back to us their favorable news!

A good woman is rare. If you should, by chance, find one, she has fallen from the sky, a die with a marvelous marking.

Venus, chilly, mourns the death of Adonis, whom long ago a boar impaled; hence the cold air pierces us through.

You who investigate the writings of Virgil without a commentary are gnawing only at the outer bark of an untouched core.

Grammarians say "like of him" and "like unto him" to separate "[I am the] like of him in manners" and "[I am] like unto him in appearance."

If any hope of rewards pleases your mind, anxious concern about the effort [to achieve it] should not deter you.

Moses is praised as the kindest of men who lived in his day, by the Lord's own testimony.

Non alius nisi ventriculus deus esse putatur
his, qui spem totam curanda in carne relegant.

Longior a domino, qui mundo proximior, sis;
si te suscipiat, quam felix!, regia caeli.

Non dominum risisse legis; quod fleverit, audis:
vir sapiens ait errorem conducere risu.

Inpatiens Heliu furibundo eructuat utre
fecundos flatus quasi mustum in ventre tonantes.

Perdunt suave quidem unguentum muscae morientes,
hoc est, perversi sancti spiraminis unguen.

Iudei dominum sic percussere maligni
in gladio linguae, gladio non materiali.

Auxiliante deo, veniunt qui, celsa merentur;
et qui non veniunt, sua se peccata recludunt.

O crucis inventrix, mea perdita quaeso ministra:
det deus inventae, det opem inventricis Helenae.

Rex in iuditio cum carne videbitur ista:
hunc omnes venturum, et qui pupugere, videbunt.

Orcestram aecclesiaeque gradus ascendere quosdam
non meritis, immo dampnata per aera pavesco.

God is thought to be nothing other than their own belly by those who place all hope in caring for their flesh.

The closer you are to the world, the farther you will be from the Lord. If the palace of heaven receives you—how lucky you are!

You do not read that the Lord laughed; you hear that he wept. A wise man says that error leads to laughter.

Eliu, no longer patient, belches out from his raging belly abundant gusts thundering like new wine in his stomach.

Dying flies spoil unguent, however pleasant; that is, perverse people [spoil] the unction of the Holy Spirit.

The spiteful Jews struck the Lord with the sword of their tongue, not with an actual sword.

With God's assistance, those come who have earned heavenly rewards. And those who do not come—their own sins exclude them.

O discoverer of the cross, pay heed, I ask you, to my losses. May God grant [me] the aid of the discovered cross; may he grant the aid of its discoverer Helena!

The King will be seen in this very flesh at the Judgment. All will see him coming, even those who pierced him.

I am beginning to fear that certain men ascend to the pulpit and to ecclesiastical ranks not by their merits, but rather through cursed money.

Solivagus gemit errando per devia turtur,
signat avis contemplativa preces heremitae;
aerem item liquidum secat ipsa columba gregatim,
dans specimen regum comitumque in terga sequentum.

Sicubi non persona potens attenditur in ius,
veris iuditiis ibi lex agitabitur ipsa.

Sunt tria sancta, quibus non sunt maiora per orbem:
omnipotens deus est, homo iustus, regna polorum;
econtra totidem tristissima monstra malorum:
ipse diabolus, auditorque homo, torridus ignis.

Mendosi sermonis amans conchilia princeps
effitiet similes sese sectando ministros.

Festinata manu substantia diminuetur;
paulatim collecta suum spectabit acervum.

Dicere quis poterit tam sanctus et integer aevi:
"Non scelus est mecum, mundusque ab sordibus assum?"

Emptor ait rerum "non sunt haec munera tanti,"
cum quibus aversus pulsanti corde triumphat.

Ve tibi terra, puer rex cui diademata prefert,
et cuius proceres indulgent mane Falerno!

Sepe piros atavi soboles videt omine tristi;
prodessent aliena magis quam rura paterna.

The lone turtledove moans, wandering through trackless ways; the contemplative bird signifies the prayers of the hermit. Likewise, thc dove cleaves the clear air in a flock, providing a model of kings and of courtiers following behind.

Wherever a powerful person is not heeded in court, there the law itself will be practiced with true judgments.

There are three holy things than which there are no greater things on earth: there is the all-powerful God, the just man, the realms of heaven. On the other hand, the direst monstrosities of evils are the same in number: the devil himself, the man who listens to him, and the scorching fire.

The prince who loves the flatteries of liars will make the ministers following him the same.

Substance hastily acquired will be diminished, that collected little by little will see itself heaped up.

Who is so holy and chaste in his life that he will be able to say, "There is no fault in me, and I am clean of blemishes?"

The purchaser of things says, "These goods are not worth that much," but when he has turned away, with a pounding heart, he gloats about them.

Woe to you, O land, in which a child king wears the crown, and whose nobles indulge in Falernian wine in the morning!

Often a descendant looks upon the pears of his ancestor with sad foreboding; another's fields might produce more than the paternal ones.

Excelsus iudex micam non sustinet auri,
in magna palea dum purgat, in igne perire.

Nescius intonsusque iacet cur carcere Ioseph?
Quod necdum ingenii patuit bona vena beati.

Huius lectoris debemus radere linguam,
qui, quotiens legit, excedit de tramite proso.

Sedulitas invita relinquit ad otia pronos:
dediscunt apices, quos turpis inertia vexat.

Hic pariter cocus et focus excessere culinam;
ne nimis esurias, aliunde diaria queras.

Haec pariter mundana via est et lubrica vita,
calcabit sine labe sua laqueos humilis mens.

Ante videre libet, quod habere in tempore debes:
serus eris partis conferre paranda et agenda.

Phaltiel hinc plorat, quod pristina redditur olim
David sponsa Michol armis illustribus empta.

Vestimur caligis ex omni parte sinistris,
adversis quotiens includimur undique fatis.

Ludus init trepidum certamen et excitat iram,
ira truces inimicitias et funebre bellum.

The judge on high does not suffer a [single] speck of gold to perish in the fire, while he is purging in a great [mass of] dross.

Why does Joseph lie in prison, unknown and unshaven? Because the good vein of his blessed genius has not yet been exposed.

We ought to clip the tongue of the reader who, whenever he reads, departs from the straight path.

Diligence that is unwillingly assumed, [soon] abandons those prone to idleness. Those whom shameful laziness vexes unlearn their letters.

Here the cook and the fire alike have left the kitchen. You should seek your daily rations elsewhere, if you don't want to go hungry.

This life is equally a worldly path and a slippery one. A humble mind will traverse the snares without falling itself.

It is desirable to see in advance what you ought eventually to get. You will be too late comparing what has to be gotten and what has to be done with what has already been accomplished.

This is why Phalti cries: because the former wife of David, Michol, is returned, she whom long ago he [David] had acquired with his illustrious weapons.

We "wear left-footed shoes on both feet" whenever we are surrounded on all sides by adverse fates.

Play begins an alarming quarrel and incites anger; anger, savage hostility and deadly war.

Uno te regnante die brevis imperii laus;
tam modico consumpta situ quam gloria fallax.

Totam nemo vides hiemem consumere vulpes:
sepe sequi post molle caput solet algor acerbus.

Ungo manus, si feceris hoc, quod poscit amicus:
delicti maculas sine, frater, xenia purgent.

Spes nummi solet iratum placare ministrum
nobiliumque thoros ascendere trudit inertes.

Qualis erat nuper, veniat mihi caseus alter:
hoc inpetrato sine fuco me utere amico.

Ante tuam domites, qui carnis deseris esum:
carne carere quid est, dum carnis amore calescas?

Laus domino soli, qui condidit omnia solus!
Omnia fundantur tam forti preside fulta.
Cautius in terris vos exercete, fideles:
desuper intentans oculatus prospicit Argus.

Modo sensus in tribus versibus.

De Ioseph

Surrexit Pharao, qui te non novit, Ioseph;
alter erat, tua qui trivit decora alta parentum.
Haec poteris qui plangis herum memorare benignum.

When you reign for a single day, brief is the praise of your rule; just as glory is deceitful, so it is consumed in a moment by decay.

Not one of you sees foxes eating the whole winter through. Often bitter cold is accustomed to follow after a mild beginning.

I will grease your palms, if you will do what your friend asks: let gifts purge the stains of your transgression, brother.

The hope of money usually placates an irate minister, and it drives foolish men to climb onto the couches of nobles.

Let another cheese come to me like the one I had recently. When this has been done, you will have me as a true friend.

First master your own flesh, you who abstain from eating meat. What use is it to go without meat, while you are hot from love of the flesh.

Praise to the Lord alone, who alone built everything! Everything is well founded, supported by so strong a protector. Employ yourselves cautiously on earth, faithful ones: from up above, a sharp-eyed Argus is watching attentively.

Now the sense [is found] in three verses.

Concerning Joseph

A Pharaoh rose up who did not know you, Joseph. He was the second, the one who destroyed the great glories of your parents. You who are lamenting a kindly lord can remember these things.

De avaris

Sacrilegus regnare diu nimis optat avarus,
auri nescit amor ferrum mortemque timere.
Hoc habet argenti et rerum possessio fulgens.

De fortuna

Commutat Fortuna vices pueriliter actas,
nunc caput hoc spolians, nunc illo in vertice condens,
non bona perpetuo: dum speras, fidere ludit.

De uno calvo

Gaudebat super invento sat pectine calvus;
quam melior foret inventus sibi pilleus unus,
calvitiem unde suam recrearet sole geluque!

De fictis amicis

Non me sic aliena manus quam ledit amicus;
plus ea tormenta in nobis sevire videntur,
quae fatiunt, quorum presumebamus amore.

Laus Dei

Quam bene disposuit mundum deus omnicreator,
nobilitans hominem ratione et divite sensu,
dans mutis breviora quidem et servire priori!

Concerning greedy men

The sacrilegious, greedy man is very eager to rule a long time. His love of gold knows no fear of the sword or of death. The glittering possession of silver and of objects causes this.

Concerning fortune

Fortune childishly changes the roles that are played, now ravaging one man, now placing another at the top. She is not good forever. While you hope, she mocks your confidence.

About a bald man

A bald man was very happy about finding a comb. How much better if he had found himself a cap with which he might provide his bald head respite from the sun and the cold!

Concerning false friends

A stranger's hand does not harm me so much as a friend does. Those torments seem to rage more within us which are created by the people whose love we took for granted.

Praise of God

How finely God, the Creator of everything, arranged the world, ennobling man with reason and copious sense, granting lesser things to dumb animals, and providing them to serve the former!

Si concussa minaretur domus ulla ruinam,
confestim fugeret, quicumque habitaret in illa:
mundo casuro cur non fugiamus ab illo?

De reis

Culpatus reus extenuat delicta patrata,
visis et factis semper facit esse minora:
et puer inmeritas causatur pendere poenas.

De Ismahele

Ismahel in saltu venandi indagine gnarus,
omnibus infensus, cuncti adversantur et illi,
bella movet late, bellis oneratur et ipse.

De Iudeis

Scissa tibi pellis fidei, Iudeus Apella;
qui nunc mendicas, olim tu regna tenebas,
post vexilla crucis, post Christum iure peristi.

De contemptu mundi

Felix, qui spernit pretiosa pericula mundi,
aurum, gemmas, cum reliquis electra metallis,
nempe timore dei sperans potiora rependi!

[Concerning fleeing from ruin]

If any house, having been shaken, were threatening collapse, whoever was living in it would immediately flee. Since the world is about to fall, why should we not flee from it?

Concerning the accused

When blamed, an accused man makes light of the crimes he has perpetrated. He always makes them out to be less than what has been seen and done. A child too complains that he is suffering undeserved punishments.

Concerning Ishmael

Ishmael was a master of hunting with a net in the woodlands. He was hostile to everyone, and all were opposed to him. He stirred up wars far and wide, and he himself was burdened by wars.

Concerning the Jews

The skin of your faith has been cut, Jewish Apella. You who now beg, once possessed kingdoms. After the triumph of the cross, after Christ, you rightly perished.

Concerning contempt for the world

Happy is the man who spurns the precious perils of the world —gold, gems, and electrum along with the other metals—in the expectation that better rewards are paid by the fear of God.

Benedictio

Sanctum sanctificans Benedictum te benedicat,
te cumulet domini benedictio, quae Benedictum,
te quoque sanctificent Gregorius et Benedictus!

De falsis promissis

Multis promissis parvam prestolor alaudam
aut hedi tinctam maculas gestantis alutam,
dedicat in pascha qualem Iudeus Apella.

De rugis

Nullus enim medicus poterit compescere rugas
albos et cani capitis prohibere capillos,
is nisi qui medicos solus prevertitur omnes.

De tedio

Vivendo atque videndo in peius proruit aetas,
otia consectans et nulla negotia curans;
incipiunt hodie, et tedet cras ferre laborem.

De monte

Mons Iovis ab Iove, quem prisci coluere profani,
dictus, non, ut vulgus ait, de calle iocoso,
quemque viatores per multa pericula repunt.

Benediction

May the one sanctifying Saint Benedict give you benediction! May the benediction of the Lord that was heaped on Benedict be heaped on you! May Gregory and Benedict also sanctify you!

Concerning false promises

After being promised many things, I anticipate a small lark or the dyed hide of a young goat with spots, the kind that the Jew Apella dedicates at Passover.

Concerning wrinkles

Surely no doctor can flatten wrinkles and prohibit white hairs on a hoary head, except he who alone surpasses all doctors.

Concerning tedium

Living and learning, our age rushes toward what is worse, pursuing leisure and not caring about business. Men begin something today, and tomorrow they are bored with the work.

Concerning a mountain

Mont Joux was named for Jove, whom the pagans worshipped long ago, not, as is commonly said, for its jovial footpath, along which travelers creep amid great dangers.

De vomitu ciborum

Vita fugit corpus victum dolitura negatum,
mors manet in labiis, ubi venter deserit escas,
predocet insanum stomachum fultura reiecta.

De leviathan serpente

Maxillam concede, deus, perrumpere fortis
Leviathan cassamque relinquere vectis et anguis,
quam prius armilla carnisque rigore forasti.

De senio

Morbus habet senium, preceps delicta iuventus;
hic columen viget, hos premit inbecilla senectus;
effetae hic carnes, ibi brachia cerno torosa.

De tonsura

Mos nostram intravit tonsurae pessimus urbem:
non sunt colla coronis, immo simillima trullis,
has perversa truces inlevit Frantia sectas.

De martyrio hodierno

Martyrio iam non potes istud tradere corpus:
quis prohibet saccos habiti vacuare peculi?
Martyrium crucis est hodie: collecta dedisse.

Concerning vomiting food

Life, suffering, flees from a body denied nourishment. Death hovers on the lips when the belly refuses food. Rejected nourishment presages an unhealthy stomach.

Concerning the serpent Leviathan

God, allow me to break through the jaw of strong Leviathan and to leave it deprived of its bar and its crook; the jaw which previously you bored through with a ring and the power of your flesh.

Concerning old age

Disease grips old men; rash youth has its own faults. Here health is flourishing; imbecile senility crushes the old men. Here there is exhausted flesh; there, I observe muscular arms.

Concerning tonsure

Tonsuring, the vilest of customs, has entered our city. The necks are not so much like crowns, but rather like ladles. Perverted France has sullied [us] with these savage habits.

On martyrdom nowadays

You can no longer hand over that body of yours for martyrdom. [But] who prohibits emptying sacks of acquired property? Martyrdom of the cross today is to have given away what you have accumulated.

De Charunte

Nolo tuae, nauclere Charon, consistere ripae
atque tua naulo fluvium transire carina;
te cupio potiores occursare ministros.

De quattuor versiculis et reliquis
indifferenter positis.

De iniusto obsonio

Rura sacerdotum Ioseph inmunia fecit
legibus obsequii popularis et absque tributis;
ecclesiae Christi fluida quatiuntur harena:
ve ve nemo locat firmae fundamina petrae!

De his qui aliena secreta querunt

Hunc, qui rimatur secreta domus alienae,
occupet amburens scabies et lepra Giezy,
sive Herodis et Antiochi merore teratur,
quos fetor crutiavit et intolerabilis ardor.
Non re salvanda sed discupis inde timeri.

De Rege Tholomeo

Quid voluit, quid vidit rex Tholomeus agendo?
Dum regno regnum sotiat, lux tertia ademit
insperata virum de morte nihil trepidantem.
Magnus in orbe labor, brevis huius fama laboris.

Concerning Charon

O shipmaster Charon, I don't want to stand around on your shore and cross over the river in your keel for a fee. I want more powerful ministers to meet you!

[Now the sense comes] from four verselets, and the remainder vary in length.

Concerning unjust tribute

Joseph made the priests' lands exempt from the laws of obligation of the people and free from tribute. The churches of Christ are tottering on shifting sand: alas, alas, nobody builds foundations of firm rock!

Concerning those who seek other people's secrets

May an all-consuming scab and the leprosy of Gehazi seize the man who pries into the secrets of another's home. Or let him be rubbed out with the suffering of Herod and Antiochus, whom intolerable foulness and heat tortured. You desire to know the house's secrets not to protect it, but to be feared thereby.

Concerning King Ptolemy

What did King Ptolemy hope for, what {profit} did he see from his activity? While he was annexing one kingdom to another, the third day carried off unexpectedly that man who had no apprehensions about death. Great is our toil in the world, brief the fame for that toil.

De pretio medico negato

Ringeris archiatro non solvens debita digno;
qua re letargum patieris, ut ante solebas.
Respondit medicus forsan commotus in iram:
"Cardiacum te faxo indignum vivere sanum,
utere nunc pretio nostro cum fine maligno!"

De malo studio

Ut numquam studium sic friget ubique scolare,
quippe domi sollertia militiaeque negatur;
lectio quid preter plorare ministrat alumnis?
Rara quidem, nauci, cum venerit, et salis expers.

[De gigantibus et muris]

Famosos postquam genuit dea Terra gygantes,
post fama et magnos reges peperit quoque mures.
Non multum a nostris abludit imago magistris,
qui apparent hodie, et qui forte fuere priores.

De parcis

Lucus enim †antifrasin† a non lucendo vocatus
et Parcae, capiti didicerunt parcere nulli:
Clothos fila trahit, Lachesis ea stamina torquet;
quae quod neverunt, Atropos, soror inpia, rumpit.

Concerning the payment denied to a doctor

You refuse with a snarl what you owe to a worthy physician. That's the reason you will suffer from lethargy, just as you used to. The doctor, aroused to anger, it may be, responds, "I will give you heartburn, who are unworthy to enjoy health. Now enjoy [the money I should have gotten as] my payment, and its unpleasant consequences."

Concerning poor scholarly effort

Scholarly effort is in decline everywhere as never before. Indeed, cleverness is shunned at home and abroad. What does reading offer to pupils except tears? It is rare, worthless when it is offered for sale, and devoid of wit.

[Concerning giants and mice]

After the goddess Earth gave birth to the famous giants and after [she gave birth to] kings great in fame, she also bore mice. This picture is not unlike our teachers, those in evidence today and those who happened to live earlier.

Concerning the Parcae

Through antiphrasis, "grove" [*lucus*] is so called from "not having light" [*a non lucendo*]; and the Parcae [the Sparing Goddesses] have been trained "to spare" [*parcere*] no one. Clotho draws out the filaments; Lachesis twists the threads; and what they have spun, Atropos, their wicked sister, breaks off.

Ad vitiosos

Nam si viveret in terris Democritus, omnes
rideret segnes, indignos pane diurno;
aut largus lacrimarum fleret Eraclitus imbre,
qualis ego aut aliquis par, qualis erat Cluvienus.

De passeribus

Audivi corvum plus iusto dicere "Cobbo";
mira dei nutu natura est dives in actu:
prodocet altilia effari dux famina verbi,
ventris amore "Pater noster" studet edere passer
ac plures inconcessas formare loquelas.

De antiquis patronis

Omnes compositi, qui nos coluere, patroni!
Longius ex quo non fuit utile vivere nobis;
exhinc debuerant veteres hanc linquere terram
et iunctis manibus pariter discedere ab urbe.
Te fusumque tuum, Lachesis, causamur iniquum,
quod superare facis mestos felicibus illis.

De echo

Esse putas, non esse, cavis dum personat, echo,
auris decipitur de vocis imagine falsa:
quae mala dicuntur, sic sunt virtutibus umbrae,
subsistentibus a! nullis et nemo creator,

Regarding corrupted men

Surely if Democritus were living on earth, he would laugh at all the lazy people who do not deserve their daily bread. Or Heraclitus, prolific of tears, would weep in torrents, as I [do], or anyone like me, such as Cluvienus.

Concerning sparrows

I have heard a crow say, more often than was necessary, "Cobbo." Nature, wondrous by God's sanction, is rich in activity. An instructor teaches birds to speak the sounds of language. Out of love for its belly, a sparrow tries to produce an "Our Father" and to fashion many words not within its power.

Concerning ancient patrons

Those patrons who cherished us are all laid to rest! From that moment, it ceased being useful for us to live any longer; after that, [all] the old men ought to have left this land and, departed from the city, side by side, with hands linked. It is you and your wicked spindle, I blame, Lachesis, because you make us, dejected, outlive those happy ones.

Concerning echo

You think nonexistence exists, when an echo resounds in the hollows; the ear is deceived by the false likeness of a voice. The things that are called evil are, in just the same way, shadows of the virtues, with no substance, ah!, and

ipse diabolus inventor, meditator abyssi,
perdidit omne bonum infra se, dum cogitat ultra.

De reptilibus

Regibus invitis et musca et reptile crescit,
absque hominum iussu surgit de pulvere pulix;
indignamur enim sortita haec plurima terrae,
crescere preterea—iam non magis illa quiescunt.
Calcanda invidia est, nequeat quae lesa nocere.

Quid calamus fatiat sapientis

Hoc calamo atque stilo sulcamus iugera campi,
quae nos aestivae recreabunt mergite messis,
mutua curamus de qua convivia laeti.
His etiam infodiet propagans vinitor antes,
atque his vere novo incidet sarmenta putator,
deinde fimum scrobibus certabit tradere pinguem,
in prelo atque aliis ut calcet vina trapetis.
Si fuerit stilus hec fatiet limatus et addet,
hic olim dominis magnum inpendebat honorem.

Quod quidam pilosum habuit cor

Callidior priscis fuit ex nebulonibus unus,
fraudes concinnans plures sub corde piloso;
verum defuncti rimantur viscera testes

nobody as their creator. The devil himself, who ponders the abyss, is their inventor. He destroys every good thing beneath him, while he contemplates what is beyond [him].

Concerning crawling things

Against the wishes of kings, flies and crawling things increase. Without any command from humans, the flea rises from the dust. We are disgusted that so many things, having been allotted to the earth, increase besides—now they are no longer quiet. Envy must be trampled underfoot; it cannot harm when it has been wounded.

What the pen of a wise man might do

With this pen and stylus we furrow the field's acres; they will restore us with the sheaf of the summer harvest, from which we, happily, arrange banquets in turn. With these also the propagating vintner will dig his rows, and with these, in early spring, the pruner will cut off the twigs. Then he will strive to apply fertile manure to the trenches, so that he may stomp out wines in a winepress and in other presses. If the stylus is polished, it will do these things and add to them. This stylus once paid great honor to its masters.

That a certain man had a hairy heart

Among the old scoundrels there was one who was more skillful, crafting many deceits in his hairy heart. But witnesses examined the innards of the man once he was dead,

inventumque nefas mirantur et hispida corda,
immo, foris quam fraudem exercuit, intus habebat.

De insipiente magistro et discipulis eius

Presbiteri insulsi super hoc responsa parabant:
"Nos docuit sapiens multorum Drogo magister,
nobis iudicibus quo non sapientior alter."
Consultus nescit, 'Sabaoth' et 'Osanna' quid esset,
ac 'Dominus vobiscum' se nescire professus!
Credo, quod docuit, proprio de nomine traxit:
deceptus decepit, fraus in fraude pependit.

De predonibus

Odit pro iusto deus omnes carpiliones,
qui miseris vitam fatiunt fetere colonis;
Arpiis similes armantur in ungue ferino,
vix spirare sinunt et sicco vivere pane.
Credimus ante deum magnis meritis fruituros:
duriter hic vivunt, ibi mollius oro quiescant!

De inmaturis maritis

Hic deberet adhuc puer ignorare, quid esset
uxor, et intactus mundis requiescere cunis:
ante maritus erit modo, quam prorumpat ab ovo.
Olim ter denis, nunc denis nubitur annis!

and they marveled at the abomination they found, that is, his shaggy heart. Indeed, the fraud he practiced on the outside, he carried within him.

About an ignorant teacher and his students

Bungling priests were offering responses about this: "Wise Drogo, a teacher of many, taught us. There is none wiser than he, if we are the judges." If asked, he does not know what *"Sabaoth"* is and *"Hosanna";* and he freely confessed that he does not know *"Dominus vobiscum!"* I believe that what he taught, he drew from his own name: Having been deceived, he deceived [others]; fraud depended upon fraud.

Concerning robbers

God justly hates all thieves, who make life stink for the poor farmers. They are armed like Harpies with a bestial claw; they scarcely allow the farmers to breathe and live on stale bread. We trust the farmers will enjoy great rewards [when they come] before God. Here they live a hard life; there, I pray may they rest more easily!

Concerning immature bridegrooms

This one, still a boy, should not even know what a wife is, and he should sleep untouched in an unsullied cradle. He will now be a husband before he breaks out of the egg. Formerly, people married at thrice ten years old; now they marry at ten.

De sterili victu fratrum

Lassos ante boves paleae iaculantur edendae,
et psallunt steriles Christi pia munera fratres
absque cibis, quos hic ventosa cucurbita pascit.
Nemo vetat servire, velint si vivere vento.

De sicca Ardenna

Ardennam valles et cingunt ardua saxa,
in pluviis heret, nimio sub sole fatiscit;
iuditio nostro semper cultore careret,
nullus carorum cupiat fieri incola terrae!

De vita otiosa

Dispeream male, si novi civilia iura!
Otior hac vita, sine fructu crustula rodo,
dormito, bibo, ventri indulgeo, totus in hoc sum;
continue ante aliud quicquam formido gehennam.

De tribus ministris, urso, lupo, vulpe

Olim defuncto cuiusdam presule sedis
consultis super hoc datur optio sola duobus.
Hic lupus et vulpes pro re responsa dedere:
“Nobis iudicibus non fiet episcopus ursus;
prepositus fratrum communes sorbuit escas,
partiri ignorans communia traxerat ad se.”
Acriter inde lupum lacerans ferus ingruit ursus.

Concerning the sterile provisions of the monks

Straw is thrown before weary oxen for them to eat, and [yet] the destitute monks sing about the righteous rewards of Christ without food. A windy gourd nourishes them in this life. Nobody forbids them to serve, if they are willing to live on wind.

Concerning the dry Ardennes

Valleys and arduous rocks surround the Ardennes. It sticks [to one's boots] in the rain; it cracks under too much sun. In my judgment, it should always lack an inhabitant. Let nobody dear to me choose to become a resident of that land!

Concerning a leisurely life

I'll be damned if I know anything about civil law! I'm at ease in this life: I nibble fruitlessly on pastries, I nod off all the time, I drink, I indulge my belly—I am totally into this. Constantly, before all else, I am terrified of hell.

Concerning three ministers: a bear, a wolf, a fox

Once when the bishop of a certain diocese died, complete discretion about [filling] his position was given to two consultants. Then the wolf and the fox gave their responses about the matter: "If we are the judges, the bear will not become bishop. As provost he gulped down the communal food of the brothers. A stranger to sharing, he hauled off the common stores for himself." Then the savage bear attacked,

Fratribus hinc memorat vulpes, vinaria custos:
"Scitis," ait, "de fratre lupo nostroque decano.
Ecce cruentatum pro fratrum stipe videtis.
Ursus in ungue fero carnem a cervice diremit,
nam de coccineo res est manifesta galero;
huius me cautam docuit rubeus galomaucus.
Stare procul liceat, dum nobis imperat, opto.
Perfidus in minimis raro in maiore fidelis!"
Huic minuatur honor, qui contrahit omnia solus.

De menbris magis iniustis

Hoc menbrum capula tibi, quod magis inpedit, inquam.
Unde mali caput? Haec duo linguam causor et inguen:
fortis et ut vir sis, tum viribus utere, victor,
si capulare velis, extingue viriliter ambo.

Quod propria domus magni sit pretii

Quo pretio possunt habitacula priva liceri?
Censeo pro magno propriis considere tectis;
priva domus, matrona laris centusse licentur
et quanto unusquisque suos metitur amores,
unde suas tegetes prisci cepere coloni.

De iuvene nostrae vitae tedente

O bene nate puer, dic, quo te lesimus umquam,
ut nostrae caperes longinquae tedia vitae?

cruelly lacerating the wolf. Hence the fox, the wine guardian, tells the brothers, "You know," he said, "about brother wolf and our deacon. Look, you see the wolf got bloodied on account of the brothers' rations. The bear tore the flesh from his neck on his savage claw: the thing is clear from his scarlet cap. His red hat has taught me to be cautious. I wish it were possible to be far away while the bear is giving us orders. One who is unfaithful in the smallest matters is rarely faithful in a greater one." Honor should be reduced for one who takes everything for himself alone.

Concerning the more unjust members

Cut off the member that impedes you the most, I say. What is the source of evil? I argue it is these two: the tongue and the genitals. If you want to be a strong man, use your strength, O conqueror. If you are willing to cut, then do away with both of them like a man.

That one's own house ought to be highly valued

At what price can private residences be valued? I reckon it a great thing to dwell under your own roof. A private home, a matron of the hearth, are valued at one hundred [coins], and at whatever amount anyone appraises what he loves. That is why the old-time farmers got their own shelters.

Concerning a young man weary of my living

Oh wellborn child, tell me, how have I ever injured you, such that you have become weary of my long life? Don't

Non nostros metire dies, si lividulus sis,
huius et aetatis nequeas contingere metam;
forte videbo tuae pereuntia menbra iuventae
atque meis calcabo tenella sarabara plantis,
inde super tumulum tero ter tibi tura polinctor;
interdum vituli senior bos tergora traxit!
Sepius his maiora deus concurrere sivit,
non erit inbecillis adhuc facturus et ista:
Pytagoras plus quam quindenum scandere ramum
miratur talem similemque per omnia mannis.
Non tendis sursum sed tabescendo deorsum:
una cicadarum fies cum rege Titono
aut terram, nisi massa neget, cum mure subibis
aut stipulam te prebebis gravitatis inanem!
Sic beo, sic ferio linguae mordacis alumnum,
hos tolera queso, ut possis, pro tempore versus,
aversum tibi nunc animum dum formo serenum:
te pingam multo melioribus atque venustis,
te reddens lepidum, mansuetum ut vellus ovinum,
omnibus ut dicas "Iam sum recinentis amicus."

De reconciliatione superioris alumni

Irritamento quidam me movit alumnus,
levis adhuc tyrunculus, antiquarius actu,
meque remorsurum temerarius ante momordit,
quem conturbavi scriptis et verbere linguae;
nunc iuvenem placare volens conchilia quaero:
strenuus et sapiens et nobilis et generosus,

number my days, even if you are a little envious, and are unable to become as old as I. Maybe I will see your limbs perishing while you are young and trample your tender little bones with my soles, then grind incense on your tomb three times, as your undertaker. Sometimes an elderly ox has carted away the corpse of a calf! Often enough God has allowed greater things than these to happen, and he will not be timid in the future in doing this. Pythagoras is amazed that you ascend beyond the fifteenth step, a man like you, so similar in every way to mules. You are not moving upward but downward, shrinking as you go. You will become a cricket, with King Tithonus; or crawl under the earth with a mouse (unless your mace should prevent you); or turn yourself into a stalk, devoid of weight. That's how I bless and how I strike down a pupil who has a biting tongue. I ask you to tolerate these verses for a spell, however you can, while I render my mind, which is now hostile to you, serene. I will paint you in verses far better and more charming, rendering you elegant, soft as the fleece of a lamb, so that you may say to all, "Now I am the friend of a recanter."

Concerning reconciliation with the above-named student

A certain student stirred me up with a provocation. He is still a lightweight beginner, [but] an old hand at action; and me, who will bite back, he rashly took a bite out of first. I stirred him up with my writings and with a tongue-lashing. Now, wishing to placate the lad, I am casting about for compliments: You are hardworking and wise and noble and eminent, the special embellishment of your family, the glory

precipuum decus es generis, laus gentis avitae,
indoles egregia atque notabilis, optima proles,
virtutum plenus, totus teres atque rotundus,
comis et ingenuus, multumque decoris habes plus:
grammaticus, rethor, geometres, scriptor, aliptes,
augur, scenobates, medicus, magus, omnia nosti;
preterea rebus te nobilitabo duabus:
retibus atque hamis fulges, piscator et auceps;
moretum cum melle liquas, contundis et herbas,
alter Ypocrates, quas monstrat mundus, olentes,
herbarum vires mensura et pondere misces,
Peonioque nihil perhibent distare magistro,
atque aiunt, qui de minimis maiora locuntur:
"Sunt equidem quaedam mustelae grana penes te,
de quibus illa solet, dum vult, revocare parentes
exanimes, penitus fatiens illos redivivos."
Hinc iam defunctos reparare putaberis arte,
si filicem incolumis granatam hoc videris anno.
Audeo opinari lignum vitale tulisse
custode averso furtivum de paradiso,
unde est exclusus quondam primarius Adam.

De colentibus nummos

Nummorum rivi, vos estis grana columbae
digna coli, pro relliquiis festiva beatis!
Propter eos multis indignis fulchra parantur,
nobiliumque thoros ascendere sepe iubentur;
hos non ars sed diva Pecunia prestat honores.

of your ancestral line, an outstanding young man of excellent and notable character, full of virtues, you are completely polished and well rounded, sociable and well mannered, and you have a great deal of beauty in addition. You are grammarian, rhetorician, geometrician, writer, wrestling coach, fortune-teller, tightrope walker, doctor, magician—you know everything! Furthermore, I will call you noble for two things in particular: you shine both with snares and with hooks, a fisherman and a fowler. You clarify mulberry wine with honey, and, a second Hippocrates, you crush the fragrant herbs that the world offers. You blend the powers of the herbs, according to weight and measure. They report that you differ from the Paeonian master in no respect, and men who say greater things about the smallest, say, "There are surely some of the seeds of the weasel in you, namely those by which, when it wishes, it calls back its deceased parents, making them entirely revivified." So, now, you will be supposed to restore the dead with your skill—provided you live to see a fern bear seeds this year! I dare to express the opinion that you have carried off the tree of life from Paradise, secretly, when the guard was looking away, Paradise from which long ago the first man, Adam, was shut out.

Concerning those who worship money

Rivers of money, you are the pure seed of the dove, pleasant beyond other blessings, worthy of being worshipped! For the sake of money, couches are prepared for many who are unworthy, and they are often called upon to mount the dining-couches of nobles. It is the goddess Money, not talent, that confers these honors.

De inmitibus magistris et pigris

Res hodie minor est, here quam fuit, atque eadem cras
defluet in peius, mox ante oculos minuetur!
Hic constare scolas video virgis sine linguis,
afficitur caro, mens medicamine nulla fovetur,
sevitia incumbit Radamanti sevior ira,
et neque sic torquet dampnatas Eachus umbras,
exagitata hydris, non sic furiatur Herinis.
Queritur a stultis, quod non docuere, magistris;
spiritus intus alet, que non virgulta ministrant,
silva tibi teritur frustra, nisi spiritus assit!
Cur tua lingua vacat parcens audita docere?
Qui non audivit, qui fit, quod scire iubetur?
Num lapidum rigor est homo, duritia aenea carnis?
Prospice, ne pereas delinquens in pereunte!
Hic sterilis rerumque capax affligitur aeque;
vidi vel didici divae plus parcere venae
semper et ingenuam parcendo attollere fibram.
Inmaturus abit, qui ceditur, iste misellus,
ante diem referens ad porthmea in ore trientem,
solvitur in cineres, olim qui profore posset;
quam nimia sanguis puerorum cede sititur,
tamquam qui patris iugulati straverit hostem!
Ingenuus nusquam nutritur ephebus ad unguem,
albus erit corvus, si strenuus exit alumnus,
perpetuoque dehinc nigros spectabis olores;
quorumdam studia et pro porro computo luctas

Concerning harsh teachers and lazy ones

Our means today are smaller than they were yesterday, and tomorrow they will trickle away to a worse state, then be diminished before our eyes. I see that the schools here rely on rods without tongues. The body is attacked, but the mind is not soothed by a curative. A savagery looms more savage than the wrath of Rhadamanthus, and Aeacus does not torture the condemned shades as much, nor is an Erinys as crazed when she's stirred up by hydras. Questions are posed by stupid teachers about material they have not taught. The Spirit fosters inside us things switches cannot provide. You waste a forest [of switches] in vain, unless the Spirit be present. Why is your tongue idle, ceasing to teach what it has learned? How can it be that a pupil who has not been instructed is ordered to know? Does man have the hardness of stones? Has his flesh the endurance of bronze? Watch out lest you destroy yourself, transgressing in destroying [another]! Here the unproductive and the capable are afflicted equally. I have learned by observation or experience to be more sparing to a God-given vein of talent at all times, and to strengthen the noble fiber by sparing. He dies young, that poor little boy who is beaten, rendering before his time to the ferryman the coin in his mouth. He is reduced to ashes, he who once could have been useful. How boys' blood is thirsted after with excessive beating, as though one were slaying the enemy of his murdered father! A noble youth is never raised perfectly. If a graduate departs with any energy left in him, he will be a white crow, and from that point onward you will always see black swans. The studies and struggles of some men I value at one leek or at the price of a

unius aut pretio lentis granoque sinapis
cassibus aut tela tenui male nentis aranae.

De ave gluttone

In terris surrexit avis de nomine glutto
absorbere volens, quae secula cuncta tulissent;
quam mundi miseram cum non tulit area pestem,
et tam dirum animal cernens deus inmoderatum,
protinus hoc pessum deiecit fulmine monstrum:
gutture disploso vacuae patuere lacunae.
Olim quisquis inexpletum par sentiat urget!

De Romanis metuentibus lupum

"Est lupus in sacco, quo tu, Romane, caveto,
vestes tolle tuas ac te ne subtrahe, sodes!"
Ille refert pavidus sanctum iurans per Osyrim:
"Quicquid habent, odi, non sunt marsuppia nostra;
non magis accedam de tristi tollere sacco,
si mihi detur et obrizum vertatur in aurum."

De multis muscis estatis

Imbribus urget hiemps: horrent incommoda muscae,
nulli ferme nocent, neque scitur, quae mala tractent;
atqui aestate calent homines, animalia passim:
et fervent scynifes et multae molis oestra,
talia multa volant, et plurima mortis imago,

single lentil; and as [much as] a mustard seed or the web of a spider who spins poorly with thin thread.

Concerning the glutton bird

There arose in the land a bird by the name of "Glutton," who wished to swallow up everything that the ages had produced. When the space of the world could not bear that wretched pest, and God was observing that so dire an animal was uncontrollable, he immediately, with a lightning bolt, laid this monster low. When its belly exploded, empty chasms were exposed. Whoever argues that this did not happen once, should experience the same!

Concerning Romans who are afraid of a wolf

"There is a wolf in the sack, Roman, beware of it; take your clothes and don't run away, please!" The frightened Roman replies, swearing by holy Osiris: "Whatever the packs contain, it's not mine, I despise it. I would no more approach and take from that sorry sack, not even if it were given to me and turned into pure gold!"

Concerning the many flies of summer

Winter oppresses with its rainstorms; the flies shudder at its unpleasantness. They harm almost no one, and no one knows what evils they are doing. But men are hot in the summer, as are the animals far and wide. Both gnats and gadflies feverishly swarm, in a multitudinous mass. Many such things fly around, and manifold is the image of death.

musca nocet pulixque adimendo psaltria somnum.
Quippe ferae, volucres querunt umbracula pictae,
mitia vina valent mollesque in tempore somni;
ad leve cogat opus, quisquis mihi talia curet!

De lupo, quod nullum haberet amicum

Cum lupus infami lesisset fauce colonos,
funesto iumenta trahens ac dente trucidans,
conspirant proceres in eum vulgusque minorum
voce, quod instarent pro dampnis, ut vigilarent.
Sic vultum veritus cunctorum scandit in altum
quam mestus scopulum; loca late lumine lustrans
"Heus," inquit, "huius quam vasta est machina mundi,
atque ego percurrens quam paucis fungor amicis!"

De lupo vulpe et alauda, quomodo partiti sunt pernas

Ergo lupus, vulpes et tertia forsan alauda
conseruere, quod inventum sibi cumque dedisset
presens fortunae donique benignior auctor,
pars divisa tribus caderet consortibus aequa.
Comminus inditium pernae fecere repertae;
hic vulpes "Mecum si senserit," inquit, "uterque,
partes dividat has, quem fert propensior aetas."

The fly harms us, and the musical flea, robbing our sleep. Indeed, the wild beasts and colorful birds seek a little shade. Mild wines and gentle sleep are healthy in this season. Whoever cares about such things, let him impose an easy task on me.

Concerning the wolf: that he has no friend

Since the wolf had injured the farmers with his dread jaw, dragging away the flocks and slaughtering them with his deadly fang, the nobles and the people from lower ranks unite against him, agreeing to be vigilant because they are alert to their losses. Thus fearing the countenance of everyone, the wolf, very sadly, climbs a high cliff. Scanning the region far and wide with his eye, he says, "Alas, how vast is the fabric of this world, and how few friends I enjoy, traversing it."

Concerning the wolf, the fox, and the lark: how they shared hams

So a wolf and a fox, and a lark as the third, as it happened, agreed that whatever discovery the ready and obliging author of fortune and of dole had granted them, an equally divided portion would fall to each of the three companions. Immediately they noticed a ham that turned up. Here the fox said, "If you both agree with me, let that one divide the portions upon whom age weighs more heavily." Prompt to

Promptula vocis "Ego haec videor," memorabat alauda,
"pone solum consumpta situ iam ponere nidum
cogor et abruptos nequeo conscendere ramos."
Sermonem excepit vulpes non irrita fraudis:
"Viximus ergo aliquid, quod victa fatebere, maius:
enumerare pilos poteris, cum protinus annos."
"At mihi sunt," lupus adiecit, "non amplius anni
quam gemini, sed tertius hoc spirabile lumen
exigat in mortem, si vobis annuo partem!"
Iustitiam frangit sic sepe potentior hostis.

Quomodo arbores questae sunt mala puerorum

Mispilus et cerasus puerorum scismata questae
ab divis quondam pacem petiisse feruntur;
respondetur eis, ne quicquam mente graventur,
tunc pacem fore de pueris, cum forte viderent
securos inopes raptu cessare potentum.
Difficilem quae prestat opem, promissio dura.

De fame auri

Auri sacra fames, quae non satiat locupletes;
quam si non saperent, quot iustos terra tulisset!
Si sic tanto opere inmensos haec urit egestas
nec modus ullus erit plures desistere posse,
optem non aures, immo aurea corda luporum.
O similem quotiens agitaret belua pestem!

speak up, the lark told them, "I seem to be the one! Consumed by decay, I am compelled to build my nest close to the ground, and am unable to scale the steep branches." The fox, not ineffectual in deceit, took his turn to speak, "I have lived somewhat longer, as, defeated, you will acknowledge: You can add up my hairs, then immediately know my years." "I," interjected the wolf, "am no more than two years old; but may my third year drive the breath of my life down into death, if I grant a portion to you two." It often happens in this way that a more powerful adversary violates justice.

How the trees complained about the boys' misdeeds

The medlar tree and the cherry once complained about conflicts with boys and are said to have sought relief from the gods. A response was given to them, not to be troubled at heart in any way: they would have peace from the boys when they chanced to see the poor people at ease, safe from the plundering of the powerful. It is a hard promise that provides no easy aid.

Concerning hunger for gold

"The accursèd hunger for gold"; it does not satisfy the wealthy. If they did not have a taste for it, how many just men the earth would have borne! If this craving burns innumerable men so strongly, and there is no way that many can give it up, I ought to desire not the ears, but the golden hearts of wolves. O how often the beast would stir up a similar disease!

De porcello et lupo

Porcellum sequitur vehemens formido ferarum,
dentibus invisis flagrans intendere rictum.
Ille prior lapsus currit per devia mestus;
quod tunc presidium caperet, nescire. Tenet grus
rura propinqua sibi. "Mi sodes, quo ruis?" inquit.
Ille refert: "Ingens me sollicitudo suburget."
Ut didicit, datur hunc pavidum occultasse sub alis.
En aderat consueta malis vesania ventris
et procul "Heus," inquit, "semper mihi grata sodalis,
quo diversus abit, scis, nostri transfuga tecti?"
Grus ait: "Accelera, spatia et non plura supersunt,
ut capias, si te cursus non tedet, agendo."
Assidue insinuans caput in sua terga reflexit,
ostentans sub se latitantem, si memor esset;
quos lupus infestos nutus non percipit esse,
hac spe frustratus sequitur vestigia cassa.
Dum loca tuta vident omni formidine pulsa,
ut meriti memor esse velit, porcum ammonet ales;
ille sub haec: "Tibi sit pro puris gratia verbis,
sed tua colla truci pereant consumpta veterno!"
Albis sepe subest verbis fucata voluntas.

De capo et columba et aquila

Instabat capus ad saltus agitare columbam,
venerat illa secans pernicibus aera pennis
ad quercum et densa vitam sub fronde tegebat.

Concerning the piglet and the wolf

The raging terrorizer of wild animals, the wolf, pursues a piglet, burning to stretch out his jaws with their hated fangs. The piglet, having gotten a head start, runs through forsaken places, sad that he does not know what aid he might find. A crane holds the lands neighboring his. She says, "Where, if you please, are you hastening?" The piglet replies: "A great cause for concern urges me onward." As soon as she learned this, she allowed the frightened one to hide under her wings. Just then that madness of belly, accustomed to evils, approached; and from afar he says, "Oh companion, always pleasing to me, do you know where the runaway from my home is wandering astray?" She replies, "Hurry, there is still a distance, and not much of one, for you to catch him, if the race does not wear you out, driving onward." Continually making insinuations, she bends her head back toward her spine, pointing out the one hiding under her, if only the wolf would pay attention. The wolf does not notice these treacherous gestures. Frustrated in his expectation, he pursues the tracks in vain. When they see that the place is safe, with all fear driven away, the bird advises the pig to remember this favor. He responds straightaway, "Thank you for your innocent-seeming words. But may your neck be damned, consumed by savage decay!" A dark purpose often hides under shining words.

Concerning a falcon, a dove, and an eagle

A falcon pressed on toward a forest to hunt a dove. She had come, cutting the air with swift wings, to an oak tree and was protecting her life under its dense foliage. Arrayed for

Agmine facto auceps, aquilam cum forte supernam
nesciret, sequitur funesto armatus in ungue;
cum sibi prestantem sensit, nimis ilico mutus
palluit, accensamque iram compescuit horror.
Ecce columba suos edebat laeta triumphos
inpense, quod preter spem securior esset;
emulus hic ales fertur dixisse tumenti:
"Sit modus in gestu! si non maiora vererer,
in morem Salium non carmina faxo tulisses."
Sepe minax metuens maiorem innoxius ibit.

De paliuro

"Non possunt," paliurus ait, "divellere trimum
me fortes in mole boves radicitus umquam,
postquam aliquot vel binis figor euntibus annis."
Uberius surgunt cultis fruticeta beatis.

De uxore infensa marito

Lite procax mulier fluvio submersa profundo,
quae stolido vixit verbis infesta marito;
quam cum labenti quesissent amne deorsum,
vir suus adiecit: "Non id de coniuge novi,
has imas tenuisse vias, at compotis ira
indefessa adeo superas obtenderat undas."
Inportuna fidem non prebent iurgia rectam.

battle, the falcon, not realizing that an eagle happened to be above him, pursues the dove armed with his deadly claw. When he noticed his superior, he was instantly silent and very pale, and terror checked his burning rage. Now the happy dove was singing songs of triumph, extravagantly, [rejoicing] that she was safe against all expectation. Here the rival bird is said to have told the boaster, "There should be moderation in your attitude! If I did not fear greater powers, I would make sure you did not sing songs like the Salii." Often one who is threatening will depart harmlessly, fearing a greater power.

Concerning the thorn bush

The thorn bush says, "Oxen, strong in their bulk, cannot ever tear me up by the roots once I have reached my third year, after I am established for a while (even for two fleeting years.)" Brambles grow up more abundantly than fruitful plants that are cultivated.

Concerning a wife hostile to her husband

A woman insolent in quarreling drowned in a deep river, who, while she lived, was hateful to her stolid husband with her words. When they were searching for her downriver in the flowing stream, her husband remarked: "This is not my experience of my wife, that she would have held a course to the lowest reaches; but she was so tireless in her rage to get her own way, that she would have gone contrary, toward the waves upstream." Distressing quarrels do not produce the proper sort of fidelity.

Quomodo ploravit gravem sibi virum uxor defunctum

Vir gravis uxori ius morti solvit avitum;
post obitum multos lacrimarum fuderat imbres
tamquam mesta viri multum de funere coniunx.
Cur in flagra gravem ploret, rogitantibus addit:
"Non queror excessisse animam de luce malignam,
ingemo plus adeo superantem tempora longa."
Letitiae interdum simulatur causa doloris.

Quomodo ursus perdidit aures et caudam

Hinc prorsus dicunt demensi corporis ursum:
tempestate nova cum primum nectara mellis
ignoraret, eum ruptis traxere priores
auribus; atque dehinc postquam libavit ofellam,
perdidit innitens imi gestamen honoris.
Experiendo colet quidam, quod primitus horret.

De uno fratre convalente et altero obeunte

Febre laborabant dudum duo corpora fratrum.
Unum morbus edax fati concivit ad urnam;
alter item parcente deo post tempora sospes.
"Quamvis oppetiit frater, maioribus," inquit,
"aestibus urebar, cum sit mihi vita superstes."
Segnius irritant aliena ut nostra dolere.

How a wife wept for a deceased husband who had been hard on her

A man who was hard on his wife fulfilled his ancient obligation to Death. After he died, his spouse poured out many rainstorms of tears as though she were very sad about the funeral of her husband. To those asking why she would weep for one dreadful in his beatings, she replies, "I do not lament that his malignant soul has departed from life. I bewail more that it survived for such a long time." Sometimes a cause for happiness looks the same as a cause for grief.

How the bear lost his ears and his tail

Here is why they say that the bear has an entirely cropped body: when the season was new, since he was at first ignorant of honey's sweetness, his elders dragged him [to it] by his ears, which were torn [in the process]. But subsequently, after he tasted a mouthful, as he struggled [against attempts to drag him away], he lost that ornament of lower dignity [his tail]. With experience, one cherishes what one at first fears.

Concerning one brother who got well and the other who died

The bodies of two brothers suffered a long time from a fever. The devouring sickness whisked one off to the fatal urn. The other who was safe after a time, since God spared him, said, "Although my brother died, I was burning with a heat greater [than his], even though there is still life in me." Another's misfortunes incite grief less readily than our own.

De viro, qui lunam fecit de pane seliginis

Quidam inpune ratus vanissimus et male sanus
sese posse aliquid furvae succurrere nocti,
doctor ut is prudens tanta incrementa dedisset
preter opinatum, quotiens se Cinthia condat,
quendam formavit de pane seliginis orbem,
ut foris expositus lumen diffunderet amplum;
cumque moras ageret, quas fixas semper habebat,
inventor probulus iurat per Castoris aedem:
"Si deberet," ait, "lucere, aliquid potuisset."
Inconcessa gemat qui stultus vota ministrat.

De quinque lineis amoris

Compages flagrantis quinque feruntur amoris:
visus et alloquium, contactus et oscula amantum,
postremus coitus, luctati clausula belli:
his in honore suo poterit desistere spado,
ni temptare suum mavult post cepta pudorem.

De eo, qui osculatus est ursum

Ignavus deforme pecus concidere iussus;
oscula sed postquam libavit, abhorruit ursum.
Cogitur inde, feri ut venabula figat in alvum:
"Labra, viri, vixdum ammovi! quo truditis?" inquit,

Concerning a man who made a moon out of wheat bread

A certain man, most worthless and scarcely sane, having recklessly imagined that he might provide the dark night with a little help (so that, wise doctor that he was, he could supply unscheduled waxings whenever the moon goddess hid herself), fashioned a kind of circle out of wheat bread so that when set up outside it might spread an ample light. And when his bread-moon continued the dark phases which it always had, this clever little inventor swore by the temple of Castor, "If it needed to," he said, "it would have shone somewhat." One who stupidly serves up promises, may bemoan that they are not fulfilled.

Concerning the five stages of love

There are said to be five key components of flaming love: sight and speech, touch and the kisses of the lovers, and finally coitus, the climax of the battle that was waged. One who has renounced sex, in his honorable state, will be able to keep far from these things, unless he chooses to put his chastity to the test after things have gotten underway.

About the man who kissed a bear

A coward was ordered to slaughter an ugly beast. But after he had kissed the bear, he shunned it. He was then urged to stick his lance in the belly of the beast. "Men," he said, "I could scarcely bring myself to touch it with my lips. Where

"Me maiora audere dehinc ne poscat amicus:
tantus enim invasit terror pro talibus ausis,
certus eram me congerie foedare inhonesta."
In minimis veritus refugit graviora timendo.

De alauda et lupo, qui credidit questum in magna voce

Dulce suum sub fronde sedens philomena canebat.
Vocis mole minor, consuetus vivere raptis
furva in nocte lupus grassando perambulat aedes,
rura, nemus, nullique datur concurrere predae;
semper in his firmata gradu vestigia pressit,
auribus explorans, si quas admittere voces
huc se precipitando queat: cum protinus audit
carmen avis noctu excubias de more colentis.
Credidit ingentem magno sub flamine questum,
accedens pede suspenso cautisque ferens se
gressibus ipse ratus rabidum tergere palatum
sorbuit, hac ventrem sperans implere capacem;
post motus graviter delusum in voce sonora
reicit et tantas demum rupisse querelas
dicitur: "O vacuus clamoso in gutture quaestus!
Nemo fidem posthac committat grandia flanti."
Sepe minor probitas tumido versatur in ore.

are you pushing me? Let no friend ask that I dare greater things after this. Such terror infused me from what I have already dared, I was sure I was going to defile myself with a filthy mass." One terrified by the smallest things, balks at more serious ones in his fear.

Concerning the songbird and the wolf who trusted that in a loud voice [there was] prey

A nightingale, sitting under a bough, was singing her sweet song. A wolf, less powerful in voice and accustomed to live on plunder, on the prowl in the dark night, ambles along through buildings, fields and groves; and he is not granted an encounter with any prey. In these places he always made firm tracks as he went, exploring with his ears whether he might pick up any sounds while rushing onward. Then all at once he hears the song of the bird keeping in her customary way her nighttime vigils. He thinks he has found a mighty prize on the basis of its strong lung power. Approaching with a light foot and moving with cautious steps, having imagined that he would sate his rabid palate, he swallowed the nightingale, hoping thereby to fill his capacious belly. Afterward, gravely disturbed that he had been deluded by her sonorous voice, he regurgitated her and is said finally to have burst out with grumblings such as these: "Oh worthless prey in a noisy throat! After this, nobody should put faith in one trumpeting grandiosities." Often little probity is to be found in a bombastic mouth.

De cote et serpente, quis prior hominem lederet

Conditus in bivio serpens sub cote latebat.
Rusticus isset iter cum forte negotia curans,
in saxo casu cogente resedit eodem;
exuviis fessus positis dehinc talia serpens
commonuisse datur: "Nostrum non cedimus hostem?
Cede prior, lapis, heus, inquam! post haec ego morsu
perstringam." Ille refert: "Iam dudum lesimus," inquit,
"Frigoris occultum serpit per menbra venenum;
tu, quoscumque voles, posthac morsus adhibeto!"
Labitur aufugiens nullis conatibus hydrus.
Quod non presumit, hortatur ledere suasor.

De lepore et vulpe, quis melioris esset augurii

Convenere lepus vulpesque in famina dudum,
cui melior concessa sui stet temporis urna.
Mox pecus auritum "Felitior ominis," inquit,
"Incedis, sodes: in pulpam agor omnibus horis;
tu tantum, dum tempestiva et idonea pellis;
post requies et grata tibi sunt otia parta."
Illa sub haec "Promissa fides, velut ipse fateris,
sed mihi non fuerat pacto iurata fideli,
credere non cogor, sed tecum perfuga tollor."
Sic fati cautis discursibus inde feruntur.
Nedum promissum, rumpuntur iura sacrorum.

Concerning a rock and a serpent: which would injure man first

Concealed at a crossroads, a snake was hiding under a rock. When a farmer, tending his affairs, happened to set out on a journey, he was led by chance to sit down on that same stone. The snake, exhausted from having shed his skin, is then said to have uttered the following exhortation: "Do we not attack our enemy? Listen up, stone! You attack first, I say. Afterward, I'll stun him with a bite." The stone replies: "I have injured him already, long since"; he said, "The hidden poison of coldness snakes through his limbs. You, then, apply whatever bites you wish!" The snake slips away, fleeing without [making] any attempts. An inciter urges us to do injury that he doesn't dare to do himself.

Concerning the hare and the fox: which had the better lot

A hare and a fox came together once to discuss which of them had been granted a better lot in life. So the long-eared animal said, "You run about, if you please, with a happier destiny. I am hunted at all hours to a pulp, you only when your pelt is in season and suitable. Afterward, rest and pleasing leisure are allotted to you." The fox responds to this, "A promise has been given, just as you say, but it has not been sworn to me in a faithful contract. I am not obliged to trust it, but fleeing I am captured along with you." Having spoken thus, they go from there on their cautious ways. Even the laws of sacred oaths are broken, let alone a [mere] promise.

De muliere, quae vidit iurgare virum et natos

Olim cum proprio natos iurgare marito
ut vidit mulier, sic fari protinus orsa:
"Absque meis pugna est, pugiles, miscete capillos,
non mea res agitur neque rerum cura mearum."
Qui simulat non esse suum, fert sepe dolorem.

De viris, qui pugnaverunt de auca et ansere

Olim ruricolae bini fecere duellum,
quos in iurgia furtivus contraxerat anser.
Hic parat infitias, dum dimicat alter ob aucam;
duram post cedem, post rivos forte cruoris
anseris hic defecit herus ceciditque supinus.
Turgidus hinc adeo congressor robore sumpto
"Perfide, quid mecum sit tendere comminus," inquit,
"disce relisus humi, quia non fuit auca sed anser;
non eadem mihi res suspecta et vera videtur."
De re collata male poenas plectitur insons.

De quattuor caluis

Quattuor ut calvi Calvo puto Monte creati
occurrere mihi, fatie cum nomine noti,
mirabar sic conflatos quae flabra tulissent,
ridebam frontes levi quoque pelle glabellas;

Concerning a woman who saw her husband and sons quarreling

Once when a woman saw her sons brawling with her husband, she immediately rose up to speak in this way: "This fight does not concern my family, you boxers. Muss up your hair. This is not my affair, nor is it my concern." One who pretends the pain is not his, often suffers it.

Concerning men who fought over a goose and a gander

Once a couple of country folks had a battle. A stolen gander had drawn them into a brawl. This one [the thief] engages in denials, while the other fights over his goose. After a hard pounding, after rivers of blood, it happened that the owner of the gander collapsed and fell on his back. Then his puffed-up adversary, when he had regained his strength, said, "You scoundrel, now that you have been struck to the ground, learn what it is to have a hand-to-hand struggle with me: for it was not a goose [I stole] but a gander. This thing did not seem suspect to me, and it seems to be true." A man, innocent though he be, suffers punishment when his case is badly presented.

Concerning four bald men

When four bald men, born, I think, on Bald Mountain, encountered me (they were known to me by face and name), I wondered what winds had brought them thus blown together. I laughed at their foreheads, also bald with smooth

cuiusdam subiit quinti mihi mentio calvi:
is plane curruca foret, si quintus adesset.

De communi bono Romanorum

Ante suum commune bonum coluere Latini
et decus hoc sollempne suos docuere minores;
interea gens et genus intractabile bello,
nec tam clara fuit cuiusquam gloria gentis.
Munere corrupti retro cessere Quirites.

De ficta scriptura thesauri

Cote super plana scripturam inpressit aliptes:
"Thesaurum inveniet sibi, qui me verterit," inquit.
Collecta ecce manu quidam cupidissimus instat
vertere mox sursum, quod clauditur ante deorsum,
quo verso nil nactus preter "Avare, volebas."

De invido vitae nostrae

Cui longinqua mei tempestas cardinis instat,
non queat optatae contingere lumina vitae:
iste ministerium cupit, ille domum, alter agellos.
Invidia tabesce, puer, quasi non moriturus;
sorte licet dubia, cunctus tamen ortus obibit!
Invidus heritio similis: pus atque venenum
nutrit et omne nefas nebuloso in pectore versat.

skin. Mention was made to me of a certain fifth bald man. If a fifth one were there, he plainly would be a cuckoo.

Concerning the common good of the Romans

Previously, the Latins cherished their common wealth, and they taught the solemn dignity of this to their young. During this time, the people and race were unmastered in war, nor was the glory of any people so outstanding. Corrupted by bribery, the Romans have regressed.

Concerning a false inscription about treasure

A stonecutter carved an inscription on a flat rock: "Whoever turns me over will find himself a treasure," it said. Look, a certain very greedy man, having collected a group [of helpers], insists on turning upward straightaway what was concealed underneath before. When it was turned over, he found nothing but "Greedy man, you were stealing."

Concerning one who envied my life

May anyone to whom the long extent of my life is threatening not attain the joys of a longed-for life himself! This man craves a priestly office; that one, a house; another, fields. Waste away with envy, child, as though you were not going to die. Even though our lot is unknown, nonetheless, everything born will perish! An envious man is like a hedgehog: he fosters pus and poison and ponders every evil in his devious

Quo me perfidia trudis, nolendo sequeris,
pro livore tuo poenas scelerum luiturus.
Quam mala te rubigo coquit, si lividulus sis!

De debilitate evi nostri

Stamina qui quondam sciolis subtilia nevi,
torqueo nunc stuppas, rem debilitatis anilem,
prima elementa docens brutae pecuaria plebis,
archadicos iuvenes in rusticitate moratos.
De visis atque auditis vix pauca recordor,
atque ea dispensans partibor herile talentum,
otia vel vitans stolidis contenta ministro.
Teste deo numquam exsecui pretium artis avare,
quod mecum novit, qui scit deus omnia solus.
Quod queo, non renuo, nequiens invitus omitto,
iam dudum vires abeunt sed nulla voluntas,
sors gravis Entello cestus artemque negavit,
preteriitque (et eo plus) quinquagesimus annus,
quod tempus poscit vietis solatia fessis;
unde ego vasorum fieri desidero custos.

De ardea, quae ubique idem est

Militiae atque domi sibi, quod fuit, ardea semper:
dicitur illuvie volucris foedissima ventris,
quae solet Esquilias alvo calcare soluta,
hinc dignum factis nomen sortita cacatrix.

heart. Wherever you push me in your wickedness, you yourself unwillingly follow. Because of your envy, you will pay the penalty for your sins. How your evil corrosiveness will roast you, if you are [even] a little jealous!

On the debility of my old age

I who once wove subtle threads for scholars, now twist flax, the work of an old woman in her debility, teaching the first rudiments to flocks of brutish plebeians, simpletons mired in their rusticity. I scarcely recall a few things I have seen and heard; and dispensing these, I will divide up the "master's talent." Forsaking even contented leisure, I minister to these dolts. As God is my witness, I never greedily exacted pay for my skill. God, who alone knows all things, knows this along with me. What I can do, I do not refuse to do; what I cannot do, I reluctantly give up. My strength is long since departed, but not my desire. A heavy fate denied to Entellus his boxing gloves and his skill. And the fiftieth year (and more!) has passed away, a time that demands solace for worn out old men. That is why I want to become a "guardian of the vessels."

Concerning the heron, which is everywhere the same

In his own home and abroad, the heron always remains what it was. It is called from the filth of its stomach the foulest bird. It used to trample the Esquiline hill, loosening its bowels. Hence, a name worthy of its deeds was allotted it: the crapper.

De rustico semper inculto

Rusticus, ut Coridon, stupet in sermone diserti,
veste incompositus nulloque lepore facetus;
rustitius tonso cui laxus calceus heret,
parvo interstitio referre videtur asello,
horret in ungue fero digitis et plemine fultis
et menbris adeo incultis ac denique barbis,
silvestremque feram, quae capta tenetur, agit se;
simplicitas cui fida comes, quae fallere nescit.
Talibus indultis pietatis opus perhibetur.

De variis nominibus per omen inventis

Quidam optata suis inponunt nomina natis,
ut possint longam de nomine ducere vitam,
atque adhibere dies vitae ipsa vocabula rentur:
hic Durand, hic Guot, Vitalis dicitur, Hartman.
Hoc tantum iuvit, tamquam nulli nihil addas;
quantum quod sequitur, credas hoc profore tantum:
inprime puncta super puncto—non linea crescit;
non magis inde ferax, si Copia vacca vocetur;
si Mulctralis, eo non plus tibi lactis abundans.
Non tamen his fruimur, quamvis optata loquamur.

De quattuor vocibus

"Arma virumque cano" commendat scire caracter;
mugitum et strepitum nec mens nec littera prodit;

Concerning an ever-uncouth peasant

A peasant, like Corydon, is dumbfounded by the speech of an eloquent man. He is disheveled in his clothing, and his wit has no charm. Countrified in his hairstyle, his shoe clings loosely to him. He's not far removed from resembling a little donkey. He bristles with his bestial nails, and blister-filled fingers, and his limbs so uncared for, and, lastly, his beard. And he behaves like a woodland beast that is held captive. Simplicity that knows no deceit is his trusty companion. When such faults as he has are discounted, he is a masterpiece of piety.

Concerning various names picked as [good] omens

Some people impose on their children names chosen so that they might lead a long life on account of the name, and the words themselves are supposed to add days to their lives. This one is called Durand, this one Guot, Vitalis, Hartman. This helps just as much as adding nothing to nothing. And you may trust that this will be just as beneficial as what follows: place many points on top of a single point—no line results. A cow will not be more fruitful if she is called "Abundance." If she is called "Milk bucket," she will not produce more milk for you on that account. Although we may name the things we wish for, still we do not [thereby] obtain them.

Concerning four kinds of utterance

The written character allows us to understand "I sing of the arms and the man." Bellowing and rattling are the product

sibilus et gemitus nam scire datur sine scripto;
quamvis sint elementa "coax," non scire potes, quid.

De bono capite et malis lateribus

Sepe caput circumvallant latera inpia herile,
nempe quod est odiosa domus servique maligni,
qui dominos ridere suos rixasque ciere
assueti cives inimica fauce lacescunt;
hos punire dei manus imminet, inclita vindex.

De lupo, modo monacho, modo populari

Discurrens obiter lupus ad predam properabat
et nactus pisces, quos ventri indulsit edaci;
reddidit elatum congesta parabilis esca
in tantum, ut monachum sese iactaret habendum.
Inde abiens pernas invenit et insuper edit.
Cur a proposito ruat atque repente recedat,
"Parcite in hoc mihi, quaeso," percunctantibus inquit,
"nunc monachus, nunc sum parto popularis in esu,
ut lepidum facilemque vocent ad edenda ministri.
Non egeo ut lauti proceres pistore cocoque,
talibus insoliti talem docuere parentes,
ut numquam fastidia delitiosus amarem.
Non vescor coctis, invisa meis mora furtis,
cruda meum magis hoc guttur stipendia poscit."

of neither thought nor writing. Hissing and sighing surely can be understood without writing. Although there might be letters in "koax," you can't understand what it means.

Concerning a good chief and bad associates

Often impious associates surround the master's head because his household is hateful and his servants malign. Accustomed to laugh at their lords and stir up troubles, they provoke the citizens with their hostile jaws. The hand of God, the renowned avenger, threatens to punish them.

Concerning a wolf, now a monk, now a layman

A wolf, running on his way, hastened toward his prey and acquired some fish, which he conferred on his voracious belly. The readily gathered meal made him so elated that he boasted he ought to be considered a monk. Departing from there, he discovered some hams, and ate them as well. To those who ask why he hurries and suddenly backtracks from his proposed way of life, he said, "Pardon me in this, I beg you. Sometimes I'm a monk, sometimes a layman in eating what has been provided, so that being a charming and easy guest, the ministers might call me to dine. I do not need, as the cultivated noblemen do, a baker and a cook. My parents, unaccustomed to such things themselves, taught me this: never to love delicacies like a voluptuary. I do not eat cooked things. Delay is hateful to my thefts. Rather, this stomach of mine demands raw rations."

De lupo, qui non vult esse venator nec piscator

Multi sectantur lepores pinguesque ferinas,
quos moneo, ne me querant, non persequor illos.
Non venor iaculis nec ventilo cornibus apros,
dentibus ante meos quos sors armavit acutis.
Captarem, si non prohiberent flumina pisces,
inter decurrunt elementa minantia mortem.
Delitias ubi speres, imminet inde periclum.

De decem porismatibus

Sputa per os homines, norgam de naribus edunt,
dant oculi lacrimas, non sunt sine sordibus aures,
posteriora suas, prebent genitalia feces,
ultima sudorem reddunt porismata largum.
Sic denos numeramus in omni corpore poros,
perfectus numerus genus hoc insectile format.

De innumerabilibus

Quod numerum excedit, nullus hominum numerabit.
Quis stellas et quis bibulas censebit harenas?
Quis numerabit aves, diverso in flumine pisces?
Quisnam herbis, quisnam arboribus sua nomina figet?
Non muscae genus et non scitur reptile terrae,
nullus gemmarum lapidumque vocabula promet.

Concerning a wolf who did not wish to be a hunter or a fisher

There are many who hunt hares and fat game. I advise them that I don't chase those animals, so they do not need to pursue me. Nor do I hunt boars with spears nor rouse them with bugles. Fate armed them with teeth sharper than mine. I would catch fish, if the rivers did not prevent me. The fish course through an element that threatens death. Where you hope for delicacies, danger is lurking there.

Concerning the ten bodily apertures

Men discharge spit through the mouth, snot from their noses. The eyes produce tears, the ears are not without their crud. The posterior and the genitals offer their own waste products, and the tiniest apertures render abundant sweat. So we count ten openings in every body; a perfect number forms this indivisible group.

Concerning uncountable things

Whatever exceeds number, no man will number it. Who will count the stars and who the thirsty sands? Who will number the birds and the fishes in different streams? Who on earth will assign proper names to the grasses, who to the trees? The generation of the fly is not known, nor that of the reptile of the land. No one will produce the names of the gems and the stones.

Quod sint parentes colendi

Qui tolerat se divite mendicare parentes,
hic stimulante fame cogetur luce pacisci,
extinguetur et in tenebris sua iure lucerna!
Indulget senibus miserando ciconia nidis,
confectos matie victu solata parentes.

De ranis et earum deo trunco

Mitem habuere deum ranae per tempora truncum;
quo temere exploso meritas dea sorbuit ydra.
Post culpas, post dampna deum petiere priorem;
Iupiter aversus spretum non reddidit ultra.
Ex quo continuas non destituere querelas,
ut redeat, frustraque suam geminare coaxem.
Qui bona non tolerat, superest graviora gemiscat.

Quomodo pecunia pepulit sophiam de turre cum vecte

Delibuta comas ingressa Pecunia turres
turritasque domos, solaria fulta columnis,
hinc indefensam pepulit cum vecte Sophiam,
precipitem trudens, moribundam ad rudera stravit.
Quod laudant proceres, dignum dixere fere omnes:
"Haec mendica quid hic faceret sine fruge fruendi,
quae raro vel numquam nostra cupita resolvit?

That parents ought to be cherished

Whoever tolerates his parents begging, when he himself is wealthy, will be compelled by hunger's sting to bargain for light; and his lantern will justly be extinguished in the darkness! The stork, demonstrating compassion, provides for its elders in its nest, comforting with nourishment its parents who are perishing of hunger.

Concerning the frogs and their god the stump

The frogs had for a time a benevolent god, a stump. When it was rashly laughed off stage, a snake goddess gobbled up the frogs, who deserved it. After their crimes, after their losses, they asked for their former god. Jupiter was unsympathetic and did not restore the spurned god again. From then on they did not cease their continual complaints that he should return; and they redoubled their croaking in vain. One who does not appreciate good things, lives to bemoan worse ones.

How money drove wisdom from her tower with a crowbar

Money with her anointed locks assailed Wisdom's towers, turreted halls, and terraces supported on columns. She drove defenseless Wisdom from the place with a crowbar. Pushing her headlong, she hurled her half-dead to the rubble. The noblemen applaud this, nearly all of them said it was deserved. "What is this beggar [Wisdom] doing here, without producing pleasure? She rarely or never grants our

Haec placet, a nobis nusquam procedat, ut absit!
Haec nos delectat magis; illa sit abdita semper,
hinc curis confecta fameque perempta facessat,
haec sit apud mediocres et non liberiores;
ista suas nobis effundat tota cruminas,
vix reliquae plebi victum vestemque relinquens!"

Quod pueri fugiunt scolas

Quaeso, quid esse putas aut unde ita olere palestram,
quod fugiunt pueri ut Rusonem debitor aeris?
Dedaleum mussant et opinantur laberinthum,
inde adeo dictum, quod magnus sit labor intus;
in quo monstrum occiditur, informis Minotaurus,
stultitiam signans, quae cesa ibi porro fugatur.

De sciniphe hiemante in aure bubali

Ignorantis eam scinifes hiemavit in aure
per cantum bubali, qua dum referente resciret.
"Quid me sollicitas vanis de laudibus?" inquit,
"nec te visentem sensi nec curo abeuntem,
non gravor adventum nec mestus tardo recessum!"
Sordescunt magnis, quae parvi mira putamus.

wishes. This other one {Money} is pleasing. May she never depart from us; heaven forbid it! This one delights us more; let that one {Wisdom} always be out of sight. Let her be on her way hence consumed by cares and destroyed by hunger. Let her reside among the ordinary people and not among the better sort. May this one {Money} pour out her money-bags entirely for us, scarcely leaving food and clothing for the rest of the people!"

That children flee from the schools

I ask you, why do you think it is, or why does school stink so much that children flee from it like a debtor fleeing from Ruso? They mutter and consider it a Daedalian labyrinth, so-called for this reason, that great labor is in it. A monster is killed in it, the hideous Minotaur, who signifies stupidity, which is slaughtered there and put to flight.

Concerning a gnat who wintered in the ear of a buffalo

A gnat spent the winter in the ear of a buffalo who was ignorant of her presence, until he learned it by her reporting it through a song. "Why do you bother me with empty praises?" he said, "I was not aware of your stay, nor do I care that you are leaving. I am not vexed by your arrival, nor in my grief do I try to delay your departure!" Things that we little folks think are notable, are as dirt to great men.

De his, qui nolunt sibi exprobrari, quod fatiunt

Arguitur culpae auditor plus quam malefactor:
audet perpetrare nefas—ego dicere culpor;
liber agit, quodcumque libet—mutire negabor.
Quod reus admittit, cur insons debita solvo?
Si taceant homines, factum iumenta locuntur;
si infodias scrobibus, cantabunt carmina cannae;
non deerunt, vel qui mussent: operare, quod optas,
quamvis dissimules, haec noxia te penes heret.
Quod facis ad cantum gallorum in nocte secundum,
mane sciet caupo, caetarius, ozima vendens.
Verus cessabit te non operante relator.

De furtu perdicum, et quomodo matres secuntur

Perdix perdici solet excipere ova latenter
atque suis nidis miscere fovenda quotannis;
mox quibus egressis rupta testudine pullis
continuat monstratas naturaliter escas,
donec se pennis audent et credere ventis;
una avium si forte sonat vox matris ad aures,
agnoscit cito, de cuius processerat ovo,
et matrem sequitur propriam nutrice relicta.
Sic latro latitans, fur furvae noctis amicus,

Concerning those who don't wish to be rebuked for what they do

One who hears of a crime is censured more than the malefactor. He dares to commit the evil deed; I am blamed for talking of it. He is free to do whatever he pleases; I am denied the right to mutter about it. For what the guilty man commits, why do I, an innocent man, pay the price? Even if men were silent, the animals talk about the deed. If you were to bury it in a ditch, the reeds will sing songs about it. Nor will there be any lack of men who gossip. Do what you wish, however much you may dissemble, the offense sticks to you. Whatever you do at the second cock crow in the night, by morning the innkeeper, the fishmonger, and the vendor of trinkets will know. The reporter of truth will fall silent [only] when you are not doing anything [wrong].

Concerning the thievery of partridges and how they follow their mothers

The partridge is accustomed to take secretly the eggs of another partridge and every year to introduce them into her nest for warming. Then, to those chicks that have emerged when the shell is broken, she naturally provides the appropriate nourishment until they dare to entrust themselves to their wings and to the winds. [But,] if by chance a single call of its [natural] mother reaches the ears of a chick, it immediately realizes from whose egg it has come, and it follows its own mother, abandoning its nurse. So the secret robber [the devil], the thief who is the friend of the dark night,

blandis excipit insidiis aliena creata;
cumque aliquis se deceptum cognoverit errans,
voce creatoris redit auditoque monente:
"Non mors iniusti mea sit sed vita voluntas!"

De lupo et agno

In rivi decursibus agnus ab amne bibebat;
desuper adveniens lupus hunc deprendit et actum,
quem temere insiliens funesto dente trucidat.
Queruntur causae, commissi noxia tanti,
quod tam cede nova pereat, qui dicitur insons;
cum facti arguitur, dixisse lupus perhibetur:
"Inferius turbavit aquam fecitque molestum
pocula me talem sursum lutulenta bibentem,
inde animi inpatiens me frena tenere momordi."
Omnes iniustos propria inpatientia vexat.

De ovo a coniugibus comesto

Hoc ritu quidam cum coniuge vixit apud nos:
inter prandendum cum ferrent ova ministri,
servorum dominus meditullia sola voravit;
quae vitans uxor callosa adamavit in ovis.
Si sic consumunt, quae spes tibi pendet in ovo?
Expectare boni quid habes, ubi nulla supersunt?

takes another's creations with alluring snares. And whenever some sinner has recognized that he has been deceived, he returns at the voice of the Creator when he has heard Him admonishing: "Let not the death of the unjust one be my desire, but his life!"

Concerning the wolf and the lamb

In the channel of a river, a lamb was drinking from the stream. Arriving upstream, a wolf perceived it and what it was doing. Rashly jumping on the lamb, he slaughtered it with his deadly fang. The reasons are sought, the offense [deserving] of such a crime. That one should perish in such an unheard-of carnage who is said to be innocent! When he is charged with the deed, the wolf is reported to have said: "From downstream he disturbed the water and made me upset as I was drinking muddy drafts upstream. So, unable to control the reins of my spirit, I ate him." Their own lack of self-control makes trouble for all unjust men.

Concerning an egg eaten by a married couple

In this manner a certain man lived among us with his wife: when the servants brought them eggs during breakfast, the servants' master ate only the yolks. Avoiding these, his wife liked the hard parts [the whites] in eggs. If they consume them in this way, what part of the egg is left for you to hope for? What good can you expect, where nothing remains?

De duobus venatoribus inique partientibus

Cum sotio gnarus venator foedera sanxit,
quicquid cepissent, dirimendum partibus aequis:
de lepore accepto pellem dedit et sibi carnem,
pellem vero sibi, carnem de vulpe sodali.
Qui nequit obscure, deceptor fallit aperte.

De noctua

Carmina dispersit volucris de nocte vocata
voce minor, quae continuat per cantica noctem.
Garrula pulsatur, vox musica non aperitur,
tollitur inprobitas in magno magna labore,
sedulitas ingens non exprimit utilitatem.
Ventilabrum sine frugibus hac ratione notatur.

De fratribus benefitium invidentibus

Dente canum quidnam me, fratres, roditis? inquam,
cur careat paleis hic bos enectus arando?
Indignum foeno atque habitis censetis agellis,
pro quibus aetatem trivi servilibus annis,
quando urebar sole gravi atque algore nivali
et trituranti ex oculis somnus fugiebat.
Nam meritus labor exigit in iuvenilibus annis,
molliter ut pascat sparsos in vertice canos;
scribitur: "Ad iuga fessa boum non ora ligabis."

Concerning two hunters dividing things unequally

A crafty hunter made a pact with his partner: whatever they should catch, should be divided in equal parts. From the rabbit they caught, he gave [his partner] the pelt and himself the flesh. But he gave the pelt to himself and the flesh to his partner when a fox was caught. A cheater who cannot deceive secretly, does so openly.

Concerning the owl

The bird named after the night spread her songs abroad, though she was inferior in voice. She spends the whole night in song. A throbbing babble, not a musical voice issues forth [from her throat]. A great annoyance [of a voice] is raised with great effort. Her enormous diligence does not produce a useful result. A winnowing fan without grain gets a black mark in the same way.

Concerning brothers envious of my benefice

Why, brothers, do you gnaw at me with the teeth of dogs? I say, why should this ox fatigued by plowing lack hay? You consider me unworthy of the straw and of the fields I've gotten, for which I spent my life in years of slavery, when I was burned alike by the heavy sun and the snowy cold, and sleep shunned my eyes while I was threshing. Surely meritorious labor in youthful years demands that one be allowed to let the sparse gray hairs on his head grow softly. It is written, "Thou shalt not bind to the yoke the weary mouths of the oxen."

De superbo iuvene et tonsura nova

Qui putat, invenies quendam levitate superbum,
quod non terra suo sit solo corpore digna.
Sextae, dum tondes, imitatur cornua Lunae
aut Irim, sole adverso de nubibus arcum;
"Dispice," ait, "si rombum feceris, inprime normam;
ne quis ad opprobrium cincinnus pendeat, aequa;
occiput hoc scurris ridendum nolo parare.
Quis videor? similisque mei perrarus habetur."
Iste periscelides, caligas, circumspicit umbras,
indignans, si non respondent omnia votis.
Instituit, quicquid deliberat, edere nutu,
calce terit terram tedetque audire loquentes,
grandia verba tonat rigidissima, plena minarum;
cum placas, magis instigas, causatur et ardet.
Aspernatur et indignatur habere parentes,
esse suos quos preter se non ambigit ullus;
"Hei mihi," tristis ait, "quod sum de talibus ortus!
Cur pater aut dux non fuit aut mihi regia mater?"
Succinctis opus est, cum dici plurima possunt;
curentur compendia, ne fastidia gignant.

Ad amicum quendam iocose

Cur alienus in Esquiliis mea gramina carpis?
Otius hinc mutato pedem, ne crura terantur,
nam te noster adusque necem iam cippus habebit!
Si capiat te nostra manus, mihi crede, peribis;
et tu, si recte sapias, oculos tuearis,

Concerning a proud young man and his new haircut

You will find a certain young fellow proud of his own frivolity, who thinks that the earth is unworthy of his singular person. While you're trimming his hair, he resembles the horns of the "sixth moon" or Iris, the bow from the clouds when the sun is opposite them. "See here," he says, "if you've made it crooked, use a ruler! Level it, so that no curl hang down to embarrass me! I don't want the back of my head to be an object of ridicule for buffoons. Who do you think I am? It is almost impossible to find my like." This fellow surveys his garters, his boots, his shadows. He is indignant if everything does not correspond to his wishes. He is determined to express whatever he is thinking with a [mere] nod. He wears out the ground with his heel, and is bored listening to others speaking. He thunders out mighty words, intransigent and full of threats. When you try to calm him, you incite him even more. He argues and flares up! He spurns his parents and is indignant to have them. (Aside from him, no one doubts that they are his own.) "Woe is me," he says sadly, "that I was sprung from such people! Why was my father not a duke or my mother not royal?" There is only need for a few words, although many could be spoken. Even brief summaries must take care that they not become tedious.

To a certain friend in jest

Why, stranger, do you traverse my turf on the Esquiline? Take your foot quickly from here, so your legs don't get broken, for my shackles will hold you till death! If my hand should seize you, believe me, you will die. And if you are really wise, you will guard your eyes. At my hands, you are go-

de nostris manibus visu cariturus et aura!
Suplitiis si muto animum levioribus ultro
propitiusque deus te iuverit atque eris insons,
nona opera in silva fies de glande legenda
aut bostar mihi purgabis manibus lutulentis
sive in pistrino te dedam lege molendi
non alia nisi, dum te exemero prorsus ab illo,
ipse subibo operi lapides volvendo molares.

De Waltero monacho brachas defendente

Mandant Waltero fratres non tradere brachas,
omnibus ablatis tacito defendere solas,
dum contingat iter fortes transire per hostes.
Interea datur experientia militis huius:
mittitur imperiis ad certa negotia fratrum.
Fors fuit, ignorans in prorumpentibus hesit
hostibus et faleras et equum tollentibus una,
mastigiam, cunctos habitus iuxtaque cucullam;
non renuit neque contendit, facere omnia sivit.
Tandem de bracis solvendis tendere coepit,
usus militia viguit, quae nota, sub armis:
dissipat assultus macta virtute repressos,
omnes disiectos ab equis sine sanguine stravit,
dicens: "Omne quidem spolium, de podice nullum
fratres his tolerant, qui fratrum nuntia portant,
tales exuvias avido vetuere latroni."
Collectis spoliis et equis ad sacra meavit

ing to lose both your sight and breath! If I change my mind, of my own will, in favor of milder punishments, and if a propitious god comes to your aid, and if you are found to be guiltless, you will become the ninth worker gathering acorns in my woods. Or you'll clean my ox stall, with your mucky hands. Or I'll surrender you to the gristmill, under no other condition than that, if I release you from that task, I will myself submit to the labor of turning the mill stones.

Concerning the monk Walter defending his breeches

The brothers gave Walter a mandate not to hand over his breeches, but to defend those, even when everything else had been taken from him without protest, whenever his journey should happen to take him among powerful enemies. Meanwhile, a test of this great soldier is afforded. By order of the brothers, he is sent on a particular business. It was fate that, unknowingly, he is mired in the midst of enemies who burst upon him, taking simultaneously his horse's armor and his horse, his whip, all his [outer] clothes, and his hood too. He did not refuse or struggle; he let them do everything. At last he began to contest over his breeches being taken. Experienced in military service, he was strong under arms, as is well known. He breaks their assaults, which he repressed with great strength. He hurled them down, dislodged from their horses, without bloodshed, saying, "Every other spoil, but none from the rear end, do the brothers allow [to be taken] from those who carry their messages. That kind of booty they deny to the greedy robber." When he had collected the spoils and horses, he traveled to the sacred

psallentum sub laude dei collegia fratrum,
tantam militiam mirantum et fortia facta
vergentis vetulique hominis nova bella moventis.

De sapientia, quae non possit auferri

Nitimini appositas, fratres, attollere gazas!
Quam deus inseruit, vigilantem nemo mamillam
auferet. Hoc etiam fieret, si vota valerent:
linquerer ingenio pariter viduatus et aura!

Qui scelus, inde timete deum, non linquit inultum!
Si sum dedecori vel quemquam crimine lesi,
ferte palam nevum, veris convincite, victum
propulsate reum, confectum vile talentum;
non metuo testem fugientem lumina luscum.

De malis Francigenis

Unde solent tempestatum ebullire procellae,
solis ab occasu orta heresis quam pessima nuper.
De quibus audistis satis et meminisse potestis,
gens inimica deo, nullius commoda honoris,
iurat per frameam atque crucem, per viscera Christi
perque animam mirandam, quod non fulminat omnes,
quod non sorbet eos iam vivos terra dehiscens.
Hinc prodeunt homines omni feritate bilingues,
corrupto cerebro, furibundae cedis haneli,

fraternity of brothers who were singing psalms in praise of God and wondering at the great military courage and brave deeds of a declining and rather aged man waging new wars.

Concerning the kind of wisdom that cannot be taken away

You should strive, brothers, to build up the treasures you are given! No one will take away the vigilant heart that God placed within us. This would also happen, if [mere] wishes prevailed: I would be left equally bereft of mind and of the breath of life.

Fear God, who leaves no sin unpunished! If I am disreputable or have injured anyone by my crime, bring the fault into the open, convict me with the truth. Drive me out when I'm overcome, a guilty man, rendered a "worthless talent." I have no fear of a one-eyed witness who avoids the light of day.

Concerning evils of French origin

Out of the West, from which storm blasts come boiling up, has recently arisen the worst sort of heresy. Men about whom you have heard a great deal and can remember, a race that is hostile to God, deserving of no honor, swears by the lance and the cross, by the bowels of Christ and by His wondrous soul—wondrous in that it does not strike them all down, that the gaping earth does not swallow them alive! From here men come forth, fork tongued in all their savagery, with corrupted brains, panting for raging slaughter.

quos malus error et exagitat manifesta frenesis.
Vita, ne verbis sis credulus hospitis huius:
ianua limen amet, custos et pessulus obstet,
ne noctu tales suspecti irrumpere possint
et pereas aut tu vel carus natus et uxor!
Interior, qui scis, quid eis persuaserit hostis?
Non feriare manus puto, quo non lingua domatur;
presumptus vigor ebrietas et crebra negabit
ausus illicitos et inexpertum scelus ullum?
Qui vult, credat eis; non ausim credere quicquam.

De putida carne nostra

Putidius nostra non est in carne cadaver:
sudor olet, sanies, flatus cunctusque meatus;
sola pii redolent domino timiamata cordis
et quibus algentem solaris veste cyboque.

Men whom a wicked sin and manifest delirium drive to a frenzy. Avoid them, lest you become a believer in the words of this enemy! Let the door hug the threshold, and let the bolt stand as a guard, lest at night such suspect men be able to break in, and lest you die (either you or your dear son and wife)! How do you know what the enemy within persuaded them to do? I do not think that hands are idle where the tongue is uncontrolled. Will their impudent vigor and frequent drunkenness prevent unlawful enterprises and [leave] any sin unattempted? Whoever wishes may trust them; I would not dare to trust them in anything.

Concerning our putrid flesh

A cadaver is not more putrid in flesh than our flesh. Our sweat stinks, our pus, our breath and every passageway. Only the incenses of a pious heart are redolent of the Lord; and through them you comfort one who is freezing with clothing and food.

BOOK TWO

The Bronze-Clad Stern

INCIPIT SECUNDUS LIBELLUS PUPPIS AERATAE.

Comminus Aeratae succedunt postera Puppis,
cuius non dolabro est sed cesa crepido securi.

QUOMODO PYTAGORAS INVENIT TRES SIMPHONIAS IN QUATTUOR MALLEIS

Pytagorae resonabat malleus absona quintus
invenientis inesse sonos in quattuor aptos.
Est modus hinc vitae certusque in limine cardo,
ultra quem citraque nequit consistere rectum:
en tibi corpus et est princeps in corpore flatus;
his sunt appendenda quidem adiectiva duobus:
haec caro queritat induvias et spiritus escas;
quae superant, absurda videntur et absona sanis.
Malleolum ecce sophos reprobat; nos, quicquid abundat.

DE PRIMO HOMINE DE PARADYSO EIECTO

Olim factus homo de terrae principe limo
nobilis intravit hortum possessor amenum,
angelica victurus et illa celibe vita;
ast ubi vipereo componit credita suasu
consilia, in peius ruere omnis fabrica cepit,
nobilitasque viri temeraria degeneravit.

HERE BEGINS THE SECOND LITTLE BOOK OF THE BRONZE-CLAD STERN.

The ensuing sections of the "Bronze-Clad Stern" follow immediately. Its bridge was cut with an ax, not with a pickax.

How Pythagoras found three concordant sounds in four hammers

One of Pythagoras's five hammers sounded discordant noises even as he found agreeable sounds in four of them. In the same way, there is a measure in life and a fixed pivot point on the threshold, on either side of which uprightness can not exist. Look, you have a body, and in charge of your body is the spirit: on these two things everything else must depend. Our flesh wants clothing and nourishment, and the spirit likewise. Whatever exceeds these things seems absurd and discordant to sane men. See, the philosopher condemns a little hammer; we condemn whatever is superfluous.

Concerning the first man tossed out of paradise

Once upon a time, a man made from the first mud of the earth entered a pleasant garden as its noble proprietor, planning to live an unmarried life and one "like the angels." But when he took as advice things believed at a snake's persuasion, all of creation began a precipitous decline, and the man's nobility degenerated into audacity. Then, having

Qui tunc mutatus sedem mutare iubetur,
stirpsque dehinc Mausolia pulverulenta subivit,
nunc caro, nunc vermis, post vermem denique pulvis.
Qui patriae memor illius se moribus ornat,
virtutes sequitur, quibus assidue decoratur,
succedet quandam invitis suasoribus aulam:
alter erit paradisus et eminus ortus ab illo,
qui prius et multum fuit ante viabilis hosti,
quique vel ingratus non subruet amplius ullum
inde hominem, quod ad hanc non aspiraverit arcem;
invidiae huc aditus non panditur ire volenti,
nec caput aut famuli possunt irrumpere claustrum,
perpetuo locus est illis munimine septus;
inde foris stabulant tabentia corda dolore,
quod norint requiem solos celebrare beatos
accensumque suum flammis crepitantibus ignem
et simul ingruere aeternis incendia penis
tormentisque suis cinctam sine fine gehennam.

De his, qui non corripiunt commissos

O vos prelati, non cura at nomine solo!
Commissos vobis niti per prona videntes,
turpis amore lucri non corripitis labefactos.
Inproperante deo poenas ultore luetis,
credite scripturis, si non mihi credere vultis:
"Qui fratres errare videt transitque videndo,
morte peremptorum cogetur pendere penas;

undergone a change himself, he was ordered to change his abode; and from that time on, his offspring have descended into dusty mausoleums. Now flesh, now worm; after the worm, finally, dust. He who, mindful of his homeland, adorns himself with [good] morals, and pursues virtues by which he is continually honored, will enter a certain palace, even though the persuaders [of evil] do not wish it. It will be a second paradise, sprung up far away from that one which previously, and much earlier, was accessible to the Enemy. And the Enemy, even though he is disagreeable, will no longer drive out any man from there, since he has no hope of reaching this citadel. No entrance is open to Envy, even though she wishes to go there. Neither the master nor his servants are able to break into this enclosure. The place is fortified against them with an enduring fortification. Outside are found hearts withering from grief, because they know that the blessed alone experience rest. And that their own fire has been kindled with crackling flames, and, simultaneously, that conflagrations loom with eternal punishments, and Gehenna, girt by its own unending torments.

Concerning those who do not reprove the people entrusted to them

Oh you who are not priests in solicitude, but in name alone! Seeing those entrusted to you downcast and struggling, you do not reprove them when they slip, because of your love of filthy lucre. You will pay the price, when God the avenger reproaches you. Believe the scriptures if you do not want to believe me: "Whoever sees his brothers erring, and though seeing, passes by, will be compelled to pay the penalty for

unde sciet se fusurum pro fratre cruorem,
qui parcit fratri correctos tradere mores."
Neglectus vestros carbones mille cremabunt,
et frustra stillantis aquae fomenta petetis.

De coco Nabuchodonosor

Succendit Nabugodonosor cocus ardua templi
in Solimis, regi dum prandia lauta pararet:
nos templum domini violamus et igne cremamus,
copia dum mentem suffocat larga cyborum.

De inmundo spiritu

Spiritus in mundo proprii nil possidet ater.
Nudi cum nudo debemus sumere luctam;
vestitus si cum nudo luctamina temptet,
sternitur indutus, quod vestibus inpediatur.
Qui nitens talem contra contenderit hostem,
is, ne succumbat, sua vestimenta repellat.
Huc nihil attulimus, nihil hinc auferre locamur,
nudis adventus, nudisque reversio certa.
Divitias mundi cur quisquam colligere instat,
quandoquidem nec stare potest, qui colligit, auctor?
Cursum quisque brevem vitae consideret huius,
suffitietque sibi contento vivere paucis.
Longa quidem desideria increpat haec brevis hora,
cogitur incassum servata pecunia multa,
cum iuxta est, quo pergitur, et non longius absit!

those cut off by death. Hence, he who refrains from transmitting correct morals to his brother shall know that he is going to pour out blood for his brother." A thousand coals will burn up your acts of omission, and you will seek the refreshment of a drop of water in vain.

Concerning the cook of Nebuchadnezzar

Nebuchadnezzar's cook torched the heights of the Temple in Jerusalem while he was preparing lavish feasts for the king. We violate the Temple of the Lord and burn it up with fire, whenever a great abundance of food chokes our mind.

Concerning an unclean spirit

The black spirit possesses nothing in the world that is its own. We ought to enter the ring naked against one who is naked. If someone wearing clothes should attempt to wrestle with a naked man, the one who is dressed gets thrown down because he is impeded by his clothes. Whoever will contend in struggle against such an enemy, ought to remove his clothing so that he not be overcome. We brought nothing here, we are in a position to carry nothing away. Our arrival was as naked men; our return will certainly be as naked men. Why does anyone strive to gather up the riches of the world, since surely the one doing the collecting cannot endure? Everyone should consider the short course of this life, and it will suffice for him to live content with a few things. This brief hour is a standing rebuke to long-term desires. A stored-up bundle of money is collected in vain since the place to which we are heading is near at hand, and may it not be further away.

De bellis adversarii

Semper bella duos movet adversarius inter,
inflammans unum convitia ferre priorem,
alterum, ut is regerat peiora repotia lesus;
acrius inde dolet, si non incendere possit
ante lacessitum, quem tunc videat patientem.
In tribus ergo modis virtus patientia surgit:
emulus intentat mixtis obprobria dampnis—
absque odio hunc tolerat patiens et deputat aequum;
hostis continuat variae temptamina rixae—
hunc sine consensu quam surda avertitur aure;
atque flagellantem dominum sine murmure portat.
Quisquis eum assidua pulsaverit et prece digna,
concite opem feret optatam in temptamine carnis.

De superbia

In rebus bene gestis sola superbia restat,
ignorata subit quasi tussis in omnibus egris.
Dum sine teste deo te commendaveris actu,
laberis in vitium fallens ab origine primum.
Preliba dominum in factis, et tutior ibis.

De vindicta Domini

"Omnis," ait dominus, "vindicta mihi tribuatur,"
quam, tecum nisi pacta sit et diluta, rependet.

Concerning the wars of the adversary

The Adversary always stirs up wars between two men, inflaming one to offer insults first, and the other, after he has been wounded, to return still worse counterpunches. Then the Adversary is bitterly pained if he cannot ignite the one previously provoked, should he see him exercising patience. The virtue of patience arises in three ways: a rival directs his taunts intermingled with injuries; a patient man tolerates him without hatred and reckons the score is even. An enemy adds the further temptations of a variety of quarrels—how the patient man turns away from him without assent, with a deaf ear! And finally, he bears without grumbling the Lord who is punishing him. To whoever urges Him with constant and worthy prayer, He will swiftly deliver the hoped-for aid in the trial of his flesh.

Concerning pride

Pride alone [among vices] is found among good deeds. It steals in unrecognized like a cough among all the sick people. While, without a witness, you are commending yourself to God for your actions, you will fall into the first vice that deceived from the beginning. Put the Lord first in your doings, and you will proceed more safely.

Concerning the vengeance of the Lord

"All vengeance," says the Lord, "is to be assigned to me." He will repay it, unless it has been settled with you and resolved.

Quodsi respondere velis per singula plagis
et commissa aliena tuis aequare flagellis,
debilitabis eum, qui sanus vivere posset,
primule subiectum tibi teque deinde trucidas
in plagis animae, conservum corpore tantum.
Hinc Salemon "Ne iustus," ait, "plus par habearis"
atque iterum "Iustus perit ad nimis alta recurrens."
Dic, ubi pax, pietas patiens, patientia, Christus,
virtutum dominus, si, perfide, nulla remittis?

De Herusalem superna

Illa Salem mater, cui nomen visio pacis,
anglorum numero constabit tota hominumque;
humanum genus hoc ad eam conscendere tantum
quantos electos ibi permansisse putamus.
Teste sacro eloquio, quod nostram ventilat aurem,
terminus est electorum positus populorum,
anglorum ut numerus caelesti in sede relictus.

De spiritu incircumscripto

Spiritus angelicus circumscriptus perhibetur;
qui deus est, incircumscriptus et abditus in se.
His poenam iudex, qui nolunt stare, minatur;
lapsis, ut surgant, veniam promittit et inplet,
lamentis aperit bonus ille sinum pietatis,
aversos ad se revocat recipitque reversos.

But if you wish to respond to blows one by one and to match another's faults with your whips, you will weaken one who could live healthy. First you destroy the one subject to you, and then yourself by the blows to your soul; he is your fellow slave only in body. Hence Solomon says, "Be not over just," and again, "A just man perisheth, resorting to things that are too high." Tell me where is peace, patient piety, patience, Christ, the Lord of virtues if, scoundrel, you forgive nothing?

Concerning the heavenly Jerusalem

That mother Jerusalem, which has the name "vision of peace," will agree entirely in its number of angels and men. We think that only as many from the human race will ascend to it as there are chosen ones [angels] who have remained there. By the testimony of the sacred word, which blows in our ear, a limit has been placed on the number of chosen people that is equal to the number of angels left in the celestial home.

Concerning the spirit who is not circumscribed

An angelic spirit is said to be circumscribed; the one that is God [the Holy Spirit] is uncircumscribed and hidden within Himself. As judge, He threatens to punish those who do not choose to stand firm. To the fallen, so that they may rise up, he promises forgiveness; and he fulfills it. To their laments, that kind Judge opens up the bosom of his mercy. He recalls to himself those turned away, and he receives those who have returned.

De terrenis crutiatibus

Crux terrena modis speratur certa duobus:
dum quis ab illicitis bonus abstinuisse probetur
et carnem macerans contemplativa sequatur;
altera, quando aliena incommoda nostra putamus,
fratribus et dum compatimur sua dampna gementes.

De quattuor percussionibus

Omne genus hominum punitur cede quaterna:
in medio propono duos, Iob atque beatum
Paulum, quos ambos exercita cura beavit
fidenterque probans dominus purgavit ut aurum:
hic nihil admisit condignum verbere tali;
alter, ut evigilet, ne qua extollentia crescat,
ut caveat lapsum, tritura fuit stimulorum.
Ex utero cecus, propria nec sorde parentum,
ut testatur ei lumen dans luminis orbes,
accepit lucem, deus ut fieret manifestus.
Iob bonus hoc plagae fertur temptamine tactus.
Languidus hinc sequitur, qui multis languit annis,
erigitur culpisque dehinc cessare iubetur.
Ut semper, Iudea suis obnoxia factis,
offendens dominum trahit inmedicabile vulnus,
cui deus "Occide," ait, "nec sit mihi cura mederi!"

Concerning earthly torments

A guaranteed earthly cross is expected in two ways. First, when any good man is proven to have abstained from forbidden things and, mortifying his flesh, is pursuing contemplative ways. Secondly, when we regard another's misfortunes as our own, and when we share the suffering of our brothers, lamenting their losses.

Concerning the four types of blow

The whole human race is punished with fourfold afflictions. As examples, I propose: A) two men, Job and the blessed Paul; the exercise of [God's] concern blessed both of them. Confidently testing them, the Lord purged them like gold. The former did nothing deserving of such a scourging. For the latter there was a threshing with goads, in order that he be vigilant, in order that no haughtiness arise {in him}, in order that he avoid a fall. B) A man blind from birth—through neither his own nor his parents' fault, as the Light that grants eyes to him bears witness—received light, so that God might be manifest. Virtuous Job is said to have been stricken by this type of painful trial. C) Next follows the invalid, who languishes for many years; he is raised up and ordered to stop sinning from that day forth. D) Judea, culpable as always through its own misdeeds, offending the Lord, contracts an untreatable wound. To it God says, "Die! Let it not be my concern to heal you!"

De hac peregrinatione

Quod volumus, cupimus, peregre hic non semper habemus,
summa salus hic queritur, at non invenietur;
est alias ea diva et suffitientia plena,
quo fur fallaces latitans non ingerit ungues,
nemo timet morsus eruginis aut tinearum.
Crimina si qua scabunt presentia, dilue presens,
malleoli quia non resonat vox, nulla securis
clangit in aede dei, nova cum Sales aedificatur,
quaeque dolavit Hyram, decoravit in arce Salemon,
illustrans templum se preside, pacifer heres.
Sanctus sanctorum sanctos servabit in aevum,
hic domus et dominus regnabunt iugiter! Amen.

De invitatione Dei

Si persona potens, si quisquam mitteret heros
pauperis ad tegetem cenae invitans epularum,
quid faceret? nonne eximie gauderet et illuc
allota fatie mutatis vestibus iret,
ne sese prior ad convivia tanta veniret?
Dives homo invitat, pauperque occurrere temptat—
invitamur et excusamus adesse vocanti,
Agnus ab arce vocat, sed adultera sponsa recusat.

Concerning this sojourn

What we want and desire, here in this foreign land we do not always have. The highest salvation is sought here, but it will not be found. It is elsewhere, that divine and full sufficiency, where the hiding thief cannot lay his deceitful claws on it, where nobody fears the bites of rust or moths. If any of your present crimes mar you, wash them away in the present; for the sound of a mallet does not reecho, no ax rings out in the house of God, when the new Jerusalem is being built. Whatever Hiram fashioned, Solomon adorned on the citadel, embellishing the Temple when he was ruler, the peace-bringing heir. The Holy of Holies will preserve those who are holy for all time. Here the house and its Lord will rule perpetually! Amen.

Concerning God's invitation

If a powerful person, if any great man, should send to a poor man's hut, inviting him to a banquet of feasting, what would the poor man do? Would he not be uncommonly happy and go there when he had washed his face and changed his clothes, so that no one might arrive at such a meal before him? The rich man invites, and the pauper attempts to arrive on time. We are invited, and we make excuses to the one calling us. The Lamb calls from the citadel, but the adulterous spouse declines.

De Arca Noae

Archa Noe fuit intus in inferioribus ampla,
reptile et hic habuisse inmunda animalia fertur;
desuper angusta, hic cohibebat aves hominesque.
Mater ita ecclesia est: nimis in carnalibus ampla,
atque in secretis et spiritualibus arta.

De Iudeis

"Sydon, frontem absconde tuam!" clamans mare dixit.
Quae Sydon sinagogam significat, mare mundum;
credidit in Christum gens, cum Iudea recessit.
Temporis eheu quam nimio torpore vacabit,
tandem perditione sua longa resipiscet,
reliquiae salvae fient in limite mundi.

De iniusta preda

Quae violenta furit cum magno preda tumultu
et vestimentum consperso sanguine mixtum
ignis erit cybus et longae combustio poenae.
Disce, homicida, deum, quam longe et predo, vereri,
crede minis vatum, ne te frustrere, malignans!
Veris inflatos de poenis vera sequentur.

De legitimo certamine

Legitime accipient soliti certare coronam,
ast aliis labor est celum conscendere durus.

Concerning Noah's Ark

On the inside, Noah's Ark was ample in its lower decks, and here it is said to have held reptiles and unclean animals. Up above it was narrow; here it contained the birds and men. Mother Church is like that: very ample in carnal things, but restricted in its mysteries and spiritual things.

Concerning the Jews

"Sidon, hide your face!" said the sea, crying out. This Sidon signifies the synagogue, the sea signifies the world. The pagan believed in Christ, when Israel withdrew. Alas, for how long a period of torpor it will sit empty. Finally it will recover from its long affliction. What remains will be saved at the end of the world.

Concerning unjust plunder

The violent taking of plunder which rages with great tumult and the garment stained with spattered blood will be food for the fire and a burning of long punishment. Learn to fear God, however late, you murderer and plunderer. Believe in the threats of the prophets, miscreant, don't deceive yourself! Truths will ensue for those inspired about true punishments.

Concerning the lawful struggle

Those accustomed to struggle lawfully will receive the crown; but for others, ascending to heaven is a hard labor.

Non est diversus; vario licet ordine mundum
disponat dominus, tamen inmutabilis idem.

De murmure iniusto

Quae patimur vel quae deus irrogat, omnia iusta;
valde quidem iniustum, si contra murmuret ullus,
cui nihil iniustum placet, a domino quia fiunt;
murmur apud sanas mentes est valde cavendum,
Israel quia disperiit pro murmure crebro.
Iob domino numquid stultum datur esse loquutus?
Sed "Dominus dedit, abstulit et placita omnia fecit,"
non dixit: "Dominus dedit, atque inimicus ademit,"
certus, quod nisi permissus nil iuris haberet;
cui semper consueta malis innata voluntas,
a domino quia fit nonnumquam iusta potestas;
quae res indicat, humana dum pellitur aede,
quod porcos nisi concessos non audet adire.

De misericordia

In nullo morum studio sic vincitur hostis,
quam cum quis caleat miserentis fomite cordis.
Iuditio multabitur absque ulla pietate,
si non hic fuerit clemens culpaeque remissor;
iuditium superat pavidum clementia fratris.

The Lord is not inconstant; even though he arranges the world in a variety of ways, nevertheless, he remains the same, unchanging.

Concerning unjust complaining

All that we suffer or that God imposes is just. Indeed, it is terribly unjust if anyone complains to the contrary. These things were brought about by the Lord, to whom nothing unjust is pleasing. Complaining must be strenuously avoided in sound minds, because Israel perished on account of constant complaining. Is Job recorded to have said anything foolish to the Lord? On the contrary, he said, "The Lord gave and took away, and did everything as it pleased him." He did not say, "The Lord gave, and the enemy took away." He was certain that, unless he were permitted, that one [Satan] could have no power. For to one whose innate will is always prone to evil things, a just power is sometimes granted by the Lord. These things are indicated by the fact that when Satan is driven from a human dwelling, he does not dare to enter the pigs unless they have been granted to him.

On mercy

In no moral effort is the Enemy conquered to the same degree as when someone is warmed with the spark of a merciful heart. In the Last Judgment, one who is not clement here and a pardoner of sin will be punished without any pity. The clemency of a brother conquers the fearsome Last Judgment.

De his, qui in paradiso nascerentur

Si primum non inficeret sua culpa parentem,
natos ad penam numquam generaret ituros;
sed, nunc plena redemptoris quos gratia salvat,
nascendi de carne forent, celum subituri
scilicet electi sine mortis tramite, soli;
nascendi non essent, quos infernus habebit.

De percussione Iob

Frustra et non frustra percussus dicitur Iob:
augetur meritis, ideo non verbera frustra;
et frustra, quoniam non commeritus perhibetur.
Tunc pellis pro pelle datur: cum cernimus ictum
cedentis contra fatiem, ut fit sepe, venire,
obvia fit manus, ut male non oculus feriatur,
et teneris obtendimus astu fortia menbris.
Radebat saniem de testa fictilis ollae:
vase (quod est) fracto confractum fictile rasit.
Teste deo cur qui multis prefertur avitis,
nunc iacet in caeno plagis detritus acerbis?
Queso, quid est, quod Iohannes laudatur abunde
voce dei, babtista suus, preco atque propheta,
et cadit in pretium saltantis vile puellae
more bovis triti, iussu regis furibundi?
Cur morte indecorat, quos vox laudantis honorat?
Idcirco sanctos in valle premit lacrimarum,

Concerning those who were born in paradise

If his own sin did not infect our first parent, he would never have begotten children heading for punishment; but only those, whom now the full grace of the Redeemer saves, would have been born of his flesh (namely, the elect who are going to ascend to heaven without the pathway of death). Those whom hell will hold, would not have been born.

Concerning the smiting of Job

Job is said to have been smitten in vain, and also not in vain. He is enhanced because of his merits, therefore the blows were not in vain. And they *were* in vain, since he is not presented as one who deserved them. "Skin is given for skin" when we perceive that a blow from one striking us is coming against our face (as often happens). Our hand is raised as an obstacle, so that our eye not be struck a harmful blow; and we intentionally offer up our strong members for the sake of the more fragile ones. Job scraped the pus with the shard of a clay pot, which is to say, he scraped broken clay [his infected flesh] with a broken vessel. With God as a witness, why is one who is favored more than many of our forefathers now lying in filth, worn down by bitter blows? I ask, why is it that John is lavishly praised by the voice of God, as His baptizer, herald and prophet, yet he is cut down as the vile reward of a dancing girl, in the manner of a worn-out ox, by the order of a mad king? Why does He dishonor in death, those whom the voice of one praising honors? Here is why He oppresses the holy ones in this vale of tears:

largius ut possint meritis excrescere summis
magnificetque magis, quos sic iaculatur in imis.
Collige, quos reprobat, miseros quae poena sequatur,
cum sic hic crutiat sanctos, quos constat amare!
Quid fatient, quo iuditio miseri ferientur,
cum, qui laudantur, tam despective premuntur?

De Sancto Augustino

Inter scriptores citus Augustinus habetur,
ut pedites prevertit equo quis miles equestris.
Nemo pedem minus offendit discursor in orbe,
verus inoffenso et multo sermone probatur,
quod solet adversum cursoribus esse citatis.

De Gregorio

Totus in angelicis Gregorius intima fixit
et calamum in cornu tinxit spiraminis alti.
Mores depinxit, contexuit allegorias;
aurea cum situla e caelo suspensa catena
egregie potavit eum de fonte superno.

De igne purgatorio

Sermo propheticus ostendit vada torrida dicens:
"Ante meum currebant ignea flumina vultum";
ille fuit, quem dicunt, purgatorius ignis.

so that they may grow greater by their supreme merits, and that He may magnify still more those whom He casts down in this manner to the lowest depths. Consider what punishment awaits the wretched ones whom He reproves, when He tortures in this way the holy ones, whom it is certain He loves! What will they do, by what judgment will those wretches be stricken, when those who are praised, are oppressed in such a humiliating way?

Concerning Saint Augustine

Among the writers Augustine is considered to be swift, as any mounted soldier outruns the infantry on his horse. No runner in the world stumbles less on foot. He is proven to be true in his abundant and faultless expression; normally it is the opposite for speedy runners.

Concerning Gregory

Gregory fixed his intimate thoughts entirely on angelic things, and he dipped his pen in the inkwell of the lofty Spirit. He depicted morals, he interwove allegories; a golden chain, with a bucket, suspended from the sky abundantly furnished him with water from the heavenly spring.

Concerning purgatorial fire

A prophetic voice pointed out the scorched waters, saying: "Fiery rivers were running before my face." That was the fire they call "purgatorial." Depending on the type of sin,

Quanta est materia atque levis contagio culpae,
tanta exsudandi dabitur mora stare per ignem.
Inde alias divina loquutio comparat ollae
peccatricem animam, sic dicens ore prophetae:
"Pone super prunas vacuam virtutibus ollam,
donec in aere suo deferveat atque calescat,
et donec stagnum commixtum defluat omne."

De igne aeterno

Inferni lacus et puteus baratrumque profundum
quam super iniustos nimis hora pavenda fatiscet,
cum miseros susceperit ore dei maledictos!
Huc descensus erit sed non ascensus in evum,
claudetur sursum se dilatando deorsum,
non spiramen erit, non liber hanelitus ulli.
Inde propheta pavens David sanctissimus orat:
"Os, deus, iste suum puteus non urgeat in me!"

Quod malum non sit creatura

Virtutum deus ipse potens, in prelia fortis,
inmunis scelerum, regimen commune bonorum,
mititiam docuit famulosque suos pietatem,
visibile atque invisibile edidit atque creavit.
Ergo malum nihil est preter privatio recti.
Huius non dominus, quia nulla creatio, factor,
ipse diabolus auctor nullorumque creator;
maiestas domini in solis virtutibus hesit,
quas docuit, fecit, factores ipse beavit.

and how easy its contamination, that's how long a period of sweating in this fire will be assigned. That is the reason that, in another passage, the divine word compares the sinner's soul to a pot, speaking thus through the mouth of the prophet, "Set a pot lacking in virtues upon burning coals, until it melts and grows hot in its bronze, and until all the base metal mixed in it flows away."

Concerning eternal fire

The lake of hell, and the pit, and the profound abyss, how it will gape over the unjust when the fearful hour has taken from the face of God the wretched who have been damned! There will be a descent to that place, but no ascent for all eternity. Extending itself downward, it will be closed off above. There will be no breath, no free inhalation for anyone. For this reason the fearful prophet, the most holy David, prays, "O God, let not the pit shut her mouth upon me!"

That evil is not a creation

God himself, powerful in virtues, brave in battles, free of sins, the common guider of good men, taught his servants meekness and piety. He produced and created what is visible and what is invisible. Therefore, evil is nothing but the absence of righteousness. The Lord is not the maker of this thing, because it is no created being. The devil himself is the author and creator of nothing. The majesty of the Lord abides in virtues alone; he taught them, he practiced them, and he himself blessed those practicing them.

De interpretatione angelorum

Voce "quis ut deus" exprimitur Michahel Latiali
dissimilemque deo fatiet, cum vicerit, hostem;
"summa dei virtus" Gabrihel sonat ore Latino,
qui volat intactae bona nuntia ferre Mariae,
hanc fore laturam dominum regemque potentem,
bella potestates contra aerias habiturum;
nam "medicina dei" Raphael datur esse vocatus,
qui sanctum domini venit curare Tobiam;
deque ministeriis aptantur nomina missis.
Angelus in Greco, quod "nuntius" ergo Latine;
angelus offitium, naturam spiritus inplet,
angelus ad tempus, sed semper spiritus actu;
"nuntius" exprimitur "princeps" archangelus, esto.
Quippe Thronos dicunt sedes astare tonantis;
nomen habent post hos Dominantes a dominatu;
primores a primatus ditione sequuntur;
ecce Potestates comitantur iure potenti;
hinc sequitur numerus Virtutum a viribus auctus.
Consistunt Cherubim, quae plena scientia format;
hinc Seraphim, quae nos incendia scire docemur.

De decem preceptis

In tabulis precepta decem sunt scripta duabus;
una quidem cohibet tria, continet altera septem.
Principio tria divino tribuuntur honori;
cetera, quae superant, ea proximus ardor habebit.

Concerning interpretation of the angels

In the Latin language, the name Michael means "he who is like God," and he will make the Enemy unlike God, when he has conquered him. "The highest virtue of God" is the sense in the Latin tongue of the name Gabriel, who flies to bring the good news to the unblemished Mary that she is going to bear a Lord and powerful king, who will wage battles against the aerial powers. Raphael is said to be called "medicine of God," he who came to cure Tobias, a holy man of the Lord. On the basis of their services, these names are appropriate for these ambassadors. "Angel" in Greek means what "messenger" means in Latin. He is called "angel" in fulfilling his commission, "spirit" in fulfilling his nature. He is "angel" from time to time, but always "spirit" in actuality. Archangel means "chief messenger": be it so! They say that the "Thrones" stand by the seat of the Thunderer. After these, the "Dominions" get their name from [his] domination. The "Princedoms" come next, [named] from the authority of their primacy. And see how, the "Powers," [named] from powerful justice, accompany them. Then follows the crowd of "Virtues," magnified in vigor. The "Cherubim" are informed by "full knowledge"; finally the "Seraphim," are what we are taught to know as "burning things."

Concerning the Ten Commandments

The Ten Commandments were written on two tablets. One of them holds three; the other contains seven. The three at the beginning are dedicated to honoring divinity; love of our neighbor will be found to encompass the remainder. Among

De quibus est primum mandatis "Israel, audi,
sculptile non fatias, quoniam tuus est deus unus";
alterum erat "Ne quere dei convertere nomen
in vanum"; sequiturque dehinc, ut sabbata servent.
Haec ternae fidei tria dicta putantur honori:
ecce monas prima occurrit de patre fateri.
De nato patris in dicto patet esse secundo,
filius ut genitus credatur nonque creatus,
sic patris aequalem debemus sumere natum;
vana creaturis connexa feruntur in istis,
in vanum non accipies aequabile Verbum
cum patre, non factum, pariter quod cuncta creavit.
Monstratur pure per sabbata spiritus almus,
qui summam requiem per se promisit agendam,
quique figuratur per sabbata tam spatiosa;
sabbata servamus tunc spiritualia digne,
si numquam facimus, quae sunt servilia famae.
Personis tribus his nulla ratione carere
hoc genus humanum poterit: pater ipse creavit;
filius eterna caro factus morte redemit;
spiritus equalis nos omnes vivificabit.
Semotim resonant aliquid pariterque operantur;
sectis nominibus licet, omnipotens deus unus.

De altera tabula

Demus, qua ratione habeat tabula altera septem;
ista quidem sunt ad solum conscripta propinquum.
Primum dignus honor debetur utrique parenti;
sanguinis effusor ne sis, datur ordo secundus;

these commandments, the first is "Hear, Israel, you should not make a graven image, since yours is one God." The second was, "Do not seek to use the name of God in vain," and then follows that they should keep the sabbaths. These commands are thought to be three in number for the glory of our Trinitarian faith. Observe that the first unit happens to speak of the Father. The Son of the Father is revealed in the second command: that the Son should be believed to have been begotten and not created. So we ought to accept the Son as equal to the Father. Vanities are said to be joined to created things. You shall not take in vain the Word which is equal to the Father, the Word which, not made himself, equally created all things. Through "sabbaths," the Holy Spirit is clearly indicated, who promised that the highest rest was to be achieved through him, and who is represented by the sabbaths that will be unending. We keep spiritual sabbaths in a worthy fashion if we never do things servile to fame. There is no way that the human race can do without these three persons. The Father himself created us; the Son, having been made flesh, redeemed us from eternal death; the Spirit, their equal, will confer life upon all of us. They signify something separately, and they carry out their work equally; although with distinct names, Almighty God is one.

Concerning the other tablet

We should explain why the second tablet has seven commandments: these were written down only concerning our neighbor. First, worthy honor is owed to both of our parents. That you not be a spiller of blood is given as the second rule. The third, as you often hear, says, "You shall not com-

tertius, ut sepe audis, "non moechaberis" inquit;
quartus "non partas furaberis alterius res";
quintus "ne coram quid falsum testificeris";
sextus "ut uxorem non concupias alienam";
septimus "ut non res studeas ambire propinqui."

Quantae virtutis sit Spiritus Sanctus

Spiritus interni solaminis ac pietatis,
si quos accendit, non casso concremat igne:
Psalmistam fecit tangens puerum cytharedum;
fit vates tactus puer armentarius Amos,
dum ramos sychomori vellicat, ecce prophetat;
afflatus Daniel iuvenis reprobat seniores
et iudex canos veris convicit iniquos;
aecclesiae fecit de piscatore magistrum;
et quos persequitur furibundae cedis hanelus,
inpletus docuit sancto spiramine Paulus;
reddit evangelii scriptorem spiritus idem
publicolam factum domino solvente Matheum.

De quolibet episcopo

Ultro sollicitus scrutetur quisque sacerdos,
quae per ovile suum de se sit opinio vulgi,
more sui domini, qui percunctatur alumnos:
"Quem dicunt homines hominis se credere natum?"
Addat et accumulet, si sanus sermo feratur;
sin turpis, pudeat, discat melioribus uti.

mit adultery." The fourth, "You shall not steal things belonging to another." The fifth, "Do not testify in person to anything false." The sixth, "That you should not covet the wife of another." The seventh, "That you should not be eager to get your neighbor's property."

How great the virtue of the Holy Spirit is

If the Spirit of internal solace and mercy sets some people ablaze, it does not burn them with futile fire. Touching the boy harpist, it made him the psalmist. The herd boy Amos, having been touched, becomes a seer. While he plucks the branches of a wild fig tree, see, he is prophesying. The young Daniel, inspired, reproves his elders, and as a judge he convicted the wicked old men with the truth. Out of a fisherman, the Spirit produced a teacher of the Church [Peter]. And those whom Paul persecutes, panting for mad slaughter, he later instructed, once he had been filled with the Holy Spirit. This same Spirit renders Matthew a gospel writer, when the Lord releases him who had been made a publican.

Concerning any bishop you please

On his own initiative, every priest ought to scrutinize earnestly what the opinion of the people throughout his flock might be of him. [He should do this] following the example of his Lord, who interrogated His disciples: "Whom do men say they believe the Son of man is?" If he receives a healthy report he should [strive to] augment and expand it. But if it be bad, he should be ashamed. He should learn to practice

Extendatur in exemplum pia vita minorum.
Non preiuditium tolerat deus, ut puto, maius,
quam fatiunt, quos constituit superesse magistros
(dico sacerdotes late per ovilia missos
et quibus est permissa suae correctio plebis):
de se prava operum prebent exempla malorum,
dum peccant, qui debuerant compescere culpas;
et plerumque, quod est gravius, rapiunt aliena,
qui sua debuerant dare. De gregibus quid agatur,
dicite, quando lupi pastores efficiuntur?
Lucra sacerdotes non querimus ulla animarum,
intenti ad studium nostrum sed mente vacamus.
Hinc scriptum: "Sicut populus, sic ipse sacerdos,"
cum nullis meritis soleat precedere vulgus.
Intus habebantur semper lapides pretiosi,
nec sumebat eos nisi festa luce sacerdos,
cum sancta ingrediens sanctorum mystica agebat:
nos, fratres, lapides sumus et domino pretiosi,
si numquam foris in mundi actibus aspitiamur;
desinit in templo domini lapis esse vel aurum,
qui foris in populo terrena negotia tractat.

De hospitalitate

Hospitibus prebere domos sumptusque iubetur,
quos non solum invitandos, magis esse trahendos.
Hinc quidam plane angelicis placuere ministris.
Susceptus legitur deus in forma peregrina.

better behavior. The pious life of children should be held out as an example. God does not endure any greater injury, I think, than what those men do whom he appointed to be teachers. I mean those priests sent far and wide among the sheepfolds to whom correction of their people has been granted. They offer of themselves depraved examples of evil deeds when they, who ought to be restraining others faults, commit sin. And what is even more serious: frequently they snatch the goods of others; they who ought to be distributing their own. What will happen to the flocks, tell me, when their shepherds become wolves? We priests are not seeking any profit of souls, but intent on our own interests we are neglectful in our hearts. So it is written, "Just as the people, so also is the priest," since he normally does not surpass the people in merits. Precious stones always used to be kept inside, and the priest did not handle them except on a feast day when, entering the Holy of Holies, he performed the mysteries. We, brothers, are the stones; and we are precious to the Lord if we are never seen outside amid the doings of the world. One who transacts earthly business outside among the people ceases to be a stone or gold in the temple of the Lord.

Concerning hospitality

We are ordered to offer our homes and provisions to strangers, who must not only be invited, but actually be dragged in. So doing, some men plainly pleased angelic ministers. We read that God has been received in the form of a stranger.

Quomodo inter filios Dei fuit Satan

Ante deum natis venientibus edite, quid sit,
quod fuit inter eos Satan, cum non penetraret
celum post lapsum nec furtim irrumpere posset.
Creditur atque ita maiorum ratione probatur:
angelus hanc libertatem tenet immo fidelis,
ut rediturus eat, domino sua nuntia portet;
carcere in aerio dumtaxat apostata ludit.
Lumina clara latere dei vibrantia ubique
non potuit, stabili sed visus in ordine rerum
ad subtile dei veniens concessit acumen,
in solis iubare ut cecus cerni perhibetur,
sole illustratur nec se videt ipse videntem.

De missa pro defunctis

Noster ad aecclesiam quotiens conventus habetur,
psalmodiam, dignasque preces, sollempnia agamus
missarum, nos corde deum meditemur et ore.
Sunt bona cuncta simul, melioribus expedit uti:
missis continuis non hostia dignior ulla,
angelico sine conventu quae non celebratur,
egressis non tale quid invenies animabus.

How Satan was among the sons of God

Explain how it could be that when His children were coming before God, Satan was among them, since he could not enter Heaven after his fall, and he could not break in secretly. This is what we believe, and it is proven so by the reasoning of our elders: an angel, or rather a faithful angel, has this freedom, that he may set out, retaining the ability to return, in order to carry messages for the Lord. The apostate one merely plays around in his airy prison. From the bright eyes, glimmering everywhere, of God, he was not able to hide; but having been seen in the immutable order of things, he submitted to the subtle acumen of God, coming [before Him]. As a blind man is said to be discernible in the radiance of the sun; he is illuminated by the sun, and [yet] he does not see the one seeing him.

Concerning the mass for the dead

As often as our assembly is held in the church, we should practice psalmody and worthy prayers, the solemnities of masses; we should meditate on God with our heart and our voice. All these things alike are good [but] it is expedient to make use of even better ones. There is no sacrifice more worthy than continuous masses; that sacrifice is not celebrated without an angelic assembly. You will not find anything so worthy for departed souls.

De die iuditii

Fratres, extremi memores estote diei,
qui veniet caros etiam diducere binos,
corpus et hanc animam, qua nunc spiramus haneli;
"Quisquis es," hinc Salemon "memorare novissima" dixit,
"quorum rite memor semper peccare timebis."
Nec procul adventus, qui dicitur esse futurus,
magni iuditii cunctis veniens manifestus,
in quo examen erit scelerum requiesque bonorum.
Haec mundi mala venturis collata nihil sunt;
nam tantum refert presens tribulatio ab illa,
quantum preco solet distare a iudice forti.
De quo proclamat quidam terrore propheta:
"Ecce dies domini iuxta est velox nimis atque,
vox ingens et vox illius amara diei,
magnus ubique pavor, tribulabitur ergo ibi fortis!
Obsitus ille dies erumnis plenus et ira,
ille dies nebulae, caliginis ac tenebrarum,
turbinis atque tubae strepitus, clangoris acerbi!"
Iudicis adventum securior opperietur,
si quis pro Christo gravius quid nunc tolerabit.

De infirmis

Infirmi cum gaudia tanta salutis amamus,
sumimus, ut purgent nos, pocula amara libenter;
displicet, in potu quicquid gustamus amarum,
sed, quam restituit, placet ipsa, a! credo, salutem:
si sint in vita presenti multa molesta,
nos oneri subdamus, ut his meliora feramus.

Concerning the day of judgment

Brothers, be mindful of the final day, which will come to separate even two things that are dear [to one another]: the body and this soul with which, panting, we now breathe. Hence Solomon said, "Whoever you are, think about the last days; rightly mindful of them, you will always be afraid to sin." Not far off is the advent of the great Judgment, which it is said will take place, becoming manifest to all. In it there will be a weighing of sins and rest for the good. The evils of the world are nothing compared to those that are coming. For the present tribulation differs as much from that one as a herald usually varies from a powerful judge. A certain prophet proclaimed about this terror: "Behold, the day of the Lord is near, and it is very swift. The sound of that day is immense, and the sound is bitter. There will be great fear everywhere; there even the brave man will be afflicted! That day is beset with hardships and filled with wrath, that day of smoke, of darkness and shadows, of the whirlwind, and of the trumpet's shriek, of bitter clanging!" If anyone will now tolerate some heavier burden for Christ, he will await the advent of the Judge in greater security.

Concerning the sick

When we are sick, when we desire the great joys of health, we happily ingest a bitter draft to purge ourselves. Whatever bitterness we taste in the dose is displeasing; but the health that it restores—that, I think, is pleasing! If there be many troubles in our present life, we should submit to the burden, so that we may win things better than these.

De apostolo

De prima ad quintam edificabat apostolus hora,
de quinta ad decimam spargebat semina verbi,
de reliquo carnis curas et pauperum agebat,
noctibus attenti mactavit munia cordis.

<De lassitudine>

Fesso in quo succurritur, ecce aliud renovatur;
cumque sedendo fatigatur, mox stando medetur;
quem somni tedet, si vult, vigilare licebit:
multa quis experiens sic in contraria currit.

De quinque clavibus sapientiae

Quinque movens, interna secans, sapientia claves
assiduas docet esse moras studiosa legendi,
multa sibi memorans pressis vincire catenis,
munditias lustrare et querere amat fugitivas,
obsequiumque suo dignum prebere magistro,
proque deo mundi vanas contempnere pompas.

De abscondito talento

"In terris abscondere" dicitur ecce "talentum"
ingenium terrenis volvere in actibus omne,
spirituale vel eternum non querere lucrum,

Concerning an apostle

An apostle used to build edifices from the first hour until the fifth. From the fifth hour until the tenth, he was spreading the seeds of the Word. The rest of the time he spent on concerns of his body and of the poor. During the nights, he performed the duties of an attentive heart.

<On fatigue>

Observe how when relief is offered to a tired man, a new problem arises. And when he is fatigued by sitting, he is cured in turn by standing. One who is tired of sleep, if he wishes, may stay awake. In this way, a person experiencing many things rushes to their opposites.

Concerning the five keys to wisdom

Offering five keys, cutting to the inner depths, studious wisdom teaches that the times for reading are continuous. Remembering to bind many things in her heart with taut chains, she loves to examine worldly things and inquire into those that escape her, to offer proper obedience to her teacher, and to despise the empty pomposities of the world in favor of God.

Concerning the hidden talent

Observe that it is called "hiding your talent in the earth," to turn all your ingenuity toward earthly activities, not to seek everlasting or spiritual profit, and also never to raise your

cor a terrena quoque numquam fece levare.
Hostia grata deo contritae afflictio carnis;
hinc Salemon ait: "Ut mors est dilectio fortis":
ut mors interimit corpus, sic nos dilectio Christi
separat a cunctis terrenis actibus aptos,
qui virtutis iter temptamus querere dextrum.

De summo pastore

Pastor ait summe bonus hoc de nomine falso
pastorum: "Non ex adverso ascendere causa
velle mei, non salvandis opponere murum
Israel ovibus neque stare in prelia vidi;
immo vos potius quam nostros pascitis agnos,
vobis, non estis mihi lucrandis animabus!"
Ficti pastoris culpas innotuit hac re.

De viatore

Valde viatorem stultum speramus haberi,
qui, dum carpit iter, pratum miratur amoenum,
deserit oblitus, quo primum intenderat ire:
sic, qui forte choris celestibus addere civem
se velit, hunc mundi non tardet blanda voluptas;
ad summum transire bonum perventio felix.

Septem modis peccata delentur

Septenis in carne modis peccata abolentur:
primus per liquidas agitur babtismatis undas;
digno martirio rubroque cruore secundus;

heart from earthly dregs. The affliction of a contrite heart is a pleasing sacrifice to God; hence Solomon says: "Love is strong as death." As death destroys the body, so does love of Christ separate from all earthly activities those of us who are suitable, namely we who are attempting to seek the rightward path of virtue.

Concerning the highest shepherd

The shepherd who is supremely good says this about the false name of shepherds, "I have not seen you wishing to rise to oppose [the foe] for my sake, nor to set up a wall to save the flocks of Israel, nor to stand in the battle lines. On the contrary, you feed yourselves rather than our lambs; you exist for yourselves, not to gain souls for me!" He made the faults of the false shepherd known in this way.

Concerning the traveler

We expect that he will be judged a very foolish traveler, who, while making his journey, admires a pleasant meadow and abandons the journey, having forgotten where he first intended to go. In the same way, let not the alluring pleasure of the world delay whoever desires to enroll himself among the heavenly choirs. To cross over to the highest good is a happy end to our journey.

Sins are erased in seven ways

In seven ways sins are abolished in the flesh. First, it is done through the clear waves of baptism; second, by worthy

tertius: extentae solando manus ad egenos;
quartus, ut eucharistia digne et sumpta verenter;
quintus, ut ad cunctos dilectio flexa propinquos;
sextus, peccator dum penitet ante malorum;
septimus: ex toto culpis ignoscere fratrum.

De Zacheo et vidua

Mactandi fuit in vidua quam magna voluntas,
Zacheo pietas tribuendi et larga facultas;
quodque habuit, totum obtulit haec: duo sola minuta.
Hic medias divisit opes miseratus egenos,
de reliquo fraudes sibi nil retinendo paciscens.

De fletu et stridore

Accipe, quid fletus, quid stridor in orbe hiehennae
esse velit: surgit de fumo et caumate fletus,
dentibus et stridor de frigoris amne nivali;
sicque malum geminant scelus expendendo merentes.

De sex gradibus rerum

Natura utilior lapidi premittitur arbor;
arbor item pecori cedit prepostera valde;
hinc homo, qui supereminet atque ea continet in se;
cum ratione capit sentire et vivere et esse;
angelus in quinto consistit cardine maior,
inmortale decus cohibens fulcitur et istis;

martyrdom and red blood; third, when consoling hands are extended to the needy; fourth, when the Eucharist is taken worthily and reverently; fifth, when love is turned toward all our neighbors; sixth, when the sinner does penance for his earlier sins; seventh, to forgive completely the faults of your brothers.

Concerning Zaccheus and the widow

How great was the desire of the widow to offer sacrifice; how extensive the piety and the wherewithal of Zaccheus to distribute! All that she had, she offered up: only two small coins. He divided his wealth in half, taking pity on the needy, expiating his offenses by retaining none of the remainder for himself.

Concerning weeping and gnashing

Hear what "weeping,"' what "gnashing" in the world of hell signifies: the weeping arises from the smoke and the heat, and the gnashing of teeth from the icy river of cold. And so they have a double woe, paying for their crime, deservedly.

Concerning the six gradations of beings

Being more useful by nature, a tree is a step up from a stone. Likewise, a tree, its station quite reversed, is below a herd animal. Next is man, who rises above and encompasses these [lower] things in himself; with reason he is able to feel and to live and to exist. An angel is greater, it takes its place in the fifth order and, possessing immortal glory, is supported

ultima consequitur dives natura, creator
cunctorum, factor cunctis prelatus et auctor,
incircumscriptus circumscribenda recludit,
qui fabricam foris et circa perlustrat et infra.

De stellione

Tardus in incessu neque compos stellio nisu,
quamvis non agilis, regalia moenia querit;
at magni volucres liquidum per inane volantes
stagna petunt et ab his calidos truduntur in ignes:
vana minus doctis mundi sapientia cedit,
quamlibet hi tardi, celum palpando requirunt;
qui properasse putant, hi longius eitiuntur.

De puella a lupellis servata

Quod refero, mecum pagenses dicere norunt,
et non tam mirum quam valde est credere verum:
quidam suscepit sacro de fonte puellam,
cui dedit et tunicam rubicundo vellere textam.
Quinquagesima sancta fuit babtismatis huius.
Sole sub exorto quinquennis facta puella
progreditur vagabunda sui inmemor atque pericli,
quam lupus invadens silvestria lustra petivit
et catulis predam tulit atque reliquit edendam.
Qui simul aggressi, cum iam lacerare nequirent,
ceperunt mulcere caput feritate remota.

by those others. Abundant nature comes last, the creator of all things, the maker and author, preferred to all things. Not circumscribed himself, he encloses everything that must be circumscribed. He pervades his creation outside, all around, and beneath.

Concerning the newt

The newt is slow in its step and not steady in its stride. Although he is not agile, he seeks out royal walls. On the other hand, great birds flying through the clear void seek out ponds; and from these they are thrust into hot fires. The vain wisdom of the world yields to the less learned. Although they are slow, they seek after heaven, feeling their way. Those who think they have been quick are tossed farther away.

Concerning the girl saved from wolf cubs

The story I tell, the country folk know how to tell with me, and it is not so much marvelous to believe as it is very true. A certain man raised a girl from the sacred font, and he gave her a tunic woven from red wool. Shrove Sunday was the holy day of this baptism. When the sun had risen, the girl now five years old set out wandering, heedless of herself and of danger. A wolf attacked her and headed for his woodland haunts; and he took her as prey to his cubs and left her to be eaten. They immediately approached her, then when they were unable to tear her to pieces, they began to caress her head, their fierceness having been allayed. The little infant

"Hanc tunicam, mures, nolite," infantula dixit,
"scindere, quam dedit excipiens de fonte patrinus!"
Mitigat inmites animos deus, auctor eorum.

De lamentis viduae

Lamentis viduae deus et dolet atque rigatur,
et stillant lacrimae in fatiem domini miserantis;
est deus indultor pius, eximius miserator,
iuditio rigidus, pietate benignus ad aequum,
iuditium domini multae confertur abysso.
Estuet in dextris tua mens et tota voluntas:
divinis ad te veniet perfectio donis.

De Iacobo fratre domini

De cruce deposito domino tandemque sepulto
Iacobus indixit iustus ieiunia tanta
velle sequi, donec sollempnes experiatur
surgendi causas; ubi se collegit ad ortum
Sol surgendo suum iamque amplius haud moriturus,
discipulo dicens apparuit opperienti:
"Vescere pane tuo, surrexi, Iacobe frater!"—
"Frater" ait non matre sua, sed stirpe propinqua,
ex quo in catalogo servatur mentio sacro,
ut scriptura det inditium prenominis huius.

De Samson

Samson ingressus Gazam fortissimus urbem
cingitur obsidione, premunt fortes inimici;

said, "Oh mice, don't rip this tunic which my godfather gave me, taking me from the font!" God, their creator, softens savage souls.

Concerning a widow's laments

God is pained by a widow's laments, and he weeps. And tears drip down the face of the Lord, who commiserates with her. God is a kind protector, an outstanding commiserator, firm in his judgment, [but] equally benign in his mercy. The judgment of the Lord is likened to a great abyss. Let your whole mind and will be inflamed for proper things; perfection will come to you by divine gifts.

Concerning James the brother of the Lord

When our Lord had been taken down from the cross and finally buried, James the Just declared that he wished to continue extensive fasting, until he should experience solemn proofs of resurrection. When the Sun [Christ], ascending, collected himself for his rising, now never again to die, he appeared to his waiting disciple, saying: "Eat your bread; I have risen, brother James!" He called him "brother" not as being an offspring of His mother but of a close relative. Mention is preserved of him in the sacred listing [of the apostles], so that scripture may provide proof of his name.

Concerning Samson

Samson, the strongest of men, having entered the city of Gaza, was surrounded by a siege; strong enemies were

de nocte exsurgens portas a cardine vellit,
clam custodibus in montes quas sustulit altos:
Christum victorem inferni per facta figurat,
qui portas fregit proceresque ad vincla coegit,
quasque animas voluit, tenebris a noctis abegit,
sic dragmam decimam in scapulis ad agalma revexit.
Hunc Samson typicum de morte sua male doctum
femina corruptrix a! viribus exspoliavit;
hic datur exemplum per vires fidere nullum
femineamque fidem capiendis viribus aptam.
Primum hominem, Samson, Salemonem femina stravit,
plasma novum, fortem, sapientem femina vicit,
debilis allisit fortem per scandala sexum.

De Moyse

Laudatur Moyses mitissimus esse virorum,
qui vixere suis domino testante diebus.
O quantum distant hodierni laude minore!
Consilium Moysi genero dedit utile Ietro
partita populi cura in commune regendi;
hic quamvis sermone dei consuetus et ore,
ille deos coleret, de ritu barbarus esset—
vinea, quid mirum, si sustentetur ab ulmo?

pressing upon him. Rising at night, he rips the doors from their hinge, and he carried them up into the high mountains, unbeknownst to the guards. Through his deeds, he prefigures Christ, the conqueror of hell, who broke the gates and constrained the princes [of darkness] in chains, and he led away from the shadows of night whatever souls he wanted. Thus on his shoulders he carried back the tenth drachma to rejoicing. Alas! a corrupting woman robbed this Samson of his strength; he represents one ill-instructed about his own death. Here we have an example that no one should put trust in strength, and that trust in a woman may result in the sapping of strength. A woman laid low the first man, Samson, and Solomon. A woman conquered the newly formed man, the strong man, the wise man. The weak sex struck down the strong one through temptations.

Concerning Moses

Moses is praised as the kindest of men who lived in his day, by the Lord's own testimony. Oh how far distant, of what lesser glory, are the men of today! Jethro gave useful advice to his son-in-law Moses when the responsibility for ruling the people was shared in common, even though this one was accustomed to the voice and countenance of God, while that one was worshipping [many] gods, and was barbaric in his religious practice. What wonder is it if a vine is held up by an elm?

De Iosue

Iosue vertit Amurreos cedendo feroces
et populis terram lactis mellisque locavit,
umbrato signans Iesum de nomine et actu,
qui victis vitiis virtutum semina sevit.

De Salemone

Salemon legitur sapiens scriptisque probatur,
pacificum vocat interpres de nominis usu;
portat et ipse vicem domini, qui est pacifer heres,
ingrediens inter hominem atque deum mediator.
Humanae mulier venatrix pessima vitae
hunc quoque corruptum malesuada virum labefecit:
Astarten coluit, simulachra caponia suplex,
insuper ad cumulum sceleris phana aedificavit,
desertor domini sapiens ita degeneravit.
Hic sexus quota pocula semper amara propinat!
Primus homo hoc morbo, Samson ceciditque Salemon—
quid non precipitet haec ydra venefica mirum?

De Abraham

Abraham pater est primus credendo fidelis,
per mathesin regnare deum cognoverat unum.
Cui deus ad votum cordis promisit aventi,
quod sobolem promissam connumeraret harenae,
stellarum numero gentes se patre coequans;
credidit ille deo et meritis reputatur amicis,
iustus amando deum meruit pater esse piorum.

Concerning Joshua

Joshua overturned the fierce Amorites, slaughtering them, and he founded for his people a land of milk and honey, signifying under a veiled name and action Jesus, who conquered the vices and sowed the seeds of virtue.

Concerning Solomon

We read that Solomon was wise, and this is confirmed by the Scriptures. The translator calls him "peacemaker" from the meaning of his name. And he symbolizes the role of the Lord, who is the peace-bringing heir, serving as a mediator between man and God. Woman, the foulest predator of human life, persuading evil, corrupted this man and led him to stumble. As a suppliant he worshipped Astarte and castrated statues. Additionally, he built sanctuaries, to increase his sin. So the wise man degenerated, a deserter of the Lord. How many cups, always bitter, does this sex serve up! The first man fell by this disease, and Samson and Solomon. What wonder could this poisonous snake not topple?

Concerning Abraham

Faithful Abraham is the first father in believing; through gazing at the stars he had learned that one God rules. God promised him, in accord with the wish of his eager heart, that he would number the offspring promised to him as the sands, equaling the peoples he fathered to the number of the stars. He believed in God and is counted among his deserving friends. A just man, loving God, he deserved to be the father of pious men.

De David

David et ipse manu fortis, misteria Christi
plena gerens, psalmista, potens rex atque propheta,
strenuus incessit primis ineuntibus annis;
spiritus assidue domini directus in illum
succendit iuvenem non destituendo senectam.
Mandibulas ursorum fregit et ora leonum,
prostravit Goliaz sumpto a torrente lapillo,
victorem nostrum tanta virtute figurans,
qui post aerias venit frenare phalanges
atque invisibilem mortis calcare draconem,
aspidis et basilisci et fortis colla leonis.
Det deus hos nobis semper superare timores!

De heremitis

Vimineos qualos texebant colaque patres
antiqui et manuum vixere labore heremitae,
hic radicibus herbarum, hic bacis lapidosis,
pluribus ad victum cedebat cornea silva,
fons aliquis puteusque profundus potus eorum;
duram post vitam requiem meruere beatam.
At nos altilibus pleni pinguique ferina,
porcis inmundis similes, ut sunt Epycuri,
Christicolae falsi, solo de nomine dicti,
factis digressi, curamus corpora tantum,
non animas matie confectas atque veterno.

Concerning David

David himself also, strong of hand, embodying the full mysteries of Christ, a psalmist, a powerful king, and a prophet, walked forcefully in his early years. The Spirit of the Lord, assiduously directed toward him, inflamed him as a young man, and did not abandon him in his old age. He smashed the jawbones of bears and the mouths of lions. He laid Goliath low, with a pebble taken from a stream, prefiguring in his great virtue our conqueror, who came afterward to rein in the airy battalions and to tread upon the unseen dragon of death, upon the necks of the asp, and the basilisk, and the strong lion. May God always grant us to overcome these terrors!

Concerning hermits

The ancient fathers wove wicker baskets and nets and lived by the work of their hands as hermits, this one on the roots of plants, this one on stony berries. For many, a cornel cherry grove provided nourishment. Any spring and deep well was their drink. After a hard life, they deserved blessed rest. But we, stuffed on fowl and fatty game, are like filthy pigs, just like Epicureans. False Christians, called Christians only in name, deviants in our deeds, we care only for our bodies, not for our souls, which are weakened by emaciation and sloth.

De exsecratione idolorum

Exsecro cultores et abominor idola cuncta,
cum famulis pereant sub caelo phana prophanis!
Corda deo figamus, opuscula cuncta sacremus
Christicolae solique sibi inpendamus honorem!
Preter eum non invenies regnare secundum,
qui celos terramque super fundarat abyssos;
quattuor ideas tryas in origine mundi
cunctarum deus expressit nutrimina rerum:
terram onerosa et aquam, subtiliaque aerem et ignem.

De Caypha

Suspendit madidum Cayphas in funibus ephot,
qui, cum vera prophetaret, fallaciter egit,
unde ex fune ruit, qui non ex corde pependit;
quo minus in vero pasca gaudebit in albis
Alleluia novum nobiscum psallere carmen.
Omnibus aspirat presens rationis imago:
quod domino lingua canitur, factis teneatur.

De suffitientia vitae

Gratia summa dei me suffitienter et apte
ditavit reliqua cessante cupidine carnis,
panniculos prebens panemque, nec amplius opto;
unde deum, non quemquam hominem formido minantem,
quorum verba, minas pluviis et comparo ventis.

Concerning the abomination of idols

I abominate all idols, and I curse their worshippers. May their sanctuaries under heaven perish along with their profane servants! We should fix our hearts on God. As Christians, we should dedicate all our works and pay honor to him alone! Besides him, you will not find a second ruler. He founded the heavens and the earth above the abyss. God, the Triad, fashioned four archetypes in the beginning of the world as the sources of nourishment for all things: the heavy ones were earth and water, the subtle ones air and fire.

Concerning Caiphas

Caiphas suspended his soaked ephod on ropes. Although he prophesied true things, he acted deceitfully. Whence the one who did not depend on his heart, perished by a rope. So he will not rejoice on the true Passover in white robes, singing a new song, Alleluia, with us. An image of reason is present to inspire all: what is sung to the Lord with our tongue should be held fast by our deeds.

Concerning what is sufficient for life

The highest grace of God has sufficiently and suitably enriched me, when all remaining desire of the flesh departs, offering rags and bread. I do not desire more. Therefore, I fear God, not some man who threatens, whose words and threats I compare to the rains and the winds. Nature gives the means to live content with few things. Those who gape

Dat natura modum contento vivere paucis;
qui mundi lucris inhiant, ut corpora curent,
non animas, ibi vinea Christi inculta laborat.

De extrema vita

Cum subeunt ad cor scelerum monimenta meorum
et recolo, quid sim, me mortis mentio turbat,
mestus eo et nequeo letari nocte dieque,
hoc mecum reputans, in qua sim parte locandus,
quae manus occurrat, quis spiritus, albus an ater.
Unde quod est iustum, deus, hoc nunc exigo de te:
ut, cum flatus in extremis exire iubetur,
non furtiva manus sed, quae fecit, moveat me,
et quae Martinum cepisti pars pia quondam,
huc assis eadem forma fugiente cruenta!

after the world's lucre, so that they are concerned for their bodies not their souls—there the vineyard of Christ suffers from lack of cultivation.

Concerning the end of life

When reminders of my sins steal into my heart, and I recall what I am, the mention of death disturbs me. I move sadly, and I cannot be happy day or night, thinking to myself about this: in what part must I be placed? Which hand will I encounter? What spirit, white or black? Therefore, this thing, God, which is just, I now require of you: that, when my breath is ordered to depart at the end, the hand that made me should transport me, not the hand of a thief. Also that you, the same gracious portion that received Martin long ago, should be present, when my fleshly form is leaving.

Note on the Text

The Latin text printed here is essentially that of Ernst Voigt *(Egberts von Lüttich Fecunda Ratis),* the only previous edition. He established the text on the basis of the sole extant complete manuscript of the work, an eleventh-century codex from the Cologne Cathedral Library (Codex 196 = Darmstadt 2440). Voigt provides a description of the manuscript (pp. v–ix); some additions and corrections are offered by Alexander Arweiler in his description of the manuscript on the website of Codices Electronici Ecclesiae Coloniensis (CEEC) at www.ceec.uni-koeln.de/. A handful of verses or excerpts from Egbert's work are preserved in other manuscripts; these are listed and discussed most fully by Wolfgang Maaz (*Enzyklopädie des Märchens,* 3:1015–16). The few passages in which I have diverged from Voigt's text are recorded in the Notes to the Text. I have adopted nearly all of the corrections and emendations suggested by Rudolf Peiper (*Egberts von Lüttich Fecunda ratis,* 423–30) and have recorded this in the Notes to the Text. I have introduced emendation otherwise in only a few cases, and I have Francis Newton, Greg Hays, Danuta Shanzer, and Kurt Smolak to thank for their suggestions and advice on these.

The excellent and complete scans of the manuscript provided on the website of the CEEC have made it possible to check readings throughout, and they were particularly valuable in transcribing the glosses to the first four hundred lines of the poem (these are edited and translated in the Notes to the Translation); though here too I have essentially followed Voigt's edition.

From verse 1009 onward, the manuscript has titles that divide the individual proverbs or stories into sections. In verses 5–1009, however, there are no markers at the beginning or the end of an individual proverb. As a general rule, verses 5–596 are single-line proverbs, and verses 597–1008 are proverbs of two lines. But Egbert is not entirely consistent about this division, and he sometimes puts two-line (and longer) proverbs in the one-line section, and sometimes four-line proverbs in the two-line section. This occasionally creates difficulty in deciding where any particular proverb ends. Egbert often bunches proverbs on the same topic (so, e.g., three successive verses mentioning cats appear at 1.336–38), or, after giving one proverb, provides one that means the opposite. Thus, many readers will want to join consecutive lines that are related, even though this disturbs the division of the poem into sections based on the length of the proverb. Voigt joined *many* more of the proverbs in the one-line section into multi-line proverbs than I have. Peiper, in his review of Voigt, criticizes him on this point, listing dozens of Voigt's pairs that he would break up. I have followed Peiper in dividing many of these; indeed, I have printed more of them separated than Peiper lists.

One reason that it is tempting to join many of these verses is that Egbert often begins a verse with the words *nam, enim,* or the like, (these are often translated here as "to be sure," "indeed," "surely"). These words imply that something has come before, from which a conclusion is now being drawn. The appearance of these words at the beginning of a verse can create the sense in the reader that the verse goes with the preceding one. When the preceding verse is on the same topic, the temptation to join the verses is especially great. But Egbert regularly begins with such words verses that cannot be joined to the preceding verse. He is not alone in this; it is to be expected in proverb collections. Proverbial sayings are generally introduced when we have told (or heard) a story or cited an example of a particular type of person or situation. So we introduce them with phrases like "and so it is that we say," "you know what they say," "it just shows," etc. This is generally the sense of the words *nam, enim,* and the like in Egbert. They do not signal that we should join the verse to the preceding one, but that there is an ellipse of a story or anecdote that would prompt us to use the proverb. Often they do not need to be translated at all.

For the first four hundred lines of Egbert's poem, my principal guide in joining or dividing the one-line proverbs has been the commentary glosses in the MS (there are no such glosses after v. 400). If the glosses join the verses or divide them, I have done the same, unless otherwise noted. The glosses are not an unerring guide to this, or to any other, aspect of Egbert's work; but they have the advantage of providing us with at least one medieval reader's understanding of the text. For the remainder of the one- and two-line sections, I have generally divided wherever I thought it was possible. Sometimes the source texts provide a guide. If there are different source texts for different verses, I have divided. But even where a single source is used for two or three consecutive verses, Egbert may have thought of the source text as providing two (or three) different proverbs. Generally speaking, unless grammar, syntax, or sense required joining verses, I have not done so, choosing to respect the headings in the MS which define one-line, two-line, three-line, and longer sections in the poem. These headings reflect the description given by Egbert in the prefatory letter. Punctuation and paragraph marks were added by later readers (see Introduction, n. 25). Although these are not sure guides to the joining or dividing of verses, they have, like the glosses, the virtue of providing us with at the least one medieval reader's interpretation.

In matters of orthography, I have sometimes introduced a classicizing spelling (so, e.g., *v* is used for consonantal *u; ae* is used for *ę,* but anywhere the MS has *e* where classical spelling would require *ae,* I have not altered the MS spelling). In general, however, I have followed the MS orthography. In matters of punctuation, I have recorded in the Notes to the Text my variations from Voigt's edition only when the alteration significantly influences the translation or interpretation of the passage in question. In minor points of punctuation (those that do not significantly change the interpretation), I have altered silently.

Abbreviations

In addition to standard abbreviations for the books of the Bible and for Latin authors and texts, the following abbreviations are used regularly in the Notes to the Text and the Notes to the Translation:

e = an early corrector of the MS.

MS = Cologne, Dombibliothek 196 (Darmstadt 2440), the sole extant complete manuscript of the *Fecunda ratis.*

Peiper = Peiper, Rudolf. Review of Ernst Voigt, *Egberts von Lüttich Fecunda ratis. Zeitschrift für Deutsche Philologie* 25 (1893): 423–430.

TPMA = *Thesaurus proverbiorum medii aevi. Lexikon der Sprichwörter des romanisch-germanischen Mittelalters.* 14 vols. Berlin, 1995–2002.

Voigt = Voigt, Ernst. *Egberts von Lüttich Fecunda Ratis zum ersten Mal herausgegeben auf ihre Quellen zurückgeführt und erklärt von Ernst Voigt.* Halle a. S., 1889.

In exceptional instances (where a word usage is very uncommon), I have cited the dictionaries in the Brepols "Database of Latin Dictionaries," using the abbreviated titles employed there: Lewis and Short, Blaise Medieval, Blaise Patristic, Du Cange, Firminus Verris. These references are to be understood as referring to the entry in the specified electronic dictionary under the word in question.

Notes to the Text

Letter to Adalbold

"A." Alboldo; see Notes to the Translation.

"E." Egbertus; see Notes to the Translation.

privatumque malui alloqui: privatumque magis alloqui *MS Voigt. The emendation of* magis *to* malui *was suggested by Francis Newton.*

videbis, praeterea *MS*: videbis mandans praeterea *Voigt*

in ventum: inventum *MS,* inventum hinc *e Voigt*

Book 1

50	(Gloss) posterioribus: posteriora *MS Voigt*
179	(Gloss) quia *MS*: quod *Voigt*
335	(Gloss) et modo quo hic: et quomodo hic *Voigt*
434	honustus *MS*: onustus *Voigt*
571	bellum *MS Voigt*: bellus *TPMA*
721–22	*I punctuate following Peiper.*
774	servilibus *MS Voigt*: senilibus *F. Seiler,* Zeitschrift für deutsche Philologie *45: 243.*
871	aiebat *MS Peiper*: aibat *Voigt*
982	aliunde *added superscript e*: hodierna *MS Voigt*
1103	Clothos *MS*: Clotho *Voigt. The peculiar spelling* Clothos *for the nominative singular is also found in other texts from the period in Liège, including Sigebert's* Passio Sanctorum Thebeorum *(2:111); so I have restored it.*
1117	iunctis *e*: uinctis *MS Voigt*
1181	hinc *Peiper*: hic *MS Voigt*
1191	caput?: caput, *Voigt; the MS has no punctuation following* caput.

1228 indoles egregia *MS Peiper*: indolis egregiae *Voigt*

1243 hinc *Peiper*: hic *MS,* hac *Voigt*

1412 potuisset *Kurt Smolak*: patuisset *MS Voigt*

Book 2

41 uidendo *MS*: tacendo *Voigt*

448 obtulit haec: duo] obtulit. haec duo *MS,* obtulit. \scilicet uidua/ haec duo *e,* obtulit: haec duo *Voigt*

Notes to the Translation

Letter to Bishop Adalbold

"Adalbold" Adalbold II, bishop of Utrecht (1010–1026); the name was variously spelled Alboldus, Adelboldus, and Adalboldus. He is consistently called Adalbold by modern scholars, but he himself did use the form Alboldus on at least one occasion in his signature in a document dated in 1007; Voigt, ix. Although *Alboldum* is the only form that appears in the MS of the *Fecunda ratis* (in the first title), it may only be spelled that way through haplography.

"Egbert" Egbert's name is not found in the MS; the attribution to Egbert of Liège *(Egbertus Leodiensis)* is based on the chapter devoted to Egbert and his poem in the *Catalogus de viris illustribus* of Sigebert of Gembloux, ch. 146.

"campaigned among the scholarly ranks" Sulpicius Severus, *Vita Martini* 2.2 (identified by Maaz, "Brotlöffel," 108n5).

"we came to know one another better" Terence, *Adelphoe* 271.

"Many people often say many things" *Disticha Catonis* 1.13 (identified by Manitius, *Geschichte* 2:539).

"in vain" Voigt follows *e* in adding *hinc* and interprets the phrase "discovered from this source (namely, from common or rustic speech"). This requires understanding a far-removed and vague antecedent, and it also implies that Adalbold had written a work derived from folk speech and had learned the futility of doing so. There is no evidence that he did. The phrase *in ventum* has, in biblical and patristic texts, the sense "in vain," "to no purpose." Egbert is describing the vanity of labor in this life and the lack of remembrance of the same. He seems to have in mind Ecclesiastes 5:15: *quid ergo prodest ei quod laboravit in ventum* (What then doth it profit him that he hath laboured for the wind?). Egbert's point seems to be that neither the writer nor the contents, but rather the dedicatee, Adalbold, will give the work its enduring importance (both through his correcting of the text and through his personal prestige).

1–4 Voigt prints (and numbers) verses 1–4 as part of the poem proper, even though they are not in any sense proverbs. The first two verses are a *coda* to the Letter to Adalbold, and I have printed them as part of the *Letter.* Verses 3–4 are a distich that introduces Book 1, parallel to the distich introducing Book 2. When the glosses were added, the one that explains the title (beginning *Incipit iste libellus,* "Here begins the little book") was written in the upper margin of folio 2r. Because it is in the upper margin, if falls, accidentally, between verses 1 and 2 (which are, respectively, the last line on folio 1v and the first line on folio 2r). It cannot apply to either. But the title itself to which the gloss applies *(Fecunda ratis)* was never added. The title should have been added between verses 2 and 3, and the gloss applies to this title.

1–2 These verses are modeled on Venantius Fortunatus, *Carmina* 7.5.34 and 7.7.35–36.

1 Gloss: *Ferunt, qui de terra Egypti vera didicerunt, quod in terra illius non pluat, sed, quoties Nilus ripas suas excedit et finitima arva abluit, postquam in alveum suum redierit, statim cultores semina iactent, deinde post paucos dies fructus colligant, et, si bis aut ter in anno effusio eius fiat, totiens serant et metant. Unde de quodam, qui ibi fuerat, legendo comperimus, qui hoc asserebat a die iacti seminis fructum in die trigesimo maturescere, et aditiens "vidi" inquit "ibi rem mirabilem: ollam ferventem ad solem et, si credi fas est, ova in meridie coquere posse in sabulo." Nam sicut Nilus effluendo finitima loca percurrit et cultores letificat, ut inde spem vivendi habeant, ita tu excurso libello et emendato, ut paucis possit prodesse, letificabis auctorem.* (Those who have learned the truth about the land of Egyptus, say that in his land it does not rain, but as often as the Nile exceeds its banks and washes the neighboring fields, after it has returned to its bed,

immediately the sowers spread seeds. Then after a few days they gather the harvests, and if there should be a flood of the Nile two or three times in a year, they sow and reap just as many times. Whence I learned in my reading about a certain man who had been there, who asserted that this harvest is ripe on the thirtieth day after the seed is spread. And additionally he says "I have seen there a remarkable thing: a pot boiling in the sun and, if it can be believed, that eggs can cook in the sand at noon." Indeed, just as the flowing Nile runs over the neighboring places and gladdens the farmers so that they have, thereby, a hope of living, in the same way, when my little book has been run through and emended so that it can benefit a few people, you will gladden its author.) The quotation and most of the information reported about Egypt derive from Sulpicius Severus, *Dialogi* 1.3.4, 1.3.6, 1.13.4.

Book 1

[Here begins the little book whose name is *The Well-Laden Ship*. First part: The Embellished Prow.] I have supplied this title based on the following gloss (folio 2r, upper margin): *Incipit iste libellus, cui nomen fecunda ratis, eo quod plena iocis et rusticis instrumentis; et sicut navicula dividitur in duabus suis partibus, prora et puppi, ita et iste libellus, cum sit unus, in medio suscipit sectionem, ut prior pars eius vulgaribus stipetur exemplis, altera propter mixturam veteris testamenti et novi aliquid altius quasi aere fulgidiore videatur obtecta.* (Here begins the little book whose name is *The Well-Laden Ship* because it is filled with riddles and rustic embellishments. And just as a little ship is divided into two parts, the prow and the stern, so also this little book, even though it is one, has a division in the middle so that the first part is filled with popular examples, and the second, because of its mixture of the Old Testament and the New, appears as something loftier, as though it were covered in shining bronze.")

3–4 A distich introducing Book 1. On the separation of these verses from 1–2 and from 5 and following, see the Introduction.

3 Gloss: *Aplustre dicitur instrumentum naviculae; qualis navicula,*

talia eius armamenta; et quia dicitur parva, ideo portat et levia. (The embellishment of a little ship is called rigging. However the little ship [is], so [is] its tackle; and because it is said to be small, so it carries light things.) The reading *diversa aplustria portat* (carries diverse rigging) is a correction in the MS. According to Voigt, the original reading may have been *aplustria levia portat* (carries polished rigging); he bases this assumption on the gloss. Voigt suggests the corrector thought the prosody of *levia* was false (i.e., the corrector assumed, as did the glossator, that the word was to be read *lĕvia,* "light," not *lēvia,* "smooth," "polished.") In the context, however, *lēvia* makes good sense and is metrically correct. Nonetheless, the meager traces of the original reading that are visible under the erasure in the MS do not seem to me to support the assumption that *aplustria levia portat* was the earlier reading, so I have not restored it to the text.

5 Gloss: *Quando in contrarium vertuntur auxilia et plus offitiunt quam iuvant, hoc utimur exemplo; ventus solet domum urere, non liberare.* (When our efforts at aiding turn out contrary [to our expectations] and harm more than they help, we use this maxim. The wind normally burns a house, it does not free it [from harm].) TPMA *Wind* 3.3.

6 Gloss: *Nichil potest fieri, quod non eveniat secundum predestinationem suam.* (Nothing can happen which does not turn out according to its predestination.) TPMA *Geschehen* 5.

7 Gloss: *Quando inpune aliquid agitur et presumptor neminem prelatum metuit.* ([This maxim is used] when something is done that goes unpunished, and the transgressor has no fear of a superior.) TPMA *Katze* 2.1.

8 Gloss: *Non laudat deus initium sed finem bonum.* (God does not praise the beginning but the good outcome.) TPMA *Ende* 1.3.1.1.

9 Gloss: *Qui se sponte commaculat furfure, dignum est, ut a canibus consumatur.* (Whoever willingly stains himself with bran, deserves to be eaten by dogs.) TPMA *Kleie* 2. Bran (a waste product of milling wheat) is a common food for dogs and an even more common food for pigs. The sense is, if you wallow in slop, don't be surprised when dogs (or pigs) attack you. The term *furfur* is glossed *quod excutitur de farina* (what is shaken out of the flour).

10 Gloss: *Cum de lupo loquimur, solet inter oves venire.* (When we speak of the wolf, he usually appears among the sheep.) TPMA *Wolf* 6.2. On *sermo caeditur* = "to converse," see Blaise Patristic.

11 Gloss: *Si ranam posueris in loco palliato, cito tibi inde saltabit in luto.* (If you place a frog in an honored place, he will quickly leap from there into the mud.) TPMA *Frosch* 1.2.

12 Gloss: *Ubi amor, ibi oculus.* (Where love is, there the eye is.) TPMA *Auge* 6.2. Voigt joins this and the following line, and the combination is common in proverbs (though both ideas also occur alone, as the examples in TPMA make clear).

13 Gloss: *Ubi dolor, ibi frequens manus herebit.* (Where the pain is, there the hand frequently will cling.) TPMA *Auge* 6.2; compare TPMA *Hand* 3.2.

14 Gloss: *Non solum inter multos sed etiam, ubi solus fueris, honore fruaris.* (Not only in a crowd, but also when you are alone, you should delight in honor.) TPMA *Allein* 2.

15 Gloss: *Qui hominem de re cara avertere velit, inde sibi odium excitabit.* (Whoever wants to turn a man away from a thing that is dear to him, will excite thereby hatred against himself.) TPMA *Rat* 4.3.

16 Gloss: *Non est perfectus amor, qui tibi fastidium generabit.* (That love is not perfect which will create [a sense of] loathing in you.) TPMA *Liebe* 3.3.3.

17 Gloss: *Sepe solet bos corium vituli ad molendinum trahere: ita et senex tenerum puerum, qui non sperat, vivendo superat.* (Often an ox is accustomed to drag the hide of a calf to a [fuller's] mill; so also an old man who did not expect it surpasses, in living, a tender youth.) TPMA *Rind* 10.2; see 1.1206.

18 Gloss: *Antequam herba veniat, sepe videtur equus mori.* (Before the [new] grass can come, it often seems that the horse dies.) TPMA *Gras* 3.2.2.

19 Gloss: *Puer rusticus domi nutritus in curte est brutus quasi pecus.* (A country boy who is raised at court is brutish like an animal.) TPMA *Erziehen* 2.3.

20 Gloss: *Qui tibi minatur malum, ea, qua poteris, debes oppositione extinguere.* (Whoever threatens to harm you, you should destroy with whatever opposition you can muster.) TPMA *Wasser* 10.2.1.

21 Gloss: *Veterem canem ante desuetum tarde coges in vinculis currere.* (An old dog that was not accustomed to it previously, you will have difficulty forcing to walk on leashes.) TPMA *Hund* 21.3.

22 Gloss: *Mora per totum annum non morantur, nec semper presto sunt pueri, qui ea manducent: ita et bona temporalia non possunt esse continua.* (Berries are not available throughout the entire year, nor are there always children at hand to eat them: so also temporal goods cannot be endless.) TPMA *Kind* 4.8.

23 Gloss: *Omnes nubes, quae videntur, non continuo pluviam prestant: ita et hominum minae ad operationem non perveniunt.* (All the clouds which are seen do not immediately produce rain: so also men's threats do not [always] come to fruition.) TPMA *Wolke* 2.

24 Gloss: *Ibi canes debent ossa rodere, ubi contingit eos latrare: sic et calones ibi panem manducare, ubi onera portare.* (Dogs ought to gnaw bones where they bark; so also porters ought to eat bread where they carry the burdens.) TPMA *Hund* 13.6.

25 Gloss: *Quicquid super plaustrum posueris, hoc ad temonem trahentium animalium venit: ita quicquid a servis delinquitur, ad correctorem familiae destinatur.* (Whatever you place on the wagon is transferred to the pole of the draft animals; likewise, whatever is done badly by the servants, is passed on to their overseer.) TPMA *Wagen (Subst.)* 4.2.

26 Gloss: *Plus quam nova veste letificantur pueri saturo ventre.* (Boys are made happy by a full stomach more than by new clothes.) TPMA *Bauch* 2.2.1.

27 Gloss: *Quamvis aves habeant corneum rostrum, tamen, quid edendum sit, sapiunt.* (Although birds have a hard beak, still they taste what should be eaten.) TPMA *Vogel* 25.

28 Gloss: *Lenis aqua sepe profunda est et ripas consumit: sic et tranquillus homo invidia torquetur et aliis malum, quod potest, machinatur.* (Slow-moving water is often deep and erodes the banks: so also a quiet man is tortured by envy and works whatever evil he can against others.) TPMA *Strom* 2.3.

29 Gloss: *Ubi non fuerit pastor, grex in dispersionem vadit.* (Wherever there is no shepherd, the flock goes astray.) Ezekiel 34:5; TPMA *Hirt* 11.

30 Gloss: *Ubi fuerit meretrix, omnes feminas sibi similes vellet et nullam earum pudicam.* (Wherever there is a prostitute, she wants all [other] women to be like her and none of them to be chaste.) TPMA *Hure* 2.1.

31 Gloss: *Mulier incesta docet natam talem se prebere, qualem se videt precedere.* (An unchaste woman teaches her daughter to offer herself the same way she sees that her mother does.) Ezekiel 16:44; TPMA *Hure* 2.1.

32 Gloss: *Vitricus sive bene sive male fatiat privigno: continuo in adversis habebit eundem <infidum>, rarissime in prosperis fidum.* (A stepfather, whether he treats his stepson well or badly, in adversities will continuously consider him unfaithful, and in prosperity will very rarely consider him faithful.) Ecclesiasticus 40:32; TPMA *Stiefsohn* 1.

33 Gloss: *Inter socrum et nurum ex antiquo rixae fuere continuae; econtra nurus nunquam letior, quam ut socrum mortuam audiat.* (Between a mother-in-law and a daughter-in-law there have been since ancient times continual conflicts; on the other hand, the daughter-in-law is never happier than when she hears that her mother-in-law is dead.) TPMA *Schwiegermutter* 2.2.

34 Gloss: *Omnes deteriores fiunt licentia.* (Everyone becomes worse through license.) Terence, *Heautontimorumenos* 3.1.74.

35 Gloss: *Ibi mures perstrepant, ubi cattus videtur abesse: tales et pueri absente magistro.* (The mice are noisy when the cat is absent: and boys are that way when their teacher is absent.) TPMA *Katze* 7.12.

36 Gloss: *A maioribus non semper minoribus iniuria est irroganda, quia ab his potentiores aut in re aut de vita possunt periclitari.* (Injury should not always be inflicted by the powerful on the weaker because from the weaker people the powerful can be endangered either in regards to their property or their life.) TPMA *Stark* 2.3.

37 Gloss: *Interdum improbae muscae leonem, bestiarum fortissimum, vel mortuum comedunt: sic et pauperes iniurioso principi si non vivo vel mortuo derogant.* (At times, wicked flies devour a lion, the strongest of the beasts, at least when he is dead: just so poor people

disparage an unjust leader, if not while he is alive, at least once he is dead.) TPMA *Löwe* 3.4.

38 Gloss: *Rubigo levioris naturae forte ferrum consumit.* (Rust, although of a lighter nature, may consume iron.) TPMA *Rost* 1.1.

39 Gloss: *Non letabitur sola venatione, cui domi contingit panis deficere.* (One who has no bread at home will not be made happy solely by hunting.) TPMA *Jagen* 3.4. According to the gloss, the sense of the proverb is essentially "one should have a backup plan"; in other words, hunting is not a foolproof means of acquiring a meal, so it is an unhappy undertaking for one who has no other food available. I have followed the gloss in my translation, not Voigt's interpretation, though there is much to recommend the latter. He cites a French proverb, *Il va à la chasse aux croûtes de pain, il mendie* (He goes hunting for crusts of bread; he is a beggar). If we follow Voigt's interpretation and the French proverb, the sense of Egbert's line would be "One who doesn't even have bread is a sad hunter [because he must go begging]."

40 Gloss: *Multi aliquando aliis bene consulunt, qui sibi non possunt nec aliis bene suadentibus credunt.* (Many people sometimes give good advice to others, although they are not able to give good advice to themselves, nor do they believe others who give good advice.) TPMA *Rat* 3.5, 4.5. I follow the gloss (and TPMA *Rat* 4.5), not Voigt's interpretation (and TPMA *Rat* 3.5).

41 Gloss: *Meticulosa res est vitulo cum forti bove luctanti: sic invalido cum fortiore rixanti.* (It is a fearful affair for a calf to wrestle with a strong ox; so also for a weak person to quarrel with a stronger one.) TPMA *Rind* 21.4.

42 Gloss: *Bos minatus ad aquam nisi sitiens bibere cogetur: ita et in malivolam animam non introibit sapientia.* (An ox driven by threats to water, unless he is thirsty, will drink only if compelled: so also wisdom will not enter [unless compelled] into a malevolent soul.) TPMA *Trinken* 2.1.2.

43 Gloss: *Quantum nocet capra in vinea, tantum et filia eius: ita, quod fatiunt mali parentes, imitantur noxii filii.* (Just as harmful as a goat is in a vineyard, so also is the goat's kid: likewise, whatever evil parents do, their wicked children imitate.) TPMA *Ziege* 7.

44 Gloss: *Iste mos inter nos antiquitus inolevit nostra potius curare quam aliena.* (This custom became normal among us long ago: to care more about our own affairs than about another's.) TPMA *Eigen* 5.2.1.

45 Gloss: *Sub magna pulcritudine corporis latet vitiosa contagio mentis.* (Under the great beauty of a body hides a vicious infection of mind.) TPMA *Haut* 5.1.

46–47 Gloss: *Stultus aliquis non magis est necessarius inter reliquos, quemadmodum nec poletrinus in comitatu exercitus et quinta rota in plaustro.* (Any fool is no more necessary among his fellows than a colt is [needed] in the company of an army and a fifth wheel [is needed] on a cart.) TPMA *Pferd* 13.3, *Rad* 5.1.

48 Gloss: *Melius viatori equum secum ad onus portandum in via ducere quam sine eo solum incedere.* (It is better for a traveler to lead a horse alongside him on the road for carrying the baggage than to go alone without the horse.) TPMA *Pferd* 15.2. *Propter* is glossed *est iuxta* (it means alongside).

49 Gloss: *Cornice inconsulta soli dabimus stipendia milvo: his, quos timemus, damus, infirmioribus nulla largimur.* (Without regard for the crow, we give tribute to the kite alone: we give to those whom we fear; to those who are weaker we dispense nothing.) TPMA *Falke* 16.

50 Gloss: *Gallina ut pura grana legat, in posterioribus trahit anteriora: ita et nos in poetarum scriptis abiectis sordidis utiliora queramus.* (A hen, so that it may select pure grain, among inferior things draws out those that are foremost; so also we, in the writings of the poets, with the sordid things cast aside, should seek the more useful ones.) TPMA *Huhn* 1.2. The Latin is unclear, but I follow the gloss in my translation. The intended sense may be that a hen finds gems in the dung in which it scratches (and if so, this is a very elliptical variant of Romulus Anglicus, 1: *de gallo et iaspide* [Hervieux, *Les fabulistes,* 2:564]). *Ut semper* is glossed *scilicet solet* (that is, is accustomed).

51 Gloss: *Si sanus sis, circa puteum noli frequenter currere, ne forte in eo contingat oppetere: ita et de maiori te non debes temere iniusta tractare.* (If you are sane, don't make a habit of running near a well, lest

you happen to die in it: so also concerning a greater matter, you ought not to conduct yourself in a thoughtless manner.). Why it should be a musician (literally, a lyre player) is unclear; perhaps the point is that a musician, because concentrating on his performance, is not paying close enough attention and risks putting himself in a potentially dangerous situation.

52 Gloss: *De iniusta noverca non sunt privignis salubria querenda consilia.* (From an unjust stepmother, stepsons ought not to seek sound advice.) TPMA *Stiefmutter* 4.

53 Gloss: *Non est spes asinis dominis carere, dum pendet follis in pariete.* (There is no hope for the asses that they will lack a lord so long as a sack is hanging on the wall.) TPMA *Esel* 12.1.

54 Gloss: *Senem frangit iracundia, et puerum necat invidia, ut Salomon ait.* (As Solomon said, "anger breaks an old man, and envy kills a boy.") Job 5:2; TPMA *Zorn* 1.8.2.1.

55 Gloss: *Qui adversus regem debet occurrere in bello, necesse est ut regem habeat in auxilio.* (Whoever must go against a king in battle, needs to have a king as his ally.) Comparing Luke 14:31, Voigt interprets *hostis* in the Late Antique and medieval sense of "army, host" (see Blaise Medieval). TPMA *König* 4.1.4. *Hostem* is glossed *scilicet se* (namely, himself,), so it appears the glossator understood the sentence as "One who makes himself an enemy to a king should have a king for an ally."

56 Gloss: *Debitor malus et inobs pro frumento solvat avenam, quia si posset mutare, invitus eandem.* (A wicked and indigent debtor may pay with straw instead of grain—I swear that if he could change, he'd be unwilling to pay with straw!) Compare TPMA *Getreide* 4.3. For *quia si* in oaths, see Blaise Patristic (also used in the glosses to 1.104, 1.115, and 1.179).

57 Gloss: *Qui perdite vivunt et sua sine temperantia devorant, aut furando aut verenter petendo ad aliena transibunt.* (Those who live like wastrels and devour their own property without restraint, either thievishly or respectfully will go through another's.) TPMA *Eigen* 5.2.7.

58 Gloss: *Hi qui minus habent, semper sua addunt ditioribus.* (Those who have less, always give their property to the wealthier people.) TPMA *Reich* 6.4.

59 Gloss: *Istud omnibus notum et vulgo visum, fatuos in scamno sedere et ex more crura movere.* (This is known to all and commonly seen, that fools sit on a bench and out of habit swing their legs.) TPMA *Narr* 14.2. *Scamnum,* "bench," could also mean "throne"; in which case the sense would be roughly "a fool placed on a throne still acts like a fool" (similar to 1.11).

60 Gloss: *Stultus, dum tacet, intelligitur aliquid esse; ubi incipit loqui, deprehenditur, cuius sit ingenii.* (A fool, so long as he is silent, is understood to be of some worth; when he starts speaking, it becomes known what intelligence he has.) Compare TPMA *Narr* 7.6.

61 Gloss: *Qui multos nummos habet in arca, omnia habet necessaria; sola deest pustella.* (One who has many coins in his chest, has all he needs; only a pimple is lacking.) TPMA *Reich* 3.1, *Geld* 2.2.1. *Pus* = an insignificant thing or something of no value at all.

62 Gloss: *Una ovis morbida totum gregem commaculat.* (One sick sheep infects the whole flock.) TPMA *Schaf* 19. I follow the manuscript punctuation of the Latin, not that of Voigt, who eliminates the comma after *ovem* and places one after *sola* (so that the sense is: "disease infects one sheep [who is] alone, then it [disease] infects the whole flock").

63 Gloss: *Imminente pluvia cornix se magis aquis immergit, sed niger color naturaliter insitus in albedinem nunquam vertetur. Sunt multi quidem qui lautiores volunt videri quam sint, sed id nulla sua ratione merentur.* (When rain threatens, the crow immerses himself more in water; but the black color naturally present in him never turns to white. There are many indeed who want to appear more washed than they are, but by none of their concern do they achieve it.) TPMA *Krähe* 1.1.

64 Gloss: *Corvus et aliae pleraeque aves propter esuriem ventris discunt hominum verba formare, sed venter, magister artis, compellit hoc facere.* (The crow and many other birds, on account of hunger of their belly, learn to form human words; but the belly, the master of skills, compels them to do this.) Persius, *Satirae, prol.* 8–14; TPMA *Bauch* 1.3, *Hunger* 4.8.2.2.

65 Gloss: *Canis invidus cum fuerit ossibus plenus, cum non ipse amplius poterit, nec aliis contingere permittit. Est enim quilibet homo qui hoc habet parcitatis vitium: id quod habet sibi soli habet, nulli partitus

amico. (An envious dog, although he has plenty of bones, even though he cannot have more, does not permit others to have them. There is many a man who has this vice of stinginess. What he has, he keeps for himself alone, sharing with no friend.) TPMA *Hund* 13.10.

66 Gloss: *Multi passeres nobiscum perpetuo perseverant, cum hirundo semel in anno redeat. Hoc datur intellegi cultiores debere esse nobiscum in servitio perseverantes quam novitios hospites.* (Many sparrows remain with us continually, while the swallow may return once in a year. This can be understood to mean that those remaining in service with us ought to be more respected than the new guests.) TPMA *Sperling* 6.

67 Gloss: *Qui aviculas delicate nutriunt, quid aliud pro diligenti cura foventibus reddunt, nisi quod stercora dicunt?* (Those who delicately care for little birds, with what else do the birds repay them for this diligent care than with what is called shit.) TPMA *Elster* 7. "What I'd rather not name," that is, bird droppings.

68 Gloss: *Antequam in utrem mittatur, vinum acessit. Hoc proverbium illis dicitur, qui nuper regimine accepto, ante incipiunt in subiectos insanire, quam bonae vitae exemplum monstrare.* (Before it can be put in the bottle, the wine sours. This proverb is said to those who, having recently undertaken a position of authority, begin to rage against their subjects before they have shown them an example of a good life.) TPMA *Wein* 3.5. *"Acessit,"* i.e., *acescit.*

69 Gloss: *Qui res perperam involutas et clausas proponit, quis melius solvit, quam qui eas ne aliis paterent conclusit?* (Whoever mistakenly proposes involved and obscure things, who better to resolve them than the one who arranged them so that they not be clear to others?) TPMA *Weben* 1.2.

70 Gloss: *Indutias unius noctis dicunt valere centum solidis.* (A truce of a single night, they say, is worth a hundred coins.) TPMA *Aufschub* 1.2.2.

71 Gloss: *Quando due res sunt dissimiles et inter se differentes, utimur hoc exemplo de maiore ad minorem: ita similes quemadmodum aper et vulpes.* (When two things are dissimilar and differ from one another, we use this example from a greater thing to the lesser: they are as much alike as a boar and a fox.) TPMA *Eber* 5.

72 Gloss: *Inter corticem et lignum nemo potest digitum inserere. Sic non debes inter patrem et filium, virum et uxorem legitimosque amicos discordiam seminare.* (Nobody can insert a finger between the bark and the wood. Likewise, you should not sow discord between a father and a son, a husband and a wife, and legitimate friends.) TPMA *Rinde* 2.

73 Gloss: *Si semper fueris usus pane farreo et reliquo bene purgato, priusquam fame pereas, meo consilio, si ad manum venerit, utere ordeaceo.* (If you have always been accustomed to spelt bread and whatever else is very pure, before you die of hunger, in my opinion, you should eat barley bread if it comes into your hand.) TPMA *Brot* 20.3.

74 Gloss: *Corvus ubi recens cadaver invenerit, importuna voce incipit crocitare et suam multitudinem provocare; quod solus totum posset habere, dummodo vellet tacere.* (A crow, when it has found a fresh cadaver, begins in a rude voice to crow and to stir up his flock about something that he could have had entirely to himself if he had chosen to be silent.) Horace, *Epistulae* 1.17.50–51; TPMA *Krähe* 23.

75 Gloss: *Non est annona, quae sine suis nascatur paleis: nec quilibet homo sine sua qualicumque animi vel mentis ratione.* (There is no harvest which is born without some chaff; nor is there any man without some sort of reason of heart or mind.) TPMA *Stroh* 1.1.

76 Gloss: *Cum quis viderit vicinam domum flagrantem, tunc poterit estimare eundem ignem comminus venturum esse.* (When anyone has seen the neighboring house on fire, then he might imagine that same fire is coming close to hand.) TPMA *Brennen* 2.1. The word *"ibi"* (which itself stands on an erasure) is glossed *scilicet sors* (namely, fate.)

77 Gloss: *Si casu aliquo tua pulmenta ad terram ceciderint, nec integra nec purgata levabis. Sic et aliquis minus sapiens, si spreto consilio ad dampnum venerit, raro in integrum restituet, quicquid inconsultus amiserit.* (If by some accident, your food falls to the ground, you will not pick it up intact and clean. So also someone who is less intelligent, if he comes to misfortune because he has spurned advice, will rarely restore intact whatever he foolishly lost.) TPMA *Ausschütten* 1.

78 Gloss: *Non est adeo canis timendus latrans, dum tunc mordere non audeat. Ita multi minantes non sunt pavendi, quorum presumptio nulla est.* (A barking dog should not be so much feared, so long as he does not then dare to bite. Likewise many who make threats should not be feared; their presumption is nothing.) TPMA *Hund* 7.12.

79 Gloss: *Dum plaustrum frumento oneratum ad molendinum venerit, folles eitiuntur in angulis. Ita minores cedunt, dum ditiores adveniunt.* (While a cart loaded with grain comes for milling, the [mere] sacks are tossed in the corners. Likewise the less powerful folks give way while the wealthier ones come forward.) TPMA *Sack* 1.4.

80 Gloss: *Qui parcus fuerit in pane dando, nimirum parcissimus erit in auro.* (Whoever is parsimonious in giving bread, no doubt will be extremely parsimonious in giving gold.) TPMA *Brot* 31.

81 Gloss: *Nullus potest tali perfrui voluptate longe positus in exercitu, qualem posset in privata domo.* (Nobody can enjoy such pleasure stationed faraway in the army as he can in his own home.) TPMA *Haus* 4.3.2.3.

82 Gloss: *Qui non potest digerere, quod manducat, ad tormentum veniet, dum languescit in ventre, quod non potest exire.* (Whoever is not able to digest what he eats, will come to torment while a thing that cannot exit is languishing in his stomach.) Compare TPMA *Schlucken* 3.

83 Gloss: *Ille locus satis vallo et propugnaculis est munitus, ubi fuerit fortium militum conglobatus exercitus.* (That place is sufficiently fortified with a rampart and barriers where there is an army of strong soldiers amassed.) TPMA *Burg* 1.7.

84 Gloss: *Neglegentibus pueris verbera debes intentare, ut corrigantur; senibus et canis, quo digni sunt, honorem impendere.* (You ought to direct beatings to negligent boys, so that they be corrected; to old and white-haired men, where they are worthy, you ought to give respect.) TPMA *Alt* 5.3.

85 Gloss: *Ille dignum et competens sibi coniugium sortitur, qui non ultra vires et caput suum sed pari suae coniungitur.* (That man is granted a worthy marriage and one suited to him who is not married be-

yond his means and over his head, but to his equal.) TPMA *Ehe* 3.1. *Competit* is glossed *convenit* (suits).

86 Gloss: *Tarde perit, quod semper perire deberet, rostrum muris. Intractabile est asperum et damnaticium, quod nobis multa dampna facit et sepe peccatis hominum fatientibus multum excrevit.* (The tooth [lit., mouth] of the mouse, which should always perish, perishes all too slowly. An intractable thing is one that is harsh and cursed; it causes us many losses and often has increased when the sins of men are active.) Juvenal, *Satirae* 3.207.

87 Gloss: *Non nocet cuneus cum pane editus, et bonus sermo meliori superimpositus.* (It does no harm when white bread is distributed with the bread, and when a good sermon is added to a better one.) TPMA *Brot* 12. For *cuneus* = white bread, or bread made of especially fine flour, see Du Cange, *3. Cuneus.*

88 Gloss: *Armillam et bonas vestes debet portare, qui eas bono suo labore meruerit.* (That man ought to wear a bracelet and good clothes who has earned them by his good work.) TPMA *Armband 1.*

89 Gloss: *Segnius irritant animos dimissa per aures, quam quae sunt subiecta fidelibus oculis. Sic melius crediderim visis quam auditis.* (Things imparted through the ears trouble our minds more slowly than things brought before our trusty eyes. Thus, I would rather believe things seen than heard.) Horace, *Ars Poetica* 180–81; TPMA *Sehen* 3.3, *Auge* 3.2.

90 Gloss: *Nemo sanae mentis, si velit mundum habere mel, infundit inmundo corio canino.* (No sane person, who wants to have clean honey, pours it into an unclean dog's hide.) See 1.225; TPMA *Hund* 19.3.

91 Gloss: *Vulgare proverbium est nichil aliud canes ad ecclesiam querere nisi multos colaphos inde reportare.* (The proverb is common that dogs look for nothing at a church other than to take away from there many beatings.) TPMA *Hund* 5.5.

92 Gloss: *Indebitam rem et negatam non potest facere gallina: in patella cibos positos venit tundere, quia non potest lingere.* (A hen cannot do something inappropriate and impossible: it comes to peck at food placed on a dish because it is not able to lick.) TPMA *Huhn* 16.

93 Gloss: *Quod suum est oculorum, longius vident in patulis campis, et vox ab auribus clarius auditur in silvis.* (The eyes see further in open places, because that is proper to them, and sound is heard more clearly by the ears in the forest.) TPMA *Ohr* 2.2.2.

94 This verse, which merely repeats verse 93, was added in the lower margin by a much later hand. It seems to me more likely that it is a later reader's addition of a similar sentiment rather than an original part of Egbert's work.

95 Gloss: *Sive lavando sive pectendo canem mundare volueris—quod fuit, inmundus erit, et tu preterea tuam in eo operam perdis.* (Whether you want to make a dog clean by washing or by combing [him], he will remain what he was: unclean. And you, furthermore, will waste your effort on him.) TPMA *Hund* 1.4.

96 Gloss: *Nec pedes a toto, nec bonus eques in asino.* (One on an ass is neither entirely a pedestrian nor a noble knight.) TPMA *Esel* 7.2.

97 Gloss: *Qui vitam suam incolumem servat, non servat inanes paleas sed munit se omni custodia meliore.* (One who keeps his life safe does not preserve worthless chaff, but fortifies himself with every better sort of protection.) TPMA *Leben* 1.7.1.1.

98 Gloss: *Qui cum asino suo vadit ad forum, cum aculeo sequatur post tergum.* (Whoever goes to market with his ass, should follow behind him with a goad.) TPMA *Esel* 26.

99 Gloss: *Hiemali tempore ubi videris candentem pruinam proxime aliquam dicunt consequi pluviam.* (In winter time when you see frost becoming white, they say that some rain will follow.) TPMA *Regen* 2.

100 Gloss: *Conviatoribus dat commedendi modicum, qui pro necessitate suum linguit cultellum.* (One who licks his knife compulsively, gives little to his companions to eat.) TPMA *Lecken* 2.

101 Gloss: *Rabidorum canum raro vidimus collectam multitudinem nec diuturnam stare generationem.* (We rarely see a large crowd of rabid dogs, nor their offspring enduring for long.) TPMA *Hund* 6.3.

102 Gloss: *Sepes indecenter stat sine spinis, nec mulierem decet incedere sine capitis sui redimiculis.* (A hedge stands indecently without thorns,

and it is not decent that a woman go around without covering her hair.) TPMA *Frau* 7.5.2.

103 Gloss: *Longam moram, ut liberetur, habet diutius expectandi, si suspenso cito non subvenis.* (He has a long delay waiting a long time to be freed, if you do not come quickly to the aid of one who has been hanged.) TPMA *Hängen* 3.

104 Gloss: *Contra hostem subdolum, quantum valeas, dimices, quia si potest, tibi non parcet; artes vero discere, quantum potes, non differas: quibus si bene usus fueris, non confunderis.* (Against the tricky enemy, you should struggle as much as you are able, because if he has the chance, he will not spare you! As far as possible, do not put off learning skills; if you use them well, you will not be left in the lurch.) TPMA *Lernen* 1.1.1, *Feind* 5.3.3. For *quia si* in oaths, see note to 1.56.

105 Gloss: *Inde magis formidat avicula, quod crebro eam in horreo tuo fueris persecutus cum scopa.* (For this reason a little bird is more afraid: that you frequently chase after her with a broom in your granary.) TPMA *Sperling* 9. The gloss treats this verse and the following one as a pair.

106 Gloss: *Et puer lapsus in igne, postea stigmata videns et recolens, semper timet eundem.* (And a boy who has fallen into a fire afterward seeing the scars and remembering, always fears it.) TPMA *Feuer* 5.3. The gloss treats this verse and the preceding one as a pair.

107 Gloss: *Qui aequa pondera gestant et tolerant, minus gravantur et inter se moleste ferunt.* (Those who bear equal weights and tolerate them, are less burdened, and between them they carry with less trouble.) TPMA *Last* 5.

108 Gloss: *Qui mel manducat, aliquando nolens aculeum patietur, quod est dicere: qui cum seniore suo bonis eius fruitur, interdum, si necessitas incubuerit, cum eo adversa tolerabit.* (Whoever eats honey, sometimes unwillingly will endure the sting; which is to say, whoever along with his lord enjoys the latter's goods, at some point, if necessity requires it, will have to endure adversities along with him.) TPMA *Honig* 4.6.1.

109 Gloss: *Fasces graves nullus potest procul pellere, quin ulciscatur proxi-*

morum dum videt iniurias. (Nobody can drive heavy loads very far away without taking vengeance when he sees the injuries done to his neighbors.) TPMA *Last* 2. The glossator treated verses 109 and 110 as a pair.

110 Gloss: *Vindictae proximorum, quocumque modo fiant, sunt dulces, sed illa dultior, quam propinquus propria manu expleverit.* (Vengeances of our neighbors, however they come about, are sweet; but that vengeance is sweeter which a relative achieves by his own hand.) TPMA *Rache* 1.1.

111 Gloss: *Qui non habet cor strenuum ad pugnandum, ad confortandum se tollat secum vel grande pedum et ponat in baculi sui spe, quod non habet in corde.* (One who does not have a strong heart for fighting, should carry with him, for comfort, a very large stick and he should put in the hope of his rod what he lacks in his heart.) TPMA *Furcht* 3.1.1.

112 Gloss: *Omnes fructus arborum imitantur generationem suam et sapore et, unde oriuntur, eo caudam vertendo, sive male sive bene sectando.* (All the fruits of trees reflect their birth, both in their taste and in turning their tail [that is, their stem] towards the source from which they were born, whether they are following well or ill.) TPMA *Baum* 5.1.1.

113 Gloss: *Stercora, quo plus moventur, tanto deterius fetent.* (Shit: the more you turn it, the worse it stinks.) TPMA *Dreck* 2.2.2.1.

114 Gloss: *Proximior est fidus et indefessus frater quam latus et sterilis ager.* (A faithful and indefatigable brother is dearer than a broad and sterile field.) TPMA *Bruder* 1.4.

115 Gloss: *Quisque serpens calcantis sinuat pedem, et inficit veneno, quia si posset et ferro.* (Every snake curls around the foot of the one stepping on it and infects it with poison—I swear that if he were able to, he'd attack it with a sword too!) TPMA *Schlange* 3.2.3. On *quia si,* see note to 1.56.

116 Gloss: *Apud rusticos usitatum proverbium: de uno lupo alterum non comprehendes.* (Among the country folk the proverb is common: from one wolf you will not capture another.) TPMA *Wolf* 10.1. The sense of *actor* is not entirely clear; my translation assumes it is equivalent to *auctor.* It might perhaps mean (although no par-

allels are known to me) "the agent who drives *(agit)* the game toward the hunter" (in plain English, "the one who beats the bushes"). Perhaps we should assume that Egbert uses the deponent *venor* here as a passive: "When a wolf is the hunter, rarely will any other wolf be hunted." That provides a straightforward and correct meaning; however, such a usage is not, to my knowledge, otherwise attested (but compare Egbert's use of an active form of *vulpinor* at 1.887.)

117 Gloss: *Qui tetigerit picem, inquinabitur ab ea.* (He that toucheth pitch, shall be defiled with it.) Ecclesiasticus 13:1. For *palpo* = "a person who touches or pats," see Firminus Verris. TPMA *Pech* 1.

118 Gloss: *Canis revertitur ad vomitum suum.* (A dog returns to his own vomit.) Proverbs 26:11; TPMA *Hund* 2.21.

119 Gloss: *Interdum stulto debes cedere, ne causam inveniat, unde adversum te iure possit irasci.* (Sometimes you ought to yield to a fool so that he not find an excuse to be justifiably enraged against you.) TPMA *Narr* 10.4.6.

120 Gloss: *Cuidam libero homini hoc nomen erat, qui benefitia sua suaviter vivendo deservivit, unde cunctis pigris et inertibus hoc proverbium inolevit.* (This [that is, Magrid] was the name of a certain free man who served his offices by living elegantly, whence this proverb became customary for all lazy and indolent people.) TPMA *Sitzen* 3.1.1.

121 Gloss: *Non protinus est aurum, quodcumque rubicundi coloris invenitur metallum: sic et qui se simulat bonum; aliud latet intrinsecus ulcus et vitium.* (Whatever red metal is found, is not suddenly gold. And the same applies to one who pretends to be good: some ulcer and vice is hiding within.) TPMA *Gold* 7.1.

122 Gloss: *Hyringus quidam erat senex emeritus et decrepitus, unde longevis dicitur, "dies tuos equiperas Hyringo," quem in aetate ultima musca precipitavit de sella.* (Hyringus was a certain old man, worn out and decrepit; hence one says to the long-lived, "you are equaling your days to Hyringus's," a man whom at the end of his life a fly knocked from his stool.) TPMA *Alt* 10.

123 Gloss: *Melior est una apis mellifera, quam quot usquam sunt muscarum genera. Si bene velis intendere, omnia haec exempla ad homines*

poteris applicare. (One honey-bearing bee is better than however many kinds of flies there are. If you want to understand this properly, you may apply all these examples to men.) TPMA *Biene* 2.1; for *per moenia* as "in the city," see Virgil, *Aeneid* 2.250 and 4.74.

124 Gloss: *Poles fuit quidam rusticus, quem dominus suus maiorem domus suae fecit; at ubi inter pares ut iudicaret consedit, ut inde alii magis timerent, in primo iuditio patrem iugulavit. Hoc exemplo alii terreantur, qui tyrannum aliquem habeant proximum.* (Poles was a certain country fellow whose lord made him the mayor of his palace. But when Poles sat among his peers as a judge, in order to make the others more afraid, in his first judgment he condemned his own father to be hanged. From this example, other people should be terrified who have any kind of tyrant as a relative.) TPMA *Gewalt* 3.2. *Poles* is glossed *proprium nomen* ("proper name.")

125 Gloss: *Eques sapiens de ponte non cadit, quia ascensor equi per hiantem pontem non transit.* (A wise knight does not fall from a bridge because one seated on a horse does not cross over a gaping bridge.) TPMA *Brücke* 3.

126 Gloss: *Omnis, qui studium suum oderit, non hoc solum odit, sed et seipsum totiusque vitae suae solatium.* (Everyone who hates his own job, not only hates it, but also hates himself and the solace of his entire life.) TPMA *Hass* 3.2.3.

127 Gloss: *Qui habent prurientem et ebullientem capitis infirmitatem, semper pilleati incedunt, ne decalvatum et verecundum caput eorum patulum videatur; unde natum est proverbium: cuius fuit capitis vitium, ille tulit galerum.* (Those who have an itching and blistering infirmity of the head always go around with a hat on so that their shorn and embarrassing head not be seen in the open. Hence arose the proverb: "The one with a diseased head wore the cap.") TPMA *Krätze* 10. A *galerus* is a cap especially associated with priests, suggesting that the proverb is a satirical jab at the clergy. *Porrigo* is glossed *est infirmitas capitis* ("it is an infirmity of the head"); *galerus* is glossed *galerus et galamaucus pillei sunt* (*galerus* and *galamaucus* are caps).

128 Gloss: *Cum gratis aliquis tibi datur equus, non debes os aperire, ut per*

inspectionem dentium numeres, quot annorum sit, quem tibi sine tuo pretio gratia aliena concessit. (When any horse is given to you for free, you should not open its mouth to count through inspection of its teeth how old it is. Another's favor granted it to you without your paying.) TPMA *Pferd* 18; see 1.845.

129 Gloss: *Cui bene semper in omnibus suis actibus evenerit, cunctis aequaliter ut sibi evenisse credit.* (One for whom, in all his actions, things have always turned out well, believes that it has equally turned out well for all others as for himself.) TPMA *Erfolg* 2.

130 Gloss: *Qui nescit de pecore docte pellem tollere, solet incautius vulnerare: ideo, qui artem non didicit, stultus est, si quando eam incohare presumit.* (One who does not know how to remove the hide of an animal skillfully, usually damages it rather incautiously. Likewise, one who has not learned a skill is a fool if he ever presumes to start doing it.) TPMA *Schinden* 2.

131 Gloss: *Si quis canem ceperit castrare uno testiculo eruto, altero dimisso, nec mundam habet manum nec opus impletum. Sic aliquis, <si> inimicum vulnerans vivum dimiserit, postea experietur mortis suae ultorem, quem antea volens reliquit superstitem.* (If anyone has begun to castrate a dog, when one testicle has been removed and the other is left, that man has neither a clean hand nor a completed job. In the same way, anyone wounding an enemy and letting him escape alive, afterward will contend with an avenger of death, whom he had earlier, willingly, allowed to survive.) TPMA *Hoden* 1.3.

132 Gloss: *Quod semper habet exosum, invitus vadit canis ad balneum: sic piger et deses renititur ad omne preceptum.* (A dog goes unwillingly to a bath, which he has always hated. In the same way a lazy and idle man resists every order he is given.) TPMA *Hund* 2.28.

133 Gloss: *Magnae est infamiae regem aut aliquem principem multorum non esse comitum.* (It is a great disgrace that a king or any prince not have a large crowd of courtiers.) TPMA *König* 3.6.1.

134 Gloss: *Sive pluat sive ninguat, hospes, ne apud extraneos tediosus exsistat, quantotius ad propria redeat.* (Whether it rains or snows, the guest, so that he not be a bore among strangers, should return to his own home as soon as possible.) TPMA *Regen* 7.1.

135 Gloss: *Equus suspiria gravia trahit, ubi diu ieiunus ad presepia vacua steterit; et omnis homo ibi servit invitus, ubi nullus paratur cibus.* (A horse draws heavy sighs when he has stood for a long time hungry at empty mangers. Also every man serves unwillingly in that place where no food is made ready.) TPMA *Pferd* 1.1.

136 Gloss: *Vetus peccatum ad novum et verecundum transit ruborem.* (An old sin turns into a new and embarrassing redness.) TPMA *Schande* 3.1.

137 Gloss: *Inflata superbia quanto ad altiora surrexerit, tanto durius cadet.* (Inflated pride: the higher it has risen, the harder it will fall.) TPMA *Hochmut* 5.1.2.

138 Gloss: *Sub alta casa sepius sunt cibaria stricta vel pauca.* (Rather frequently, under lofty houses there are few and limited meals.) TPMA *Dach* 8. *Tholis* is glossed *est eminentior locus in domo* (it is a high place in a house.)

139 Gloss: *Melior est ager fertilis auro pretioso vel gemmis.* (A fertile field is better than precious gold and jewels.) TPMA *Acker* 1.1.

140 Gloss: *Odium dei vel aurum preponderat omne metallum.* (The hatred of God, or gold, outweighs every metal.) TPMA *Gold* 6.2.

141 Gloss: *Quod hodie fit et pre oculis habemus, inde certi sumus; quid cras futurum sit, ignoramus.* (What happens today and we have before our eyes, about that we are certain. What is going to happen tomorrow, we do not know.) TPMA *Heute* 3.2.

142 Gloss: *Potores desiderant vinum; musca, quod suum est potius morbum quam vinum.* (Drinkers like wine; the fly prefers that which is proper to it, disease rather than wine.) TPMA *Fliege* 5.1.1.

143 Gloss: *In primo partu suo pulcher conspicitur asellus, quanto longiori, tanto deformiori aevo.* (When it is first born, the little donkey seems pretty. However much older he is in age, he is that much uglier.) TPMA *Esel* 5.1.

144 Gloss: *Si quis pro sapone caput vendiderit, triste est mercimonium et omni campsatione* (sic) *dirissimum.* (If anyone will sell a life for soap, it is a sad business and the most dire of any exchange.) TPMA *Haupt* 1.6. The term *campsatio* is marked as hapax by Voigt; I follow his suggestion that it is equivalent to *cambiatio.*

145 Gloss: *Breviter et cito deus succurrit his, qui per somnium graviter*

laborant: cum experrectum facit, de periculo statim eum exsolvit. (Soon and swiftly God aids those who labor heavily through a dream: when he wakes someone up, he immediately frees him from danger.) TPMA *Traum* 4.

146 Gloss: *Cum deus bono cultori locum dederit, ut boves strenuos emat, ipse profecto dat, et tamen per cornua non ministrat.* (When God has given to a good farmer the opportunity to buy strong oxen, certainly he himself gives this, and yet he does not supply them by the horns.) TPMA *Rind* 4.2.

147 Gloss: *Qui uno tempore duas vias tendere voluerit, aut bracae rumpuntur aut ipse insanis coxis distenditur.* (One who wants to go two ways at one time—either his britches are torn or he himself is split apart, with his hips no longer healthy.) TPMA *Weg* 18.5.

148 Gloss: *Immundas aves asserimus, quae suos stercorant nidos: his plerique similes, qui nullam rem servant honestam.* (We assert that birds which shit in their own nests are unclean. Many men are like them: they do not preserve their estate honorably.) TPMA *Nest* 5. Voigt joins this verse to the following one.

149 Gloss: *Pelex legitimae uxori superaddita nec factis nec nomine digna, meo iudicio ad reliquas conpescendas in spinis esset urenda.* (A concubine in addition to a legitimate wife is honorable neither in name nor in fact. In my opinion, she must be burned among the thorns to keep the others in their place.) Voigt joins this verse to the one preceding it.

150 Gloss: *Stultus, quocumque se verterit, iugiter dampna offendit, quorum omnium ipse sibi caput exsistit.* (A fool, wherever he turns, continually suffers losses, of which he is himself the chief cause.) TPMA *Narr* 8.8.2.

151 Gloss: *Gallinam cum pullis si ad farinam admiseris, tibi dampna irrogat, et quae multis prodessent, sola dissipat.* (If you have given a hen and her chicks access to the flour, she inflicts losses on you; and what could have benefitted many, she alone wastes.) TPMA *Huhn* 3.3.

152 Gloss: *Sumptuosa coniunx et voratrix effetum et debilem reddit maritum: dispergit omnem victum, pretiosas vestes et vasa vendit usque ad salinum, cunctaque viri sui bona mergit in baratrum.* (An extrava-

gant and voracious wife renders her husband effete and weak. She disperses his entire sustenance, she sells precious clothes and vessels up to and including the saltcellar, and she sinks the entire property of her husband in the abyss.) TPMA *Frau* 1.14.1.1.

153 Gloss: *Nusquam gravius bellum agitur quam inter homines, et vicissim inter emissarios; quia agitantur invicta discordia, ideo pugna est inremissa.* (Nowhere is war waged more grievously than between men, and next between stallions. Since they are stirred up by uncontrolled discord, for that reason the battle is unrelenting.) TPMA *Pferd* 30.

154 Gloss: *Nunquam erit aurum tam rubicundum aut ita purgatum, quod non detur pro penuria panum.* (Gold will never be so red or so pure that it would not be given up on account of a lack of bread.) TPMA *Not* 1.5.2; compare TPMA *Brot* 1.4.

155 Gloss: *Quid curae est tibi, cuius esse vacca dicatur, dum in tuos usus lac totum fundatur?* (Why is it a concern to you, to whom the cow is said to belong, so long as all the milk is flowing for your use?) TPMA *Rind* 8.1.

156 Gloss: *Cum capellae desint, quae transseant* (sic), *cur ultra modum de ponte fatiendo eris sollicitus?* (Since there are no goats which could cross over it, why are you concerned beyond measure about building a bridge?) TPMA *Brücke* 1.

157 Gloss: *Ante poteris penes te invenire bilinguem et mendatia fingentem quam consequi celerius iterantem loripedem.* (You will find next to you a two-tongued inventor of lies before you can catch up to a lame man, who moves more swiftly.) The sense is, a liar is so quickly caught that you will catch him sooner than you will catch up to a lame man, even though the latter walks slowly (a lie slows one down more than a limp). TPMA *Lügen* 4.2.

158 Gloss: *Cum pro aliquo pisce piscem vendideris et aliud pretium non dederis, suspicari poteris alterutrum eorum olacem esse aut aliquo vitio preditum: ita et in reliquis rebus istud poteris arbitrari.* (When you have sold a fish for another fish and have not given a different price, you might suppose one or the other of them stinks or has

some blemish. So also in other things you might imagine the same.) TPMA *Fisch* 9.

159 Gloss: *Qui iurem superfluum hauserit, tanto distensiorem ventrem habebit.* (Whoever has drunk extra sauce, will have a belly distended that much more.) TPMA *Suppe* 9.

160 Gloss: *Ubi domi sumus, foris exclusum citius obliviscimur, quem intus non videmus.* (When we are at home, we rather quickly forget the one excluded outdoors whom we, inside, do not see.) TPMA *Vergessen* 4.2.

161 Gloss: *Nomen et gloria operatoris ad illum magis pertinet, qui dictando disponit, ut fiat, quam qui manu operatur, ut sit.* (The name and glory of the maker pertains more to that one who, by ordering [it], arranges that it be made than it does to the one who works with his hand to make it.) See Franco of Liège, *De quadratura circuli,* ed. M. Folkerts and A. J. E. M. Smeur, "A Treatise on the Squaring of the Circle by Franco of Liège," *Archives internationales d'histoire des sciences* 26 (1976): 59–105, 225–53, at 77–78: *An non ille auctor qui incitator? Ille utique auctor.* (Is not the instigator the author? He is in every way the author.) TPMA *Meister* 4.

162 Gloss: *Hoc potest fieri bono ingenio, quod nequit menbrorum robore forti vel ligno.* (A thing can be made by a good mind, which cannot be made by the oaken strength of the limbs or by wood.) TPMA *Weise* 4.1. *Asser* is glossed *asseres sunt laterculi fortes in tecto* (*asseres* are the strong wooden parts in the roof).

163 Gloss: *Non sunt vera verba nec lacrimae, quas fundit mulier ebria.* (They are not true words nor true tears which a drunken woman pours out.) TPMA *Frau* 1.3.2.4.

164 Gloss: *His porcis, quos habemus, debemus pascua nostra consumere: ita nos privatis uti servientibus, qui meliores habere non possumus.* (We should use up our pastures with the pigs we have. Likewise, we who cannot have better ones, ought to enjoy our own servants.) TPMA *Schwein* 21.

165 Gloss: *Aves, quae priusquam volare possint deserunt nidos, aut ita, ut moriantur, corruunt aut sese, quandiu vivunt, debiles reddunt: ita, qui priusquam discant docere volunt; qui antea magistri non fuerant veri-*

tatis, postea fient erroris. (Birds that leave their nests before they can fly either fall so that they die or render themselves weak for their entire lives. Likewise, those who want to teach before they learn. Those who were not previously teachers of truth, afterward will become teachers of error.) TPMA *Vogel* 3.1.

166 Gloss: *De hoc versiculo ita scriptum est: nolite serere margaritas inter porcos neque sanam doctrinam inter stultos derisores.* (About this verse, it is thus written: don't sow pearls among pigs nor sound doctrine among mocking fools.) TPMA *Schwein* 1.2.

167 Gloss: *Ille ales caeteris delicatior est, qui alios devorat: ita divites cultiores, qui suffocant minores.* (That bird is more luxurious than the others, who devours the others. So also are the more extravagant rich people, who suffocate the less fortunate.) TPMA *Vogel* 25.

168 Gloss: *Ubi est multitudo ministrorum, ibi minor proventus redit ad dominum.* (Where there is a multitude of ministers, there less revenue is rendered to the master.) The terms *ministri* and *dominus (Dominus)* might also be rendered "minsters" and "the Lord" (i.e., the proverb may be a criticism of priests). TPMA *Dienen* 9.9.5.

169 Gloss: *Qui, quod scit vel audierit, totum foras in vulgus efflaverit, inter consecretales non est admittendus amicos.* (The one who blabbers outdoors among the mob everything he knows or has heard must not be admitted among trusted friends.") See 1.247; TPMA *Wort* 17.3.

170 Gloss: *Caecus, qui male videt, male percutit; errat in verbere, qui non illustratur ex lumine.* (A blind man, who sees badly, strikes badly. That one errs in his blows, who is not illuminated by light.) TPMA *Schlagen* 17.

171 Gloss: *Ad votum raro crescet tibi faetura gregis alienis fota in tectis.* (The newborn who is raised under another's roof will rarely grow according to your wishes.) TPMA *Stall* 3.

172 Gloss: *Quae ad salutem hominum pascua deus donare voluerit, tollere non poterit unquam gelu aut nix.* (The pastures which God has chosen to give for the health of men, neither cold nor snow can ever take away.) TPMA *Schnee* 14.

173 Gloss: *Qui aliud cogitat, aliud dicit, errat in voce, quia dissipatur in corde.* (One who thinks one thing and says another, errs in his speech because he is dissipated in his heart.) TPMA *Verstehen* 1.

174 Gloss: *Ubi non est vigilans pastor, ibi lupus acervatim dilaniat agnos.* ("Where the shepherd is not vigilant, there the wolf tears apart the lambs in droves.") TPMA *Hirt* 4.

175 Gloss: *Inter duas sellas sessor aliquis, quod non speravit, in terram cadit.* (Anyone who sits between two stools, contrary to his expectation, falls to the ground.) TPMA *Stuhl* 4. *Sella* can mean "seat" or "stool"; but in the Middle Ages it also frequently meant "saddle."

176 Gloss: *Macris canibus et fame peremptis adprime non venaberis, quia nullus est in suis vigor medullis.* (With dogs that are skinny and exhausted from hunger you will not hunt very well because there is no vigor deep within them.) TPMA *Hund* 10.6.

177 Gloss: *Capus et accipiter ad vacuam manum non tam libenter convolant quam ad illam escis et carnibus plenam.* (A falcon and a hawk do not fly so happily to an empty hand as to one full of food and meat.) The word *auceps* normally means "bird catcher" (i.e., a person); here it is applied to a bird who is a hunter of other birds. TPMA *Hand* 11.1.

178 Gloss: *Colonus aliquis sub malo patrono diffidentiam habitandi habens casam, quae bene stabat, precipitat et ad dominos mitiores asportat.* (Under a bad landlord, any tenant farmer having a house difficult to live in, which used to be stable, wrecks it and moves to milder lords.) TPMA *Trauen* 1.3, *Zweifel* 1. My translation follows the interpretation in TPMA.

179 Gloss: *Nobilis aliquis dives, dum sua dilapidari non videt, minus dolet; quia si coram se fieret, tolerare non posset.* (Any rich nobleman, so long as he does not see that his property is becoming dilapidated, is less pained. I swear if it happened before his eyes, he could not bear it.) TPMA *Auge* 5.2. On *quia si,* see note to 1.56.

180 Gloss: *Piscis et avis ossa habent; rapum, quod est hortorum herba, unde holus conficitur, sine ossibus nascitur.* (A fish and a bird have bones. A turnip, which is a garden plant from which a vegetable dish is prepared, is born without bones.) TPMA *Rettich* 3.

181 Gloss: *Cadentibus stillis lapis cavatur, et utendo anulus minuitur.* (A stone is hollowed out by falling drops, and a ring is diminished by use.) Ovid, *Ex Ponto* 4.10.5; TPMA *Ring* 1.3, *Stein* 1.4.1.

182 Gloss: *Saxum, quod in aquis volvitur, muscum non colligit: et instabilis non ditabitur, qui sine cessatione de loco ad locum movetur.* (A rock which rolls in waters does not collect moss. And an unstable person, who endlessly moves from place to place, will not become rich.) TPMA *Stein* 4.

183 Gloss: *Utiliora sunt pecorum vicina et herbosa pascua longissimis a nobis adeo pratis.* (The neighboring and grassy pastures of the flocks are more useful than those meadows that are most distant from us.) TPMA *Wiese* 3. "Nearby reed," literally, "A reedy neighborhood."

184 Gloss: *Interdum dura resistunt aliquid resecantibus, cum penitus mollia minuuntur.* (For a time, hard things resist somewhat those things that are cutting them, while soft things are greatly reduced.) TPMA *Hart* 2.5.

185–86 Gloss: *Quotiens continua adversa nuntiantur, sicut de Iob legitur, hoc exemplo uti possumus.* (As often as constant adversities are announced to us, such as we read about in the case of Job, we can use this example.) TPMA *Gerücht* 1.2 *(50).*

187 Gloss: *Qui fidem sinceram non habet, nec ullo sacramento cohibetur.* (One who has no sincere faith will not be inhibited by any oath.) TPMA *Eid* 1.10.

188 Gloss: *Calvus est et frigoris et caloris impatiens.* (A bald man is vulnerable to both cold and heat.) TPMA *Kahl* 7.

189 Gloss: *Mus, cum vix foramen possit intrare, malleum sibi nectit in cauda.* (A mouse, although he is scarcely able to enter his hole, binds a mallet on his tail.) TPMA *Maus* 4.2; see 1.1213. The word *massa* here is equivalent to *matia* (mace, mallet, hammer); see Blaise Medieval, *matia.* The expression "to have a mace/mallet tied to the tail" is similar to our "millstone around the neck."

190 Gloss: *Veteris amici veterisque viae nunquam te immemorem fatias pro novis et incognitis.* (You should never make yourself forgetful of an old friend and an old road for the sake of those that are new and unknown.) TPMA *Freund* 5.8.3.

191–92 Gloss: *Quod lupus invaserit, nisi vi cogente invitus dimittit, et preda in fine non bene cantabit.* (What a wolf has attacked, he unwillingly gives up unless compelled by force; and his prey, in the end, will not sing well.) TPMA *Wolf* 8.1.

193 Gloss: *Ubi aurem lupi videris, comminus caudam esse scias: ita et perfidus amicus; qualem se in prima necessitate ostenderit, talem fore in secunda tibi poteris estimare.* (When you have seen the ear of the wolf, you may be sure his tail is nearby. So also a faithless friend: however he shows himself the first time you are in need, so you may judge he will be in the second instance.) TPMA *Wolf* 6.5.

194 Gloss: *Prius, si poteris, lupum debes arcere, quam caulas tuas possit irrumpere.* (If you can, you ought to fend off the wolf *before* he breaks into your sheepfolds.) TPMA *Wolf* 15.2.

195 Gloss: *Si quis de se ipso confidens iunioris se minas contempserit, illi dicere poterit: tantum te modo timeo minantem, quantum cum te natum non vidissem.* (If anyone, confident in himself, has despised the threats of one younger than himself, he might say, "I fear you now threatening me as much as I did back when I had not yet seen you born.") TPMA *Drohen* 4.

196 Gloss: *Sic de aliquo iracundo dicimus: cum aliquis plus quam opus sit irascitur, fel terrae et absintium vocamus ad comparationem herbarum amarissimarum.* (We speak thus about someone who is angry. When someone is more angry than is necessary, we call him "Gall of the earth" and "wormwood" by analogy with the most bitter herbs.) TPMA *Wermut 1.*

197 Gloss: *Hoc proverbium apud sapientes dicitur: Perdat agrum, qui non vult solvere censum.* (This proverb is spoken among wise men, "One who does not want to pay his tax may lose his field.") TPMA *Acker* 1.4.

198 Gloss: *Quanto altior gradus, tanto difficilior casus.* (The loftier the promotion, the more difficult the fall.) TPMA *Fall* 3.20.6.

199 Gloss: *Animi moderator expugnatore urbium fortior est.* (The one who controls his own spirit is stronger than the conqueror of cities.) TPMA *Herr* 14.1.

200 Gloss: *Quid mirum, si tu offendis in verbis, cum animal cadat, quod in quatuor pedibus stat?* (Why is it a wonder if you stumble in words,

when an animal, which stands on four feet, may fall?") TPMA *Fuss* 4.2. See 1.220.

201 Gloss: *Ad tua dampna male hospitem in parte domus suscipis, qui te postea de tota expellat.* (You err by receiving in part of your house, to your own detriment, a guest who afterward drives you from the whole thing.) TPMA *Schwelle* 3.

202 Gloss: *De multis verum videtur: quanto nobilior genere, tanto humilior actione.* (It seems to be true about many men: however much more noble they are by birth, so much the more humble they are in their behavior.) TPMA *Hals* 3.1.

203 Gloss: *Interdum pauperis utile consilium alicuius vincit regis ingenium.* (Sometimes the useful counsel of some poor man surpasses the ingenuity of a king.) Ecclesiastes 4:13; TPMA *Weise* 8.6.

204 Gloss: *Illum deum benignum dicimus, qui bona largitur ad manum.* (We call that god benign who distributes goods directly.) TPMA *Gott* 26.7.

205 Gloss: *De sana pelle raro putredo aut sanguis videtur exire.* (From healthy skin, rot or blood rarely seems to exit.) TPMA *Gesund* 1.1.2.

206 Gloss: *Qui sanum cum panno ligaverit digitum, item solutum inveniet sanum.* (Whoever has bound a healthy finger with a bandage, likewise will find it healthy when it is uncovered.) TPMA *Finger* 13.

207 Gloss: *Ironice dicitur de malo cantore, cuius vox inter fratres male discordat: Hic bene cantat.* (It is said ironically about a bad singer whose voice is badly discordant among the brothers, "*Here* he is singing well.") I take *hic* to be the adverb ("here, "at this time," or "in this place") rather than the demonstrative ("this"). The sense is, "[if you think this singing is bad] you should hear him on other occasions (or 'elsewhere')." TPMA *Mönch* 9.

208 Gloss: *De cocleare interdum cadit, quod ad os tuum sumendum porrigis.* (Sometimes what you are holding out to take in your mouth falls from the spoon.) TPMA *Mund* 16.2.

209 Gloss: *De insolito amico dicitur. "Volo" inquit inventus amicus, "iste insolens dicat, de qua terrarum parte adveniat."* (This is said of a

friend rarely encountered. "I want," says the friend he's come to visit "this rarely encountered friend to tell me from what part of the earth he comes.") TPMA *Kommen* 3.5.

210 Gloss: *Quod manus non rapiunt, in domo inventum parietes reddunt.* (Whatever hands do not steal, the walls return when it has been found in the house.) TPMA *Hand* 17. This is said when objects that were lost are later rediscovered.

211 Gloss: *Lector sive cantor, si in mendicitate fuerint positi, male legunt et nequius cantant.* (A reader or a singer, if they have been forced to beg, read badly and sing even more wretchedly.) TPMA *Singen* 1.1.

212 Gloss: *Musa mendicans facit inutile carmen. Epos utile carmen, inde epica pagina, id est laudabilis.* (A beggarly muse makes a worthless poem. An epic is a worthwhile poem, whence we have the expression "an epic page," that is, a laudable one.) TPMA *Singen* 1.1.

213 Gloss: *Eiusdem sensus est et iste versiculus.* (This verse also has the same meaning.) TPMA *Singen* 1.1. *Defrudat* is glossed *id est mutilat* (that is, mutilates.)

214 Gloss: *Waltherus monachus factus fratrum mandata inter hostes de non reddendis bracis custodit.* (Since Walter has been made a monk he observes the commands of his brothers regarding not giving up his breeches among enemies.) = 1.1717; see 1.1717–36. This story about Walter of Aquitaine, the hero of the Medieval Latin epic called *Waltharius,* is also recorded in the *Chronicon Novaliciense.* The sense is that one should turn the other cheek, but only up to a point. TPMA *Hose* 1.

215 Gloss: *Melius est homini, ut non sit natus, quam inter homines male nutritus.* (It is better for a man that he not have been born than that he be badly raised among men.) TPMA *Erziehen* 1.2.

216 Gloss: *Utilius est modesta sapientia aliquid inchoare et perficere quam repentina et inconsiderata fortitudine rem bene ceptam subvertere.* (It is more useful with measured wisdom to begin something and to complete it than to subvert by sudden and thoughtless power a thing that was well begun.) TPMA *Weise* 4.1.

217 Gloss: *Dum prandemus, nulla inutilia, sed honesta debemus et Deum*

decentia loqui. (While we dine, we should say no useless things, but those that are honest and befitting God.) TPMA *Tisch* 1.6.

218–19 Gloss: *Mos est puerorum insolitam rem et inauditam in pariete cum carbone notare, ut ibi sit novitatis signum, sicut olim adversa notabantur nigris lapillis et prospera albis.* (It is the custom of boys to mark on the wall with charcoal a thing that is uncommon and unheard of, so that there may be a sign of its novelty, just as they long ago marked adverse things with black stones and lucky things with white ones.) TPMA *Kohle* 12. See Pliny, *Hist. nat.* 7.40.41; Persius, *Satirae* 2.1; Martial, *Epigrammata* 9.52.4; Sedulius Scotus, *In Donati artem maiorem* (ed. B. Löfstedt *CCCM* 40B): 130.34.

220 Gloss: *Cadit equus, quamvis sit quatuor pedum, et contingit aliquando frangere collum.* (A horse falls down, even though he is a quadruped; and he happens sometimes to break his neck.) TPMA *Fuss* 4.2. See 1.200. *Asturco* is glossed *est equus ambulatorius* (it is a walking horse.)

221 Gloss: *Inaures ferreae fortes quidem sed pretiosae non sunt.* (Earrings made of iron are certainly strong, but they are not precious.) TPMA *Eisen* 9.

222–23 Gloss: *Qui vera loquitur, hoc proverbium illi congruit, ut Sybyllae similis dicatur aut Apollini, qui consulentibus semper vera responsa canebant.* (This proverb suits one who tells the truth, he may be said to be similar to the Sibyl or to Apollo, who always sang true responses to those consulting them.) Juvenal, *Satirae* 8.125–26.

224 Gloss: *In alta domo dei non aliud presbiter cantare poterit, quam quod scit et quod didicit.* (In a lofty cathedral of God, the priest cannot sing anything other than what he knows and what he has learned.) TPMA *Kirche* 3.

225 Gloss: *Iste versiculus se ipsum exponit.* (This verse is self-explanatory.) See 1.90; TPMA *Hund* 19.3.

226 Gloss: *Qui utile consilium dat et malum pro amore amici non laudat, ille sic dicat.* (One who gives good advice and does not praise evil out of love of his friend may speak thus.) TPMA *Honig* 4.5.3.

227 Gloss: *Hoc dicit vulgus: Frigidus implet horrea Maius.* (The people say, "A cold May fills the granaries.") TPMA *Mai* 1.

228 Gloss: *Qui in aquis morari vult, vitalis sibi comes erit, si quam navim*

secum habebit. (He who wishes to remain in the water, will have a vital companion if he has some sort of boat with him.) TPMA *Schiff* 10. *Ratis* is glossed *connexio trabium* (a joining of timbers.)

229 Gloss: *Furere incipit, cum malus servus equum ascendit.* (Craziness begins when an evil servant mounts a horse.) TPMA *Pferd* 14.2.

230 Gloss: *Numquam avis tam alte volat, quin aliquando ad terras descendat.* (A bird never flies so high that he does not descend at some point to the ground.) TPMA *Vogel* 2.1.

231 Gloss: *Mundus oculus omnia munda querit.* (A clean eye seeks everything clean.) TPMA *Salbe* 1.2.1.

232 Gloss: *Non ideo tacet bos et humano sermone non utitur, quod satis magnam non habeat linguam.* (The reason an ox is silent and does not use human speech is not that it does not have a large enough tongue.) TPMA *Rind* 1.1.

233 Gloss: *Cuius materiae sit et quam bene cocta et quo figulo compacta, ex testa deprehenditur olla.* (A jar is understood from a shard: of what material it is made, how well baked it is, and by what potter it was fashioned.) TPMA *Scherbe* 1.

234 Gloss: *Edacitas et pinguis venter extenuat sensum, ebrietas et luxuria mentis parant interitum.* (Gluttony and a fat stomach dull our senses; drunkenness and wantonness cause death of the mind.) TPMA *Essen* 5.10.1.

235 Gloss: *Qui non sapit et recti cordis intentionem non habet, cur inter fratres regiminis honorem querit?* (One who is not wise and does not have the intention of a good heart—why does he seek the honor of governing amongst his brothers?) TPMA *Ehre* 10.2.

236 Gloss: *Melior est digitus sanus quam oculus lippus.* (A healthy finger is better than a bleary eye.) Augustine, *Enarrationes in Psalmos* 130.8; TPMA *Finger* 16. *Prevertit* is glossed *antecedit* (surpasses.)

237 Gloss: *Sedulus dicitur a sedendo et opus aliquod utilitatis exercendo.* (A person is called sedulous from sitting and working at some useful task.) See 1.120. This proverb involves an etymological pun in Latin on *sedulus* (sedulous) and *sedere* (to sit). Sedulius Scotus, *In Donati artem maiorem,* 241.5: *sedulus dicitur assiduus studiosus et dicitur a sedendo quia qui bene studet diu sedet* (a sedulous person is one who is assiduously studious and it is derived from

sedendo [sitting] because one who studies well, sits for a long time.) *Curagulus* is glossed *id est curiosus* (that is, diligent.)

238 Gloss: *Non potest canis diu, quin devoret, bene olentibus cibis caltiatus incedere: ita devorator filius bona patris sibi relicta cito solet consumere.* (A dog with fragrant food for shoes cannot walk very long before he eats them; so also a wastrel son usually consumes the goods of his father that are left to him.) See J. Werner, *Lateinische Sprichwörter und Sinnsprüche des Mittelalters*[2] (1966) 86: *Si fortasse canis vestitur planta placenta, Tempore non longo durant sibi calciamenta.* (If a dog happens to be dressed in shoes made of cake, his sandals will not last long.) TPMA *Hund* 11.7.

239 Gloss: *Unusquisque canis acrior est in suo sterquilinio, quam sit in ignota domo.* (Each and every dog is more aggressive on his own dungheap than he is in an unknown house.) TPMA *Hund* 2.10.

240 Gloss: *Lupus numquam bene, nisi cum moritur, facit* [see Publilius Syrus, A.23]; *ideo suam nunquam pellem mutabit.* (A wolf never does anything good, except when he dies. For that reason, he will never change his skin.) TPMA *Wolf* 4.1.

241 Gloss: *Proprium nomen operatricis feminae; et cum omnia mundana transeant, etiam suorum operum nihil inconsumptum remansit.* (This is the proper name of a craftswoman. And since all earthly things pass away, also none of her works remained uncorrupted.) TPMA *Berta* 1.

242 Gloss: *Otiosae manus ad vellendum corpus tandem se vertunt, quia, quod aliud facerent, non didicerunt.* (Idle hands eventually turn themselves to tearing at the body because they have not learned anything else to do.): listed under TPMA *Kratzen* 3; but the sense of the gloss is much closer to TPMA *Hand* 7.3: *Otia palmarum faciunt dorsum scabiosum.* (Idle periods for the hands make the back rough.)

243 Gloss: *Rex, in quam partem voluerit, per vim legem convertit.* (A king, by force, makes the law face whatever direction he likes.) TPMA *König* 4.3.1.2.

244–45 Gloss: *Qui minorem non metuit, fortiorem offendit; quem quoque si sine metu transierit, utrisque in graviorem incurrit adversarium.* (One who did not fear a lesser adversary, meets a stronger one; if he also passes him by without fear, he runs into one more serious than either of the others.) TPMA *Bär* 4.4.2.

246 Gloss: *Quae possessio nostra non est, ad alterum dominum vel possessorem transibit.* (Whatever possession is not ours, it will pass to another lord or possessor.) TPMA *Eigen* 1.1.

247 Gloss: *Qui conmissa secreta tacere non poterit, minime carus erit.* (The one who cannot keep quiet about secrets entrusted to him, will be the least dear.) See 1.169; TPMA *Wort* 17.3.

248 Gloss: *Qui per simultatem iurat, non erit alienus a culpa, quem reatus dolositatis accusat.* (One who swears dishonestly will not be free from fault: the charge of fraud indicts him.) TPMA *Eid* 2.2.

249 Gloss: *Nullus unquam latronum in furcis penderet, si ipse sibi iudex existeret.* (None of the thieves would ever hang, if he were his own judge.) TPMA *Richten* 12.7.

250 Gloss: *Sunt plerique, qui multa bona pollicentur verbis, et factis non implent; hi figurate dicuntur albas apes promittere.* (There are many who promise many good things in word and do not fulfill them with deeds. These men are said figuratively to promise white bees.) TPMA *Versprechen* 8.2.

251 Gloss: *Aquila dixisse fertur ad aucam: "Ludimus iocum antiquum ad te nostrorum de more parentum."* (An eagle is reported to have said to a goose, "We play the old game for you, in the manner of our parents.") TPMA *Adler* 5.3.

252 Gloss: *Qui monitore indiget, de itinere malo, quod ceperat, ad melius quantotius sese convertat.* (One who lacks a guide, ought to turn himself from the bad path he has started on toward a better one as soon as possible.) Compare TPMA *Umkehren* 2, *Weg* 15.2 and 16.2; Horace, *Epistulae* 1.18.67; Juvenal, *Satirae* 1.60.

253 Gloss: *Vestis a carne calorem suscipit atque eum iterum corpori reddit.* (Clothing takes its warmth from the flesh and returns it again to the body.) TPMA *Kleid* 3.1.2.

254–55 Gloss: *Nostri maiores his, qui nunc sunt, et corpulentiores et melioris fidei fuerunt.* (Our elders were both larger and of better faith than these men who are here now.) Juvenal, *Satirae* 15.70; TPMA *Schlecht* 2.1.1.2.

256 Gloss: *Qui fuerit centum annorum, cum deliquerit et se per pueritiam

peccasse dixerit, ad maledictionem transibit, quia se non recte purgavit. (One who was one hundred years old when he sinned and said that he sinned through childishness will go to damnation because he did not purge himself properly.) See Isaiah 65:20. TPMA *Kind* 10.

257 Gloss: *Stultitia est hominis et summa vanitas ita per legem velle promissa expetere quasi debita ex propriis donis ante collata.* (It is the stupidity of man and the greatest nonsense to want to pursue promises in this way through the law as though they were debts previously conferred by personal gifts.) TPMA *Versprechen* 6.1.

258 Gloss: *Non est eadem mens puero minanti et asino onus portanti.* (The boy who is leading it and the ass who is carrying a load are not of one mind.) TPMA *Esel* 8.1.

259 Gloss: *Raro invenitur ulla infirmitas, cum qua se tussis non misceat: hic mos est discordantibus et bella tractantibus.* (Rarely is any infirmity found with which a cough has not joined itself. This is customary for those who are quarreling and conducting wars.) See 2.84; TPMA *Husten* 1.

260 Gloss: *Fama semper habet currere, nunquam quieta stare, sed ubique terrarum altas turres terrere.* (Rumor always has to run, never to stand still, but everywhere on earth to terrify high towers.) TPMA *Gerücht* 1.1.

261 Gloss: *Infrunitus est, qui nequit exsaturari, et cui nemo potest ad suffitientiam ventris ministrare.* (The insatiable man is one who is not able to be full and whose belly nobody is able to serve enough to satisfy.) TPMA *Narr* 8.7.

262 Gloss: *Qui moderate et cum mensura vivere non vult, cum bona parata defecerint, velit nolit cum dedecore vivet.* (One who does not wish to live moderately and with measure, when the goods that are available run out, whether he wishes it or not, will live dishonorably.) TPMA *Mass (Mässigkeit)* 3.9.

263 Gloss: *Hospitem, qui mane ad te venerit, et pluviam matutinam, horum neutra non sunt apud te diu mansura.* (The guest who comes to you in the morning and the morning rain—neither of them will remain with you for long.) TPMA *Morgen (Subst.)* 6.3.

264 Gloss: *De eodem folle particulam sumas, unde eius foramen resartias: de suo, non de alieno, debet quisquam sumere, qui vult debitoribus foenerata persolvere.* (You should take a piece from the same sack to mend the hole in it. It is from his own [money bag], not from another's, that every person ought to take if he wishes to pay to his debtors what was loaned at interest.) TPMA *Sack* 5.2.

265 Gloss: *Canis, quod sibi precipitur, caudae committit, unde datur intellegi: dum futili servo et pigro necessaria res a dominis fuerit commendata, nequiori se fatiendam tradit, et neuter eorum naviter explebit; de quorum factis hoc proverbium ad canem convertitur.* (A dog assigns to its tail whatever it is ordered to do. From this we may understand: when a necessary task has been assigned to a useless and lazy servant by his masters, the servant passes it along to be done by an even more worthless servant; and neither of them will complete the task diligently. From the actions of these servants, this proverb is transferred to a dog.) TPMA *Schwanz* 9.6.

266 Gloss: *Cum pauper factus fuerit dives, continuo ad avaritiam transit, metuens ne perdat ea, quae nimia tenacitate coartat.* (When a poor man has become rich, he immediately turns to avarice, fearing lest he lose those things that he clutches with excessive tenacity.) TPMA *Arm (Adj.)* 6.9.

267 Gloss: *Ille pannus erit latissimus, qui omnium ora, ne diversa loquantur, obstruxerit.* (It is a very broad cloth indeed that obstructs everyone's mouths, so that they cannot say various things.) TPMA *Mund* 17.2.2.

268 Gloss: *Sepius secretum, quod domi inter familiares loquimur, etiam foris incauti, dum non speramus, prorumpimus.* (Frequently, a secret which we talk about at home among our family members, we also blurt out thoughtlessly outside the house when we are not intending to.) TPMA *Haus* 5.3.3.

269 Gloss: *Qui patrem alterius occiderit, aliis bonis suis pacificet, quia eundem patrem vivum non reddet.* (One who has killed the father of another, will pacify that person with other things, because he cannot return the same father to him alive.) TPMA *Tod* 4.2.1.2.

270 Gloss: *Cum vas fuerit plenum, quod superinfundis, excedet.* (When a vase has been filled, whatever extra you pour into it, will overflow.) TPMA *Voll* 1.1.

271 Gloss: *Cum tibi gratis datur aliena pellis secanda, dum licet, largas incide corrigias, quia ex antiquo more minus alienis quam nostris est indulgere.* (When someone else's leather is given to you for cutting, while it is possible, cut large strips from it, because by ancient custom, it is less [damaging to us] to be profligate with another's property than with our own.) TPMA *Haut* 7.1.

272 Gloss: *Sunt multi, qui res bene gestas potius destruunt, quas reedificare non possunt.* (There are many people who prefer to destroy things well done, which they cannot rebuild.) TPMA *Brechen* 9.

273–74 Gloss: *Infirmitas carnis suspecta est magis quam ad vitam tendere ad interitum mortis. Longus languor proximam significat mortem.* (Infirmity of the flesh has been supposed rather to tend toward death than toward life. A long debility indicates that death is near.) TPMA *Krank* 1.2.1.

275 Gloss: *Unicuique carum sibi foret bono quo calleret ingenio, si se artifice polleret in uno.* (To each and every person, it would be a precious thing for him to be sharp-witted if it [sc. sharp-wittedness] flourished in him alone as the only trickster.) TPMA *List* 4. I follow the interpretation in TPMA, not in Voigt.

276 Gloss: *Divites pauperibus sua vendunt suffragia, pauper vero sua non vendit sed emit.* (Rich men sell their favors to the poor; but the poor man does not sell favors, rather he buys them.) TPMA *Verkaufen* 9.

277 Gloss: *Vicissitudo et mutatio fit omnium rerum.* (Vicissitude and change happen to all things.) TPMA *Ändern* 21.

278 Gloss: *Cum canis canem commederit, vicina inter eos rabies surgit.* (When dog eats dog, a similar rage surges between them.) TPMA *Hund* 2.25.

279 Gloss: *Album ponis in albo, cum ova posueris in farinis: ita fit, cum aliqua simillima iungis.* (You put white on white when you place eggs in flour. The same occurs when you join any very similar things.) TPMA *Weiss* 14.

280–81 Gloss: *Cum olim aliquis insaniret, fune ligatus post se funem trahebat, ut inde alii discerent, ab insano qua se ratione caverent. De cane est idem sensus.* (Long ago, when someone was insane, bound by a rope, he dragged the rope behind him so that from it others would learn to beware in some fashion of the insane person. The proverb about the dog has the same meaning.) TPMA *Narr* 13.5, *Hund* 16.3. *Signatur* is glossed *scilicet signum dat* (that is, it provides a sign.)

282 Gloss: *In curvo pedo, quod pastor portat in collo, intellegitur, quo vivat offitio.* (From the curved crook which the shepherd carries on his shoulder one understands by what trade he makes his living.) TPMA *Stock* 6. *Pastor* could be understood as "bishop" instead of "shepherd."

283 Gloss: *Peccatum ibi cessat, si quis pro eo poenam consequi timeat.* (Sin then ceases to occur, if someone fears that punishment will follow because of it.) TPMA *Strafe* 1.1.

284 Gloss: *Ubi fuerit humilitas, virtutum regina, ibi nulla deest sapientia.* (Where there is humility, the queen of the virtues, there no wisdom is lacking.) TPMA *Weise* 9.2.

285 Gloss: *Tempore necessitatis consilii nostri sepe querimus adiutorem, qui magis nocet quam iuvat.* (In a time of need, we often seek a counselor who harms more than he helps.) TPMA *Rat* 11.

286 Gloss: *Stultus, dum bene consulitur, ante dampna consultorem non audit; qui, postquam dampnatus fuerit, tunc vel invitus cedit.* (A fool, while he is being well counseled, does not listen to his counselor before he suffers harm. After he has been harmed, then, albeit unwillingly, he yields.) TPMA *Narr* 8.11.2.

287 Gloss: *Novum aliquid aut inutile in plaustro reliquis eius menbris quiescentibus inportune resonat: ita stultus in placito aliis silentium indicentibus solus vociferat et usque ad tedium clamat.* (Anything new or dysfunctional on a wagon creaks unpleasantly, while the remaining parts of it are silent. So also a fool in court proceedings, while others are enjoining silence, alone speaks and clamors tediously.) TPMA *Wagen (Subst.)* 6.1.

288 Gloss: *Cui prosperum omne bonum succedit, in conclavi suo securior dormit.* (One whom all good luck follows, sleeps more carefree in his chamber.) TPMA *Schlafen* 4.2.4.

289 Gloss: *Puerulus parum cesus diutius plorat.* (A small child, when beaten too little, cries for a longer time.) The sense is that a child not used to being punished cries louder (essentially: "spare the rod and spoil the child.") TPMA *Schlagen* 4.1.

290 Gloss: *Si sanctorum merita non quesieris, eorum suffagia fidutialiter non mereris.* (If you have not sought out the services of the saints, you do not rightfully deserve their aid.) TPMA *Heilig* 26.

291 Gloss: *Studium suum perdit, qui in asino quasi in equo currere velit.* (One who wants to race on an ass as though on a horse is wasting his effort.) TPMA *Esel* 7.1.

292 Gloss: *Fatuus, quod cogitat, semper verum putat.* (A simpleton always imagines that whatever he thinks is true.) TPMA *Narr* 6.7.

293 Gloss: *Qui habet habundantiam piperis, si voluerit, etiam cum pultibus miscebit.* (One who has plenty of pepper will mix it even with his gruel if he feels like it.) TPMA *Pfeffer* 3.

294–95 Gloss: *Qui rixas odit, aliis tumultuantibus prohibebit; et qui eas amat, alios, ut itidem faciant, provocat.* (One who hates brawls, will stop them when others are raising a tumult. And one who loves them, provokes others to do the same.) See 1.775–76; TPMA *Kampf* 3.4.3, *Zorn* 1.7.1.

296 Gloss: *Si in flumine fueris tempestate surgente, quantotius navim ad littora coge.* (If you are in a river when a storm is rising, steer your boat toward shore as quickly as possible.) TPMA *Ufer* 3.

297–98 Gloss: *Longi servitii mercede non persoluta hoc versiculo potest uti; et si debitor non dat, deus omnium bonorum redditor ipse persolvat.* (When a reward for long service has not been paid, this verse can be used. And if the debtor does not give, God himself, the remunerator of all good men, may pay.) Juvenal, *Satirae* 3.124; TPMA *Dienen* 5.5.

299 Gloss: *Virgo postquam lapsa fuerit, virgo esse non poterit.* (After a virgin has fallen, she cannot be a virgin.) TPMA *Jungfrau* 2.2.

300 Gloss: *Si defitiunt, qui tecum iurent, preterea te propinqui non deserant.* (If your oath helpers abandon you, your relatives should not desert you as well.) TPMA *Eid* 1.9.

301 Gloss: *Haec est superflua vanitas quenquam hominem sublimiorem*

se estimare, quam possit evincere. (This is excessive vanity that any man consider himself more sublime than he can demonstrate that he is.) TPMA *Sein* 7.4.

302 Gloss: *Qui perditos gemit oculos, non gemitus effundit vacuos.* (One who bemoans that his eyes have been lost, is not pouring out meaningless moans.) TPMA *Auge* 1.2.

303 Gloss: *Non bene heret in vasculo pix, quae funditur in umido.* (Pitch does not stick well if it is poured on a wet vase.) TPMA *Pech* 2.

304 Gloss: *Canibus conparantur cinici, luxuriosis cinedi.* (Cynics are compared to dogs; *cinaedi* to wanton people.). This proverb not only teaches the meaning of these two Latin terms with similar looking roots (that is, in the medieval spelling, the root of each word, *cin-*, looks identical, although the Greek roots are not the same), but also exemplifies the idea expressed in our proverbs "You can't tell a book by its cover," "Things are not always what they seem." Things that seem similar on the outside can be entirely different inside. In this case, the two terms that appear to be related, have diametrically opposed meanings (here "hard/harsh" and "soft"; or, alternatively, "frugal" and "luxurious"). See 1.322, 1.341–43, 1.364–66, etc. *Cinici* is glossed *cinici parci vel canini* (*cinici* are chary or canine); *cinedi* is glossed *cinedi molles et effeminati* (*cinedi* are soft and effeminate).

305 Gloss: *Paucis egent, qui parce vivere volunt, et pluribus indigent, qui perplura desiderant.* (Those who want to live parsimoniously, lack few things; those who desire many things, lack many.) Boethius, *De consolatione philosophiae* 2.5.63; TPMA *Arm (Adj.)* 6.1.

306 Gloss: *Ad paupertatem cito se potest perducere, qui incessanter vino voluerit estuare.* (One who constantly seeks to be inflamed by wine is able to reduce himself quickly to poverty.) TPMA *Wein* 1.13.2.

307 Gloss: *Ignavus, qui non vult operari, continue servit mendicitati.* (A lazy person, who does not want to work, is constantly a slave to poverty.) TPMA *Faul* 3.1.

308 Gloss: *Cum tuba ad bellum perstrepat, si non miles antea peniteat, ibi seram penitentiam inchoat.* (When the trumpet sounds for the

battle, if a soldier has not repented beforehand, he begins his penitence too late at that point.) Juvenal, *Satirae* 1.168–70; TPMA *Trompete* 1.

309 Gloss: *Cum in expeditione exercitus annum continuet, non omnis incolumis revertitur, nisi ibi aliquis moriatur.* (When an army spends a year on campaign, not everyone returns safe, but some die on it.) TPMA *Heer* 2; see 1.839–40.

310 Gloss: *In divitis domo aluntur servi superbi.* (In the home of a rich man, haughty servants are nourished.) TPMA *Haus* 4.5.1.

311 Gloss: *Laudo calvum, sed non eum in toto capite depilatum.* (I praise a bald man, but not the one whose entire head is depilated.) TPMA *Kahl* 7.

312–13 Gloss: *Magnum decus est eum a servitute liberum, ubi caput est generosum; ignavus et obscure natus ille potius est servitio obprimendus.* (It is a great glory that one be free from servitude when the person [concerned] is noble; the one who is a coward and obscurely born ought rather to be oppressed by servitude.) TPMA *Frei* 4.7.

314 Gloss: *Sarcina ulcerat equum retro in lumbis, antea sessor in armis: ita contingit pauperi, cui nusquam est bene.* (The pack wounds the rear of the horse in its loins, the rider wounds him up front on his shoulders. So it goes for the poor man, for whom it does not go well anywhere.) Horace, *Sermones* 1.6.105–6.

315 Gloss: *Violentus et legis effractor omnibus subditis negata iustitia facit iniuriam.* (A violent man and breaker of the law causes injury to all his subjects when justice has been denied.) TPMA *Gewalt* 8.1.

316 Gloss: *Quandiu putredo fuerit intus, non sanabitur corpus; qua eiecta convalescet infirmus.* (As long as rot is within, the body will not become healthy; when it has been ejected, the sick man convalesces.) TPMA *Wunde* 4.3.4.

317 Gloss: *Non est recti consilii in omni negotio, dum res prepostera velit esse prima.* (It is not a good plan in any business when the later thing wants to be first.) TPMA *Wagen (Subst.)* 4.5.

318 Gloss: *De una filia non debes tibi duos generos parare: ita de re uni homini promissa non debes alteri suspitionem dare.* (From a single daughter you should not get yourself two sons-in-law. Likewise,

concerning a thing promised to one man you should not give hope [of acquiring it] to another.) TPMA *Schwiegersohn* 1.

319 Gloss: *Qui suam habet uxorem, eius postea non poterit habere sororem.* (One who has a wife, will not afterward be able to have her sister.) Mark 6:18. There is an additional gloss in the manuscript on this line: *Glos, gloris est soror uxoris* (*Glos* means the sister of your wife.). This interpretation of *glos,* however, is not attested elsewhere; *glos* normally means the wife of your brother.

320 Gloss: *Quis potest scire vias hyrundinis in hoc aere tota die volantis?* (Who can know the paths of the swallow flying in the air all day long?) TPMA *Schwalbe* 5, *Weg* 11.2.

321 Gloss: *Tria sunt, quae sulcantur: aer, aqua et terra; sulcis vero in duobus elementis cito clausis terra suum non claudit.* (There are three things that can be furrowed: air, water, and earth. But while the furrows in two of these elements are swiftly closed up, the earth does not close up its furrow.) TPMA *Weg* 11.2.

322 Gloss: *Glosae sunt.* (These are glosses.) The point is, "words that look alike, have different meanings"; see the note on 1.304. *Lens, lendis* is glossed *vermiculus in capite* (a little worm on the head.)

323 Gloss: *Convivae suo debet in necessitate succurrere, qui suis epulis vult continuus interesse.* (One who wants to continue taking part in his meals, ought to aid his host when he is in need.) TPMA *Tisch* 4. For *conviva* = "host," see Blaise Medieval. *Plagarum* is glossed *plaga quando vulnus significat, longa; quando partem mundi, brevis* (when *plaga* means "wound" [the first syllable is] long; when it means "part of the world" [it is] short).

324 Gloss: *Idem sensus est iste versiculus.* (This verse has the same meaning [as the preceding one].) TPMA *Tisch* 4.

325 Gloss: *Rana turpem profert sonum sed carmen nullum mellitum.* (A frog produces an ugly sound, but no sweet song.) TPMA *Frosch* 1.3.

326 There is no marginal gloss on this line. The phrase *hac tempestate* (in this life) has an interlinear gloss: *in tempore sibi concesso* (in the time allotted them). Voigt joins this verse to the previous one. TPMA *Frosch* 1.3. The sense is "ugly" people complain all the time.

327 Gloss: *In monasterio fratrum pueris bene legentibus et cantantibus inponitur iugum pro his, qui ita non possunt; utiles vocamus vitulos, minus capaces asellos.* (In a monastery of brothers, a yoke is placed on the boys who read and sing well because of those who cannot do so. We call the useful ones "the little bulls"; the less capable ones, "little asses.") The point seems to be that the boys who sing well have to carry those who don't (who only mouth the words, so as not to destroy the harmony). TPMA *Rind* 25.5.

328 Gloss: *Quoties fratribus digna stipendia non dantur, monitori eorum pretium aliquod impenditur, ut taceat: quod vocatur os in gulam proiectum, et cunctis fratribus venit ad dampnum.* (Whenever the proper stipends are not given to the brothers, some bribe is paid to their overseer, so that he keep quiet: this is called "a bone tossed in the throat," and it is harmful to all the brothers.) TPMA *Knochen* 3.4.

329 Gloss: *Propter iniustam mercedem non clamat prelatus ad fratrum utilitatem.* (The guardian does not clamor for the benefit of the brothers on account of an unjust payment.) Compare TPMA *Hund* 13.5: "A dog can be appeased with a bone and be made quiet." Voigt joins this to the preceding verse. The formatting of the glosses indicates they are separate verses, though the import is certainly similar.

330 Gloss: *Ibi non decet anulus, ubi est unguis et digitus sordidus.* (A ring doesn't look good on a dirty finger and fingernail.) TPMA *Ring* 1.

331 Gloss: *Bonum est prius abstinere a vitiis, qui vult pro deo abstinere ab escis.* (It is good to abstain first from vices, for the one who wants to abstain for God's sake from food.) TPMA *Fleisch* 2.7.

332 Gloss: *Cum omnia bona confluant vobis, necesse est, ut ad nos corporis necessaria vel minima profluant.* (Since all good things are pouring out for you, it is necessary that at least the minimal necessities of the body trickle down to us.) TPMA *Regen* 9.2.

333 Gloss: *Qui iuxta viatorum tramitem edificat, multos habet magistros, qui sic aut sic facere dictent.* (One who builds near a pathway that has traffic, has many masters who will tell him to do this or that.) TPMA *Weg* 13.

334 Gloss: *Qui se vera dixisse fatetur, illi ironice obicimus "ideo te rex, ut*

solus vera loquereris, reliquit." (At one who claims that he has spoken the truth we ironically throw out this proverb: "That's why the king left you here, so that you alone can speak the truth.") This saying does not seem to be attested elsewhere.

335 Gloss: *In circino formamus circulos, et modo quo hic dicitur, a puncto usque ad punctum.* (With a compass we form circles, and in the way that it is described here: from one point to another point.) See 1.1541. The sense of the proverb seems to be that some things are accomplished little by little, through skill, effort, proper tools, etc.

336–37 Gloss: *Multi volunt strenue vivere, sed nullum laborem subire. Nam et cattus est adeo superbus, qui suos per se non queritat victus.* (Many people wish to live busily, but undertake no work. A cat is excessively proud who does not seek his food for himself.) TPMA *Katze* 9.1. Voigt joins this pair to the following verse.

338 Gloss: *Licet farinam arbitreris, interdum aliud habetur in arca vel urna.* (Although you may think it is flour, sometimes something else is held in the box or jar.) TPMA *Mehl* 6. This is a version of the proverb about a lazy (or old, or clever) cat (or weasel) covering itself with flour and hiding in the flour jar in order to get the mice to come to him.

339 Gloss: *Infans a matre ova rogitat; dum modo sibi dentur, unde habeantur, non curat.* (An infant asks his mother for eggs. So long as they are given to him, he does not care whence they are gotten.) TPMA *Kind* 5.6.

340 Gloss: *Ex deformi matre et inhonesta non nascitur venustus et nobilis infans.* (From an ugly and dishonorable mother, a beautiful and noble child is not born.) TPMA *Affe* 1.9.

341–44 On these verses, compare the note to 1.304. The present verses are further examples of words that look as though they ought to mean something other than what they do mean (*optio, -onis,* m., "soldier," looks like *optio, -onis,* f., "option"; *uclupa, -ae,* f., "ridge," looks like it might be related to *lupa, -ae,* f., "wolf"; *vopiscus, -i,* m., "surviving twin,"—especially if it were in the accusative case—looks as though it could be related to *vobiscum,* particularly since in Medieval Latin *b* and *p* are frequently interchanged.)

341 Gloss: *Iste versiculus glosa est.* (This verse is a gloss.) Isidore, *Etymologiae* 9.3.41, 9.5.21.

342 The otherwise unrecorded Latin word *uclupa* (which is written over an erasure in the MS) has an interlinear gloss: *ferest. eminentior pars domus* (top/ridge, upper part of a house.) See Paris, "Review," 560n2.

343 Gloss: *Vopiscus dicitur filius, qui est cum altero geminus et illo aborto vivus nascitur* (A son who is the twin to another and who, after that other one has been aborted, is born alive is called a "surviving twin.") *Penes* is glossed *id est apud te* (that is, within yourself.)

344 Gloss: *Velites sunt pedites, qui in auxilio equitum ad bellum vadunt.* (*Velites* are foot soldiers, who stride into battle in aid of the knights.) TPMA *Ritter* 1.12.

345 Gloss: *Milvus ex antiquo more furtivus de pullis gallinae semper suos consuevit nutrire.* (The kite, a thief by ancient custom, has always had the habit of feeding its own chicks on the chicks of a hen.) TPMA *Falke* 16.

346 Gloss: *Quis sapiens emet pecuniam quam non videt et in sacco reclusam?* (What intelligent person will buy money which he cannot see and which is sealed up in a bag?) TPMA *Sack* 13.5.2.2.

347 Gloss: *Mures ad saccum mendici liberius currunt, quem sub sera positum non inveniunt.* (Mice more happily run to the money bag of a beggar, which they do not find put under lock and key.) TPMA *Maus* 5.2.

348 Gloss: *Vatrax est aranea tortis cruribus nata, et hic propter glosam posita.* (A vatrax is a spider born with twisted legs; and it is put here as a gloss.). See the note on 1.304. *Ede* is glossed *scilicet dic* (that is, tell); *vatrax* is glossed *tortis pedibus* (with twisted legs).

349 See the note on 1.304. *Cymex (cimex)* is glossed *vermis in pariete* (a worm in the wall), *exiguus mus* is glossed *vocativus* (vocative case), and *capronus* is glossed *capite pronus* (hanging/drooping from the head). Voigt joins this verse to the preceding and interprets both of them as admonitions to students ("little mouse" being, in his view, a term of endearment used of young students). Horace (*Sermones* 1.10.78) uses *cimex* (bug) as a term of reproach, parallel to English "louse." Isidore (*Etymologiae* 12.5.13) lists *cimex* under

"worms of the flesh." Voigt takes *capronus* as a reference to the students having their heads bent over a book, studying intently.

350 Gloss: *Resolutio glosarum.* (Explication of glosses.) TPMA *Kleie* 4.

351 Gloss: *Ve illis, qui usque ad obitum suum luxuriose vivunt.* (Woe to those who live wantonly until they die.) TPMA *Wollust* 1.2.

352 Gloss: *Dando et recipiendo mater et filia inter se fiunt amicae.* (By giving and receiving, a mother and daughter become friends with one another.) TPMA *Geben* 2.8.2.

353 There is no marginal gloss on this line, but an interlinear gloss on *dosinus* reads: *frequentior color iste invenitur in asinis.* (this color is rather frequently found in asses.) TPMA *Esel* 11.2.

354 Gloss: *Catarrum est morbus narium; unde qui hunc dolorem patitur vix anhelat et magnum impedimentum sustinet.* (Catarrh is a nose disease. Hence, one who suffers from this discomfort is scarcely able to breathe and sustains a great obstruction.)

355 Gloss: *Aviarium est, ubi aves nutriuntur, et hoc maxime in silvis agitur.* (An aviary is where birds are raised, and this especially is done in the woods.) TPMA *Vogel* 14.

356 Gloss: *Multi festinant ad infamiam vitae suae uti pisces ad nimias aquas.* (Many people rush toward disgrace in their lives like fish to abundant water.) Juvenal, *Satirae* 3.308; TPMA *Eile* 8.

357 Gloss: *Hinc solet secundus maritus irasci, si qua mulier virum laudat priorem.* (A second husband generally gets angry if any wife praises her prior husband.) TPMA *Mann* 10.

358 Gloss: *Si quis equorum faleras super scrofam posuerit, cito cum eis ad volutabrum transire videbit.* (If someone places the armor of horses on a sow, he will soon see her go with them to wallow.) TPMA *Schwein* 3.2.

359 Gloss: *Ligneus canis nec poterit nec bene ridebit: ita vir umbrosus raro videbitur letus.* (A wooden dog cannot and will not laugh well. Likewise, a gloomy man is rarely seen happy.) TPMA *Lachen* 1.

360 Gloss: *Filix et reliqua frutecta uberius surgunt quam boni fructus, pro quibus incessanter laboramus.* (The fern and other briars surge up more abundantly than the good produce for which we incessantly labor.) Horace, *Sermones* 1.3.37; TPMA *Acker* 4.2.3.

361 Gloss: *De femina, quae luxuriae causa per plateas circumvolat vaga-*

bunda. (Concerning a woman who for the sake of wantonness flits around through the public squares as a tramp.) TPMA *Hure* 4.1.

362 Gloss: *De amico iam ex longo tempore non viso, quo suscipitur gaudio.* (Concerning a friend not seen for a long time now and the joy with which he is received.) TPMA *Arm (Subst.)* 6.

363 Gloss: *Aranea cito tabescit, si quis eam vel facillimo tactu contigerit.* (A spider's web quickly disintegrates if someone touches it even lightly.) TPMA *Spinne* 4.1.

364–66 Gloss: *Magister qui fueris, dic famulis tuis distantiam inter* cio, cis *et* cieo, cies, *et in similibus multis, quid inter* candidum *et* album, *inter* alterum *et* alium, *ut eos fatias regulares.* (You who are a teacher, tell your charges the difference between *"cio, cis"* and *"cieo, cies"*; and in many similar instances, what the difference is between *candidus* (whitened) and *albus* (white), between *alter* (the other) and *alius* (another), so that you may make them instructed according to rules.) See the note on 1.304.

364 The same distinction between *cio* and *cieo* (not made by modern Latin dictionaries) is found in the *Orthographia Bernensis,* vol. 2, ed. H. Hagen, *Grammatici Latini, Suppl.* (Teubner, 1870): 296.

365 The second example, *candidus* and *albus,* is somewhat different from the other two. The words do not look alike, rather they both describe something which looks as if it is the same thing, but which is not entirely identical. The same distinction is made by Alcuin, *Orthographia* (ed. H. Keil, *Grammatici Latini* 7: 296.23), and in many other grammatical works: *Album natura, candidum cura facit* (Nature makes a thing white, effort makes it whitened.)

366 A definition commonly found in grammatical works, e.g., *Differentiae sermonum,* ed. Hagen, *Grammatici Latini, Suppl.* 279.

367 Gloss: *Omnes aves non sunt accipitres, et omnes homines non continuo milites, et clerici non equaliter sapientes.* (All birds are not hawks, and all men are not automatically soldiers, and all clerics are not equally wise.) TPMA *Vogel* 13, *Gelehrt* 2.1.

368 Gloss: *Coclear ex pane utendo consumitur: sic omnis res frequenti usu minuitur.* (A spoon made out of bread is consumed by use. Like-

wise everything is diminished by frequent use.) TPMA *Löffel* 7. See Maaz, "Brotlöffel," 108–10.

369 Gloss: *Illi, qui litteras aut syllabas mutilando pronuntiant, intellectum auditoribus suis non prestant.* (Those who pronounce letters or syllables in a mutilated fashion, do not provide understanding to their listeners.) TPMA *Kohle* 8.

370 There is no gloss on this line. Voigt joins it to the preceding verse. See Ovid, *Metamorphoses* 10.653–55. Compare TPMA *Wind* 9.8: "Lighter than the wind."

371 Gloss: *Multa dicuntur et fiunt, quae melius esset nescire quam scire.* (Many things are said and done which it would be better not to know about than to know about.) TPMA *Wissen* 2.17.2.

372 Gloss: *Omnis culpa plus nocet fatienti quam audienti et patienti.* (Every crime harms the one doing it more than the one hearing it or suffering from it.) TPMA *Dulden* 1.3.2.3, *Sünde* 3.3.2.

373 Gloss: *Qui tirannidem suam aut immitem potestatem contra subiectos exercent: si enim, quam cito transit, adverterent, non utique inchoarent.* (Those who exercise their tyranny or unbridled power against their subjects—surely if they recognized how quickly it passes away, they would never start.) TPMA *Gewalt* 9.

374 Gloss: *Bos non ideo tacet, quod linguae satis non habeat: sic et boni plurima propter pudorem conticescunt, quae inutilia sciunt.* (An ox is not silent because he does not have enough of a tongue. Likewise also good men are silent about many things, which they know to be harmful, out of modesty.) TPMA *Rind* 1.1.

375 Gloss: *Mos est convivarum dicere, cum invitatus ad prandium venire non vult, "Bonus annus nobis veniat, si amicus venire recusat."* (It is the custom of diners, if someone has been invited to a meal he does not wish to attend, to say, "A good year will come, if a friend refuses to come.") TPMA *Einladen* 4.

376 Gloss: *Vulteius eligans [sc. elegans] iuvenis ab urbe Roma ad villam, ut ibi moraretur, transivit, et cum ibi ditaretur multis peculiis, villam prefecit urbi; sed cum non multo post oves et pecora clade perirent, cepit villam odisse et urbem preferre et ad eam quantotius redire. Namque de eo ibi est longa ratio, hic brevibus verbis est conprehensa.* (Vulteius, an

elegant young man, moved from the city of Rome to a villa, in order to live there. And when he was flourishing there with a great many cattle, he preferred the villa to the City. But when not much later his sheep and cattle died from a disease, he began to hate the villa, and to prefer the City, and to return to it as quickly as he could. There is a long account of him there [sc. in Horace, *Epistulae* 1.7]; here it is summarized in a few words.) The long account is in Horace, *Epistulae* 1.7.55–95.

377 Gloss: *Melius est dare quam accipere.* (It is better to give than to receive.) Acts of the Apostles 20:35; TPMA *Geben* 10.2. See 1.559.

378 Gloss: *Quanto propius ad ignem accesseris, tanto magis ustionem senties.* (The closer you get to the fire, so much the more you will feel its burning.) TPMA *Feuer* 1.2.

379 Gloss: *Lignum, ubicumque ceciderit, ibi erit: lignum pro homine ponitur, qui, qualis in fine fuerit inventus, sive bonus sive malus, tale habebit premium et eum non mutabit locum.* (Wood, wherever it will have fallen, will remain there. "Wood" is a metaphor for "man," who, however he is found to be at the end [of his life], whether good or bad, so he will be rewarded. And he will not be able to change his place.) Ecclesiastes 11:3; TPMA *Baum* 9.7.

380 Gloss: *Minae nostrae et superbia nostra, quam hic exercemus, cum morimur, ad nichilum redigitur, et qualis haec potestas nostra sit, ostendetur.* (Our threats and our haughtiness, which we exercise here, when we die, are rendered nothing; and what this power of ours is like will be revealed.) "Flower of grass:" see Psalms 102:15; Isaiah 40:6; 1 Peter 1:24; TPMA *Heu* 3.2.

381 Gloss: *Qui cum cocleare pulmenta non levat, os suum fatigat.* (One who has no food on the spoon he raises to his mouth, torments his mouth.) TPMA *Trügen* 19.

382 Gloss: *Qui didicit a pueritia, spes est, cum quesieris, in eo aliquam reperire scientiam.* (One who has learned from childhood—there is hope of finding some wisdom in him, when you look for it.) TPMA *Wasser* 1.

383 Gloss: *Qui stultum docueris, odium tibi potius quam amorem inpendet.* (You who have taught a fool, will earn hatred rather than love.) TPMA *Erziehen* 2.4.1.

384 Gloss: *Familia domus obliviscitur ignem struere, cum coeperit manducare, et ideo dicitur ignem ibi non esse sed ad vicinos transisse.* (The household staff forgets to keep the fire going when it has begun to eat, and so it is said that the fire does not remain there but has gone to the neighbors.) TPMA *Feuer* 15.

385 Gloss: *Puer quilibet et docendus est et ammonendus in tenella aetate, ut discat necessaria, quod iam concretus non potest facere, si velis tum temporis constringere.* (Every boy must be taught and admonished at a tender age so that he learn the necessary things. He cannot do that once he is formed, even if, at that time, you wish to force him.) TPMA *Eisen* 3.1.

386 Gloss: *Male vestitis frigora sunt noxia, sed magis semper illa matutina.* (Cold is harmful to those who are badly clothed, but the morning cold is always more harmful.) Horace, *Sermones* 2.6.45; TPMA *Kalt* 3.2, *Kleid* 3.1.1.

387 Gloss: *Hi, qui plus habent, non debent a minoribus supplementum querere.* (Those who have more should not seek a supplement from the poorer people.) TPMA *Wolle* 1.1.2.2.

388 Gloss: *Dum id scire querimus, quod magis officit quam prosit, plus quam opus sit scimus, cum tantum modo bona scire debeamus.* (When we seek to know a thing which harms us more than it helps, we are learning more than is useful, since we ought to learn only good things.") Romans 12:3; TPMA *Wissen* 3.1. The proverb might be rendered in different ways (e.g., "It is the better part of wisdom to know [what is] bad"); my translation follows the interpretation of the line given in the gloss.

389 Gloss: *Sunt quidam, qui ad onera ferenda aptiores inveniuntur.* (There are certain people who are found to be more suited for carrying loads.) Juvenal, *Satirae* 3.251–52; compare TPMA *Last* 7.1: "The burden should correspond to one's strength and not be excessive." "Has a name," the etymology of Corbulo's name, is said to be from *corbis* (basket), but "has a name" also means "earned his fame," from his ability to carry a great load.

390 Gloss: *Filius stultus oneri est patri et dolor matris, quae genuit eum.* (A stupid son is a burden to the father and a pain to the mother who bore him.) Proverbs 17:25; compare TPMA *Eltern* 3.

391 Gloss: *Omnem puerum, qui invitus discit, nulla eum scola iuvare poterit.* (No school will help any boy who is unwilling to learn.) TPMA *Schüler* 3.3.

392–93 Gloss: *Ad viles pelles et teneriores luterum preparamus, fibrum ad honestiores.* (We prepare an otter for inexpensive and thin hides, for more noble ones, we prepare a beaver.) The otter's fur is used as a trim on inexpensive garments; the beaver's fur is used in more costly garments.

394 Gloss: *Raro latent vultures cadavera regionum et gluttones prandia seniorum.* (The carrion in a region is rarely unknown to the vultures, and the feasts of the nobles are rarely unknown to the gluttons.) TPMA *Aas* 1.2.1.

395 Gloss: *Nunquam de his bene loquimur, quibus nulla prospera optamus.* (We never speak well about those for whom we wish no prosperity.) TPMA *Liebe* 1.4.8.2.5. *Euge* is glossed *vox salutantis* (a word of a well-wisher.)

396–97 Gloss: *Quaelibet mulier inde cariorum habet filium, qui patrem habuerit vivum.* (Every woman holds her son more dearly on this account, that he has a father who is still living.) TPMA *Mutter* 6.

398 Gloss: *Qui aliter vivit quam predicat, restat ut eius predicatio contempnatur.* (One who lives otherwise than he preaches, it is inevitable that his preaching be despised.) TPMA *Hören* 11; compare *Predigen* 2.4. *Previus* is glossed *anterior* (before); *veretur* is glossed *timet* (fears).

399–400 Gloss: *Omnia superflua nocent, quod illi videntur sequi, qui longiora necessitate traxerint vestimenta.* (All excessive things are harmful. Which is what they seem to be pursuing, those people who trail unnecessarily long clothing.) TPMA *Mönch* 1.2. *Syrmata* is glossed *syrma extrema pars vestis* (syrma is the train of a piece of clothing.)

401 Gloss: *Qui moderate bibit, aliquo modo compos est mentis; qui multum, concitat lites.* (One who drinks moderately, is sound of mind in some measure. The one who drinks a lot, stirs up quarrels.) TPMA *Gefäss* 13.7.

402–3 1 Kings 10:10–12; TPMA *Saul* 4. From this point onward, the manuscript does not have glosses for each line, but there are, occasionally, interlinear glosses of a word or two.

404 TPMA *Hochmut* 2.5.

405 Psalms 9:23.

406 Psalms 36:16; TPMA *Wenig* 1.3.1.2.1.

407 TPMA *Lob* 10.

408–9 Tobit 12:7.

410 Ecclesiasticus 21:19.

411 Proverbs 19:5.

412–13 TPMA *Geben* 3.3.

414 TPMA *Faul* 1.6.

415 TPMA *Rauch* 1.6.

416 TPMA *Fisch* 2.1.

417 *Disticha Catonis* 1.18; TPMA *Glück* 15.9.

418 Proverbs 9:8; TPMA *Narr* 8.6.2.

419 TPMA *Gut (Adj.)* 4.3.1.

420 Gregory the Great, *Moralia* 3.9; TPMA *Gift* 2.1.1.

421 TPMA *Viel* 5.2.1.

422 TPMA *Verbergen* 7.5.

423 2 Corinthians 9:7; TPMA *Geben* 5.2.

424 TPMA *Schimmlig* 1.

425 Proverbs 1:17; TPMA *Vogel* 6.1.

426 Proverbs 3:9.

427 Proverbs 3:28; TPMA *Freund* 3.10.3.

428 TPMA *Fall* 3.20.4.

429 Proverbs 5:9; TPMA *Ehre* 15.

430 Proverbs 8:11; TPMA *Weise* 5.2.

431–32 Proverbs 10:8, 10:14; Ecclesiastes 21:18–23; TPMA *Weise* 13.7.2.

433 Proverbs 10:19; TPMA *Wort* 13.8.

434 TPMA *Almosen* 2.2. The manuscript reads *honustus;* Voigt altered this to *onustus.* I have returned to the manuscript spelling, which highlights the pun on *honor* and *honustus.* On *honor* = alms, see Voigt, *ad loc.*

435–36 Proverbs 10:27; TPMA *Gott* 32.8.

437 Proverbs 11:28; TPMA *Reich* 4.1.

438 Proverbs 13:24; TPMA *Rute* 2.

439 Proverbs 16:1; TPMA *Gott* 15.1.

440 Proverbs 18:21; TPMA *Zunge* 4.1.

441 Proverbs 19:14; compare TPMA *Frau* 3.1.2.

442 Proverbs 17:10; TPMA *Schlagen* 24.

443 Proverbs 31:31.

444 TPMA *Reich* 5.2.3.

445 TPMA *Brot* 7.2.

446 TPMA *Regen* 11.

447 Ecclesiasticus 20:26.

448 TPMA *Sarg* 1.

449 TPMA *Teufel* 7.10. *Talliolas* is glossed *ligationes pedum* (bindings of the feet). On *taliola* = "little snare," see Blaise Medieval.

450 TPMA *Hermelin* 1.

451 Proverbs 25:27; TPMA *Honig* 2.2.2.1.

452 TPMA *Nacht* 3.2.4.

453 TPMA *Huhn* 3.1.

454 TPMA *Dienen* 9.1.3.2. *Calones* is glossed *ministri qui ligna portant* (servants who carry wood).

455 TPMA *Arm (Adj.)* 6.5.

456 1 John 2:15–16; see Augustine, *In Epistolam Joannis,* tract. 2 (Migne, *PL* 35, col. 1994).

457 TPMA *Gnade* 13.

458 *Biteriscus* is an alternate spelling of *bitriscus* (kinglet), see Blaise Medieval.

459 Voigt joins this verse to the preceding. He suggests the latter has to do with a children's song or game in which they imitate the song of a bird.

460 See, e.g., Psalms 33:2.

461 Ecclesiastes 1:8.

462 Psalms 146:9; TPMA *Krähe* 21.

463 TPMA *Käse* 9; see 1.827. The point is, a greedy man is so stingy that he will not even give hardened, dried out cheese that is inedible to the dogs.

464 TPMA *Mord* 4.

465 TPMA *Schnell* 4.

466 TPMA *Esel* 14.1.

467–68 Ephesians 6:10–17.

469 Ecclesiastes 7:11; TPMA *Sein* 8.4.

470 TPMA *Wagen (Subst.)* 1.5.

471–72 TPMA *Erschaffen* 2.

473 Juvenal, *Satirae* 3.125.

474–75 TPMA *Pferd* 9.2. *Epiredium* is defined by Lewis and Short as "a thong by which a horse is attached to a cart." Firminus Verris says it is a small vehicle. It could be either here.

476 TPMA *Ziege* 14.

477 Sallust, *Bellum Catilinae* 7.

478 TPMA *Dieb* 3.5. This line is glossed *Non debet furari, qui nescit celare* (He should not steal, who does not know how to conceal).

479 Ecclesiasticus 25:3; TPMA *Arm (Adj.)* 6.10.3.

480 Esther 13:17, 14:9.

481 ≈ 1.1157; TPMA *Arm (Adj.)* 3.2.

482–83 TPMA *Herr* 1. *Carabus* is glossed *parva navis* (little ship); *lembus* is glossed *navicula* (small ship).

484 See 1.1522–25; compare TPMA *Reiher* 2, note 2.

485 TPMA *Winter* 5.2.

486 TPMA *Krebs* 2. Voigt joins this verse to the preceding.

487 TPMA *Busch* 6.

488 Prudentius, *Psychomachia* 777; TPMA *Schlange* 5.1.1.

489–90 Compare *Vitae patrum* 5.12.10.

491–92 Job 40:10–28; see 1.1060–62.

493–94 Radbod cannot be identified with certainty, and the sense is obscure; see Voigt's note to the verses.

495 TPMA *Viel* 4.3.2.

496 Juvenal, *Satirae* 13.140; TPMA *Huhn* 15.4.

497 Ambrose, *De Cain et Abel* 2.1.3; TPMA *Schlagen* 8.

498–500 TPMA *Kind* 3.3.1.

501 See 1.456; TPMA *Sehen* 16.

502–3 Compare Luke 22:26; TPMA *Geiz* 9, *Herr* 8.2.2.

504 TPMA *Drohen* 1.

505 TPMA *Verschwenden* 1.6.

506–7 TPMA *Lügen* 5.1.

508 TPMA *Lehre* 4.1.

509 Luke 14:28.

510 Proverbs 29:2; TPMA *Volk* 3.3.

511 TPMA *Hund* 21.2.

512–14 Compare TPMA *Gast* 3.

515 TPMA *Geben* 23.

516–17 TPMA *Vogel* 25.

518 TPMA *Schwein* 3.3. "Ornaments": *phalerae* can be military medals or the type of trappings worn on the forehead and breast of horses (horse armor). It could mean either here.

519 TPMA *Bock* 4.

520–21 See 1.981–82; compare TPMA *Spät* 3.2.2: "Coming late to eat."

522 Galatians 6:2; Augustine, *Enarrationes in Psalmos* 129.4: *dicuntur cervi, quando transeunt freta in proximas insulas pascuae gratia, capita super se invicem ponere; et unus, qui ante est, solus portat caput et non ponit super alterum; sed cum et ipse defecerit, tollit se ab anteriore parte et redit posterius, ut et ipse in altero requiescat; et sic portant omnes onera sua, et perveniunt ad quod desiderant.* (Deer are said, when crossing water going to neighboring islands for the sake of pasturage, to go single file, each one placing its head on the one in front of it. The one in front alone holds his head up and does not place it on another. But when he gets tired, he moves to the back of the line, so that also he may rest on another. And so they all carry burdens, and they get where they want to go.) TPMA *Hirsch* 7.

523 Perhaps a variant of the proverb "Wait till a roasted dove flies into your mouth" (TPMA *Fliegen* 14), or of "Roast a water bird far from the flame" (TPMA *Vogel* 17).

524–25 Proverbs 30:19; TPMA *Weg* 11.2.

526–28 Job 5:25; TPMA *Stern* 6.1.527: *inextricabilis error* (Virgil, *Aeneid* 6.27) = labyrinth.

529 Gregory the Great, *Homiliae in euangelia* 1.10.3; TPMA *Gott* 33.3.

530 Proverbs 29:15; TPMA *Kind* 3.6.4.1.

531 Ecclesiastes 4:9; TPMA *Allein* 1.2.2.

532 Ecclesiastes 5:4; TPMA *Versprechen* 3.3.

533 Ecclesiastes 9:4; TPMA *Hund* 32.1.

534–35 Ecclesiastes 12:11; TPMA *Stechen* 6, *Wort* 34.30.
536 Ecclesiastes 12:13.
537 Proverbs 21:30.
538 Gregory the Great, *Homiliae in euangelia* 1.12.1; TPMA *Lehre* 5.2.
539 = 2.437; TPMA *Gut (Adj.)* 1.1.
540 TPMA *Gott* 28.24.
541 TPMA *Friede* 2.3.
542 TPMA *Gnade* 6.2.
543 Ecclesiasticus 5:4; TPMA *Gott* 19.3.
544 1 Kings 22:9–22.
545 TPMA *Erlaubnis* 3.
546–47 546 = 1.929, 2.518. 547 ≈ 2.520; Numbers 12:3; compare Arator, *Historia Apostolica* 1.108.
548 Psalms 11:2.
549 1 Kings 18:24.
550 Gregory the Great, *Moralia* 3.9; TPMA *Gift* 2.1.2.
551 Sallust, *Bellum Jugurthinum* 35.10; TPMA *Seele* 3.5.
552 Compare Commodian, *Carmen* 303 (ed. J. Martin, *CCSL* 128).
553 Proverbs 14:4; TPMA *Rind* 3.2.
554 Voigt joins 554 and 555.
555 TPMA *Weise* 3.2.
556 Ecclesiasticus 1:13; TPMA *Gott* 32.5.
557 TPMA *Welt* 1.5.
558 TPMA *Herz* 15.
559 TPMA *Geben* 10.2; see 1.377.
560 Proverbs 16:32; TPMA *Sieg* 10.4.
561 TPMA *Tod* 1.2.2.5; compare Horace, *Epistulae* 2.2.178; Isidore, *Etymologiae* 11.2.32.
562 Gregory the Great, *Homeliae in euangelia* 2.39. Gregory relates the story of three sisters, Tharsilla, Aemiliana, and Gordiana, who all became nuns. But while the first two stuck to their vows and died in grace, Gordiana strayed further and further in her ever-increasing love for the world, and finally sunk so low as to marry her tenant farmer.
563 Genesis 30:31–35. Laban was the father of Leah and Rachel, whom he gave to Jacob as wives. Jacob asked that all the spotted

goats and the black lambs in Laban's herds be given to him as reward for his service to Laban. Laban agreed, and Jacob managed the breeding of the herds so that the best animals of the next generations were spotted and black. Thus he ended up with the best of the flocks and Laban with the weaker animals.

564 1 Kings 25:2–11. For *habendus est* = *habebitur,* see Voigt. Nabal was a rich and ornery man with many flocks. David spared his flocks and protected his shepherds. When Nabal refused hospitality to David's messengers, David set out to attack him. Nabal's wife, Abigail, persuaded David not to kill Nabal, but when Nabal heard that his wife had saved him, he was stricken and soon died.

565 2 Kings 2:18. Asahel was the swiftest runner in David's camp, and he pursued Abner during a battle between Abner and David. He refused to give up the chase and was killed by Abner.

566 Psalms 32:16; TPMA *Kampf* 1.14.3.

567 Virgil, *Georgica* 4.429–44. *Diversa* is glossed *portenta* (monsters).

568 TPMA *Schwach* 2.3.1. Voigt thinks the one leading the weak is, per force, the leader, and that he ought to take pity on the weak (so he would render the line: "the one who draws the weak to himself, should have pity on them.") I follow instead the interpretation in TPMA ("one who has weak followers is dragged down by them").

569 TPMA *Pfeffer* 9. See 1.293.

570 TPMA *Stachel* 2.5.

571 TPMA *Scherz* 2.3. I translate the verse as it appears in the manuscript, since it makes tolerable sense as such. Voigt tentatively suggests emending *bellum* to *bellus* and placing the comma after *bellus* instead of after *est*: "While the sport is still attractive (while the joke is still pretty), you ought to give it up."

572 The sense of this verse eluded Voigt, and it eludes me. It is added in the manuscript by a later hand and is written over an unrecoverable erasure. "The gifted one" *(Donatus)* could refer to the short grammatical treatise by the Late Antique author (called the *Ars minor*). But how reading his work could subvert justice is unclear.

573 TPMA *Rot* 9. An example of a commonly expressed medieval prejudice against redheaded people (compare TPMA *Rot* 1); "mouse" is perhaps used in the same sense as in 1.349, i.e., "boy" or "student."

574 TPMA *Dieb* 18.

575 TPMA *Offenbar(en)* 6.2.

576 Compare TPMA *Tag* 1.1: "Alternation between day and night."

577 Lactantius, *Institutiones* 3.28; Gregory the Great, *Moralia* 23.27.

578 Ecclesiasticus 15:9.

579 Jerome, *Commentarii in quattuor epistulas Pauli: Ad Galat.* (Book 3, Migne, *PL* 26, col. 412C).

580 TPMA *Ameise* 4.

581 TPMA *Schön* 8.1.

582 Virgil, *Aeneid* 2.49; TPMA *Furcht* 1.1.2.9.

583 TPMA *Wolf* 37.

584 TPMA *Laus* 1. *Polipes* is glossed *est pediculus a multis pedibus* (it is a louse; its name is derived from having many feet).

585 TPMA *Ändern* 5. The Latin is a wordplay on *motio* (movement) and *promotio* (promotion, advancement).

586 TPMA *Schlemmen* 1. A bird called *glutto* (glutton) is not attested outside of Egbert. The point of this verse seems to be that even though "birds of a feather flock together" (TPMA *Gleich* 1.2.2), a hungry bird does not want any other hungry birds near him. See 1.1281–87.

587 TPMA *Tod* 1.1.2. See 1.1501.

588 TPMA *Dorn* 5.4. The reference is to the "thorn of worldly lust" according to Voigt, or to "the thorn of falsehood and deceit in the world" according to TPMA.

589 TPMA *Freund* 1.1.4.

590 Matthew 25:32–34; TPMA *Ziege* 11.

591 TPMA *Getreide* 6.2. The proverb is used ironically of someone/something that is *not* growing—or is decreasing (like grain at harvest time, which has either stopped growing, having reached its maturity, or is actually being mowed down).

592 TPMA *Narr* 8.5.1. The Latin involves a pun on *follis,* "bellows" (puffed up with empty air), and *follis* (*follus*), "fool."

593–94 Horace, *Sermones* 1.7.8–20; TPMA *Stark* 3.

595 TPMA *Mutter* 2.7.

596 TPMA *Ja* 5. *Dedicat* is glossed *affirmat* (he affirms).

597–98 TPMA *Mühle* 13; compare also TPMA *Mahlen* 1: "Whoever comes to the mill first, mills first."

599–600 TPMA *Fuss* 1.2.2; *Pferd* 1.2.2.

601–2 TPMA *Blut* 1.5. These lines are obscure. Voigt's explanation, that *itis* (Itys) stands for *hirundo* (swallow), and that this was confused with *hirudo* (leech), and, further, that the passage is related to Horace, *Ars Poetica* 476, is unconvincing. *Itis* is glossed *avicula rupia* (the small bird called "rupia"), but there is no attestation of *rupia* as the name of a bird species. Perhaps *rupia* is a corruption of *rubeus (rubius, robeus)* and means "red," (the gloss would then mean "a small red bird"). The verb *minuo* can mean "to let blood"; the combination of the word with *sanguis* in 602 suggests the lines might be about bloodletting.

603–4 TPMA *Fuchs* 1.2.

605–6 Voigt associates this, unconvincingly, with 1.338. I take it is a version of TPMA *Halm* 4.2.1 ("Draw straw before a young cat") and *Halm* 4.2.2 ("Draw straw in vain before an old cat"). The proverb "To draw straw before a cat" means to distract it from its purpose, to deceive it, by dangling straw (or a straw broom) in front of it, but not letting the cat capture it. A kitten is easily persuaded to follow the straw's wanderings, but an old cat is not.

607–8 TPMA *Hemd* 4. *Ependima* is glossed *sarroch* (shawl); *interulae* is glossed *camisia* (shirt).

609–10 Compare Persius, *Satirae* 5.116–17. "What the fox has," that is, a black stripe. Egbert has combined several proverbial concepts of deception, the fox's tail (TPMA *Fuchs* 14.1), the deceptive face or eyebrow (TPMA *Gesicht* 3; *Augenbrave 1*), cosmetics (TPMA *Farbe* 6, 7).

611–12 Voigt argues that the Ada referred to in this verse is the queen of Caria, sister to Artemisia, brother to Hidrieus. What source Egbert would have had for this otherwise unrecorded report that she sang songs about her imprisoned brother (not husband) is unclear. *Ada* is glossed *proprium nomen* (a proper name).

613–14 TPMA *Kleid* 3.2.1.

615–16 Compare Horace, *Carmina* 2.19.4 *(capripedum Satyrorum);* Jerome, *Epistulae* 36.16.

617–18 TPMA *Faul (verdorben)* 2.

619–20 TPMA *Axt* 9. The point is, an ax handle should be made from hard wood.

621–22 TPMA *Maus* 4.1.

623–24 TPMA *Schmied* 5.

625–26 Compare TPMA *Tugend* 1.3.

627–28 TPMA *Coitus* 3.

629–30 TPMA *Frau* 1.15.1.

631–32 TPMA *Hunger* 9, *Koch* 6.

633–34 Compare TPMA *Baum* 6.5, *Feigenbaum* 1.

635–36 TPMA *Hund* 4.4.

637–38 Genesis 11:7. The Hebrew word "Babel" was interpreted by the Church Fathers as *confusio* in Latin (confusion, discord); see Jerome, *Liber interpretationis hebraicorum nominum* (ed. P. de Lagarde, 3.18).

639–40 TPMA *Pferd* 4.2.

641–42 TPMA *Gefäss* 13.3. There may be a pun on the two meanings of *ius*: *iuris ratione* might mean "in the customary way/by legal right" or "for the sake of the juice." The common version of the proverb is "Whoever holds the platter by the handle (or, 'has a good grip on it'), turns it where he will."

643–44 The sense is obscure. *Billardum* is glossed *proprium nomen* (a proper name), but no story of anyone with that name being killed with an ax is known. The expression *ventris fultura* is related to Horace, *Sermones* 2.3.154. Here and in 2.2, Egbert scans *dolabra (-um)* with a short penult.

645–46 A precise parallel is not known. *Comes* might mean "companion" or "Count." The Latin *magirus* for "cook" is extremely rare; Egbert probably knows it from the *Testamentum porcelli.*

647–48 TPMA *Hof* 2.3.

649–50 TPMA *Tod* 1.2.1.3.

651–52 TPMA *Binden* 4.3.

653–54 TPMA *Pferd* 2.3.

655–56 TPMA *Spinne* 4.1. "The Lydian spider" refers to Arachne, who was turned into a spider by Athena after a spinning competition. *Lide* is glossed *nomen araneae* (the name of a spider); *casses* is glossed *telas* (webs).

657–58 TPMA *Pfeife* 12.

659–60 TPMA *Horn* 4.3.

661–62 TPMA *Fuchs* 12.4.

663–64 *Butzo* is glossed *proprium nomen* (a proper name), but neither he nor his story is known. See 1.885.

665–66 TPMA *Traum* 4.

667–68 TPMA *Feder* 7.10.1.

669–70 TPMA *Geld* 2.7.

671–72 TPMA *Löwe* 13.3. The dog-fly is an allusion to the fourth plague in Exodus 8:21–31.

673–74 TPMA *Narr* 28. As in Juvenal, *Satirae* 9.102, the name Coridon here is used as a typical appellation for a simpleton farmer. *Pollinis* is glossed *pulvis exiens de fornace* (dust that comes from a furnace).

675–76 Jerome, *Epistulae* 43.2; TPMA *Geld* 9.7.

677–78 TPMA *Fasten* 11.

679–80 Voigt says verse 680 concerns pederasty. I see no justification for this statement and assume the point is that the bed of an adulteress is more disgraceful than her kiss.

681–82 TPMA *Herr* 8.2.1.

683–84 TPMA *Glauben* 1.1.3.

685–86 See 1.438. Similar sentiments are found at TPMA *Lernen 133* ("Seldom does anyone learn without punishment"), *Lernen* 4.3 ("Learning requires work and endurance"), *Rute* 4 ("The rod casts out the stupidity [of a child] and brings wisdom and virtue").

687–88 TPMA *Lehre* 6.1. *Electus* might mean "handpicked," "carefully chosen" (i.e., for being a slacker).

689–90 TPMA *Bart* 1.1, *Narr* 13.6.1. The sense is, not everyone with a beard is a philosopher; fools grow beards too. It is not always wisdom (prudence) that puts hair on cheeks; stupidity can do that as well.

691–92 TPMA *Arm (Adj.)* 2.3.2.

693–94 See 1.65. Similar sentiments are found at TPMA *Hund* 2.19 ("A dog prevents other animals from eating"), *Hund* 2.12 ("A dog is always at the door and wants to enter"), *Hund* 13.10 ("A dog is jealous of the bones of another").

695–96 The corruption of Rome by Jugurtha is related by Sallust (*Bellum Jugurthinum* 8.1, 28.1).

697–98 TPMA *Bauch* 2.2.4.

699–700 TPMA *Drohen* 11.

701–2 Compare Virgil, *Eclogae* 8.29–30, and TPMA *Nuss* 11. Neither the sense nor the connection of the two verses is entirely clear.

703–4 TPMA *Küche* 3.

705–6 See 2.396–401; Gregory the Great, *Homeliae in euangelia* 1.3.3; TPMA *Gesund* 1.4.1.

707–8 TPMA *Zorn* 1.1.1.3.

709–10 TPMA *Maus* 1.5.

711–12 TPMA *Wolf* 10.2.

713–14 TPMA *Kohl* 7. *Ebulum* is glossed *amara herba* (a bitter herb), but it is unclear whether any specific herb is intended here; Lewis and Short give the ancient meaning as "danewort" (i.e., *sambucus ebulus,* or dwarf elder), but Du Cange equates it with "hellebore." The latter gives some point to Egbert's *delira,* so I have followed that meaning. If Voigt is correct to connect this with Jerome, *Epistulae* 7.5 ("The lips have a 'lettuce' to match when a donkey eats thistles"), then the point might be that a crazy old woman with shriveled lips is eating shriveled cabbage boiled in hellebore (which makes one crazy).

715–16 TPMA *Eile* 3.10.

717–18 TPMA *Haar* 19.9.

719–20 TPMA *Bastard* 2. *Vitricus* here, as in Ovid, *Am.* 1.2.24, does not have its normal meaning of stepfather. It means, instead, the man who actually fathered the child but who is not the man married to the mother of the child. The (cuckolded) husband is referred to here as *pater.* In Ovid, Mars is called the *vitricus* of Cupid, because he sired the boy through his adulterous relationship with Venus; Vulcan is the husband of Venus, so the *pater* of Cupid.

721–22 Compare TPMA *Wolf* 6.2. The translation and interpretation was suggested by Gregory Hays. Voigt interprets differently and unconvincingly. I follow Peiper's punctuation of these verses.

723–24 TPMA *Nachbar* 2.4.2.

725–26 TPMA *Tod* 2.2.2.1. See 1.1048–50.

727–28 TPMA *Kröte* 3.

729–30 Numbers 19:15; Job 32:17; TPMA *Gefäss* 2.3.

731–32 TPMA *Narr* 6.10, 13.4.

733–34 On the harmless innocence of the dove, see Bede, *Homeliae in euangelia* 1.12. The sentiment of this distich is similar to TPMA *Falke* 12 ("Joining the falcon and hawk with the dove"), namely, that an innocent person who associates with a vicious one will suffer. *Hanelat* = *anhelat* (pants, strives).

735–36 TPMA *Mai* 1.

737–38 No stories of birds stupidly losing eggs are known, other than the stories of the ostrich doing so. But I do not follow Voigt in joining this distich to the following one and in interpreting *fiscedula* generically as "bird" (and therefore equivalent to *strutio,* "ostrich," in the next line). The glossator took *fiscedula* as a specific small bird, not as anything related to an ostrich. The punctuation and the added paragraph marks in the manuscript indicate that the medieval readers considered these two distichs as separate proverbs. *Fiscedula* is glossed *avis quae vocatur sceppa* (the bird which is called *"sceppa"*); *menceps* is glossed *sine mente* (without a mind).

739–40 Job 39:13–18; *Physiologus* (B), ch. 8.

741–42 Compare Psalms 2:9. Voigt joins this distich to the one that follows, but the punctuation and paragraph marks indicate that the medieval readers took them as separate distichs.

743–44 Romans 13:4.

745–46 Augustine, *Enarrationes in Psalmos* 132.12; TPMA *Rad* 2.2.

747–48 Compare Augustine, *De agone christiano* 3; Gregory the Great, *Homeliae in euangelia* 29.5.

749–50 For the general sentiment of this and the following distich, Voigt compares Augustine, *Sermones supp.* 97 (*PL* 39.1932).

751–52 Voigt joined this distich to the preceding one, but the punctuation and paragraph marks indicate that the medieval readers took them as separate distichs.

753–54 Compare Proverbs 28:15, 30:26.

755–56 TPMA *Wald* 10; compare Juvenal, *Satirae* 15.147–58.

757–58 Juvenal, *Satirae* 11.1–2.

759–60 TPMA *Schaden* 13.

761–62 TPMA *Ende* 1.1.2.

763–64 TPMA *Wind* 9.9.

765–66 TPMA *Fundament* 1, *Haupt* 1.3.

767–68 TPMA *Kuckuck* 7. The cuckoo surreptitiously places its eggs in the nest of other birds so that another mother will incubate them. Once the young cuckoos are born, they consume the foster mother as prey. *Curruca* may refer not to a specific species, but to any small bird whose nest and incubating services are used by the cuckoo. The warbler is only one such host species.

769–70 TPMA *Frau* 7.3.5.

771–72 1 Thessalonians 5:19–20.

773–74 TPMA *Biegen* 4.2.

775–76 See 1.294–95; TPMA *Zorn* 1.7.1.

777–78 TPMA *Singen* 17, *Wasser* 8.5.2.1.

779–80 TPMA *Frau* 4.1.6.3.

781–82 TPMA *Ei* 2.4; compare John Cassian, *De institutis coenobiorum* 4.20. *Perfidus* is glossed *infidelis* (faithless); *instructor* is glossed *ministrator* (waiter).

783–84 TPMA *Trinken* 7.2.

785–86 Horace, *Epistulae* 1.1.39.

787–88 TPMA *Wein* 4.2.

789–90 Exodus 1:14; 7. "Canopic," = Egyptian.

791–92 TPMA *Zorn* 1.4.1.

793–94 TPMA *Richten* 7.3.

795–96 TPMA *Neid* 1.9. Voigt joins this distich to the following one, but the punctuation and paragraph marks indicate that the medieval readers took them as separate distichs.

797–98 TPMA *Neid* 1.9.

799–800 Ecclesiastes 2:14; Jerome, *Commentarius in Ecclesiasten* 2.4.

801–2 Compare, e.g., Alcuin, *De virtutibus et vitiis* 32.

803–4 Gregory the Great, *Homeliae in euangelia* 2.26; TPMA *Glauben* 1.1.2.

805–6 John Cassian, *De institutis coenobiorum* 10.23; Gregory the Great, *Regula pastoralis* 3.15; TPMA *Faul* 4.1.8.

807–8 Proverbs 15:1; TPMA *Wort* 11.3.

809–10 Genesis 8:6–11; Augustine, *Quaestiones in heptateuchum* 1.13.

811–12 Avianus, *Fabulae* 5; TPMA *Esel* 15.1.

813–14 Voigt says that *peregrinus* refers to the Cynic philosopher Peregrinus Proteus (second century BCE). Where Egbert would have found any account of him giving away what he had is unclear. *Peregrinus* need not refer to a specific individual; if it is interpreted as "pilgrim," the first verse would read: "The beggar who gives what he has imitates a pilgrim." But we should expect a pilgrim to receive, not to give, charity. Gregory Hays suggests interpreting *peregrinus* as Christ (as in Luke 24:18). See 1.423.

815–16 Compare TPMA *Bauer* 3.1.3.2.1. Voigt compares Virgil, *Aeneid* 12.9–46.

816 ≈ 1.1697. *Adolere* is glossed *crescere* (to increase); *meracam* is glossed *amaritudinem* (bitterness).

817–18 *Crabrones* (wasps, hornets) is glossed *muscae quae de asinis nascuntur* (flies that are born from [the corpses of] jackasses). See 1.123: "One bee in a city is preferable to countless flies."

819–20 That is, it does not leave at all. See 1.205; TPMA *Gesund* 1.1.2.

821–22 TPMA *Essen* 12.2.

823–24 *Curruca* (warbler) is proverbial for cuckold. See 1.767–68; Juvenal, *Satirae* 9.70–82; TPMA *Kuckuck* 7.

825–26 "Little worms," that is, lice. TPMA *Laus* 1.

827–28 TPMA *Käse* 9; see 1.463.

829–30 The story of the golden bough is told at Virgil, *Aeneid* 6.137–55; compare TPMA *Lehre* 5.1 (99), *Predigten* 2.3 (31).

831–32 *Nebris* is glossed *purgata pellis* (a smooth hide); compare TPMA *Arm (Adj.)* 10.9, esp. 874.

833–34 TPMA *Kuss* 17. The implication is that the person is skinny enough to place his/her head in the narrow space between a goat's horns.

835–36 TPMA *Gross* 2.3.2.2.

837–38 TPMA *Haken* 5. This proverb is about a wooden pruning hook; "its parents" = "the trees that bore it."

839–40 TPMA *Heer* 2; see 1.164, 1.309.

841–42 TPMA *Bauer* 12.

843–44 Compare 2 Maccabees 11:28–33.

845–46 TPMA *Pferd* 18; see 1.128.

847–50 Petrus Chrysologus, *Sermones* 5; "husks" = chaff (pig food). I follow (with some reservations) Voigt in joining these two distichs. The punctuation in the MS does not indicate that they should be joined.

851–52 TPMA *Aas* 1.2.2.

853–54 TPMA *Kleie* 2. "Husks" = chaff (pig food). *Porcorum siliquas* is glossed *scripta poetarum* (the writings of the [pagan] poets); see Jerome, *Epistulae* 21.13; Paulus Diaconus, *Homeliae* 1.87. For *follis* = "dry pods," see R. E. Latham, *Dictionary of Medieval Latin from British Sources, "follis* 2" (London, 1975).

855–56 Proverbs 18:23; 1.855 ≈ 1.1696.

857–58 Compare TPMA *Teil* 2.3.2.

859–60 Compare TPMA *Beutel* 3.1, 3.3; *Bringen* 2: "Whoever comes is welcome, whoever brings something is even more welcome."

861–62 Compare TPMA *Name* 3.8, *Tod* 5.3.2.1.

863–64 TPMA *Ende* 1.3.3.

865–66 TPMA *Jahr* 1.3.1.

867–68 See 1.218: "Unfamiliar things are marked with charcoal"; the sense is that the puppy is a distraction of no particular interest, but any excuse will suffice for avoiding something one does not want to do.

869–70 TPMA *Pferd* 11.1.

871–72 Curtius, *Historiae Alexandri Magni* 9.11.34.

873–74 Ecclesiastes 7:40; TPMA *Ende* 1.3.3.

875–76 TPMA *Aachen* 3; compare *Köln, Rom* 1; see Einhard, *Vita Karoli* ch. 17 (on the basilica built at Aachen by Charlemagne), and ch. 22 (on the palace): *Delectabatur etiam vaporibus aquarum naturaliter calentium . . . Ob hoc etiam Aquisgrani regiam extruxit.* (He took pleasure also in the vapors of naturally hot springs . . . for this reason as well he built a palace at Aachen.)

877–78 TPMA *Taub* 2.2, *Schelten* 8.11. See 1.418.

879–80 Juvenal, *Satirae* 6.556; Virgil, *Aeneid* 6.127.

881–82 TPMA *Hirt* 4.

883–84 Augustine, *Enarrationes in Psalmos* 127.10.

885–86 *Drances* is the verbose councilor of Latinus in Virgil, *Aeneid* 11.122–391. He advises against war, being no warrior himself.

887–88 Matthew 2:3–16; Luke 13:32. Egbert may have coined the (otherwise unattested) verb *vulpino, -are* (to pursue like a fox, to trick like a fox) which appears to be an active, transitive form of *vulpinor, -ari.*

889–90 Gregory the Great, *Homeliae in euangelia* 2.35.1; TPMA *Schlecht* 1.2.1.

891–92 Matthew 23:24. See Gregory the Great, *Moralia* 1.15.

893–94 Gregory the Great, *Moralia* 2.20.

895–96 Deuteronomy 16:21; see Jerome, *Commentarius in Ecclesiasten* 10.9. The groves (and the leaves of their trees) were understood by Jerome to refer to the fruitless words of empty (or false) rhetoric. The perfect subjunctive appears instead of the present subjunctive in 896.

897–98 Tobit 12:8; compare Augustine, *Sermones* 64.12, and *Enarrationes in Psalmos* 42.8.

899–900 Compare Apocalypse 2:11, 20:14, 21:8.

901–2 Wisdom 4:3.

903–4 Jeremiah 6:13, 8:10.

905–6 Hebrews 4:13.

907–8 TPMA *Fleisch* 2.1.

909–10 See 1.408–9; Tobit 12:7; compare TPMA *Verbergen* 7.4.

911–12 TPMA *Donner* 1.

913–14 On the fifteen (7 + 8) steps to the temple, see Ezekiel 40:22–37; Gregory the Great, *Moralia* 35.8; Gregory the Great, *Homiliae in Hiezechihelem prophetam* 2.7.7–2.9.2. The fifteen steps may refer to the seven virtues (Isaiah 11:2) and the eight beatitudes (Matthew 5:3–10).

915–16 See, e.g., Deuteronomy 6:5; Matthew 22:37; Matthew 5:6; Isaiah 58:11.

917–18 See 1.1717–36; Psalms 67:20.

919–20 If *tessella* is "die" (sing. of "dice"), *caractere miro* might mean "with a lucky number." But *tessella* (diminutive of *tessera*) could perhaps be "tablet, painting, sign, ticket, tile," or the like. TPMA *Frau* 1.4.1.1; Juvenal, *Satirae* 2.40.

921–22 Macrobius, *Saturnalia* 1.21.1–6; see also Hyginus, *Fabulae* 248.1. Macrobius says that Adonis represents the sun, and in the winter months when the days are shorter, he is in the underworld and Venus mourns him. During this period, it is colder on earth.

923–24 TPMA *Kern* 6.

925–26 The different grammatical constructions in Latin distinguish between inner and outer similarity. See, e.g., Keil, *Grammatici Latini* 4.570; Isidore, *Differentiae* 1.1.309. The basic idea is that two constructions, using the same word and so appearing at first to be the same, have, upon closer analysis, important differences.

927–28 Gregory the Great, *Homeliae in euangelia* 2.37.1; TPMA *Arbeit* 2.3.

929–30 = 2.518–19 (and 929 = 1.546). Numbers 12:3; see note to 1.546.

931–32 Philippians 3:19; TPMA *Bauch* 1.5.

933–34 Compare Gregory the Great, *Dialogi* 3.15; Smaragdus, *Diadema monachorum* ch. 47; TPMA *Welt* 1.5.

935–36 Compare Benedict of Aniane, *Concordia regularum* 48.31; Salvianus, *De Gubernatione Dei* 6.5.29.

936 Ecclesiastes 2:2; TPMA *Lachen* 5.1.1.

937–38 Job 32:18–20.

939–40 Ecclesiastes 10:1; Gregory the Great, *Moralia* 18.43.; TPMA *Fliege* 3.4.

941–42 Augustine, *Enarrationes in Psalmos* 56.12.

943–44 1 Timothy 2:4; compare Prosper, *De vocatione omnium gentium* 2.28.

945–46 See, e.g., Ambrose, *De obitu Theodosii* 40–51.

947–48 Apocalypse of St. John the Apostle 1:7.

949–50 See 1.1250–52; *Orcestram* is glossed *id est pulpitum* (that is, the pulpit). Compare TPMA *Pfaffe* 3.5.

951–54 See, e.g., Bede, *Homeliae in euangelia* 1.18; Heiric of Auxerre, *Homeliae per circulum anni,* 24. The punctuation in the MS separates these verses into two distichs.

953 TPMA *König* 3.6.1.

955–56 TPMA *Richten* 15.

957–60 Paulinus Aquileiensis, *Liber exhortationis,* ch. 50 (Migne, *PL* 99.253B–54A). The punctuation in the MS suggests that these four lines belong together.

961–62 Proverbs 29:12 *Princeps, qui libenter audit verba mendacii, omnes ministros habet impios* (A prince that gladly heareth lying words, hath all his servants wicked); TPMA *Herr* 8.2.2. According to Voigt (p. 243), we should understand *conchilia* (*conchylia*) here as "stains" or more specifically "vices" (which stain us purple). TPMA takes it as "gatherings of men," i.e., more-or-less equivalent to *consilia* (the opening of the Psalms is rendered by some Patristic and medieval writers in the form *"in concilio impiorum"*). Even though the intended meaning of *conchilia* is debatable, the sense of the lines is clear from the source text, Proverbs 29:12. See 1.1225.

963–64 Proverbs 13:11. TPMA *Reich* 9.1. *Suum spectabit acervum,* literally, = "will look upon its own heap."

965–66 Proverbs 20:9. TPMA *Sünde* 2.1.

967–68 Proverbs 20:14. TPMA *Kauf* 1.6.

969–70 Ecclesiastes 10:16. Egbert has altered the biblical passage from "*eat* in the morning." TPMA *Kind* 7.2.

971–72 Voigt relates these verses to Virgil, *Eclogae* 9.50 (with Servius, *ad loc.*) and 1.73–78. But compare TPMA *Birnbaum* 2: "One can tend a grandfather's pear tree too long." Many pear trees stop producing edible fruit after three or four decades, so a grandfather's pear trees, which still must pass through the ownership of the father, are of dubious value to a grandson. The distich appears also to be a variant of "the grass is always greener."

973–74 Matthew 3:12; Augustine, *Enarrationes in Psalmos* 47.11, 21.2.5.

975–76 Psalms 104:17–20.

977–78 This seems to be a playful elaboration of Mark 9:42–46; the reader's tongue scandalizes, so it should be cut out. Compare TPMA *Zunge* 12.2 ("Evil and corrupted tongues should be cut off"), *Zunge* 12.3 ("There are many tongues one would wish were shorter"), *Hand* 177.

979–80 Compare TPMA *Lernen* 4.3. I follow Voigt in taking *invita* as *molesta.* For *apices* = *apices litterarum,* see Blaise Patristic, *apex* 3.

981–82 See 1.520–21; TPMA *Spät* 3.2.2: "Come late to eat."

982 "Elsewhere": I follow the variant inscribed by *e* over *hodierna* (daily), which reads "*vel aliunde*" (alternatively, elsewhere). Since *hodierna diaria* ("daily daily rations") is redundant, and not otherwise attested, it seems to me likely that the exemplar had *aliunde* in the text, and that *hodierna* was inserted as a gloss (not a variant) on *diaria.* A later scribe then misinterpreted the gloss as a variant and entered it in the text. The original reading was later added between the lines as a variant. I have restored *aliunde* to the text, since the line has no clear sense in relation to the preceding one if *hodierna* is retained.

983–84 *Vitae patrum* 5.15.3.

985–86 Voigt interprets these lines as specifically about pregnancy (taking *partis* as "when [the children] have been born"). He is followed by TPMA *Gebären* 18. I take *partis* in a different and more general sense and as *dative; confero* + acc. + dat. = "compare x to y," as in *ut parva magnis conferamus* (Augustine, *De civitate Dei* 22.6, quoting Cicero, *De re publica*). The sense is, One should plan in advance instead of lamenting afterward what has happened (and could have been avoided by foresight).

987–88 1 Kings 18:20–27, 25:44; 2 Kings 3:13–16.

989–90 TPMA *Links* 2.

991–92 Horace, *Epistulae* 1.19.48–49.

993–94 Voigt relates this distich to Phaeton. But compare Ausonius, *De XII Caesaribus,* 9, about Vitellius, who was emperor for only a short time: *Vitae ut sors, mors foeda tibi, nec digne, Vitelli, qui fieres Caesar: sic sibi fata placent. umbra tamen brevis imperii; quia praemia regni saepe indignus adit, non nisi dignus habet.* (As was the fate of your life, so was your death putrid; you were not worthy, Vitellius, to be Caesar: so it pleased the Fates. It was a brief semblance of rule, because an unworthy man often approaches the prize of a kingdom, but only a worthy man can hold it.)

995–96 TPMA *Fuchs* 20.

997–98 Ecclesiasticus 20:31. Compare TPMA *Salbe* 2.1.1; *Richten* 6.1. The sense is, I will reward you if you do what I ask; you can use the reward to assuage your guilt.

999–1000 See 1.1248–52. TPMA *Geld* 1.27.

1001–2 TPMA *Käse* 11.

1003–4 TPMA *Fleisch* 2.7.

1005–8 These verses are not a proverb, but a short prayer following the original thousand-verse poem; see Introduction. On Argus (Juno's guard, who had one hundred eyes), see Servius, *In Aeneidem* 7.790.

1009–11 Exodus 1:8; *decora alta parentum* (great glories of parents) = the male offspring.

1012–14 Lucan, *Pharsalia,* 3.118.

1015–17 Horace, *Carmina* 1.34.12–16, and Ps.-Acro, *Scholia in Horatium, ad loc.;* TPMA *Glück* 3.1.1, 3.7.1.

1018–20 TPMA *Kamm* 1.

1021–23 Gregory the Great, *Homeliae in euangelia* 2.35.3. TPMA *Freund* 1.6.2.

1024–26 Augustine, *Enarrationes in Psalmos* 144.13

1027–29 Gregory the Great, *Homeliae in euangelia* 1.4.2. This passage lacks a heading in the manuscript.

1030–32 Gregory the Great, *Regula pastoralis* 3.11; "undeserved punishments" = punishments that he considers undeserved.

1033–35 Genesis 21:20, 16:12.

1036–38 See Horace, *Sermones* 1.5.100, and Ps.-Acro, *Scholia in Horatium, ad loc.*

1039–41 Boethius, *De consolatione philosophiae* 2.M.5.1 and 28–30. Psalms 18:10–11.

1042–44 These verses apply the standard formulas of benedictions and prayers (see *Corpus benedictionum pontificalium latinarum* and *Corpus orationum*) to Saints Benedict and Gregory.

1045–47 TPMA *Versprechen* 5.8; the sense is, From a lot of promises, one expects little, or cheap, return. *Alutam* is glossed *est pellis capreae tincta* (it is the dyed hide of a goat).

1048–50 A variant of 1.725–26.

1051–53 *In peius ruere:* Virgil, *Georgica* 197–203; *ferre laborem: Disticha Catonis, monosticha* 53. *Incipiunt* is glossed *aliquid boni* (something good).

1054–56 There is more than one *Mons Jovis;* according to Voigt the reference here is to the Great Saint Bernard Pass. Given the dangers of the place emphasized in line 1056, *iocosus* may be a euphemism (or apotropaic).

1057–59 Gregory the Great, *Homeliae in euangelia* 1.15.2.

1060–62 Job 40:21; Isaiah 37:1; "its bar and its crook" *(vectis et anguis):* from Isaiah (*loc. cit.*); I follow the Douai-Rheims translation of the passage. The meaning is obscure and the passage variously rendered. See 1.491–92.

1063–65 Gregory the Great, *Homeliae in euangelia* 1.1.5. As the source passage in Gregory shows, this is about the decline of the world, which parallels the decline of the human body in the course of time (the young body is healthy and has strong limbs; the old one is feeble and has weak limbs).

1064 *Hic* is glossed *in iuvenibus* (among the young men).

1065 *Hic* is glossed *in senibus* (among the old men).

1066–68 Voigt says this refers to the rising popularity of lay tonsuring in Egbert's day.

1069–71 1069 is reminiscent of 1 Corinthians 13:3; for the remainder, see, e.g., Remigius, *Commentarium Einsidlense in Donati Artem Maiorem* (ed. Hagen, *Grammatici Latini, Suppl.* 227.23): *Condite gaza poli, saccos vacuate gazarum* (Store up treasures in heaven; empty your sacks of [earthly] treasures).

1072–74 These verses, "Concerning Charon," were added in the lower margin of fol. 28r (in the section of four-liners). Verses 1093–96, "Concerning Poor Scholarly Effort," were added in the lower margin of the facing page, fol. 27v, by a different hand (at the end of the section of three-liners). Voigt swapped the placement of these two poems so that each would appear in a section in which it had the proper number of lines.

1072–74 On Charon, the ferryman of the Underworld, see, e.g., Virgil, *Aeneid* 6.326–29.

1075 The rubric in the MS before verse 1075 reads "DE QUATUOR VERSICULIS ET INIUSTO OBSONIO." This is not only a subtitle for the beginning of the four-liners, but also a title for the specific poem that follows (vv. 1075–78). Voigt combined the rubric here with the one that appears before 1097: "DE QUATUOR VERSICULIS ET RELIQUIS INDIFFERENTER POSITIS"; and he separated out the final phrase, "([DE] INIUSTO OBSONIO)," to stand as the title for 1075–78.

1075–78 Genesis 47:22–26; Matthew 7:24–27; the "obligation of the people" was to render one-fifth of their crop annually to the pharaoh.

1079–83 See Juvenal, *Satirae* 3.113. On Gehazi, see 4 Kings 5:20–25; on Herod (= Herod Agrippa I), Acts of the Apostles 12:21–23; on Antiochus (= Antiochus IV Epiphanes), 2 Maccabees 9:5–12.

1084–87 1 Maccabees 11:1–18.

1087 Horace, *Sermones* 2.8.66.

1088–92 *Ringeris* is glossed *caninum verbum* (a canine word). Voigt compares Horace, *Sermones* 2.3.142–61.

1093–96 See note to verses 1072–74, above. Compare Odo of Cluny, *Occupatio,* praef. 10–11: *Prorsus ubique bonum / Friget iners studium / iam nimis; Frivola quisque cupit, / Nullus honesta petit, / pro dolor!*

1095 Compare Horace, *Sermones* 2.5.69.

1096 *Rara* is glossed *scilicet lectio* (namely, reading); *nauci* is glossed *inutilis* (useless).

1097 The manuscript here repeats the title that appears (partially) before verse 1075, and there is no title in the manuscript for verses 1097–1100. I have supplied a title.

1097–1100 Voigt considered this a version of the Romulus fable (2.5 *"Mons parturiens"*) about the mountain groaning excessively in labor, then giving birth to a mouse. Genesis 6:4.

1099 Compare Horace, *Sermones* 2.3.320.

1101–4 Isidore, *Etymologiae* 1.37.24, 8.11.93; TPMA *Wald* 4. The construction of the accusative in *antiphrasin* is unclear and unparalleled. Grammarians regularly use the phrase *per antiphrasin* (for Greek *kat' antiphrasin*), but not the accusative alone in this way. Voigt's text requires scanning the final syllable of *antiphrasin* as long; he calls this lengthening of Greek words because of ictus (p. 255; the same is required for *Lachesis* in v. 1103).

1105–8 Horace, *Epistulae* 2.1.194, and Juvenal, *Satirae* 10.28–30, with the scholia *ad loc.* (ed. O. Jahn [Berlin, 1893], 172).

1108 Juvenal, *Satirae* 1.80. Cluvienus was a bad poet to whom Juvenal ironically compares himself.

1109–13 Persius, *Satirae, prol.,* 8–9, and especially the scholia *ad loc.* (ed. Jahn, 56). According to Voigt, *Cobbo* is a nickname for *Jacopus* (either the bird's or his master's name). Kurth ("Review," 80) says that Cob was the only name for the crow in his day in the German idiom of Luxembourg.

1114–19 Horace, *Sermones* 1.9.27–28.

1119 *Mestos* is glossed *nos* (us); *illis* is glossed *scilicet prioribus* (namely, the earlier ones).

1120–25 Compare Augustine, *Solil.* 6.12; Gregory the Great, *Moralia* 3.9.

1126–30 See 1.1581–86. TPMA *Fliege* 3.2; Psalms 103:25.

1127 On *pulex,* see Firminus Verris: *dicitur a "pulvis" quia ex pulvere nascitur* (it is named from "dust" because it is born from dust), and Isidore, *Etymologiae* 12.5.15.

1128 *Indignamur* is glossed *blasphemamus* (we curse).

1131–39 For the metaphor of writing and pruning, see Horace, *Sermones* 1.10.64–74, and *Ars Poetica* 445–50.

1134 *His* is glossed *scilicet stilis* (namely, styluses).

1140–44 Valerius Maximus, 1.18.15 (*de externis*); see Maaz, "Brotlöffel," 110–14.

1145–51 Drogo is glossed *proprium nomen: insipiens presbiter* (a proper name: an insipid priest); *consultus* is glossed *presbiter* (the priest). Egbert derives the name Drogo from the noun *Drog* (deceiver, defrauder); see J. and W. Grimm, *Deutsches Wörterbuch* (Leipzig, 1860), col. 1426: "Drog, *m.* betrüger, homo nequam."

1152–57 *Carpiliones* is glossed *predones* (robbers).

1154 On the Harpies, see, e.g., Virgil, *Aeneid* 3.210–62.

1157 ≈ 1.481.

1158–61 Compare TPMA *Alt* 6.5.1.2.

1162–65 TPMA *Rind* 5.4; "windy gourd," see Juvenal, *Satirae* 14.58; "live on wind," TPMA *Wind* 10.11.

1164 *Ventosa cucurbita* is glossed *mali prepositi* (of the evil provost).

1166–69 I take "sticks . . . cracks" (1167) to refer to the soil, clinging like clay in the rain, and cracking when baked by the sun.

1170–73 See Horace, *Sermones* 1.9.38–39, 1.6.110–30.

1174–89 See 1.1311–27. Egbert has taken the elements of the fable of the division of spoils among companion hunters and applied it to an election. The version of this fable by Odo of Cheriton (20. *De leone et lupo et volpe et venatoribus*) is particularly close to Egbert's rendition. See Ziolkowski, *Talking Animals,* 245–46.

1180–82 I follow the punctuation and interpretation of Peiper (*hinc* instead of *hic* in 1181, removing the quotation marks on 1180, and adding a colon after 1181). I additionally removed the question mark after 1182.

1190–93 Matthew 5:27–30, 18:8–9; Mark 9:42–46. Egbert has altered the biblical injunction to cut out the eye, the hand, or the foot (if they should cause you to sin), suggesting instead that the most serious offenders are the tongue and the genitals. Compare TPMA *Glied* 7; *Zunge* 7.1.

1194–98 TPMA *Haus* 4.3.1. *Liceri* is glossed *appretiari* (to be valued); *centusse* is glossed *centum assibus* (one hundred coins).

1199–20 *Sarabara* is glossed *ossa* (bones, see Du Cange: *crura, tibiae*); *polinctor* is glossed *procurator funeris* (an undertaker, funeral director); *mannis* is glossed *burdonibus* (mules). The general model for this poem, and the next, is Horace, *Carmina* 1.16. See also 1.1497–1506.

1206 TPMA *Rind* 10.2; see 1.17.

1209–10 The Greek philosopher Pythagoras described the path of human life as similar to the letter *Y.* In youth it is straight, like the shaft of the letter (not knowing virtue or vice), but then it diverges into two branches. Every person has to choose either the steep right branch of virtue or the easy, left branch of vice. On the "fifteen steps," of virtue, see 1.913–14.

1212 Tithonus was granted immortality but not everlasting youth; he continued to grow older and more shriveled, until he was turned into a cricket.

1213 TPMA *Maus* 4.2; see 1.189 and the note there on *massa.*

1214 See 1.606, 1.667–68.

1221–47 The general model for this poem, like the preceding one, is Horace, *Carmina* 1.16. The humor of the poem lies in the positive-sounding descriptive terms being taken from negative and satirical sources.

1223 See Horace, *Epod.* 6.4.

1226 See Juvenal, *Satirae* 7.191.

1229 See Horace, *Sermones* 2.7.86.

1231–32 Juvenal, *Satirae* 3.76–77.

1225 On *conchilia,* see note on 1.961.

1235 "Mulberry wine with honey": a newly fashionable drink.

1236 The Greek physician Hippocrates is here presented as an herbalist.

1238 See Avianus, *Fabulae* 6.7. The master is Apollo, patron god of physicians, or Asclepius.

1239 Juvenal, *Satirae* 4.17.

1240–42 The weasel was said in the Middle Ages to be knowledgeable about herbal remedies, with which it was even able to raise the dead; see Alexander Neckam, *De naturis rerum,* 2, ch. 123.

1244 Egbert is mocking his friend by saying that the latter will be able to raise the dead when he has seen a fern's seed. The fern was said to have no seed; see Pliny, *Hist. nat.* 27.77: *Filicis duo genera nec florem habent, nec semen* (There are two kinds of fern; they have neither flower nor seed).

1245 The "tree of life" is the only plant that might be expected by a believer to actually raise people from the dead; Egbert suggests that his friend must have stolen it.

1246 "guard" = Michael the Archangel.

1248–52 "seed of the dove" in 1248 = one of the seven virtues of the dove was that it ate only the choicest seed; see, e.g., Haimo of Halberstadt, *Homiliae* 16.

1251 See 1.1000.

1252 Compare Juvenal, *Satirae* 1.112–14.

1253–54 Juvenal, *Satirae* 3.23–24.

1255 Compare Proverbs 29:15: *Virga atque correptio tribuet sapientiam* (The rod and reproof will give wisdom). Egbert's point is that the rod alone is being employed, not the rod along with oral instruction/reproof.

1257–59 Rhadamanthus and Aeacus are judges in the Underworld; Erinys is one of the avenging Furies.

1268 *Venae* is glossed *his qui sensum habent* (to those who have sense).

1271 Juvenal, *Satirae* 3.265–67.

1276 See 1.63; compare TPMA *Krähe* 1.1, 1.2.

1277 Juvenal, *Satirae* 6.1651; compare TPMA *Schwan* 1.

1278–80 TPMA *Spinne* 4.2.1.

1279 Matthew 13:31–32.

1281–87 See 1.586 and the note there.

1288–93 Phrases from Horace, *Sermones* 1.4.85 and *Epistulae* 1.17.60, appear in verses 1288 and 1290, respectively; but a more general source and the point of this poem elude me. That Romans should fear a wolf seems paradoxical (a wolf nurtured their founder and namesake). Why a wolf would be (or would be said to be) in the sack is a mystery. The origin or ownership of the clothes in the sack remains unclear.

1294–1302 Compare TPMA *Fliege* 4.

1303–10 Fredegarius, *Chronica* 4, ch. 38; see J. Janota, "Peter Schmieher. 3. Die Wolfsklage," in *Die Deutsche Literatur des Mittelalters: Verfasserlexikon,* ed. K. Ruh et al. 2nd ed., vol. 8 (Berlin, 1992), cols. 766–67, and Ziolkowski, *Talking Animals*, 28–29.

1311–27 See 1.1174–89. *Romulus* 1.6.

1317 *Propensior* is glossed *longior* (longer).

1327 TPMA *Gewalt* 8.1.

1328–33 A version of the Aesopian fable of the tree beaten by boys in order to get its nuts, known in Latin, e.g., through the pseudo-Ovidian, *De nuce.*

1334–39 Virgil, *Aeneid* 3.56–57; TPMA *Hunger* 8.2. The meaning of 1338 is obscure. One might well wish for the large ears of a wolf in order to hear better, but the meaning of "the golden hearts of wolves" is a puzzle. The "beast" in 1339 is presumably greed.

1340–60 A variant of *Romulus* 4.3.

1359 *Veterno* is glossed *morbo* (disease).

1360 TPMA *Wort* 14.2.1.

1361–73 A variant of *Romulus* 3.5.

1372 Horace, *Carmina* 4.1.28, 1.36.12; the *Salii* were dancing and singing priests of Mars who led a procession through Rome in March.

1374–77 See 1.360.

1374–75 TPMA *Dorn* 6.

1377 TPMA *Busch* 11.

1378–84 See T. Wright, *A Selection of Latin Stories, from Manuscripts of the Thirteenth and Fourteenth Centuries* (London, 1842), 10 *(De muliere contraria viro suo).*

1383 On *obtendo* = "go," see Firminus Verris: *contra tendere, pergere, ire, ambulare.*

1392–97 See Werner, *Lateinische Sprichwörter und Sinnsprüche des Mittelaltesr*[2], no. 33. TPMA *Bär* 4.

1398–1403 TPMA *Leid* 13.2

1404–13 There is no known parallel for this very puzzling poem. Compare TPMA *Versprechen* 4.1, 4.2. My interpretation owes much to Greg Hays and Kurt Smolak.

1410 Kurt Smolak has suggested emending *fixas* to *fixus* (= "when set up, when affixed [to a wall, a tree, etc.]"); *morae* (dark phases) of the bread-moon is sarcastic (since it never shone, it was always in its "dark phase").

1414–18 On the five steps to love, see E. R. Curtius, *European Literature and the Latin Middle Ages,* trans. Willard R. Trask (Princeton, 1953), 512–14. Egbert's direct source is either the commentary of Aelius Donatus on Terence's *Eunuchus* (*Commentum Terentii,* IV.2.10; ed. P. Wessner [Leipzig, 1902], 405) or Porphyrius on Horace's *Odes* (*Scholia Horatiana, Carm.* 1.13.16; ed. W. Meyer [Leipzig, 1874], 18).

1414–16 TPMA *Coitus* 1.

1417 "One who has renounced sex": for *spado* = "a voluntary abstainer," see Blaise Patristic, II.2; Matthew 19:12; Ambrose, *De virginitate: Denique cum dixisset et sunt spadones qui se ipsos castraverunt propter regnum caelorum, ut ostenderet hoc non mediocris esse virtutis* (And lastly when he said "and there are spadones who have castrated themselves for the kingdom of heaven" so that he could show that this is not an insignificant virtue); *De viduis: Et sunt spadones qui se ipsos castraverunt; voluntate utique, non necessitate, et ideo magna in iis continentiae gratia* ("And there are *spadones* who have castrated themselves for the kingdom of heaven;" entirely by choice, not out of necessity, and therefore there is in them an outstanding grace of continence).

1419–26 This poem is extremely puzzling. No precise parallels are recorded. Is the bear alive or dead? If it is alive, is it tame (e.g., a dancing bear) or wild? Is the coward to kill it or butcher it? Does "kiss" have a metaphorical instead of a literal meaning (and if so, what is that metaphorical meaning)? Compare TPMA *Bär* 4.1.5. Kurt Smolak makes the attractive suggestion that a verse (or two) has fallen out after 1419. *Concidere* (slaughter) could be understood sexually (to lie with), as could *osculari* (to kiss), *venabula* (shaft, rod), *figo* (poke), and *alvum* (bowels, belly, womb); the bear, like the coward, is male, so it would be anal sex that is implied. Verses 1.1414–18 describe *oscula* (kisses) as immediately preceding *coitus,* increasing the likelihood that the story of the kissing of the bear would be (and perhaps should be) interpreted sexually by the reader.

1419 "Coward": see 1.699–700, where *ignavus* is one destined to be covered in *stercus* (as in v. 1425).

1420 *Oscula libavit,* from Virgil, *Aeneid* 1.256, literally means "tasted its kisses"; Servius's gloss to the passage reads *leviter tetigit* (lightly touched).

1422 *Labra . . . ammovi,* from Virgil, *Eclogae* 3.43 and 3.47, literally means "moved my lips to it."

1427–43 Compare TPMA *Trügen* 7.7; E. Hoefer, *Wie das Volk spricht: Sprichtwörtliche Redensarten,* 8th ed. (Stuttgart, 1876). The use of *alauda* (lark) in the title, given that the bird in the poem is a *philomena* (nightingale) is a puzzle. Voigt takes *alauda* generically as "some bird."

1444–54 Perhaps a variant of *Romulus* 4.14.

1455–65 See 1.1311–27 and 1.1664–67.

1466–70 A similar moral is found in 1.76 and *Romulus* 4.6. The woman who refuses to acknowledge the violence going on between her husband and sons is presented as a stereotype. Her failure to admit the truth does not prevent her suffering.

1471–80 The situation seems to be that the owner of a bird said to the person who stole it, "You stole my goose." The thief replied, legalistically, "I did not steal your goose," since he believed it was a gander he had stolen. After the ensuing brawl, the thief explained the discrepancy to the beaten owner of the bird. The moral is that even when you are in the right, you need to get your facts straight.

1473 *Infitias* is glossed *negationes* (denials).

1481–86 "Bald Mountain": according to Kurth ("Review," 79) *Calvus Mons* is Colmont (near Tongres).

1486 "Cuckoo": the point is obscure.

1487–91 On the general theme of the decline of the Romans, see Horace, *Carmina* 2.15; Sallust, *Bellum Catilinae* 10 and 12.

1489 Virgil, *Aeneid* 1.339.

1492–96 For *aliptes* = "sculptor, stonecutter," see DuCange, "aliptes."

1497–1506 Compare Terence, *Hecyra* 593–97, where the mother-in-law says much the same thing, suggesting that the present lines might be a variant on 1.33. See also 1.1199–1220.

1501 TPMA *Tod* 1.3.1.

1502 TPMA *Neid* 1.13. The hedgehog is proverbially wicked; see *Physiologus* (B-Isidore), ch. 13.

1507–21 Compare Boethius, *De consolatione philosophiae* 1.M.1.1–2; Persius, *Satirae* 3.9; Juvenal, *Satirae* 7.160.

1512 "Master's talent": Matthew 25:15–29.

1518 "Entellus": see Virgil, *Aeneid* 5.387–400.

1521 "Guardian of the vessels": see Numbers 8:24–26 and Haimo of Halberstadt, *Homeliae* 17: *praecipitur, ut levitae usque ad quinquagesimum annum ministrent, post annum vero quinquagesimum custodes vasorum fiant* ("it was ordered that the Levites should minister up to their fiftieth year, but after the fiftieth year, they should become the guardians of the vessels).

1522–25 See 1.484.

1524 "The Esquiline peaks": the Romans executed criminals on the Esquiline Hill, and it served as a burying ground for poor slaves. Scavenging birds preyed on the corpses there.

1526–34 "Coridon": see 1.674, and Virgil, *Eclogae* 2.56.

1528 Horace, *Sermones* 1.3.31–32.

1533 Compare Virgil, *Georgica* 2.467–74.

1535–44 The German names are all derived from words signifying a positive trait: Durand (Enduring), Guot (Good), Vitalis (Vital), Hartman (Hearty).

1541 See 1.335; TPMA *Punkt* 2.

1545–48 Four different kinds of sounds are differentiated: articulated, unarticulated, written, unwritten; see Priscian, *Institutiones Grammaticae* 1.1. "Koax" is the croak of the frog.

1549–53 See 1.681–82.

1549–50 TPMA *Herr* 16.

1554–67 Title: "layman" *(popularis)* can mean either layperson or secular cleric (a cathedral canon as opposed to a cloistered monk). Compare TPMA *Wolf* 2.2; Ziolkowski, *Talking Animals,* 198–203.

1568–74 The wolf, preferring to dine on easily captured domestic sheep, argues that he lacks the skills required to be a hunter or a fisher. And he advises (1569) the men who might hunt him in order to prevent his taking their game that he is not a hunter, and they can leave him alone. Compare Horace, *Sermones* 2.2.1–22.

1575–80 Medieval accounts of the body's apertures usually include nine, omitting the sweat pores; compare TPMA *Fenster* 5. Egbert adds one, in order to arrive at the perfect number ten; on which, see, e.g., Gregory the Great, *Moralia* 1.16.

1581–86 See 1.524–29, 1.1126–29.

1582 TPMA *Stern* 6.

1587–91 Proverbs 20:20. On the stork, see, e.g., Ambrose, *Exameron* 5.16.55; Cassiodorus, *Variae* 2.14.

1592–98 *Romulus* 2.1.

1598 TPMA *Gut (Adj.)* 6.2.

1599–1611 Egbert's tower of Wisdom is modeled on the temple of Wisdom in Prudentius, *Psychomachia* 814–77 (whence also the description of money as having anointed locks, 312).

1612–17 Horace, *Sermones* 1.3.86 describes a Roman moneylender and writer named Ruso, who compelled his debtors to listen to him reciting his work. Daedalus was a Greek inventor, who created the labyrinth to imprison the Minotaur; Egbert puns on an etymology of *labyrinthus,* that it has *labor intus* (labor inside it); see Johannes Balbus, *Catholicon.*

1618–23 *Romulus* 4.18.

1624–34 Compare Persius, *Satirae* 1.119; Juvenal, *Satirae* 9.103–8.

1629 Alludes to the story of Midas and his ass's ears.

1632–33 TPMA *Wissen* 6.12.

1633 *Ozima* is glossed *vilia munuscula quae in foro ven<d>untur* (cheap little gifts which are sold in the market).

1635–47 *Physiologus* (B), ch. 25.

1647 Ezekiel 33:11.

1648–57 *Romulus* 1.2.

1653 TPMA *Schaf* 14.

1658–63 This tale resembles the English nursery rhyme "Jack Sprat." Compare Horace, *Sermones* 2.4.12–14.

1660 TPMA *Ei* 2.4.

1664–68 On unequal spoils, see 1.1311–27; see also 1.1455–65 (hare and fox as prey).

1669–74 See 1.207 on poor singing.

1669 A pun on owl *(noctua)* and night *(nox).*

1674 "Winnowing-fan without grain": i.e., a lot of fanning of air to no purpose.

1675–83 See 1.1162 and TPMA *Rind* 5.4.

1683 Deuteronomy 25:4; TPMA *Rind* 6.2.

1684–1703 1686 "horns of the sixth moon": i.e., his expression is like a crescent moon, the bloodred moon of the sixth seal (see Apocalypse of St. John the Apostle 6:12): in other words, his face is one great red frown of disapproval.

1692 "Shadows": the sense is unclear.

1696 ≈ 1.855.

1697 ≈ 1.816.

1703 Horace, *Sermones* 1.10.9–10; Alain de Lille, *Summa de arte praedicandi* 55: *Sit autem sermo compendiosus, ne prolixitas pariat fasti-*

dium (Speech should be curtailed, lest the excess of it produce boredom).

1704–16 Compare Horace, *Sermones* 1.8.

1704 See note on 1.1524.

1706 For *cippus* = "shackles," see Du Cange.

1712 "Ninth worker": see Horace, *Sermones* 2.7.118.

1714–16 "No other condition": i.e., under no condition whatsoever.

1717–36 See 1.214. This story about Walter of Aquitaine, the hero of the Medieval Latin epic poem *Waltharius,* is also recorded in the *Chronicon Novaliciense.*

1737–40 The references to wisdom and treasure, as well as the allusion to Juvenal, indicate that these verses are another take on the frustrated teacher; see 1.1097–1100, 1.1253–80.

1738 Compare Juvenal, *Satirae* 7.159.

1741–45 This section follows the preceding one with no interruption and no new title. It is not clear whether the two sections belong together. I follow Voigt in assuming they do not.

1741 Job 24:12.

1742–43 Compare Jerome, *Epistulae* 125.19.

1744 "Worthless talent": Matthew 25:15, 25:18, 25:24–30.

1745 "One-eyed witness": the sense seems to be that any legitimate witness with two eyes, able to see clearly, cannot impeach the speaker, so only a half-blind witness, hiding in the shadows could testify against him—and the speaker has no fear of that happening.

1746–64 Voigt (*Egberts,* xi) identifies the heresy described in this section with the Neo-Manichaeism condemned at Orléans in 1022, but there are no theological indications to that effect in the poem (in fact, as Voigt himself admits, there are indications to the contrary). Voigt's interpretation of these lines is rejected by Paris, "Review," 560–62. See also Heinrich Fichtenau, *Heretics and Scholars in the Middle Ages, 1000–1200,* trans. Denise A. Kaiser (University Park, Pennsylvania, 1998), 19–20.

1765–69 Compare Gregory the Great, *Homeliae in euangelia* 1.10.6.

1767 Compare Gregory the Great, *Moralia* 1.36.

Book 2

1–2 The first two verses are introductory, paralleling the distich that opens Book 1 (1.3–4).

2 "With an ax, not with a pickax": i.e., it was made of wood not of metal [that is, it was not dug out of the earth with a pickax or a mattock]; "bridge" *(crepido)* could be a foundation, a rim, or a promontory; the precise meaning here is not entirely clear, but it should refer to the bridge of the stern, where the pilot stood.

3–11 The story of Pythagoras testing the sounds of hammers and discovering a discordant sound is found in Boethius, *De musica* 1.10.

5–6 Horace, *Sermones* 1.1.106–7.

7 Sallust, *Bellum Jugurthinum* 1.1.

9 Matthew 6:25; Augustine, *Enarrationes in Psalmos* 105.15.

12–35 Genesis 2:7–3:24; Voigt compares Paul Diaconus, *Homeliae* 1.174, 1.173, 1.135.

14 "Like the angels": the reference is to the celibate life in heaven, described, e.g., in Matthew 22:30 and Mark 12:25.

36–46 Julianus Pomerius, *De vita contemplativa* 1.20.

41–44 Ezekiel 33:8.

45–46 Luke 16:24; Romans 12:20.

47–50 Nebuchadnezzar's cook was named Nabuzardan; see 4 Kings 25:8; Gregory the Great, *Moralia* 30.18.

51–54 There is a gap of five lines in the manuscript after verse 50. Voigt numbered the missing lines, apparently assuming that a poem of four lines (plus title) was missing. It is also possible that a poem of that length had been incorrectly inserted at this point and was later removed. I have retained Voigt's numbering.

55–69 55–60: Gregory the Great, *Homeliae in euangelia* 2.32.2.

55 "Black spirit": see 1.805.

57 TPMA *Nackt* 3.2.

61 1 Timothy 6:7.

62 Job 1:21; TPMA *Nackt* 1.1.

63–69 Gregory the Great, *Homeliae in euangelia* 2.32.4; see 2.588–95.

70–82 Gregory the Great, *Homeliae in euangelia* 2.35.6 and 2.35.9.

72 *Repotia* is glossed *est pocula quae post constitutos dies fiunt* (it is a drink which happens after the established days); that is, it is a continuation of the drinking onto successive days. See Ps.-Acro, *Scholia in Horatium* (*ad Sermones* 2.2.60): *Repotia sunt . . . mutuae invitationes,* from which it seems that Egbert uses the term to mean something like "return the favor."

75 "In three ways": namely, patience with an inferior *(emulus),* who is to be treated as an equal; patience with an equal *(hostis),* who is to be ignored and not argued with; and patience with a superior *(Dominus),* who is to be accepted without grumbling.

83–87 TPMA *Hochmut* 5.5; Augustine, *De natura et gratia* 27.31.

84 See 1.259; TPMA *Husten* 1; Virgil, *Geo.* 3.496–97.

85–87 Colossians 3:17; Matthew 6:33.

88–98 Deuteronomy 32:41; Romans 12:19; Ambrosiaster, *Commentarius in Pauli epistulam ad Romanos* 12.19.

88 TPMA *Rache* 6.1.

89 "Unless . . . resolved": i.e., unless the punishment has already been agreed upon by the Lord and remitted.

95–96 Ecclesiastes 7:17, 7:16.

99–105 Gregory the Great, *Homeliae in euangelia* 2.34.11.

99 Galatians 4:26; Jerome, *Commentarii in Ezechielem* 5.16. The etymology of Jerusalem as *visio pacis* is ubiquitous in patristic writings; see, e.g., Jerome, *Liber interpretationis hebraicorum nominum* 50.9.

106–11 Gregory the Great, *Homeliae in euangelia* 2.34.13, 2.34.15, 2.34.17.

112–16 Gregory the Great, *Homeliae in euangelia* 2.33.3, 2.37.5.

117–32 Gregory the Great, *Moralia, praef.* 5. The order and interpretation of the four afflictions in Gregory is 1) the sinner is stricken so that he be punished without end (Judaea), 2) the sinner is stricken so that his faults be corrected (the lame man), 3) someone is stricken not to purify previous faults but to prevent future ones (Paul), 4) someone is stricken to manifest the power of God (Job and the man blind from birth).

122–23 2 Corinthians 12:7.

124–26 John 9:1–7.

127 Job 29:15.

128–29 John 5:5–14.

130–32 Jeremiah 30:14–15.

BOOK 2

133–44 Ps.-Augustine, *Liber exhortationis, vulgo de salutaribus documentis* 57 (= Quodvultdeus, *Sermo 12,* ch. 12).

136–37 Matthew 6:19–20.

138–44 3 Kings 6:7, and Hrabanus Maurus, *Commentaria in libros quattuor Regum* 3.6.

143 Holy of Holies = Christ; see Daniel 9:24–25.

145–52 Gregory the Great, *Homeliae in euangelia* 2.36.3.

153–57 Gregory the Great, *Homeliae in euangelia* 2.38.8.

158–63 Isaiah 23:4; Gregory the Great, *Moralia, praef.* 2.

161–63 Isaiah 10:21–25; Romans 11:25–32.

164–69 Isaiah 9:5.

168 Horace, *Sermones* 2.3.31.

170–73 2 Timothy 2:5; 1 Corinthians 12:4–11.

172–73 Isidore, *Sententiae* 1.1.4.

174–86 Gregory the Great, *Moralia* 2.18, 2.17, 2.10.

179–81 TPMA *Gott* 28.18.

180 Job 1:21.

187–91 Augustine, *Enarrationes in Psalmos* 143.7–8.

192–97 Gregory the Great, *Moralia* 4.31, 4.29.

198–220 See 2.121; Gregory the Great *Moralia* 3.3, 3.4 3.7.

221–25 See 1.715–16.

223 TPMA *Stossen* 3.

224–25 Compare Gennadius, *De viris illustribus* 38.

226–30 227,: Isidore, *Etymologiae* 2.27.1.

229 "Golden chain": see Macrobius, *In somnium Scipionis,* 1.14.15; Acts of the Apostles 10:11–16.

231–40 Caesarius of Arles, *Sermones* 167.6.

232 Daniel 7:10.

238 Ezekiel 24:11.

241–48 Caesarius of Arles, *Sermones* 167.5.

248 Psalms 68:16.

249–57 Psalms 23:8; Gregory the Great, *Homeliae in euangelia* 2.34.9; Prosper of Aquitaine, *Liber sententiarum* 177.

253–55 Augustine, *Soliloquia* 5–6.

254–55 See 1.1120–25.

256 "Blessed those practicing them": see Matthew 5:3–12.

258–77 Gregory the Great, *Homeliae in euangelia* 2.34.9.

263 "Aerial powers": the fallen angels of the lower air (as opposed to the "ethereal powers" higher up).

266–70 Gregory the Great, *Homeliae in euangelia* 2.34.8.

271–77 Gregory the Great, *Homeliae in euangelia* 2.34.10.

278–304 Exodus 20:4, 20:7, 20:8; Deuteronomy 5:8, 5:11, 5:12.

278–95 Augustine, *Sermones* 9.

296–98 Augustine, *Sermones* 4.

298 Leviticus 23:3.

305–13 Exodus 20:12–17; Deuteronomy 5:16–21; Augustine, *Sermones* 9.

314–25 Gregory the Great, *Homeliae in euangelia* 2.30.8.

316 1 Kings 16:18.

317–18 Amos 7:14–15.

319–20 Daniel 13:45–61.

321 Matthew 4:18–19.

322–23 Acts of the Apostles 9:1–22.

324–25 Luke 5:27–28.

326–52 Gregory the Great, *Homeliae in euangelia* 1.17.14–18.

326–32 Matthew 16:13.

344 Isaiah 24:2; Hosea 4:9.

346 Lamentations 4:1. Egbert interprets the "stones" as gemstones; the priests are the jewels of the church.

353–56 Gregory the Great, *Homeliae in euangelia* 2.23.1–2.

353 Isaiah 58:7.

355 Hebrews 13:2.

356 Luke 24:13–29.

357–68 Gregory the Great, *Moralia* 2.4.

367–68 TPMA *Blind* 5.2.

369–75 Hincmar of Reims, *De cavendis vitiis et virtutibus exercendis* 2.10.

375 2 Maccabees 12:44–46.

376–95 Gregory the Great, *Homeliae in euangelia* 1.1.6.

379–80 Ecclesiastes 7:40.

383 Gregory the Great, *Homeliae in euangelia* 1.12.4.

388–93 Zephaniah 1:14–16.

396–401 See 1.705–6; Gregory the Great, *Homeliae in euangelia* 1.3.3; TPMA *Bitter* 2.2.

402–5 It is unclear which apostle is meant and whether the "building" in 402 is real or metaphorical.

406–9 There is no title for this section in the manuscript, but it is distinguished from the previous passage by an enlarged capital letter. Augustine, *Enarrationes in Psalmos* 102.6; TPMA *Müde* 3.

409 Horace, *Sermones* 1.2.24.

410–15 The five keys to wisdom described here are 1) reading, 2) remembering, 3) questioning, 4) respect for the learned, 5) fear of God. Compare *Monumenta Germaniae historica, Poetae* 5.3:651–52.

416–24 Gregory the Great, *Homeliae in euangelia* 1.9.1; Matthew 25:18.

420 Gregory the Great, *Homeliae in euangelia* 1.10.7; Psalms 50:19.

421 TPMA *Liebe* 1.3.2.

421–23 Gregory the Great, *Homeliae in euangelia* 1.11.2; Canticle of Canticles 8:6.

425–31 Gregory the Great, *Homeliae in euangelia* 1.14.2–3.

426–28 Ezekiel 13:5.

429 Ezekiel 34:8.

430–31 Gregory the Great, *Homeliae in euangelia* 1.14.2–3.

432–37 Gregory the Great, *Homeliae in euangelia* 1.14.6. Perhaps *speramus* (432) should be emended to *spernamus.*

435–36 Compare Juvenal, *Satirae* 3.3.

437 = 1.539: TPMA *Gut (Adj.)* 1.1.

438–45 Compare John Cassian, *Collationes* 20.8, where the list includes twelve means of wiping away sins.

446–50 Augustine, *Enarrationes in Psalmos* 125.11; Luke 21:2–4, 19:2–8.

451–54 Matthew 13:42; Job 24:19. Bede, *In proverbia Salomonis* 3.31.369.

455–64 Isidore, *De differentiis rerum* 36–40.

458 Gregory the Great, *Homeliae in euangelia* 2.29.2; "to feel and to live and to exist": that is, man shares with the herd animal the ability to feel; with the tree, to live; with the stone, to exist.

461 "Last": i.e., the final and highest state.

465–71 Gregory the Great, *Moralia* 6.10.

472–85 These verses presenting an early form of the "Little Red Riding Hood" story have been much discussed. A full and nuanced treatment is offered by Ziolkowski, *Fairy Tales,* 100–24, with bibliography.

486–92 Ecclesiasticus 35:17–22.

486–87 TPMA *Witwe* 2.

490 Psalms 35:7.

493–502 Gregory of Tours, *Historiarum libri* 1.21.

497 *Sol* is glossed *Christus* (Christ).

501 "Sacred listing": Matthew 10:2–4.

503–17 Judges 16:1–21.

503–10 Gregory the Great, *Homeliae in euangelia* 2.21.7. The "tenth drachma" refers to mankind, created to make up the tenth order after the fall of Lucifer and his angels; see Gregory the Great, *Homeliae in euangelia* 2.34.6.

515–18 See 2.539–41, where Adam, Samson, and Solomon again serve as examples of the destruction caused by women.

518–25 518 = 1.546; 518–19 = 1.929–30; 520 ≈ 1.547.

518 See note to 1.546.

521–25 Exodus 18:17–24; Gregory the Great, *Regula pastoralis* 2.7.

525 TPMA *Ulme* 1; Moses is described as *mitissimus* ("kindest, most gentle," but also "softest"); so he is like a vine, needing support (from the elm tee).

526–29 Joshua 10; Lactantius, *Institutiones* 4.17.

530–41 Ecclesiasticus 47:15–21.

530–33 Augustine, *Enarrationes in Psalmos* 71.1.

531 Jerome, *Liber interpretationis hebraicorum nominum* 63.5.

534–38 3 Kings 11:1–10; 4 Kings 23:13; Gregory the Great, *Moralia* 12.18.

539–41 See 2.515–18.

539 Gregory the Great, *Moralia* 12.37.

542–48 542: Romans 4:11. Prudentius, *Psychomachia, praef.* 1.2.

543 Genesis 15:5; Ambrosiaster, *Commentarius in Pauli epistulam ad Romanos* (γ) 4.17.1–2. *Mathesin* is glossed *id est doctrinalem scientiam* (that is, doctrinal knowledge).

544–46 Genesis 22:17.

547 James 2:23.

549 Jerome, *Liber interpretationis hebraicorum nominum* 68.13.

549–50 Cassiodorus, *Expositio Psalmorum* 26.20.

551 1 Kings 16:18.

552–53 1 Kings 16:13.

554–55 1 Kings 17:34–50.

556–58 Augustine, *Enarrationes in Psalmos* 33.1.4.

558–59 Psalms 90:13.

561–71 Jerome, *Epistulae* 125.11.

563–64 Virgil, *Aeneid* 3.571–72.

566 See 1.481.

567 Juvenal, *Satirae* 5.114–16; Virgil, *Aeneid* 1.215.

568 See 1.847–50.

572–75 Compare Jerome, *Commentarii in Ezechielem* 2.6.377–86.

576–80 On Platonic "ideas" and the four elements, see, e.g., Calcidius, *Commentarius in Platonis Timaeum* 20–22; Augustine, *De Genesi ad litteram* 3.4–7.

578 *Ideas* is glossed *imaginationes* (mental images); *tryas* is glossed *scilicet trinitas* (that is, the Trinity).

581–87 Egbert's story of Caiphas (the high priest of the Jews who condemned Jesus; Matthew 26:57–65) and ropes is not attested elsewhere. Neither the syntax nor the meaning of the poem is clear.

581 "Soaked ephod": perhaps = soaked in the blood of Christ, Matthew 27:25. The Jewish vestment, here red with blood, is contrasted with the white Christian baptismal cloth *(in albis)* in verse 584. "On ropes": perhaps a clothesline, where it could dry out.

582 John 11:49–53.

583 Matthew 27:5; Acts of the Apostles 1:18. Voigt assumes the subject from 583 onward is Judas, not Caiphas. If so, we must probably assume a line has fallen out of the text.

586 "Image of reason": biblical exegetes sometimes interpret the ephod allegorically as "reason."

588–95 See 2.63–69; Gregory the Great, *Homeliae in euangelia* 2.32.4.

591–92 TPMA *Wort* 9.1.

596–605 The closing prayer.

599 Prosper, *Epigrammata* 59.1.

600 Horace, *Epistulae* 2.2.189; Sedulius Scotus, *Collectaneum miscellaneum* 80.11.20.

603 Psalms 35:12.

604 *Pars pia* (gracious portion = God): see Luke 10:42; Lamentations 3:24; Psalms 72:26, 141:6.

604–5 The peaceful calm of Saint Martin at his death is mentioned, for instance, by Sulpicius Severus, *Epist. 3 ad Bassulam;* see Maaz, "Brotlöffel," 108.

Bibliography

Edition

Voigt, Ernst. *Egberts von Lüttich Fecunda Ratis zum ersten Mal herausgegeben auf ihre Quellen zurückgeführt und erklärt von Ernst Voigt.* Halle a. S., 1889.

Secondary Sources

Arweiler, Alexander. *Egbertus Leodiensis. Fecunda ratis. Cod. 196*. Codices Electronici Ecclesiae Coloniensis (CEEC). http://www.ceec.uni-koeln.de/

Balau, Sylvain. *Les sources de l'histoire de Liège au Moyen Age.* Brussels, 1903.

Brunhölzl, Franz. *Geschichte der lateinischen Literatur des Mittelalters.* Vol. 2. Munich, 1992.

Brunhölzl, Franz, and F. J. Worstbrock. "Egbert von Lüttich." In *Die Deutsche Literatur des Mittelalters: Verfasserlexikon,* edited by Kurt Ruh. 2nd ed., vol. 2, cols. 361–63. Berlin, 1980.

Genicot, Léopold, and P. Tombeur. *Index scriptorum operumque latino-belgicorum medii aevi:nouveau repertoire des oeuvres mediolatines belges.* Part 2, *XIe siècle,* edited by P. Fransen and H. Maraite, 47. Brussels, 1976.

Hervieux, Léopold. *Les fabulistes latins depuis le siècle d'Auguste jusqu'à la fin du Moyen-Age.* 5 vols. Paris, 1884–1899.

Kurth, Godefroid. *Notger de Liège et la civilisation au xe siècle.* Paris, 1905.

———. Review of Ernst Voigt, *Egberts von Lüttich Fecunda ratis. Moyen Age* 3 (1890): 78–80.

Maaz, Wolfgang. "Angstbewältigung in mittellateinischer Literatur." In *Psychologie in der Mediävistik,* edited by Jürgen Kühnel, Hans-Dieter Mück, Ursula Müller, and Ulrich Müller, 51–77. Göppinger Arbeiten zur Germanistik 431. Göppingen, 1985.

———. "Brotlöffel, haariges Herz und wundersame Empfängnis: Bemerkungen zu Egbert von Lüttich und Giraldus Cambrensis." In *Tradition und Wertung. Festschrift für Franz Brunhölzl zum 65. Geburtstag,* edited by Günter Bernt, Fidel Rädle, and Gabriel Silagi, 107–118. Sigmaringen, 1989.

———. "Egbert von Lüttich." In *Enzyklopädie des Märchens,* edited by Kurt Ranke. Vol. 3, cols. 1010–19. Berlin, 1981.

Manitius, Max. *Geschichte der lateinischen Literatur des Mittelalters.* 3 vols. Munich, 1911–1931.

———. "Zu Egberts von Lüttich Fecunda ratis." *Romanische Forschungen* 4 (1891): 426.

Paris, Gaston. Review of Ernst Voigt, *Egberts von Lüttich Fecunda ratis. Journal des savants* (Sept. 1890): 559–72.

Peiper, Rudolf. Review of Ernst Voigt, *Egberts von Lüttich Fecunda ratis. Zeitschrift für Deutsche Philologie* 25 (1893): 423–30.

Rädle, Fidel. "Adalbold von Utrecht." In *Die Deutsche Literatur des Mittelalters: Verfasserlexikon,* edited by Kurt Ruh. 2nd ed., vol. 1, cols. 41–42. Berlin, 1978.

Sigebert of Gembloux, *Catalogus Sigeberti Gemblacensis monachi de viris illustribus.* Edited by R. Witte. Lateinische Sprache und Literatur des Mittelalters 1. Bern a. M., 1974.

Thesaurus proverbiorum medii aevi. Lexikon der Sprichwörter des romanisch-germanischen Mittelalters. 14 vols. Berlin, 1995–2002.

Ziolkowski, Jan M. *Fairy Tales from Before Fairy Tales: The Medieval Latin Past of Wonderful Lies.* Ann Arbor, 2007.

———. *Talking Animals: Medieval Latin Beast Poetry, 750–1150.* University of Pennsylvania Press Middle Ages Series. Philadelphia, 1993.

Index

Let. denotes *Letter to Bishop Adalbold.* The letter *t* following a number denotes the title preceding the verse.